Praise for *The Night Singer*

"Readers will readily engage with Hanna, a no-nonsense, dogged, and thoughtful investigator. Mo is off to a strong start."
　　　　　　　　　　　　　　　　—Publishers Weekly

"Johanna Mo has established herself as one of Sweden's most reliable crime writers. Quality is guaranteed when you get one of her books in your hands. . . . The characters are brimming with life and are of flesh and blood, it feels like they come straight out of real life."
　　　　　　　　　　　　　　　　—Dast Magazine

"I can barely wait for the next book in the Island Murders series. I already knew that Johanna Mo was a great writer, but here she has undoubtedly hit a bull's eye."
　　　　　　　　　　　　　　　　—Norra Skåne

PENGUIN BOOKS

THE SHADOW LILY

Johanna Mo was born in Kalmar, Sweden, and now lives with her family in Stockholm. She has spent the past twenty years working as a literary critic, translator, and freelance editor, and is now a full-time writer. *The Night Singer* was her English-language debut.

To access Penguin Readers Guides online,
visit penguinrandomhouse.com.

THE
SHADOW
LILY

JOHANNA MO

Translation by Alice Menzies

PENGUIN BOOKS

PENGUIN BOOKS
An imprint of Penguin Random House LLC
penguinrandomhouse.com

Originally published in Swedish as *Skuggliljan* by
Romanus & Selling, Stockholm

LIBRARY OF CONGRESS CATALOGING-IN-PUBLICATION DATA
Names: Mo, Johanna, author. | Menzies, Alice, translator.
Title: The shadow lily / Johanna Mo ; translation by Alice Menzies.
Other titles: Skuggliljan. English
Description: [New York] : Penguin Books, [2022] |
Series: The island murders trilogy 2 | Originally published in Swedish
as Skuggliljan by Romanus & Selling, Stockholm.
Identifiers: LCCN 2021046688 (print) | LCCN 2021046689 (ebook) |
ISBN 9780143136699 (paperback) | ISBN 9780525508205 (ebook)
Subjects: LCGFT: Detective and mystery fiction. | Novels.
Classification: LCC PT9877.23.O25 S5813 2022 (print) |
LCC PT9877.23.O25 (ebook) | DDC 839.73/8—dc23
LC record available at https://lccn.loc.gov/2021046688
LC ebook record available at https://lccn.loc.gov/2021046689

Printed in the United States of America
1st Printing

Set in Sabon LT Pro
DESIGNED BY MEIGHAN CAVANAUGH

THE SHADOW LILY

THE LAST DAY

He looks around before he steps into the garden. A door opens farther down the street, and he pauses. The remnants of a laugh carry through the warm late summer air. The tall hedges are blocking his view, but he sees a woman with a floral dress and long dark hair emerge through one of the openings. She tosses a bag of trash into the bin. The green lid slams shut, and his heart skips a beat as she turns around to head back inside. For a split second he is convinced she must have spotted him, because she stops, gazing in his direction. But then she shakes her head and disappears behind the hedge.

He doesn't dare move until the woman is back in her house. A few quiet steps, and he reaches the front door. The key sticks in the lock, and he decides she must have given him the wrong one on purpose. A wave of stress-fueled nausea courses through his body. He hates that he got mixed up in this crap because he is incapable of saying no. Because he wanted to be nice.

This can't go on. He needs to put a stop to it, for Hugo's sake.

The key finally turns, and the door swings open. He fumbles for the light switch in the hallway. The bulb on the ceiling comes on, flickers, and goes out.

Damn it.

Time isn't on his side, but there is no reason why this should take any longer than fifteen minutes. Then he can leave the house, walk back to his car, and drive home.

Without taking his shoes off, he makes his way past the fireplace and into the kitchen. He flicks the switch on the wall, but nothing happens. He glances at his watch—6:57 p.m.—and can't decide what to do while he waits. With a sigh, he slumps to the floor and hugs his knees. Maybe he should just forget the whole thing, clear off now. But no, he doesn't dare.

A few minutes later the front door opens, and he jumps up so suddenly that the room sways and he has to brace himself against the wall. He staggers out into the hallway.

"We need to be quick," he says. "I'm in a hurry."

He stops dead and stares at the person in the doorway.

"What are you doing here?"

The initial surprise transforms into panic, his brain unable to piece together the swirling fragments. The anger on the face in front of him. The determination. Why? His heart is in his mouth, his field of vision shrinking. A single clear thought manages to break through: *Please, help.*

SUNDAY, AUGUST 18

1

Hanna Duncker chose a seat that would give her a view of the entrance and told the waiter to just bring her a glass of water. She wanted to wait for her company to arrive before she ordered.

She remembered her father's friend Gunnar as a heavy drinker, like her father, though Gunnar had always had a more on-and-off relationship with the booze. She had no idea how he felt about it now. He had been reluctant to meet when she first reached out to him. They hadn't seen each other since Lars's funeral last autumn, and she had barely managed to talk to him that day. She had asked if he wanted to buy the house—he had lived in it during all the years Lars was in prison, after all—but he said no. Gunnar and her father had been friends for as long as Hanna could remember, ever since they worked for the same company in Kalmar.

Three mourners. No one else had come to the funeral. Hanna and Gunnar and the woman he brought with him, and she was only there for moral support. Neither Lars's parents nor her brother Kristoffer had bothered to show up. She no longer had any contact with her grandparents, who now lived in Norway, and Kristoffer was in London.

The door opened, but it was a young couple. The woman turned to the man and laughed loudly, like someone newly in love. Her curly red hair fell over her face, and she quickly pushed it back.

Hanna swallowed. Fabian, her ex, had uploaded an ultrasound image to his Facebook page a few days ago. He and his partner—the preschool teacher he had started seeing just a few weeks after he dumped Hanna—were having a baby. She had spent several minutes staring at the grainy image, unable to tear her eyes away.

The young couple had booked a table. To celebrate their one-year anniversary, apparently. So much for having only just met. Hanna watched them head upstairs.

The door opened again, but there was still no sign of Gunnar. The man who came in was in his sixties, and his left arm was hanging oddly, his left leg reluctant to bend. Hanna suspected a stroke. He walked over to another man around the same age, and they shared a long embrace. What if Gunnar had changed his mind?

Hanna had spent the summer looking into the murder and robbery of Ester Jensen: the murder her father Lars had been convicted of in 2003. Or, more accurately, she had spent a week reading the investigation and the rest of the time trying to process everything she had learned. Lars's DNA had been found inside Ester's burned-out shell of a house, his fingerprints on the gas can discarded outside. There was no ignoring that kind of evidence. How could she ever have thought he might be innocent?

Hanna had only started working for the Kalmar police in May, which meant she hadn't had much of a summer break, and mulling over her father's crimes had ruined most of it. In an attempt to keep herself busy and dull her anxiety, she had started renovating her little house in Kleva. She put up wallpaper in the living room, painted the ceiling and woodwork white, and created a pale green feature wall in the bedroom on the first floor. She had decided not to touch the floral wallpaper in the kitchen. The house now looked a little less shabby, but both the toilet and the tiny shower room off the hallway still needed work.

She checked the time on her phone. Gunnar was ten minutes

late. Her childhood friend Rebecka had sent another picture from her last-minute trip to the Canary Islands with her family. Rebecka's son Joel had been found dead at the rest area in Möckelmossen this spring, and it had been Hanna's first investigation since moving back to Öland. She and Rebecka had grown up together, and it had been strange to see her again after so many years— particularly under such sad circumstances.

Hanna opened the image of Molly on the beach, an ice-cream cone in one hand. The soft white ice cream had dripped down onto her skin, and she was laughing. The young girl seemed to have taken the loss of Joel much better than her mother. Rebecka had called Hanna in tears on several occasions.

I can't do this anymore.

And yet somehow her friend had survived. The trip to the Canary Islands wasn't just a chance to get away from everything back home; it was also an attempt to save her marriage.

Gunnar finally opened the door fifteen minutes after the agreed time, wearing jeans and a rust-colored T-shirt. Only ten months had passed since Hanna had last seen him, but that was at a funeral. He looked much better now: tanned and rested, his graying hair cropped short. Gunnar was a few years younger than Lars, which meant he must be just shy of sixty. He sat down opposite her.

"Sorry I'm late," he said.

"No problem. I'm glad you came."

The waiter hurried over to take their orders. Gunnar asked for a Coke with his pizza, and Hanna did the same—though what she really wanted was a glass of red wine.

"Nice hair," said Gunnar.

"Thanks."

Hanna's hair had been longer at the funeral, but she had since had it cut. Her sweeping fringe was now the longest part, reaching to just below her cheekbone. A few months earlier, someone had called her Brienne of Tarth. Hanna hadn't had any idea who that was at the time, and while she still hadn't watched any *Game of Thrones*, she could definitely see the resemblance in terms of her height, hair color, and style—though Hanna wasn't quite so broad-shouldered.

"I hear you got a job with the Kalmar police," Gunnar continued.

Hanna nodded. His tone was curious, not critical, but she hadn't come here to talk about her work.

"I read the investigation," she said.

"Aha," said Gunnar, studying her. He didn't say anything else, though a slight crease appeared on his brow.

That crease told her he knew exactly which investigation she meant.

"Did you and Lars ever talk about what happened to Ester?" she asked.

"No. I tried, but he didn't want to."

Hanna swallowed her disappointment with a mouthful of cola. She regretted not ordering the wine.

"What are you up to these days?" she asked.

That was where she should have started, she realized: with small talk. Like any normal person who cared about others. A memory of a Christmas came back to her. The six of them together in the kitchen. Her, Kristoffer, their parents, maternal grandmother, and Gunnar. He often used to join them for Christmas lunch. He had worn a knitted sweater with reindeer on it that year, and had let Hanna try it on. It came all the way down to her calves.

"I'm living in an apartment in Norrliden," said Gunnar. "I needed to get away from Öland."

Hanna herself had fled to Stockholm, but after sixteen years there she had decided to return to the island. She assumed he must have suffered his fair share of gossip. In some ways it had probably been worse for him, because he had stayed—and in Lars's house, at that. The killer's house, as she had heard people call it. She hadn't managed to find his new address, just a phone number.

"Are you working?"

"Yup, in a care home. And Leticia and I got ourselves a Russian Toy."

"A what?"

"It's a little dog."

"I had visions of nesting dolls."

"No, no." Gunnar grinned.

The waiter came over with their pizzas, and they ate quietly for a few minutes. Gunnar much more eagerly than Hanna.

"Was it Leticia who came to the funeral?" she asked in an attempt to get the conversation going again.

Gunnar had introduced her at the time, but Hanna had forgotten the woman's name the minute he said it.

"Yeah."

"A girlfriend, a job, and a pooch. Not bad."

Gunnar smiled, and Hanna was surprised by just how painful she found it. Why couldn't her father have stopped drinking and straightened his life out, found himself a job and a new partner? If he had, Ester would still be alive today. It struck her that Lars's death must have come as a relief to Gunnar—not that he would ever put it like that. He was the only person who had stood by him and genuinely tried to help.

Gunnar's face quickly grew serious again.

"Sorry I sounded so skeptical when you called and asked to meet, but I . . ."

He trailed off, his eyes wandering. His gaze eventually seemed to settle just to the left of Hanna's head.

"I've got my life in order, and I didn't want to be dragged back there."

Those words could just as easily have come from Kristoffer.

Hanna hadn't spoken to her brother since May, when she called him after meeting his old friend Axel Sandsten as part of the investigation into Joel's death. Axel was Joel's father, and for a while he had been their prime suspect. She had left Kristoffer a message a few weeks ago, wanting to discuss the investigation into their father, but he still hadn't called her back. So far the only other person she had confided in was Ingrid, her neighbor.

"You seeing anyone?" asked Gunnar.

"No."

"Not that you have to, of course," he hurried to add when he noticed her reaction.

Hanna cut a piece of pizza, but left it on her plate.

"I was in a relationship, in Stockholm," she said. "But it didn't work out."

"No, sometimes they don't. Leticia and I have been together almost four years now."

"That's great."

"But we've got our problems."

Hanna suspected he was only saying that for her sake, and that they were like the couple celebrating their one-year anniversary upstairs. That was the impression she had gotten at her father's funeral.

"Lars would've been proud of you."

This time it was Gunnar trying to meet her eye, but Hanna continued hacking at her pizza. Everything to do with her father was one big battle. Having a murderer be proud of you wasn't exactly something to strive for, and yet . . . until she was twelve, Lars had been a fantastic father. Attentive and encouraging. It was her mother's death that had made him fall apart.

"Surely he must have said something?" she said, looking up.

"About what happened, you mean?"

Hanna nodded.

"Please," she begged, sensing Gunnar's hesitation. "I know Dad set the house on fire and that he probably killed Ester, too. But I need to know why. All that violence. . . ."

Hanna couldn't go on. The fire had destroyed most of the evidence, but there was no hiding Ester's twenty-odd broken bones. Gunnar pushed the last piece of Vesuvio into his mouth and chewed slowly.

"Once, when he was drunk, I heard him say that he never should have . . ."

He trailed off and turned to look out the window. A group of teenagers were walking by outside. They were laughing, one of the girls so much that she had to steady herself on her friend.

"Please," Hanna repeated. "What did he say?"

"That he never should have protected him."

"What did he mean by that?"

"I'm not sure, but . . ."

Gunnar turned back to her. His eyes seemed to be begging her not to make him go on.

"You have to tell me," she said.

She sounded angrier than intended, but he couldn't clam up now.

"There's only one person Lars would've gone to prison to protect," said Gunnar. "Well, other than you."

2

Her swimsuit was still damp, and Lykke Henriksen shivered as she pulled it on. She had forgotten to hang it up to dry after she rinsed it out earlier. Swimming in the strait was something she did every morning and evening. The water was no more than a hundred or so meters from the house, and taking a dip was the only thing that could clear the fog from her head. She had fallen back into her old ways, and she didn't like it. But she needed to take control. Everything was up in the air, particularly after the shitty day she'd had.

Lykke pushed her feet into her Crocs, opened the door between the kitchen and the garden, and walked over to the washing line to unclip her towel. She draped it over her shoulders, then turned around and started walking toward the water. It was after eight, and the sun was already kissing the horizon. In another thirty or so minutes, it would be gone. She could live like this, if she wanted to. Maybe it would be just as well if she gave up her apartment in Uppsala and moved here on a permanent basis, especially now that she didn't have a place in the research program. But what would she do for work? The job market wasn't exactly red-hot for a twenty-four-year-old biologist specializing in butterflies.

As though to taunt her, a large skipper took off from one of the toad lilies lining the low stone wall around the patio. It was a male, its wings more golden than brown, and she watched the butterfly flutter back and forth in front of her before disappearing on its way.

Lykke continued toward the shore. There was neither a wall nor a hedge on the western edge of her property, but it was easy enough to see where her garden ended and the common land began. The grass on the common land had been mowed recently, whereas hers had been left to grow since she arrived on the island. She hadn't had the energy to cut it.

For once there was almost no breeze, and the sun had been shining all day. The forecast had said there was cooler weather on the way, and that was also how the future felt: like a cold front approaching. The only thing she didn't know was whether the next storm would be worse than the one she had left behind.

Once Lykke had crossed the road, she turned back to look at the house. She probably wouldn't have to work for a year if she sold it. But she needed a job. Something to fill her time and her mind. And she still wasn't sure whether she would be able to let the house go. When her mother died three years earlier, the house in Grönhögen became hers. It was her mother's childhood home. Her grandmother's, too. Lykke rented it out through Airbnb for most of the year, but she had wanted it all to herself that summer, while she worked out what to do next. Getting around Öland without a car was tricky, so she had bought an old Škoda for a few thousand kronor. Grönhögen did have a grocery store and a restaurant, and there was a bus to the mainland, but the buses were fairly infrequent and involved making a transfer along the way, and she hated feeling like she was trapped.

Lykke put down her towel on a rock, stepped out of her Crocs, and slowly waded out into the water. There was a jetty down by the harbor, but she preferred swimming here, despite the rocky seabed. She also went to the quarry every once in a while. Barely anyone swam there when she was younger, but these days it was almost always packed during the summer months. The water was deep and turquoise, and you could jump in from the rocks. People seemed to go there purely to take pictures for Instagram. Swimming in the lake where her mother used to take her as a child was now impossible. The golfers had taken over, hitting ball after ball into the water from the shore.

The sun had been shining all day, but it hadn't managed to warm the strait. The water was only up to her knees, but Lykke could feel its chill spreading through her body and she braced herself. The shallows stretched out a long way here, and the rocky floor made it difficult to walk. The memory of driving a knife into his tire suddenly overpowered her, making her gasp. Puncturing the rubber had been harder than she expected, probably because she was shaking so much, but she hadn't given up until she heard the hiss of air escaping.

Lykke hurried forward in an attempt to shake off the memory. She slipped and came close to losing her balance, but her foot hit a sharp rock and the pain kept her upright. Before long she let her body fall forward into the water. She took a few hesitant strokes and then ducked beneath the surface.

She welcomed the coldness now. It obliterated everything else.

MONDAY, AUGUST 19

3

The first thing Hanna Duncker did when she got to the station in Kalmar was grab a coffee. Gunnar's words had been bouncing around in her head all night, and she had struggled to sleep.

There's only one person Lars would've gone to prison to protect. Well, other than you.

Hanna had stormed out of the restaurant after he said that, knocking over a glass of water in passing. He was talking about Kristoffer, and the idea that her brother might have killed Ester Jensen was even more unlikely than their father having done it. Why would Gunnar say such a thing? There was no escaping the evidence. Lars had been in the house where Ester died, and his fingerprints were on the gas can. Could it be that Gunnar found it even harder to accept that Lars was guilty than she did? They had been friends for over thirty years, after all. Or was it to do with Kristoffer? Gunnar had been furious when he failed to show up at the funeral.

Her father's friend had called and messaged her yesterday evening, but Hanna had been too upset to reply. *I was just repeating what Lars said*, he wrote in his last message.

Hanna's coffee cup was full to the brim, and it came dangerously close to sloshing over the edge as she began to climb the stairs. She paused and slurped from the cup, pulling a face at both the temperature and the taste.

I never should have protected him.

But why should she trust Gunnar? He could be lying. He could even have been involved himself.

Hanna had to get Kristoffer to talk to her somehow, about both Gunnar's claim and the investigation. She regretted having read the files, but what was done was done. The interviews with her father had been particularly difficult to get through. He was more than happy to talk about himself, but clammed up the minute the questions turned to Ester Jensen. He had admitted to killing her, but claimed that he hadn't meant to. Refused to say why.

Hanna slowly made her way up to the investigation room with her coffee, and was surprised to see that Erik Lindgren was already there. She usually had the office to herself when she got to the station this early.

"Trouble sleeping?" she asked.

"Yup," said Erik. "Pretty much every single muscle is aching."

Given how tanned and fit Erik was, Hanna had thought he must be a surfer the first time she saw him. His dark blond curls had probably contributed to that impression. Erik had taken part in Ironman Kalmar this past weekend. It was an overcast day, no more than around sixty-eight, but Hanna had gone to cheer him on with their colleagues Daniel and Amer. Amer had left after just a few hours, saying he needed to get home to his family, but she and Daniel had stayed until the very end. Erik was desperate for company at the moment. His wife and daughter had been in India for nearly six weeks, and wouldn't be home until Friday.

Hanna sat down at her desk and started going through her emails. She usually liked this time of day. The calm. Drinking coffee and getting a handle on everything that had happened since she'd last left the office. There wasn't much to catch up on today. She was in charge of an assault investigation, but the witness she was chasing still hadn't been in touch. Perhaps they never would. The victim was a nineteen-year-old male, and he had likely lost sight in one eye.

Her thoughts drifted back to Gunnar, to why he had said what he had. If she really wanted to understand, she knew she couldn't keep ignoring him. Her first attempt at a message sounded too accusatory, so she deleted it and started again. Closed her eyes and hit send:

I'm sorry about yesterday.

He replied immediately:

Yes. This was why I wasn't sure about meeting. I knew you'd ask.

Hanna stared at his words. She had no idea how to respond, and jumped when a new message arrived:

I know this is hard.

Anger flared up inside Hanna. No, Gunnar didn't know, no one did. He had managed to put Lars and the difficult years behind him and move on. With that thought, the sense of shame hit her like a recoil. Gunnar had helped Lars more than she ever had.

Amer came into the office.

"Our hero!" he said. "How're you feeling?"

Hanna was on the verge of blurting out something stupid when she realized he was talking to Erik.

"About as well as I deserve."

"Agreed," said Amer. "But you did it, in any case."

After thirty kilometers of the final run, they had seen Erik approaching with a pained look on his face. They had cheered and whistled, encouraging him to keep going. And they had celebrated with a beer in one of the tents afterward.

Daniel and Carina came in, both stopping to chat with Erik. Daniel's face was slightly pink, the way Hanna's skin always looked after spending too much time in the first spring sun. She wondered what he could have gotten up to yesterday. During after-work drinks recently, he had launched into a long tirade about just how bad the sun was for the skin.

Carina, on the other hand, had clearly spent a large part of her summer outdoors, likely in the garden she loved so much. Things were still chilly between the two women. Carina had made it perfectly clear how much she disliked the fact that Lars Duncker's daughter had been given a detective job with the Kalmar police. Her cousin was Ester Jensen's daughter Maria—though they were related through their fathers.

Their boss, Ove Hultmark, popped his head into the room.

"Sorry to interrupt," he said. "But since everyone is already here, we might as well start the morning meeting."

The morning meeting was almost always held in a pre-booked room, but the rest of their meetings generally took place in the investigation room. Hanna took a seat in the meeting room and studied the lines on Ove's face. He had decided to stop smoking just over a week ago, but Hanna suspected that wasn't the reason for his dogged expression. Nor the fact that they had forgotten to ask if he wanted to come along to the Ironman on Saturday. The relative calm of the past few weeks was likely about to come to an abrupt end.

Ove brought up two images. One was a passport picture of a man in his forties, the other a snapshot of a younger woman sitting on the floor, stacking building blocks with a toddler. The woman was wearing a pale blue summer dress, the boy a T-shirt and a diaper. Sunlight was flooding in onto the wooden floor around them. At the moment the photograph was taken, the child had turned to the camera with a laugh, but the woman's focus was on the child. It was a great picture.

"Forty-three-year-old Thomas Ahlström and his son Hugo were reported missing late last night," said Ove.

"How old is the boy?" asked Hanna.

"Fourteen months. It was Thomas's wife who called it in. She caught the train back from Gothenburg yesterday, and her husband was supposed to pick her up at the station, but he never showed. When she got home she realized that both he and the boy were gone."

"What kind of state was the house in?"

"No idea," said Ove. "All I know is that the car was also missing. The woman's name is Jenny Ahlström, she lives in Hulterstad. I want you and Erik to go over there and talk to her."

4

According to the GPS, Hulterstad—on the southeast coast of Öland—was a forty-minute drive away. Erik reclined the passenger seat and closed his eyes. Both his body and his mind were exhausted. There had been several moments during the Ironman on Saturday when he had wanted to give up. In fact, toward the end of the run, his colleagues' cheers had been all that kept him going.

Erik was proud that he had reached the finish line. The run was, without doubt, one of the hardest things he had ever done. He had video-called Supriya and Nila from the beer tent afterward. They could barely hear one another, but for his daughter's sake he had panned across the tent with the camera on his phone. Supriya had looked so happy for him, and she had confessed that she hadn't thought he would actually manage it.

Exhaustion tugged reality from under his feet, and Erik suddenly found himself running across the Teen Hath Naka crossing in Mumbai. It wasn't the crazy traffic that made him realize he was dreaming, but the tractor that drove by with Hanna and Daniel in its trailer. They were both shouting to him, but he couldn't hear what they were saying over the blaring of horns. Given how angry they looked, it was probably just as well. A much softer voice cut through to him, dragging him back to reality. He rubbed his mouth and sat upright.

"Was I snoring?"

"Yup," said Hanna.

Erik gazed out at the countryside racing by. A combine harvester was working its way through some sort of crop he didn't recognize. The field beside it was full of stacked white bales. The flat, open landscape stretched out for miles all around them.

"How much farther is it?"

"Just a few minutes."

His thoughts drifted back to Supriya, and Hanna seemed to sense it.

"Almost Friday," she said.

"Yeah."

The word tugged at his chest, and he had to take a deep breath.

"The longest we've ever been apart before is one week," he said once he had composed himself.

Erik occasionally regretted not going to India with them, but the truth was that he just couldn't take that much time off work. Supriya's mother had suffered a heart attack during a visit to Sweden earlier that year, and her desire to be there for her parents was the reason she had spent the summer in India. Her mother was doing much better now.

Hanna drove into the small community. The way the farms and houses were arranged along the main road was a vestige of medieval times; Erik remembered that from a radio documentary he had heard. The villages on Öland sometimes consisted of no more than a few houses, but he saw both a church and a handwritten sign announcing that Hulterstad had overnight accommodation.

After a few hundred meters, Hanna turned off the main road and pulled up in front of a white stone house. Erik could make out what looked like a sports field at the end of the gravel track. His desire to live in the countryside had faded somewhat recently, partly because he knew he would never be able to convince Supriya to make the move, but perhaps more so because he had realized that he would never be happy living somewhere so isolated. Their current home in the Varvsholmen area of Kalmar, within walking distance of the city center, was comfortable. Part of the dream of living in the countryside was becoming self-sufficient, and since he had stopped reading about how to do that, it had freed up a huge amount of time. Erik had bought a guitar a few weeks ago, and was now following a course he found on YouTube.

A WOMAN—SHE HAD TO be Jenny Ahlström—hurried out onto the steps. She looked several years older than she did in the picture with her son, and was wearing a long cardigan over a top and jeans. It was a blustery day, but the sun was shining and Erik was in a T-shirt. Hanna clutched her left arm. Back when they first met, Erik had assumed she must have some kind of injury there, but when he asked her about it she had shown him her tattoo of a nightingale. She often sought it out during stressful situations.

"Have you found them?" Jenny called over as they got out of the car.

They quickly made their way toward her.

"I'm afraid not," said Erik.

As they came closer, he noticed that her pupils were huge, her top inside out. She likely hadn't slept all night.

"I just don't understand where they could be," she said. "What if—"

"Why don't we sit down inside?" Hanna interrupted her.

Jenny stared at them like she wanted to argue, but she turned around with a sigh and led them into a large living room with an open hearth. The pieces of a train set were scattered across the floor. The room was sparsely furnished, and Erik got the sense that they hadn't lived there for long. Jenny slumped onto the sofa and pulled her cardigan tight around her. He and Hanna each took a seat in an armchair.

"I just don't understand," Jenny mumbled again. Her hands were restless, straightening her cardigan, smoothing her hair, moving back to her cardigan.

"When did you last hear from Thomas yesterday?" asked Erik.

"I called him at about half past two, and we texted sometime around four, just before I got on the train. I sent him a message as I was approaching Kalmar, but he didn't reply. He was supposed to pick me up from the station, but he never showed. To be perfectly honest with you, I was annoyed, because I thought he'd fallen asleep. I waited for fifteen minutes, but then I got fed up and took a cab."

"How did he sound when you spoke at half past two?"

"Like his usual self. I mean, it's hard to say, because I accidentally woke Hugo. They'd been to the playground in Skogsby."

Erik steeled himself for the question he knew he had to ask:

"Is there anything to suggest that Thomas has been depressed lately?"

"Are you saying he might have . . . ?"

Jenny stared at the two officers with wide eyes. The fear in them tugged at Erik's heart, and he did what he could to reassure her.

"That's just a standard question," he said. "It's something we ask whenever anyone is reported missing."

Jenny hurried to shake her head.

"No, I really don't think so. And even if he was feeling down, he'd never hurt Hugo. Never!"

Jenny's voice had gone up an octave, and she was clutching her cardigan so tightly that her knuckles had turned white. Erik hoped that what she had said was true, of course, but the car was missing and there hadn't been any serious accidents on the island the day before. Suicide was one of the two most likely explanations. The second was that Thomas had, for whatever reason, decided to leave. Perhaps he felt like he needed to be alone—though that was probably less likely given that his wife had been away. Going missing was not, in itself, a crime, but the Ahlströms had joint custody of their son, and child abduction was an offense that carried a prison sentence.

"We aren't suggesting anything," said Hanna. "Right now we're just trying to gather as much information as we can."

"You should be out looking for them instead."

"Yes," said Hanna. "But this is where we start. Do you know of anywhere Thomas likes to go when he needs to think?"

"No."

Jenny turned toward the open hearth, as though she couldn't bear to look at them. Erik could feel the fear and frustration in her straight, tense back. In the trembling of her lips.

"Has Thomas fallen out with anyone?" he asked.

The third possibility was that someone had hurt him and Hugo, though statistically speaking it was less likely.

"He's just started his paternity leave," said Jenny. "And he was really looking forward to spending more time with Hugo. He hasn't been particularly happy at work."

"What does he do?"

"He's an assistant real estate agent at a firm in Färjestaden."

Erik wrote down the name of the company.

"Why isn't he happy there?"

"He doesn't get on with one of his colleagues."

Jenny was still facing the open fire, but her back was no longer quite so straight. She turned to look at them, grief written across her face.

"I'm sorry, but that's all I know," she said. "Thomas didn't want to let on that he was unhappy."

"Why not?" asked Hanna.

"Because the job is so important to him. It's his first permanent position."

Jenny clamped her hand to her mouth and closed her eyes.

"What is it?" asked Erik.

But she simply shook her head. It took her a few seconds to compose herself enough to be able to answer.

"Thomas has another child," she said. "I just found out."

"How?"

"His daughter sent a letter."

THE LAST DAY

The plank of wood has cut off all blood to his legs, and Thomas gets up and stamps his feet to get it flowing again. He feels an unpleasant tingling sensation as his muscles start to wake up. Hugo is busy digging with a red plastic spade, and casts only a quick glance back to make sure his father isn't planning to run off. They don't have a sandpit at home, so Thomas decided to leave early in order to stop off in Skogsby and let his son play. Hugo tips the sand into his bucket, though most of it misses, and then looks up.

"Cookie?" he asks.

His bright blue eyes are wide with expectation.

"Yes," Thomas replies, sitting back down on the edge of the sandpit.

A woman who has brought her slightly older daughter to play gives him an encouraging smile. Thomas smiles back.

Hugo pushes his spade into the bucket and produces a little sand. He empties it into Thomas's outstretched palm. Thomas pretends to eat it and then heaps up the sand in a small pile beside him. The wooden plank is already covered in other, similar heaps. A few have been decorated with leaves, others with stones and pinecones. Hugo drops his spade and starts digging with his chubby little hands instead.

"Choccit!" he says, pressing his fist to his mouth.

His tiny body tenses, and he retches. It takes Thomas a moment to realize what is happening, and he throws himself toward his son, pushing a finger between his lips and digging around in his mouth. Hugo's arms are flailing. The woman is quickly by his side, trying to help.

"He put something in his mouth," is all Thomas manages to say.

The fear is worse than anything he has ever experienced before. The idea of losing Hugo. Of having to tell Jenny that he killed their son. The seconds seem to run between his fingers. He has no idea what to do. Should he turn him over and thump him on the back? Hugo's arms have stopped flapping. His eyes, so full of excitement just a moment ago, are now staring up at him in desperation. The boy's face is so pale. He can't breathe. His eyelids flutter, and all Thomas can see are the whites of his eyes. His body grows limp, heavy.

Oh God. He's dead.

Thomas feels like throwing up, but he swallows. He remembers that you aren't supposed to poke around in their mouth like this. That it could inadvertently push whatever is stuck deeper.

No, no, no, I've killed him.

Thomas pulls Hugo across his lap and starts hitting him between the shoulder blades. The woman holds out her arms. Maybe she knows how to do that Heimlich thing. But right then, Thomas manages to dislodge whatever was stuck.

He stares down at the wet black lump his son thought was a sweet. It's a dead beetle. Thomas rolls Hugo over and feels like screaming to vent his anxiety. Nothing happens. The boy's body is as limp as ever, his eyes still closed.

But then he coughs. His cough is followed by an angry howl, and his face quickly regains its color.

Thomas wraps his arms around the boy, who is now crying. The sound is the most beautiful thing Thomas has ever heard. In order to cry, you need to be able to breathe.

The woman opens her mouth, and Thomas comes close to hissing at her. He doesn't like being thought of as a bad parent just because he has the wrong genitals. And he doesn't want a lecture on keeping a better watch over his son. He already knows.

"Uff, that was awful," says the woman. "My daughter almost choked on a coin last week. She came through to me in the bathroom with her face all blue."

The girl has now left the sandpit and is making her way over to the swings. The woman gets up and hurries after her. Thomas clutches Hugo to his chest, but his son is bored of hugging.

"Owow!" he says.

Thomas lowers him to the sand and lets him keep digging, this time with his eyes locked on his tiny hands. He doesn't love anything the way he loves this little boy. He loves Jenny, of course, but there is no comparing the two. He feels himself smiling when he thinks back to the moment he first laid eyes on Hugo. Pink and wrinkled and sticky. When he first heard him cry.

His son holds out a spadeful of sand and Thomas takes it, raising it to his mouth and smacking his lips.

How could he have turned his back on all this the first time around?

5

The letter from Thomas's daughter Lykke was handwritten and stretched to one side of A4. In it, she wrote that she was living in her mother's house in Grönhögen, that she had inherited it after her mother's death. That she would like to meet Thomas if he was interested. The words themselves were mild, but the letters were large and eager. In one place, her pen had actually broken through the yellow lined paper.

"How did you react when Thomas showed you this?" Hanna asked, passing the letter to Erik.

"He didn't," said Jenny. "I found it a few weeks ago."

"Where?"

"In that box over there." Jenny nodded to the low Billy bookcase she had retrieved the letter from. "And I wasn't snooping. The lid fell off while I was cleaning."

"Was there an envelope?"

"No," said Jenny.

The letter wasn't dated, meaning they couldn't be sure how long Thomas had been in possession of it.

"Did you confront Thomas?" asked Hanna.

Jenny twisted her wedding ring on her finger. It was a smooth gold band, and it was obvious that it was too tight. The skin around it was bulging. She had likely put on weight since the wedding.

"I wanted to," she said. "That's partly why I went to stay with my friend in Gothenburg over the weekend."

"Partly?"

"Yes, I needed to get away. Without Thomas and Hugo."

Realizing what she had said, Jenny's face twisted.

"I just wanted to be on my own for a few days. To find myself again, you know? Things have been so intense since Hugo was born."

"In what sense?"

Jenny took the question as an accusation.

"I've barely slept through the night in over a year. When things were really bad, he was waking up every hour. I take it you don't have kids?"

"No," said Hanna.

A memory of Fabian came back to her. Trailing a finger along her collarbone, moving downward, looking up at her and asking whether she wanted children. If she had reacted differently that day, perhaps it would have been her and Fabian going to the midwife for an ultrasound. Erik's voice broke through the memory.

"Can we take this with us?" he asked, holding up the letter.

"Yes," Jenny replied after a brief pause.

She turned to Hanna:

"Sorry. I'm stressed. I just really want them to come back."

"We do, too," said Hanna.

Was Thomas's disappearance voluntary or not? Right now, finding out was their top priority.

"You said that things have been intense since Hugo was born. How has that affected your relationship with Thomas?"

Jenny sighed and let go of her wedding ring, massaging the bridge of her nose instead.

"The lack of sleep really got to us," she said. "Neither of us have parents nearby to help out, and I suppose we've probably taken it out on each other a bit much. But we have a good relationship. There's no way Thomas would run off with Hugo. Or . . ."

Jenny lowered her hand but left the sentence hanging.

"Where do Thomas's parents live?" asked Erik.

"Växjö. Mine moved to Malmö."

"Does Thomas have anyone he can talk to?" asked Hanna. "Aside from you, I mean."

"Mille Bergman," said Jenny. "They've been friends since school."

"Is Mille a nickname?"

"Nope, that's his real name."

Hanna asked for the details of the friend Jenny had visited in Gothenburg, but Jenny's hands were shaking so much that she dropped her phone onto the fluffy gray rug. Hanna bent down and picked it up.

"What's her name?"

"Valerija Leko. We studied economics together at Linnaeus University in Kalmar."

Hanna brought up Valerija's contact details on Jenny's phone and sent them over to herself, then asked whether there was anything else Jenny could tell them about Thomas, about their relationship. Jenny shook her head.

"I can't handle any more of this. It's like a nightmare, and I just want to wake up."

Jenny's eyes moved around the room. Perhaps she was searching for anything that looked out of place. Something that might prove this wasn't really happening.

Hanna moved over to the sofa beside her.

"I know this is hard," she said, "but it's vital that we know as much as possible about you and Thomas. It could be crucial to us finding him and Hugo."

"There's nothing else to know."

Hanna suspected it was her question about their relationship that had made Jenny falter.

"Finding out he had a daughter must have come as a shock?" she said in an attempt to muscle her way through to something else.

"What do you think?" Jenny's voice was sharp with irritation.

"That it must have come as a shock," said Hanna.

Jenny began turning her ring again, more roughly this time. She tried to push it along her finger, but it got stuck. Without warning, she let go of the ring and slumped forward, her head resting heavily in her hands.

"I don't understand why he didn't say anything," she sobbed. "Did he think I couldn't handle it?"

They sat quietly, listening to her cry. After a moment or two Erik got up and went out into the hallway. He came back with some tissues and held them out to Jenny.

"We need to take a look around the house," he said.

Perhaps he thought Hanna had been too hard on her. Jenny's only response was to nod and grab one of the tissues. Erik went off to the bathroom and Hanna took the kitchen. The sink was full of dirty plates and glasses. On the stove, there was a pan of dried-up pasta and a greasy frying pan. At the very top of the trash can, she saw a couple of burned slices of sausage. Something red underneath caught her eye, and Hanna grabbed a spatula from a pot by the sink and pushed the pieces of sausage to one side. The red object was a piece of bloody paper towel, and she noticed the white wrapper of a small bandage beside it. Hanna went back out to Jenny.

"What was the kitchen like when you got home yesterday?"

"The leftovers from dinner were still on the table, like he'd just got up and left. I started tidying everything away, but I didn't have the energy."

"Did you clean up any blood?"

"Blood?"

Jenny stared at her in horror.

"Yes—but I'm only talking about a small amount."

"No."

Jenny tossed her used tissue onto the coffee table and pulled another out of the pack, pressing it to her eyes. Erik came back into the living room.

"Do you have an attic or a basement?" he asked.

"A basement," said Jenny. "But it's only accessible from outside."

Erik and Hanna exchanged a quick glance. The basement could wait until they were done in the house.

"Do you know what Thomas and Hugo were wearing when they disappeared?" Hanna asked.

"No. Actually, maybe."

Jenny showed them a couple of pictures on her phone. Both were of Hugo. In one, he was on the slide outside the house, and in the other he was holding an ice pop in the kitchen. He was wearing a green-and-blue-striped T-shirt and a pair of shorts. Without a word, Erik turned back out into the hallway, returning with both items of clothing.

"These were in the washing basket."

The sight of the T-shirt and shorts was too much for Jenny, who was now on the verge of falling apart. Her eyes began to drift around the room again, but it was like she couldn't quite focus on anything. Hanna gave her a concrete task to cling on to.

"Could you go through their clothes? You might be able to work out what they were wearing."

Jenny looked up at her, and Hanna's words became a life buoy that she fought her way over to.

"I'll try," she said quietly.

"Does Thomas have a computer?" asked Erik.

"Yes." Jenny opened a drawer in the coffee table and passed the laptop to Erik.

"Could we take this away with us, too?"

Jenny nodded, though it was by no means certain she had actually heard him. Hanna wondered whether she really had been too hard on her after all.

"Is there anyone we can call?" she asked.

"What do you mean?"

"Anyone who can come over and be with you."

"No," said Jenny. "I'd like you to go now, so I can check through their clothes."

"We'll be in touch," said Hanna, getting to her feet.

"Please, you have to find them!"

They carried Jenny's desperate plea back out to the car with them. Erik put the laptop into an evidence bag in the trunk, and they then searched the basement. Hanna had once been called out to a house in the Stockholm suburbs after a woman reported her husband missing. She had found him in the garden shed. The autopsy showed he had died of a heart attack.

The basement was a storm cellar, and they opened both of the sloping doors. Erik went in first, pulling on the cord for the bulb on the ceiling. The damp space was full of moving boxes, stacked in the center of the room. There were some rickety metal shelves holding cans of paint and brushes against one wall. One quick loop around the boxes was all it took to determine that neither Thomas nor Hugo were there. Hanna hadn't really thought they would be, considering the family car was missing, but they had to be sure.

"So, to Grönhögen?" Erik asked once they were back outside, the doors firmly closed.

"Yeah, probably best to speak to the daughter first, then drive up to the real estate agent in Färjestaden."

"How far is it?"

"About twenty minutes with you driving."

Erik snorted and got behind the wheel.

"Did you notice anything in the house?" asked Hanna.

"Their toothbrushes were still there. And all their clothes, too."

Hanna shared her impressions from the kitchen. If Thomas had voluntarily disappeared with Hugo, it likely hadn't been planned. She dismissed Erik's question about whether they should have seized the bloody paper towel as evidence. A wound that required no more than a small bandage wasn't of interest to them. It was clear the blood belonged to either Thomas or Hugo. Hanna tried calling both Valerija Leko and Mille Bergman, but neither picked up, so she tried Ove instead, bringing him up to speed about Thomas's surprise daughter.

"What do you think?" he asked.

Hanna sighed, casting her mind back to the dried pasta and the pieces of burned sausage.

"It looked like they ate dinner, got up, and left."

"What does your gut tell you?"

"Do you really want guesswork?"

"No," said Ove. "Not really, but you know . . ."

"Yeah."

That was all Hanna said; the boss didn't want to hear any stabs in the dark. Investigations involving children as young as Hugo always stirred up emotions. What they feared most was that Thomas had murdered or injured his son and then committed suicide, but as things stood they didn't know nearly enough. Something else could easily have happened.

"I spoke to Växjö," said Ove. "They're sending a unit out to Thomas Ahlström's parents."

They ended the call, and Hanna gazed out at the sparse grassland of the alvar speeding by outside. The air was growing hazy, hugging the barren landscape. One of her first deaths had been a father who killed his own child before taking his own life. "Extended Suicide." "A Family Tragedy." The newspapers had been full of those euphemistic headlines, but it was murder, nothing less.

6

Lykke wiped the sweat from her forehead with the back of her hand. She was on her knees in front of the flower bed by the patio. Her stomach and back were aching, but she didn't want to give up. Couldn't. Right now she needed to shut out anything unrelated to digging up the damned docks.

She drove the spade into the ground, struggling to make her eyes focus. Irritated, she dug harder. Lykke had never thought of herself as a garden person. Sure, she had planted plenty of things, but she had never let it engross her like this. Maybe this was the type of job she should be looking for? Something where she had to physically exert herself.

"You bloody idiot," she hissed. "Who are you trying to kid?"

When Lykke got back to the house after her swim that morning, she hadn't known what to do with herself. Starting her battle against the overgrown garden was the only thing that had stopped her from scoffing down the bar of chocolate in the fridge. She had bought it solely to prove to herself that she could resist the urge. She had been living on vegetables, beans, and fruit since spring, but now? Lykke didn't know how she would ever be able to eat again. The future no longer felt like a cold front approaching. It was a ferocious storm, tossing her around like an autumn leaf.

The spade hit a rock, and Lykke swore. A memory of the knife in the tire immediately reared its head, but she forced it back. What she saw in its place was much worse, because it was the sight that had started everything. Her standing outside the house, looking in through the window. Seeing the woman and the child.

Lykke drove the spade into the ground again, and this time it cut through the soil without any resistance. She pushed it beneath the dock plant, dug around. Only once the roots began to loosen did the memory of the woman and the child fade away. With a laugh, she tossed the dock onto the pile of weeds.

This was a battle she could win.

Lykke heard a car on the other side of the hedge. She was sure it would drive on by, but it came to a halt. A door slammed and footsteps crossed the gravel. They sounded like they knew where they were going. What if it was Thomas's crazy wife? Lykke could barely breathe. She gripped the handle of the spade.

Two people came around the corner. A man and a woman. They were both wearing jeans, the man in a T-shirt and the woman a button-down. They looked like fitness instructors. From their movements alone, she had a sneaking suspicion of what their ID badges soon confirmed.

"We're from the police," said the woman, introducing herself as Hanna Duncker.

Fear made Lykke clumsy, and she dropped the spade.

"What's going on?" she asked, though she knew exactly why they were there.

"Could we sit down and talk?" the male officer asked.

He had said his name, but Lykke had forgotten it already. He wasn't smiling, but he had a kind face—though she had learned that appearances could be deceiving. She got up, dizziness making her reel. The man held out a hand to support her, and she had no choice but to take it to avoid falling.

"Are you okay?" he asked.

"Low blood pressure," she mumbled.

Lykke pulled away from him and brushed the dirt from her jeans. She nodded to the patio she had already tidied up. She had found the wooden furniture for next to nothing online a few years earlier, and had painted it white.

"What's going on?" she asked again the minute they were sitting down.

"It's to do with your father, Thomas Ahlström," said the man.

"Sorry, what did you say your name was?" she asked. "I've forgotten."

It was so hard to remember everything.

"I'm Erik and this is my colleague Hanna," he said. "Your father Thomas was reported missing yesterday, along with his son Hugo."

"I know." Lykke forced the words out.

"How did you find out?" asked the female officer.

Her gaze was so piercing that Lykke felt like she had to look away.

"His wife called me last night," she said. "Shouting and screaming and calling me all kinds of things. I eventually got her to tell me who she was and why she was so angry. She was convinced Thomas and Hugo were here."

"Are they?"

"No."

Lykke stared down at the flower bed. If the officers would just go, she could get back to pulling up the docks. She didn't want them to spread into the flower bed where the toad lilies were. Her mother had grown them, and Lykke had loved the purple-flecked flowers since she was a girl. She and her mother used to call them shadow lilies, because they were proof that beautiful things could grow in the shade. They also brought butterflies into the garden.

It had been after ten when Jenny called, and it had been horrible, the way she had ranted and raved. How could someone Lykke had never even met hate her so much?

7

"Why don't you have any contact with your dad?" asked Hanna.

Lykke Henriksen turned to face her, but it was as though her eyes weren't really taking anything in. She slowly pulled the rubber band from her light brown hair and then tied it up in exactly the same way, in a loose bun at the nape of her neck. Her jeans and tank top were both grubby, and she had a streak of dirt on her forehead. She was twenty-four, according to the national registration database, but Hanna thought she seemed younger.

"Lykke," she said.

When the girl said yes, she repeated the question.

"You'll have to ask him why we don't have any fucking contact."

Her anger flared up and then faded away. Lykke looked down at her hands. Rubbed at the dirt.

"Sorry," she whispered. "It just makes me so angry sometimes. He abandoned Mom and me when I was only a few months old."

"When did you send him the letter?" asked Erik.

"A few weeks ago."

"Could you be more specific?"

"At the start of July."

"What made you decide to write it?"

Lykke's eyes briefly met Erik's before she turned back to the flower bed. It was clear she was struggling to focus.

"I don't know," she eventually said. "It's the first time I've spent the summer on Öland in ages, and I . . . I usually live in Uppsala. I felt lonely, I guess. My mom isn't around anymore, and I've always wondered why he left us."

Hanna didn't have any parents, either. Her mother had died of cancer when she was just twelve, and that had caused her father to spiral out of control and start drinking. Kristoffer had spent more and more time away from the house; he had wanted to be anywhere that wasn't at home. And their father had died last autumn.

"When did your mom die?" she asked.

"Almost three years ago," said Lykke. "A car accident."

She was still staring at the flower bed, and it bothered Hanna that she seemed so evasive. Still, at least they were getting something resembling answers out of her now. Perhaps Lykke'd had bad experiences dealing with the police. Perhaps Hanna and Erik reminded her of the officers who had broken the news of her mother's death. Hanna followed her gaze. The bed was full of large speckled flowers, purple and white.

"Those are beautiful," she said.

"They're toad lilies."

"Did Thomas reply to your letter?" asked Erik.

"Yes, he phoned me."

Lykke's mouth was a straight line. Her father was clearly a sensitive subject, but the question was why. Lars had abandoned Hanna and Kristoffer in every sense but the physical, and it still hurt that he had chosen the booze over them. Was Thomas the reason for Lykke's state of mind now?

"What did he say?" Erik pressed her.

"That he could come over, but I wasn't sure I wanted him to."

Lykke folded her arms. Her entire body seemed to be screaming that she didn't want them there.

"Why not?" asked Hanna.

"I don't know," Lykke snapped.

They sat quietly, studying her, but she didn't go on.

"So you never managed to see him?" asked Erik.

"No."

Her answer came quickly, on an exhale. Hanna sensed there would be no point in pushing her right now.

"What did you do yesterday?" she asked, as though she were asking about something like the weather.

"Not much. Went swimming."

Lykke gazed out at the strait, and Hanna followed her eye. The air was clearer here than in the middle of the alvar, and they were so far south that the mainland was barely visible on the other side. She would have loved a view like this, but her house would have cost more than twice as much if it were this close to the water.

Hanna placed her card on the white wooden table. "Give us a call if you remember anything else."

Lykke nodded, and they got up to leave. Hanna glanced back just before turning the corner. The young woman was still sitting on the patio, and seemed to be staring down at the card.

"We're going to have to take a closer look at her," Erik said the minute they were back in the car.

"Agreed."

Hanna checked her phone. Neither Valerija Leko nor Mille Bergman had returned her call, so she sent Ove a quick update about their meeting with Thomas's daughter and then dialed Jenny's number. She answered on the first ring.

"Have you found them?"

"No, unfortunately, but I wanted to ask you a question. Who did you call when you realized Thomas and Hugo were missing?"

"Mille, because I thought he might know something. Then my parents and Valerija."

"Anyone else?"

"I guess you must've talked to his daughter," she sobbed.

"We have," said Hanna. "Why didn't you mention that you'd called her?"

She kept her voice soft, without any hint of accusation.

"I was so stressed it didn't cross my mind."

Jenny's version of events didn't involve any angry outbursts. All she had wanted to know was whether her husband and son were with Lykke. Hanna summarized the call for Erik once she hung up, but it was like talking to a brick wall.

"What's up?" she asked, sounding more irritated than intended.

She wasn't used to Erik ignoring her.

"Sorry," he said. "I'm just starving. Are there any good lunch places in Färjestaden?"

You idiot, Hanna scolded herself, failing to hide her feelings from her cheeks. She had always found it difficult when other people paid either too much or too little attention to her. The officers who had come to arrest her father represented the dividing line between the two extremes. Before that day, she had always lived in Rebecka's shadow. Her friend was twenty centimeters shorter than her, but she was the one everyone noticed, the one everyone wanted to be around. But after her father's arrest, suddenly it was Hanna everyone stared at.

"We can eat here in Grönhögen," she said, starting the engine. "So you don't have to wait so long."

"Thanks."

Hanna pulled up outside Kvarnkrogen. The restaurant was in an old windmill, and it had just opened for the day. The family waiting in line ahead of them were clearly on holiday. The mother and father were both carrying colorful beach bags, and the two children were being noisy. A brother and a sister, possibly around as close in age as she and Kristoffer were. The girl was laughing, but not the boy. It felt like there was an argument brewing.

"Would you please settle down?" their father snapped, and for a few seconds his words actually seemed to have worked.

Once, when Hanna and Kristoffer were around that age, the family had driven down to Spain on holiday. They had probably never fought as much as they did during that week on the Mediterranean. They had drawn a line between the beds in their shared room and each had forbidden the other from crossing it. She remembered their mother telling them off whenever they behaved like little despots, encouraging them to be there for each other instead. Their days had been spent by the pool. Kristoffer had pushed Hanna in, but when he realized she had hurt herself on the edge of the pool, he had jumped in after her. Looking back now, twenty-five years later, the trip seemed fantastic. Because no matter how Kristoffer occasionally behaved, she had always been able to trust him.

"What do you fancy?" asked Erik.

Hanna ordered a smoked salmon salad, Erik a pizza. They sat down in the shade on the patio.

"Are you telling me you've never been to Grönhögen before?" she asked.

"Nope. But Nila would definitely like this place. Getting to eat pizza in an old windmill."

"Have you shelved your plans to move to the countryside?"

It had been several weeks since Hanna had last heard Erik mention it.

"Yeah. To be perfectly honest with you, I don't know what I was thinking. I'd lose my mind. I'm all about the guitar now. You don't know how to play, do you?"

Hanna laughed, but she quickly realized he was serious. She could just picture him with a guitar. He felt like the type who would crack out a few tunes the minute a party got boring.

"No, the only instrument I can even slightly play is the recorder."

Erik had begun wolfing down his pizza the minute it arrived, and polished off the entire thing in no time at all.

"You don't want another?" she asked.

"I'm fine, thanks."

He leaned back in his chair, grimacing slightly as he stretched out his legs. Hanna still felt ashamed for having snapped at him. She stared down at the table, trying to ward off the nineteen-year-old who had watched her father being led away by the police. Whom people had suddenly started talking and having opinions about, even when she was present.

"I read through the investigation into Ester Jensen's death," she said.

"Why?" asked Erik.

"I need to know exactly what happened."

"And are you any the wiser?"

Hanna began gushing about the evidence, about the fact that her father's DNA had been found in the house, his fingerprints on the gas can outside. But also about what Gunnar had said. She hadn't planned to mention that, not to Erik, but she didn't want to be that nineteen-year-old anymore. The one who had never managed to speak up, who had never dared open up about how it felt when her father became the object of everyone's hatred. It had taken Hanna many years to realize just how much of a shock the entire thing had been. The shock had tossed her to one side, separating her from everyone and everything.

"Uff, sounds rough," said Erik. "What are you going to do now?"

She felt herself becoming irritated again. How could Erik be so calm? It was as though he didn't really care. Hanna felt so terribly alone. In this, in everything. No matter how hard she tried, she would always be floating around in her own little world.

"I've got no goddamn idea," she said.

8

Erik got behind the wheel for the drive to the real estate agent in Färjestaden. He was more or less used to Hanna's rash driving style by now, but she seemed to need a break. Erik could understand why she was so irritable. The evidence against her father was strong, and her brother was hardly the alternative suspect she had been hoping for. On top of that, a father and son were missing. What he didn't know was how she had wanted him to react to the things she had told him. Still, at least she was talking to him now. When they first started working together three months ago, it had been a struggle to coax anything unrelated to the job out of her.

"Should we call ahead to see if there's anyone there?"

"I don't think that's necessary," said Hanna.

Erik agreed with her. He had only really asked in order to have something to say. The weeks without his family had left him even less keen on silence than before. Time seemed to pass much more slowly when no one was speaking.

Friberg Properties was on Storgatan, directly opposite the harbor in Färjestaden, and Erik found a free parking space right outside the low white stone building. With its restaurants and gift shops, the harbor was a tourist magnet, but the area around the real estate agency was more like a miniature industrial park. Only two of the five desks were occupied when Hanna and Erik stepped into the office, and a woman immediately got to her feet and came over with an unconvincing smile plastered across her face. Erik glanced over at Hanna. They made a pretty unlikely couple. Perhaps the woman thought they had come in to sell the house after their marriage had hit the rocks.

"How can I help?" she asked.

The woman was in her thirties, wearing a white blouse and smart trousers. Her strawberry-blond hair was tied up in a high ponytail, and her face was dotted with small, pretty freckles. She had green eyes, one with a pale brown fleck. There was a cautiousness about her that Erik didn't typically associate with real estate agents.

"We'd like to speak to Karl Friberg," he said.

The woman's smile stiffened and disappeared completely as they produced their ID.

"What is this regarding?" she asked.

But Erik didn't have time to reply before the man was there: a wiry sixty-something in jeans and a shirt. He couldn't tell what color his short dark gray hair had once been, but the fact that his green eyes had the same brown fleck as the woman's told Erik they were likely related.

"I'm Karl," said the man. "Excuse the way I'm dressed; I hadn't planned to come in to the office today. Why don't we sit down in the contracts room?"

He led them through to a tiny room, no more than a few square meters in size. The air inside was stale, and Karl turned on a pedestal fan.

"The AC's on the blink," he explained.

"Must've been tough last week?"

There had been a heat wave on the island, with temperatures climbing above eighty-six, but cooler days were now approaching. Erik had sent a picture of the week's forecast to Supriya that morning—a series of dark clouds and rain—begging her to bring back some sun from India.

"No, it was working then."

They sat down at the oval table, which had two seats on either side. There was a bowl of toffees in the middle, the company's name on the wrapper, plus a jug of water and a few empty glasses. Erik reached for the jug and helped himself, then glanced over at Hanna, who shook her head. He drained his glass in a few quick gulps.

Karl's phone started ringing, the name Madeleine flashing up on the screen.

"My wife," he explained, rejecting the call. "Can I get you anything else to drink? Coffee?"

"No, thank you," Erik and Hanna replied in unison.

"We're here regarding one of your employees," said Hanna. "Thomas Ahlström. He was reported missing yesterday."

"Okay . . . ," said Karl Friberg. "What do you mean, missing?"

"I'm afraid we can't go into any details," said Erik. "When did you last see him?"

Karl pushed back his chair, as though he needed more room to process what he had just been told.

"Friday two weeks ago," he said. "Thomas worked his last day here. Before going on paternity leave, I mean."

The door to the office was open, and Erik got up and closed it. The woman was staring at her computer screen, but he was fairly sure her focus was on their conversation. Karl Friberg seemed to relax once the door was closed. He even smiled at the two officers.

"We've been told that Thomas didn't get along with one of your staff," said Erik.

Karl's smile froze.

"Believe me," he said, "I would know if that was the case. Who told you that?"

"I'm afraid we can't say."

"This is a small family business, and I'm very particular about the atmosphere in the office."

"How many employees do you have?" asked Hanna.

"There are four of us right now."

"Who?"

"Three real estate agents. Me, my son Hektor, and my daughter Selene." Karl nodded to the glass wall. "That's her over there. And then there's Thomas, who is an assistant."

"So Thomas is the only person working here who isn't part of the family?"

"At the moment, yes, but the number of staff varies. We're looking for a temp to replace him right now."

"Where is Hektor today?" asked Erik.

"He's doing a valuation in Långöre. He just left, so it'll probably be a while before he's back."

Erik wasn't sure where Långöre was, but he thought it was farther north, on the other side of the island.

"What made you come in to the office today?" Hanna spoke up.

"We've got someone coming to fix the air-conditioning," said Karl. "So I wanted to be here for that."

"What's your impression of Thomas?" asked Erik.

Karl poured himself a glass of water and took a couple of sips before he replied.

"He's charming. Our clients like him."

"And his performance?"

"Good."

Karl Friberg peered out at his daughter and gave a deep sigh before turning back to them with glassy eyes.

"I hope you find him," he said.

"We do, too," said Erik.

As they left the room, Selene glanced nervously over at them. She had definitely heard that her colleague was missing while the door was open, but perhaps she had heard the rest of their conversation, too.

"When did you last see Thomas Ahlström?" Erik asked her.

Selene stared up at them like she didn't understand the question.

"Sorry," she said. "It's just sounds so awful that he's missing. I can't believe it."

"Yes," said Hanna, then she repeated Erik's question.

"It was . . . two weeks ago, on the Friday. That was his last day before he went on paternity leave, so I bought a cake for our coffee break."

"Is there anything you can tell us about him?"

"No. Like what?"

Her cheeks flushed slightly, and she peered around the room, but Karl had disappeared into what was probably the office pantry. Through the door, Erik could make out a coffee machine and a metal canister on the worktop.

"Anything."

"He's considerate," said Selene. "And funny."

"How did he feel about going on paternity leave?" asked Erik.

"It was all he could talk about during that coffee break. He was really looking forward to it."

The front door opened, and a man in his forties came in to the office. Karl reappeared from the pantry.

"I'm glad you could come in at such short notice," he said.

This had to be the man who had come to repair the air-conditioning, but his toolbox was the only thing suggesting he was any kind of technician. He was wearing jeans and a Kalmar FF soccer shirt, and his breath stank of booze.

THE LAST DAY

Thomas wrestles Hugo into the car. The boy is already cranky with hunger, and he squirms in protest. Thomas's phone starts ringing just as he manages to fasten the seat belt. He worries that it might be Selene, calling to cancel their lunch, but it's Jenny.

"How are you both?" she asks.

"Good."

He knows he should tell her about what happened in the playground, that Hugo almost choked. But the terror still feels much too fresh, and if he lets it out he'll fall apart. Hugo almost died, and Thomas is ashamed. He needs to be more alert.

"What are you up to?"

"Just playing in the garden, but we're about to head inside for something to eat."

The lie slips right out of him. Thomas doesn't want to reveal who he is going to meet. He places a reassuring hand on Hugo, who is trying to wriggle out of the car seat.

"You're still coming to get me later, aren't you?"

Jenny sounds so happy and relaxed that some of her calm rubs off on him. They have been together for six years, and there are times when he still feels amazed that someone like her wants to be with him.

"Nothing could keep us away," he says.

Jenny's train doesn't get in until a quarter past eight, which is roughly when they usually put Hugo to bed, but Thomas wants to be there. Her little trip has been good for them. Taking care of Hugo on his own for a few days has really helped him understand certain things. It isn't entirely his fault that Jenny shoulders so much of the responsibility. She has trouble letting go. Thomas is the one on parental leave, but she gets in touch several times a day—and claims that *he* is overprotective. They need to start talking about things like this, about how they can better share their parenting responsibilities.

"I can't wait," says Jenny.

"Me neither," says Thomas. He casts a quick glance at Hugo, who has managed to pull one arm free. "Listen, I need to go, Hugo is trying to climb up the slide."

"See you this evening," says Jenny. "I love you both."

"And we love you."

Thomas straightens Hugo's seat belt and then hurries to get into the driver's seat. The boy calms down as soon as the car starts moving. The drive to Färjestaden takes just under eight minutes, and Thomas talks to his son in an attempt to keep him awake. It'll be better if he naps after they eat. Maybe he should have told Jenny he was meeting Selene, but it's only lunch. And he doesn't want to extinguish the spark between them. They have been sending each other cute little messages since yesterday evening, the kind they used to send in the early days. Jenny has got it into her head that Selene is interested in him, and though he suspects she might be right, he has managed to convince her that she's just imagining it.

Thomas is lucky, and manages to find a parking space down by the harbor. He wanted to go somewhere that wasn't too expensive for lunch, so he and Selene are meeting at Hasse's. For a fast-food joint, the food is great.

"We're going to see Daddy's friend," he says, lifting his son from the car.

They aren't far from Hasse's, so he doesn't bother taking the buggy out of the trunk. Instead, he swings the changing bag over his shoulder.

"Friend," Hugo parrots. "Mille."

"No, not Mille. Daddy's friend Selene."

He doesn't really like saying her name, but the chances of Hugo repeating it to Jenny must be tiny. His son's focus is already elsewhere.

"Boats!" he cries.

They have been to the harbor before, to eat and look at the boats.

"Yes," says Thomas, holding him up to get a better view. The restaurant is in the other direction, and Selene is already there. She waves to them. She has her hair down for once, hanging loose over her shoulders. It suits her, but Thomas doesn't like the fact that she seems to have made an effort for his sake. The moment they come close enough, she reaches out and strokes Hugo's cheek, her strong perfume catching in Thomas's nose.

"God, he's so sweet. I just can't help myself."

"Yeah, he is." Thomas smiles.

"Imagine having such a little cutie pie."

Thomas doesn't like the way she sounds when she says that.

"What do you fancy?" asks Selene. "I can go and get it."

"A burger. The extra-large. With fries and a cola."

Thomas scans the seating area for a high chair, and soon spots one made from red plastic. He carries it over to a free table and lowers Hugo into it. But his son immediately wants to get up and toddle away.

"Boats!" he shouts.

"No, we're going to eat now," Thomas tells him.

There is a bag of corn puffs in the changing bag, and he quickly digs it out. Hugo takes the puff Thomas holds out to him and starts gnawing on it. He has forgotten all about the boats for now.

Selene comes back with their food, and she laughs when she sees Hugo. The boy really does eat with his entire face, and his cheeks are covered in yellow crumbs. The bag of corn puffs is empty, so Thomas gives him one of his french fries instead. He has some baby food in the bag, but decides not to bother taking it out. Hugo can have a few fries and some burger bun now, and eat the jar of pasta and meat sauce later. They've almost switched him over to normal food now anyway.

"How much do I owe you?" Thomas asks.

"It's on me."

"No."

"A hundred and two kronor."

Selene gives him the exact figure because she thinks he's being ridiculous, but Thomas doesn't want to be in debt to her. Hektor has been nagging him for his money every single day—though the amount he owes Hektor is a little more than a burger lunch.

"So, how's paternity leave?" asks Selene.

"Strange," says Thomas. "But nice."

Selene doesn't have any children, though he knows she wants them. She watches with a big smile as Hugo pushes pieces of crumbled bun into his mouth. Half of it ends up on the floor, and a couple of gulls land on the wooden fence surrounding the patio area. Thomas swats them away, but they soon swoop back.

"And how is Jenny?"

"Good. Her train from Gothenburg gets in tonight."

"Has Mommy been out having fun on her own?" Selene asks in a baby voice, poking Hugo in the belly. He laughs so hard that he drops the rest of the bread, and one of the gulls raises its head in expectation.

"Stop it," says Thomas.

Selene gives him a confused glance, and he blurts out something about being worried Hugo might choke on his food. He can't bring himself to tell her just how close they came that morning.

Selene has met Jenny only once. His wife brought Hugo in to the office to show him off when he was just a few months old. Everyone was there, but Selene was the only one who asked to hold him, and Jenny had been upset by the way she fussed over him. For whatever reason, Selene seems to struggle to make her relationships last. The latest one ended in spring, and before that she was with his friend Mille for a while.

When they finish eating, Thomas grabs a couple of coffees. He makes sure he puts his cup down well out of Hugo's reach.

"How are things at the office?" he asks, though he doesn't really want to know.

"The same as ever," says Selene. "Dad has been working way too much and Hektor keeps sneaking off whenever he can. I don't know what's wrong with him. He doesn't give a shit about everything Dad does for us."

Thomas has no real desire to talk about Hektor, so he just nods along. It's incomprehensible to him that two such different people could be siblings. Selene might be frustrated with her brother right now, but she usually defends him. Apparently he really stepped up to help their mother when she was ill.

"It's better when you're there," she goes on.

"Five months will pass in no time," Thomas says with a smile.

He hopes that Hektor won't still be working there by the time his paternity leave ends in January. It's so obvious that he doesn't want to be a part of the firm, and Thomas can't understand why he doesn't just find a job elsewhere. Yes, he has his conviction hanging over him, but he probably doesn't even want the kind of job where they'd have to run a background check.

Selene pulls faces at Hugo, making him laugh. Thomas realizes that he can't drag this out any longer, no matter whether it spoils the mood.

"Do you have the keys?"

He hates having to ask Selene for this, especially now that it feels like he has abandoned her at work. Everything was much easier when he could handle things himself. Still, it'll all be over soon. This is the last time. For Hugo's sake, he needs to stop.

Selene rummages through her handbag and passes an envelope to him. She holds on to it for a few seconds before letting go with a sigh.

"Why do you need them?" she asks.

"I'm sorry, but I can't say."

Selene swallows. She looks like she might be on the verge of tears. Without thinking, Thomas reaches out and puts his hand on top of hers.

"I promise you'll have them back by tomorrow evening at the latest," he says.

"I've got my dance class then. Can't you give them back during the day?"

Thomas stares down at his hand. He knows he should take it away.

"That won't work, I'm sorry," he says.

"Do you really need them today? It's not good for them to be out of the office for so long."

"I need them tonight," he says. "Before I pick Jenny up from the station at eight."

"Is Mille forcing you to do this?"

"No, absolutely not."

Selene starts chewing on her lower lip, the way she often does when she is struggling with something.

"One of the window ledges is broken. To the right of the front door. You can push the keys in there."

"Thanks," he says, squeezing her hand briefly before pulling back.

Selene turns to Hugo and gives him a sad smile.

"The family are arriving at ten o'clock on Tuesday," she says. "So if the keys aren't back by then . . ."

"They will be, I swear. Don't worry."

9

"Thoughts?" Erik asked once they had left the office.

"We need to find out whether there's anything to this apparent conflict."

Hanna turned around and peered in through the window. Her eyes briefly met Selene's before the real estate agent looked away. Selene's anxiety had been so tangible that Hanna had left her card, telling her to call if anything came up. It was still too early to say what that anxiety was about, but it was clear Selene had a father who cared about her. Hanna found herself wondering what it would have been like to work with her own family. It was hard to imagine the Dunckers running a real estate agency—or any other business, for that matter.

"Time to track down Hektor?" asked Erik.

"Yup. If you drive, I'll call him from the car. It would be good to get ahold of him before anyone else."

"Sure."

When Hektor Friberg failed to pick up, Hanna left a message telling him to call her back as soon as possible.

"What now?" Erik asked once she hung up.

"There's no point driving all the way to Långöre on the off chance of finding him," said Hanna. "And we also need to hand in Thomas's laptop. Let's head back to Kalmar."

Her phone beeped. It was Ove, wanting a debrief at the station. *We're on our way*, she wrote as she told Erik what the boss wanted.

"Have they found something?" he asked.

"I don't know."

The traffic over the bridge was slow. The Swedes had started to return to work after the summer, but August was the month in which the Germans typically arrived in their camper vans. Hanna gazed out across the water. She was happy here, in a way she had never been in Stockholm. And she realized that she was now in much better shape to cope with whatever lay ahead of her than before. Hanna had struggled with Erik at first. She had thought he was too curious, too intense. But she found it easier not to get worked up now—even if it did still happen from time to time. Her irritation over his reaction to what she had told him about Gunnar and the investigation had already passed. No one could tell her how she was supposed to handle it. She would have to work it out for herself.

Her phone started ringing, but it wasn't Hektor Friberg as she had hoped. Instead it was Valerija Leko, the friend Jenny had visited in Gothenburg.

"You tried to reach me?" she said, in a thick Kalmar accent.

"Yes."

After going through what the two women had done over the weekend, Hanna turned to what she was most interested in:

"How would you describe Jenny and Thomas's relationship?"

Valerija took a deep breath.

"Why do you want to know?"

"Just answer the question."

"They love each other."

That wasn't really an answer, something Valerija seemed to realize without Hanna needing to point it out.

"I mean, they argue sometimes, but no more than any other couple."

"What do they argue about?"

"The usual. Who does what at home. Jenny was exhausted after maternity leave, because Thomas didn't help out enough. Hugo almost never wakes him up. Jenny is back at work now, but more often than not she's still the one who gets up at night."

"Do you think he could have run off with Hugo?"

"No, it's nowhere near that bad. Something must have happened. Jenny got a real shock when she found out about his daughter, but she hadn't told him that she knew."

They were approaching the end of the bridge, and Hanna cast one last glance out at the water.

"What did Jenny say about his daughter?"

"She was mostly upset that Thomas hadn't said anything. Why keep a child a secret, you know?"

"What's your impression of Thomas?" asked Hanna.

"What do you mean?"

"Could you describe his personality?"

"Easygoing," said Valerija. "Irresponsible."

It didn't sound like she was particularly fond of him, perhaps because she saw what other people thought of as charm in a different light. *Charming* was the first word Karl Friberg had used to describe him.

"Have you noticed any changes in him recently?" Hanna asked.

"I mean, it's been a few weeks since I last saw him," said Valerija. "I went over to Öland to see them. I spent most of the time with Jenny and Hugo, but I guess Thomas was his usual self."

"So there was nothing to suggest he might have been depressed?"

"No, not at all."

Hanna knew it wasn't quite that simple. You couldn't always tell if life had become too much for a person, and it didn't always take something major to tip the balance. A series of small setbacks could be enough to push someone over the edge, and that could easily be what had happened to Thomas. Hanna thanked Valerija and ended the call. Erik pulled into the parking garage at the station.

"I need coffee," he said.

"Me, too."

While Erik dropped off Thomas's computer with forensics, Hanna went to the cafeteria to grab two coffees. There was a line, and she got to the investigation room just after Erik. The rest of the group was already there. Everyone but Ove shared an open office space divided down the middle by a partition wall. Daniel and Carina sat opposite each other on one side, and Erik's and Amer's standing desks were on the other. Hanna sat at a desk in one corner. There was a large table in front of the partition wall, and they had now gathered around it in the same configuration: Daniel and Carina on one side, Erik and Amer facing them, Ove by himself at one end.

"Take a seat," he said, as though she needed the encouragement. Once she was sitting beside Erik, he continued: "Hanna, why don't you start?"

She pushed one of the coffee cups over to Erik and noticed Amar raise an eyebrow. *What about me?* it seemed to be saying.

"Thomas's wife told us that her husband had some kind of falling-out with a colleague at the real estate agency where he works," said Hanna. "But according to his boss there, everything was rosy. The two other agents are his children. We've spoken to the daughter, but not the son."

"Thanks for the summary," said Ove. "I hope the actual interviews were a bit more thorough?"

"Of course," said Erik.

"Jenny Ahlström's friend Valerija Leko told us that they don't argue any more than the average couple," said Hanna. "I still haven't spoken to Thomas Ahlström's friend Mille Bergman, who was the first person Jenny called when she discovered they were missing. I'll try to reach him again once we're done here."

"Good," said Ove. "Considering Thomas has Hugo, our priority is to track them down. We've got an alert out for the car. I've requested bank transactions, call lists, and a trace on his mobile phone. Thomas probably had his phone with him, but it's good that we've got his laptop now, if nothing else. Daniel?"

"Yeah, I'm actually related to Thomas Ahlström."

Carina swung around to face Daniel. Everyone else sat quietly. Since she transferred to Kalmar, Hanna had often thought of Carina as a kind of bonus mother to her much younger colleague.

"Only distantly," he continued. "He's my mom's second cousin."

"What does that mean again?" asked Amer.

"Second cousins share a great-grandparent," Carina explained.

"Mom's maiden name was Ahlström," said Daniel. "It's not the most unusual surname, but I thought I'd ask if she knew who Thomas was."

"Was she able to tell you anything about him?" asked Erik.

"No, Mom doesn't have much contact with her family."

"Why not?"

Hanna thought the question was a little intrusive, but she could understand why Erik had asked it. There could be some kind of conflict there, something that was relevant to the investigation.

"Because they never learned sign language," said Daniel. "Mom's been deaf since birth. But she said she'd ask my grandpa."

"Okay, good," said Ove. "And just to be clear, since the relation is so distant, I don't think it matters."

He looked around the room, but no one had any objections. He fixed his eyes on Daniel again.

"Unless you think it's a problem, I'd like you to take a closer look at Thomas's daughter Lykke Henriksen."

"Absolutely," said Daniel.

"I also wanted to let you all know that Missing People are now involved," Ove continued. "With a bit of luck their searches will lead to more tips. They're heading out this afternoon."

"How did it go with his parents?" asked Hanna.

"Our colleagues from Växjö spoke to them," said Ove, "but they haven't heard from their son."

"Did they know that Thomas was missing?" she continued.

"Yes. Missing People had already been in touch."

"Not Jenny?"

"No."

"Don't you think that's strange?"

"Maybe," said Ove. "We'll just have to keep working and see what comes up."

His words were followed by the scraping of chairs. Hanna was already halfway to her desk when the boss stepped in front of her.

"Hanna, could you come with me for a moment?"

10

Hektor Friberg still wasn't picking up, and Erik thought it was slightly odd that a real estate agent was ignoring his phone. Hanna had asked him to try again from a new number before she disappeared into Ove's office. Erik hoped nothing had happened. Ove had sounded so serious.

Erik considered calling Karl to check whether he had spoken to his son, but he decided to hold off. He looked up at Amer instead.

"Fancy seeing a film tonight?"

"I can't," Amer replied, his eyes not leaving his screen. "My wife is having dinner with her sister, so I've got to get the little brats into bed."

Amer had two children, a four-year-old son and a six-month-old daughter. Once his fingers stopped dancing across his keyboard, he took a step back so that he could peer around the partition wall.

"Anyone free to babysit Erik tonight?" he asked Daniel and Carina.

Both replied with a quick no, too busy with their work to appreciate the joke. Daniel had gone home with someone after the Ironman during the weekend. It was completely out of character, and Erik was incredibly curious to know who the man was.

"Not funny," he said.

"Come on," Amer replied with a laugh. "It is a bit. But you heard them, you'll have to fend for yourself tonight."

Erik didn't feel like going home to an empty apartment. Maybe he would go to the cinema on his own, or ask someone else. He had spent quite a bit of time with a guy he met in the supermarket over the past few weeks, another grass widower. He brought up the Filmstaden home page and scrolled through the list of screenings. The first title he clicked on was a horror film, yet another movie about Halloween—though it did sound interesting that it was set in 1960s America. Still, Erik didn't feel like watching horror. The title of the next film was two women's names, but when Erik realized it was a romantic drama about two Romany women he closed that tab, too. Anything romantic would just make him feel sad. He gave up his search. Maybe he could go to a bar instead, though he had eaten out a bit too often lately. He had no intention of ever repeating the Ironman, but he still wanted to keep working out and watching what he ate.

"Four days to go," said Amer. "You'll survive."

"Honestly, I doubt it."

One part of Erik felt like jumping on a plane to Mumbai that evening, but he knew that was just his nerves talking. Supriya had already pushed back her return trip once, claiming that her mother had a doctor's appointment she wanted to be there for. They had argued, with Erik wondering why one of her brothers couldn't go instead. *You know what it's like*, she had told him. And of course, he did—he knew that Supriya was the one who was expected to step up—but he didn't think it was fair to make Nila miss the first week of school. Erik tried to resist, but he just couldn't do it. He sent a message to his wife.

You're still coming home on Friday, aren't you?

Her reply took a few minutes to arrive.

Why wouldn't we?

She had added a smiley face in a party hat. Supriya's choice of emojis was often confusing.

I don't know, he wrote. *But I really can't wait to see you both. And we can't wait to see you.*

Erik made do with sending a pulsing heart. Amer looked up at him as he put down his phone.

"We can't wait, either," he said.

Erik's phone started ringing, and though he could see that it wasn't Supriya, he couldn't quite manage to hide the longing from his voice as he answered with his name.

"I know what he was wearing," said a woman's voice.

"Jenny?"

She was in such a rush that she hadn't said who she was.

"Yes. Hugo was wearing his favorite red T-shirt and a pair of rainbow leggings."

"And Thomas?"

"Jeans, I think. He's almost always wearing jeans. And probably one of his T-shirts. Gray, maybe."

"How sure are you about Hugo's clothes?"

"Very. I can't find them anywhere. And those leggings are almost new. They must have been on their way to pick me up. I think Thomas wanted to get Hugo dressed up to—"

Her voice broke, and the sound of Jenny's sobs cut right through Erik. The fact that they had dressed up didn't necessarily mean they were on their way to get her. It could just as easily be a sign that Thomas had decided to end his life. Erik had been called out to more than one suicide in which the deceased was smartly dressed.

"Do you have a picture of Hugo in those particular clothes?" he asked.

It took Jenny a second or two to compose herself enough to reply.

"Yes, I'll send it over."

11

O ve nodded for Hanna to take a seat in the chair by his desk, and once she was sitting down he tore a pink Post-it note from the pad in front of him and handed it to her.

"That's the number for the woman leading the local Missing People group."

Hanna looked down at the note: Freya Amundsdottir.

"I've made you our contact person," Ove continued.

Hanna felt like arguing—there were other people on the team far better suited to that kind of task—but she knew it would be futile. Ove had likely chosen her because she was the only member of the group who lived on Öland, or because he thought she needed to sharpen her social skills.

"Call her and introduce yourself."

"Of course," said Hanna, adding the number to her contacts. "But I'm guessing this isn't why you wanted to talk to me?"

He could easily have sent the number in a message, or given it to her during the team meeting.

"You're right," said Ove. "I've received an anonymous email about you."

Ove was looking at her as though she should know what he was talking about, but Hanna had no idea. From the tilt of his head and the way he turned slightly in his shabby desk chair, she could tell he was concerned. When she first joined the team, he had asked Erik to keep an eye on her—a request that her colleague had divulged to her—but she hadn't heard any more about it since.

"Saying what?" she asked.

The boss sighed and turned his chair so that they were sitting face-to-face. Hanna's heart began to race, and she got a flashback to the interview he had held with her when she was nineteen. When he leaned in and told her what her father had done. The way he had carefully studied her face as he said the words: *We have proof. There's no doubt he's guilty.*

At the time she had been completely incapable of processing everything, but she now saw his words as cuts. They had severed any possibility of her staying on the island. She had decided, right there and then, to leave Öland after she graduated from high school.

"The sender claims to have seen you outside the station on Friday afternoon."

"Okay. . . ."

Hanna didn't know what he expected her to say.

"You were in your car," Ove continued, "and you pulled a bottle of whiskey out of the glove compartment. You took a couple of big swigs from it and then drove away."

Hanna stared at her boss, struggling to accept that this was really happening. In the end, it was Ove who broke the silence.

"You then reversed into a seventeen-year-old boy. Well, according to the sender, anyway."

"What the hell?" said Hanna. "Do you actually believe any of this?"

"No, it doesn't sound like you."

"I haven't been drunk driving," said Hanna. "And I definitely haven't reversed into anyone."

"No, no."

His tone irritated Hanna.

"You can always check the CCTV footage."

Ove pulled an apologetic face, and Hanna realized he already had—though the cameras likely didn't cover much of the parking lot.

"Sorry," he said. "But these are serious accusations, I had no choice but to take it seriously. Especially since . . ."

The boss paused, his eyes seeming to appeal to her.

"Especially since what?" she asked.

"The time matches when you left on Friday, and someone really did reverse into a seventeen-year-old in the parking lot. Are you sure you didn't see anything?"

"No. Obviously I would have stopped if I had."

Hanna's mind was spinning. What did this mean? She folded her arms and tried to think back to Friday, but couldn't remember a thing. It was just another day when she had left the station and driven straight home to Kleva.

"Is the boy okay?" she asked.

"He came out of it with a few cuts and some bruising on his thigh. A passerby was there to help him right after it happened."

"Did either of them see the car?"

"The boy only had time to register that it was gray."

Hanna's car was gray, but the color was hardly unique.

"So what happens now?" she asked.

"Nothing, for the time being," said Ove. "The email is the only thing pointing to you, and since it's anonymous we can't question the sender. Can you think of anyone you might have fallen out with, anyone who could have sent it?"

The first name that popped into Hanna's head was Ester Jensen's daughter Maria, who, earlier that year, had sent her a series of messages saying that she should have stayed in Stockholm. But it didn't add up. Maria couldn't know what time she left the station, or that someone really had been knocked down. Carina could always have told her, of course. She might even be behind the whole thing—she and Hanna hadn't really spoken since they returned from their summer breaks. But despite everything, Hanna struggled to believe that Carina could really be so cruel. This was about her father, she was sure of that. He was the reason people disliked her. Ove's eyes were still fixed on her, and she knew she had to say something.

"No. But hang on . . . when was the message sent?"

"This morning. Why?"

Hanna shook her head. For a moment she had wondered if it could have been Gunnar who sent it. She didn't want to tell Ove that she thought it was linked to her father, but there was a question she had been wanting to ask him ever since he became her boss. Ove was the one who had led the investigation back then, and he was also the person who had given her a copy of the files before the summer. *There's no doubt.* That was what he had told her, but it wasn't necessarily true.

"Did you ever have any doubts about how Dad allegedly killed Ester Jensen?"

Ove leaned back in his chair and glanced down at the drawers of his desk. As far as Hanna knew, he no longer had any cigarettes in there, though he could always have picked up the habit again. Investigating missing children was difficult.

"So you've read the files?" he said.

"Yes."

"What do you think?"

"The violence doesn't make sense. Yes, he drank and so on, but he was never actually violent."

Ove glanced at his screen. For a moment, Hanna didn't think he was going to answer her. The only explanation she could come up with was that Lars had suffered some kind of psychosis, but he didn't have any history of that, either. And he had undergone a brief psychiatric examination, which had declared him fit and healthy.

"Yes, I reacted to the violence, too," said Ove. "But the evidence . . . that made it very hard not to go after him as the killer."

"I understand that, but was there anything to suggest he wasn't acting alone?"

"You've read the investigation."

"Yes, but . . ."

Ove sighed. He knew as well as she did that there were certain things that never made it into the paperwork. Hunches, for example.

"As you already know, the fire destroyed almost everything. We found other traces of DNA there, but we didn't put much weight on it."

Hanna turned to look out the window. All she could see was the road and the large parking lot on the other side. The one where someone had reversed into a seventeen-year-old boy. Was it the same person who sent the email claiming it was her?

"You know what people's houses are like," Ove continued. "And Ester Jensen often had visitors."

"I know."

Ester Jensen had been active in both an artists' and a gardening collective. After her death, the newspapers had been full of people talking about what an incredible person she was. Saying how terribly unfortunate and awful it was that she was dead. And it was. *How the hell could you?* That was the first thing Hanna had said to her father when she was finally allowed to see him.

She considered asking Ove about Gunnar and Kristoffer, but hanging her brother out to dry didn't feel right. She might be able to come up with a reason for him to look into Gunnar, but right there and then she couldn't think of a single one.

"Do you think you'll be able to drop this now?" asked Ove.

"Yes," Hanna hurried to reply.

She still wanted to limit the number of people who knew she

had started her own halting investigation into the murder. It had been a few months since her last threatening phone call. Among other things, she had heard the sound of fire on the other end of the line. Whoever was making those calls had likely realized that it wasn't the right way to break her—and that person was probably the one now emailing Ove instead.

"Have you had any more contact with Maria Jensen?" he asked.

"No."

Ove thought it was Maria who had texted and made the threatening phone calls, but Hanna was convinced it was someone else.

"You need to tell me if someone is threatening you again."

"Of course," said Hanna, defiantly holding his gaze.

It bothered her that he didn't seem to believe her. Ove's phone started ringing, and the little Hanna could hear of the call kept her in the room.

"One of Jenny Ahlström's neighbors just called the police," he said once he hung up. "He saw her walking down the middle of the road and went out to try to talk to her. It seems she's gone out to search for Thomas and Hugo herself; she doesn't seem to be coping very well at all."

Hanna got up.

"I'll go over there."

12

The only thing Lykke had managed to do since the police left was to throw a load of washing into the machine. She had almost no clean clothes left. She was now lying on the sofa, staring up at the clock on the wall that told her the cycle was done. The shock that had washed over her when the two officers appeared in her garden and held up their ID was still lingering like a faint nausea. It had mixed with Jenny's awful phone call on Sunday evening. Or maybe it was her damn hunger making her feel queasy. Her thoughts kept flitting around like butterflies with nowhere to land.

No, this wasn't working anymore. Lykke slowly sat up and waited for the dizziness to pass before she made her way over to the fridge. After staring at the bar of chocolate for a few seconds, she slammed the door.

There were two apples in the fruit bowl, but as she picked up the top one a swarm of fruit flies rose up into the air. Both were rotten.

"Fucking heat," she muttered.

If she wanted something other than the chocolate to eat, she was going to have to go to the supermarket. Lykke tipped the two apples into the trash with a sigh. She put the bowl in the sink and filled it with water, then pulled on her sneakers and went out into the garden. The spade was still lying where she had left it by the flower bed, but the garden would have to wait until tomorrow.

As though her problems would have disappeared by then.

Lykke had been so sure he was serious. One image after another popped into her head: the woman and the child in the window, the knife in the tire, him pressing her up against the wall, her just trying to defend herself.

Everything was going to come out now, and they wouldn't believe her.

The grocery store was only a few hundred meters away, and Lykke said hello to everyone she passed. That was what most people did around here, both permanent residents and visitors. There was a long line outside the ice-cream kiosk. She had eaten a scoop of licorice ice cream a few weeks ago, and the thought almost made her throw up.

On the bulletin board by the main entrance, someone had put up a petition. A new holiday resort had been given planning permission in Grönhögen, and a lot of people were upset. Lykke stopped to add her name to the list.

Inside the grocery store, she grabbed a carton of smooth tomato soup to heat up on the stove. She didn't have a microwave, and the people who rented her house sometimes complained about that, but she didn't think there was either the space or the need for one. Lykke picked up a watermelon, a couple of apples, and a cucumber, so she wouldn't need to leave the house again tomorrow if she didn't have the energy. She had just turned around to head over to the checkout when the lights went out with a soft whirr.

A power cut. Damn it.

The customers switched on the flashlights on their phones, using them to make their way down the aisles. But without power, no one could pay for anything. Lykke stood still in the darkness, listening to the conversations going on around her. Family members calling to check how widespread the outage was. The whole of Grönhögen at least, by the sounds of it. Discussions about whether anything could be done. Absolutely nothing, so why did they all sound so excited?

Once a few minutes had passed without anything happening, Lykke put back the things she had picked up and left the store. The power cut was a clear sign that she wasn't meant to eat. She would hold on to her control for a while longer yet.

Why had she written that letter? Deep down, she knew the answer: Because she had so desperately wanted to make a connection. To find someone who could fill the void. All her life she had longed for a father. She hadn't given him her number, but Thomas had called her eight days after she sent the letter, and she hadn't been prepared for how his voice would make her feel. Utterly fucking terrified. After just a minute or so, she had told him she needed to think and hung up.

And now he was gone. Little Hugo, too.

Lykke had seen Missing People's post on Facebook. So many people on Öland had shared it.

When she got back to the house, she opened the fridge door and stared at the bar of chocolate for a moment before closing it again. Only then did she realize that the power was back on. But she'd had enough excursions for one day.

Damn hunger.

Lykke opened the drawer in the pantry and found a pack of salted crackers one of her guests must have left behind. She snatched it up before she had time to change her mind. The movement was enough to make the room sway. There was a part of her that knew she shouldn't be doing this. She had spent a few weeks in the hospital during her teens.

She filled a glass of water and carried it through to the living room, where she turned on the TV. Thomas's and Hugo's faces were the first thing she saw. The picture of Thomas was the same one she had seen on the Missing People post, but the image of Hugo was new.

The reporter was talking about their disappearance, appealing for tips. She said that these were likely the clothes Hugo had been wearing. Lykke's eyes were locked onto the photograph. Her little brother was straddling a red plastic car, his toes only just touching the ground. He was wearing a red T-shirt and a pair of rainbow leggings, staring at the camera with a look of frustrated concentration on his face.

Lykke closed her eyes to make the picture go away. There was no way she would be able to manage a single cracker now.

13

Hanna drove through Hulterstad at a crawl, but there was no sign of Jenny. She turned around in the yard outside a farmhouse, and when she reached the turnoff to the Ahlströms' house, she pulled in. Perhaps Jenny had given up on her search after all. Every single light in the house seemed to be on, but no one answered when she rang the bell, and Jenny wasn't picking up her phone. Hanna tried calling the neighbor who had called the police instead.

"I'm glad you're here," he said. "She wouldn't listen when I tried to convince her to go home. I'm worried she might end up getting hurt."

"Do you know where she went?"

"I think she was heading for the water."

The Baltic Sea was always just "the water" this side of the island. Hanna had only ever passed through Hulterstad on the way to and from Ottenby, so she missed the turnoff and had to do a U-turn. This time she spotted the little white sign announcing that Görans dämme, the coastal wetlands, were only a kilometer away.

The gravel track was perfectly straight, flanked by low stone walls and fields. Light clouds had started to gather in the blue sky overhead. No matter which way Hanna looked, the trees were nothing but lonely dots in the horizon—though the ground couldn't be quite flat, because she couldn't yet see the sea.

After roughly three-quarters of a kilometer, there was a sign directing all unauthorized traffic into a small parking area, but Hanna ignored it and continued straight ahead. The Baltic Sea soon came into view, appearing like a revelation. On a slight rise up ahead, she spotted a figure. It had to be Jenny. Hanna crossed the cattle grid and pulled over, got out of the car. A few of the freely grazing cattle raised their heads, but Jenny didn't turn around.

"Hugo!" she shouted.

His name was carried off in the wind, which was stronger here than it had been back in Hulterstad.

One of the worst cases Hanna had ever worked on had involved pulling a drowned three-year-old out of a lake on the outskirts of Stockholm. She rarely questioned her choice of profession, but she had that day. The boy's entire family had been on the beach with him, his mother, father, and older sister.

Hanna walked toward Jenny, repressing the image of the dead child. His T-shirt and shorts, clinging to his little body. His blue lips. There was nothing to suggest that they would find Hugo like that.

After a few meters the grass gave way to sand and rocks. Hanna made her way up to Jenny in a couple of strides. The wind was blowing the waves toward them. They were around twenty kilometers south of the small village where she grew up, but the wind and the sea were exactly the same.

"Hugo!" Jenny shouted again.

Hanna reached out and touched her arm.

"Come on," she said.

Jenny swatted her hand away.

"I need to find them."

Her despair hit Hanna like a heavy squall, and she waited until she had recovered.

"Let us do that."

"But no one is even out looking!"

This time her words were carried by anger rather than despair. Hanna swallowed and steeled herself.

"We're focusing our efforts on the car," she said. "Finding the car is our best shot at finding Thomas and Hugo."

She sounded more confident than she felt. The car really was their best shot, but almost twenty-four hours had now passed, and they still hadn't found a single trace of it. The sad truth was that they had absolutely no idea what had happened. Whether anything *had* even happened. Thomas might simply have taken Hugo and disappeared. It was hard to believe that a person could do that to their partner, but people weren't always rational.

A couple of great black-backed gulls screeched as they took off. Hanna's grandmother had always said that meant a storm was on its way. The two women stood quietly, watching the birds fly away.

"I was going through Hugo's clothes," said Jenny, so quietly that the wind almost swallowed her words. "And suddenly I had an image of him with his leg stuck in the cattle grid, howling in pain. And then I saw him lying in . . ."

She nodded out to the water.

"Hugo isn't here," said Hanna.

Jenny wrapped her arms around herself. "I don't think so, either. But those images of him felt so real."

Hanna reached out to her again, and this time Jenny didn't bat her hand away.

"Please, let's go."

"I've been trying to get Missing People to start searching," Jenny mumbled, as though she hadn't heard her. "They must think I'm such a pain."

"Believe me, they understand."

With a sigh, Jenny began walking over to the car. Hanna followed her. As she turned the car around to drive back to Hulterstad, Jenny's gaze was fixed on the water, and it looked like she was fighting back those images again.

"Thomas likes coming here with Hugo," she said. "You asked about special places."

"Have you thought of any others?"

"I don't know if it counts as special, but Thomas's parents have a summerhouse in Timmernabben, and they're not there right now."

"Why didn't you call his parents when you realized he and Hugo were missing?"

"Because I knew he wasn't with them."

"How could you know that?"

"Their relationship was really bad. *Is*, I mean. Oh God."

Jenny raised her hands to her face, and Hanna gave her a few seconds. They would soon be back on the main road, and it felt like time was running out, like she had only the short drive back to the house to get answers.

"In what sense is it bad?"

"They don't know him," said Jenny. "They still think of him as he was when he was younger."

"Which was?"

"Restless."

"Which of his colleagues do you think Thomas had issues with?"

Jenny shrugged, but once Hanna rephrased the question she said, "Selene, maybe."

They pulled up outside the Ahlström house.

"Do you want me to come in?"

"I'm sure you have better things to do than babysit me."

"Do you promise to stay at home, then?" asked Hanna.

"Yes."

Jenny gripped the door handle, then paused and looked Hanna straight in the eye.

"It's so awful, not knowing anything. Where they are, what might have happened. . . ."

Hanna could only nod in reply, and after climbing out of the car, Jenny slammed the door.

Timmernabben was on the mainland, around forty kilometers north of Kalmar, so rather than drive over there Hanna called the information in to Ove. He promised to send a couple of officers out right away.

She then spent at least fifteen minutes staring at the door to the Ahlström house, but it remained closed. It was after five, she realized, which meant there was no point going back to the station. Though it was a pretty big detour, she decided to drive north, through Gårdby, before heading west to Kleva. The sea had woken a longing in her, and she needed to shake off Jenny's despair.

Hanna slowed down when she reached Gårdby. She was always careful to stick to the speed limit in the villages. She drove through the community without looking for anything in particular, past the school and the church that had always been there. Her gaze touched briefly upon her childhood home. The killer's house . . . There was no stopping the memories now. She had fallen off her bike not far from the church. Their mother had wanted them to avoid the main road, so they stuck to the smaller lanes. Hanna had been sprawled on the ground, tears pouring down her cheeks, and Kristoffer had stopped, dropped his bike, and sat down beside her. When she failed to stop howling he had pointed to a shimmering green beetle crawling across the gravel. Told her it was an expert grub hunter and that it was endangered. That it was probably the very last one. The beetle had made her forget she was upset.

Hanna pulled up outside her friend Rebecka's house and sat there for several minutes, unsure of what to do. As though to give herself an excuse, she took a picture of the house and sent it off to her.

Everything's OK here.

Rebecka's reply came a few seconds later.

Thanks, I know. The mother-in-law has been checking every day!

Followed by:

What are you doing there?

Hanna thought for a moment before she wrote back:

Just passing by.

There was a knock on the window, and Hanna jumped. Standing outside was a bearded man with a bicycle, and he was smiling at her. He was wearing jeans and a grandad shirt, the material clinging to his chest. It took her a few seconds to place him. She wound down the window.

"Isak, right?"

Isak nodded. He was a teacher at Gårdby School, and Hanna had met him during the investigation into Joel Forslund's death. The first thing she had noticed was that he was taller than her. His goatee was now a full beard, and it suited him better. His helmet was pushing his brown hair down onto his forehead. He smiled again, and Hanna grew nervous at what his smile woke in her. She searched for something suitably friendly to say.

"What are you doing here?"

"I don't live far away," said Isak. "I was just on my way home from a friend's place, but when I saw you I thought maybe you needed help with something. I heard about the missing man and his son."

"Thanks, but there's no need," said Hanna. "I'm not here on police business. I was just checking the house."

"How are they doing?"

"They're okay," said Hanna.

That was just what you said. She didn't think Isak knew Rebecka particularly well, but she wasn't sure.

"Or maybe not okay," she added. "But better, in any case."

Isak studied her, a smile still playing on his lips.

"I should get going," said Hanna.

"See you around, maybe."

Hanna nodded, wound up the window, and hurried to pull away.

See you around, maybe. She twisted and turned his words in her mind. Why had he said that? And in that slightly amused tone? Hanna glanced at her reflection in the rearview mirror, but she looked like her normal self. There was nothing on her face.

When she reached the church she chose to turn west, even though it was a slightly longer route. She just wanted to get out of Gårdby as fast as she could.

On that summer day thirty years ago, she and Kristoffer had pushed their bikes home from the church. Her mother had cleaned up her knee and then baked some frozen cinnamon buns. All four of them had sat down at the kitchen table, and her father had taken every chance he could to touch her mother. Losing her had been more than he could handle. Despite that, Hanna wanted nothing more than for someone to want to touch her like that. But Isak? She barely knew the man. His smile popped back into her head, and she stepped on the gas.

14

As Hanna pulled into Kleva, she saw her neighbor Ingrid walking along the lane. Everyone was out walking that evening, it seemed. Ingrid was wearing an anorak, and her silver-gray hair—which had grown so long over the summer—was tied up in a ponytail. Hanna pulled over and wound down the window.

"Are you just back from work?" asked Ingrid.

"Yeah, things are pretty hectic with the missing boy and his father."

And a teacher from Gårdby, she thought, though she didn't say that last part aloud. She felt utterly drained after the visit to her home village. Isak had woken a longing in her that she just didn't have the energy to deal with right now. Seeing her childhood home had also been unexpectedly tough. The gulf between how life there had once been and how everything had turned out.

"It must be hard," said Ingrid. "I did an extra-long loop on my walk this evening, but I didn't see anything of interest."

Ingrid went out walking every day, just like Hanna. Sometimes they did it together. For an eighty-one-year-old, Ingrid was surprisingly sprightly—though she did have trouble with one hip. Hanna's phone buzzed. It was Ove, letting her know that a patrol car had been out to Timmernabben and that the summerhouse was empty.

"Have you eaten yet?" asked Ingrid.

Hanna shook her head. Since her salmon salad at the restaurant in the windmill, all she had had was coffee. Ingrid opened the car door and climbed in.

"If you come back with me, I've got some leftover meat loaf and potatoes."

"That sounds fantastic."

Was Isak a good cook? The sudden thought made Hanna's cheeks flush. Ingrid gave her a strange look, but she ignored it.

Hanna parked the car outside her own house, and they walked over to Ingrid's together. Everything in her house was roughly twice the size as in Hanna's. She had an old display cabinet in the kitchen, and there were copper pans and hand-painted plates on the walls. It soon transpired that meat loaf and potatoes weren't the only things Ingrid had left over; she also served up gravy, sweetened lingonberries, and her own pickled cucumber. And a glass of milk. It took Hanna no more than a few minutes to devour the lot.

"That's all I had, I'm afraid," said Ingrid.

"It was delicious, thank you. I couldn't manage another bite."

Despite Ingrid's protests, Hanna carried the empty plate over to the sink and did the washing up. Ingrid didn't have a dishwasher. Isak's smile came back to her again, almost like a jolt in her chest, and she wanted to get rid of it.

"What do you know about Thomas Ahlström?" she asked.

She often asked Ingrid about the people from Öland who cropped up in their investigations.

"Not much."

Ingrid got up and opened one of the kitchen cabinets. She took out a couple of big floral teacups, set them down on a tray, and added a tea bag to each. Hanna reached for the kettle and filled it with water.

"What does that mean?" she asked.

"A woman from my sewing circle used to live next door to a girl he was seeing."

"In Grönhögen?"

"Yes, exactly."

Ingrid rummaged around in her overflowing pantry and found a few biscotti, which she tipped into a bowl.

"What did she have to say about him, then?" Hanna asked.

The water had boiled, so she poured it over the tea bags.

"That he was trouble when he was younger, but that he seemed to have turned things around."

"Trouble how?"

"He used to drink too much and get up to no good. I'm sorry, it was just gossip. Nothing concrete."

They took their tea through to the sofa in the living room. Ingrid's description of a young Thomas could apply to plenty of bored teenagers on the island. The older woman reached for a biscotti and dipped it into her tea.

"Has something happened?" she asked.

"What do you mean?"

"You seem low. I know it must be tough, with the missing boy and his father, but is there something else on your mind?"

Hanna sipped her tea. She didn't want to talk about Isak, the aching longing for what her parents had once had. That wasn't what Ingrid had noticed, after all. It was the ever-present sorrow Isak had stirred up. Her loneliness. The fact that she had lost both her mother and her father, and to a large extent also her brother. Ingrid already knew that she had read through the case files, that there was evidence against Lars, but Hanna wasn't sure whether she had the energy to go through the rest right now. She took another sip of her tea. Blew on it, though it wasn't necessary, then slowly lowered the cup.

"I spoke to Dad's friend Gunnar yesterday," she said.

"And . . . ?" Ingrid tried to coax more out of her when she failed to go on.

"He claimed Dad was protecting someone." Hanna stared down at the tea, directing her words at the dark liquid. "And the only person he would have been willing to protect, other than me, is . . ."

She didn't get any further, simply couldn't say it, but there was no need.

"Your brother," Ingrid filled in.

"Yes. But I honestly don't believe it," Hanna hurried to say. "Maybe Gunnar only said that to protect himself."

Ingrid studied her, and Hanna didn't like the hint of doubt she could see in her eyes.

"Gunnar has never liked Kristoffer," she went on, attempting to erase it.

Ingrid helped herself to another biscotti, dipped it into her tea, and chewed slowly, like she was debating with herself.

"You should talk to Ester's daughter again," she eventually said.

"Why?"

"I think she has a better idea of what the murder was really about than she's let on so far."

Maria was the last person Hanna felt like talking to. It had been awful when she and Erik went over there in the spring. Maria hated her for what her father had done. Perhaps she was the one who had sent the anonymous email after all. Perhaps she had been hoping it would lead to Hanna being fired. To her moving back to Stockholm.

"And you should definitely talk to Kristoffer."

Hanna knew she needed to talk to Kristoffer, but she kept putting it off. She thought back to the way he had sat down beside her on the road that day thirty years ago. How patiently he had waited for her to calm down. How he had distracted her in order to stop her tears.

Hanna stayed with Ingrid for almost an hour, talking about everything other than the investigation and her brother. Ingrid's son had temporarily dropped his crusade to make her move into a home, but one of her grandchildren was struggling. She was about to graduate from her program in industrial economics, and had started to question whether she had made the right choice. Working within trade and industry no longer seemed quite so appealing. Ingrid had told her it was never too late to change her mind, and had been given a telling-off by her son. In the end it was Ingrid who told Hanna to go home; Hanna had more important things to be doing, she said.

Hanna paused in her narrow hallway, glancing over at the tiny shower room. She knew that if she took a shower now, she would never make the call, so she grabbed her phone and dialed Kristoffer's number. His muted hello made her heart race.

"I've read through the investigation," she said as she walked through to the living room, which was so small there was no room for anything other than a sofa and a TV.

"What investigation?"

"Into Ester Jensen's murder."

The silence that followed was like a frozen expanse of water. Hanna stared at the pale gray wallpaper. She was glad she had eventually settled on one without a pattern, because she hadn't managed to hang it straight.

"Why?" Kristoffer asked.

Hanna chose to ignore his question.

"But it doesn't add up. Dad wasn't violent. He never would have hurt her like that."

Her gaze landed on the sofa, but rather than slumping down onto it Hanna began pacing back and forth.

"There were sides to him you didn't know about," said Kristoffer.

Hanna was five again, sitting at the kitchen table with a cinnamon bun. Beside her, her father's feet sought out her mother's beneath the table.

"What is that supposed to mean?" she asked.

"Exactly what I said."

Hanna knew she shouldn't raise her voice, but she did:

"And what about you? Do you have any sides I don't know about?"

She couldn't bear Kristoffer's attempts to ruin the few bright memories of her father she had left. The new silence that followed made her brother feel even more distant.

"I saw Gunnar yesterday," she continued, her voice much sharper than intended. "And he heard Dad say that he *never should have protected him.*"

Hanna wanted Kristoffer to hit something, to lose his temper, to explain how everything really fit together. But he didn't. Instead he started crying. Ragged, sniffling tears. And she felt her own anger ebb away.

"Please, Kristoffer, what is it?" Hanna begged him.

But her brother didn't reply. He hung up. Hanna was left staring at her phone, trying to make sense of what had just happened.

TUESDAY, AUGUST 20

15

Hanna came a hair's breadth from scraping the rear bumper of a black Volvo as she pulled up in the small parking area outside the station. She turned off the engine and remained sitting in the car. After Kristoffer hung up on her last night she had immediately phoned him back, convinced the line must have gone down by mistake, but he hadn't picked up. Hearing her brother cry had left her shaken. She could remember only two other occasions on which she had heard him cry: when their father told them their mother was ill, and at her funeral. His reaction had cracked the defenses Hanna had built up so carefully over the years. Maybe there was something in what Gunnar had said after all.

No, her father hadn't confessed to murder to protect Kristoffer.

Hanna beat the wheel with her palms and screamed to herself. A woman cutting between the parked cars peered in through the windshield, and Hanna attempted to smile, though she knew it hadn't quite worked. She vaguely recognized the woman, and guessed she must work at the station. After a quick shake of the head, the woman hurried away.

Hanna dug her fingernails into her palms. Ove would probably get another complaint email now, one with some substance to it this time.

Hanna glanced over at the station, where the woman was now

approaching the main entrance. She needed to focus on the investigation right now. One of the local papers had splashed the case across its front page that morning, asking: "Where Are Thomas and Hugo?" A journalist from *Expressen* had also been in touch, wanting a comment. *Call our press spokesperson*, Hanna had snapped, slamming down the phone.

There were so many things she wanted to ask Kristoffer, because nothing made sense. The idea that he might have killed Ester Jensen felt just as improbable as their father having done it. Kristoffer had never been violent, either, or not as far as she knew. It made her so angry that he refused to talk to her, though she knew she could have handled the conversation better. Hanna wished she hadn't raised her voice, and she probably should have asked completely different questions.

Her phone started ringing, and she found herself hoping it was him. How many messages had she left with him yesterday? It had to be somewhere around ten, both voice mails and texts. She didn't recognize the number, but it was Swedish. Possibly another journalist, she thought, hitting the green button.

All Hanna could hear was the sound of someone sobbing, and panic gripped her heart. Were the threats starting again?

"Hello?" she whispered.

"He's dead," a soft voice stuttered.

"Who is?"

"Thomas. Oh God, he . . . he's on the floor."

Hanna thought she recognized the voice, but she was far from sure.

"Sorry, who is this?"

"Selene. From Friberg Properties."

"Selene." Hanna used her name, because that typically helped a person calm down. "Where is Thomas?"

"On the floor."

"Yes, you said that. But where is this floor?"

"In a house in Södra Möckleby."

Hanna swallowed.

"And Hugo?"

"I don't know . . . ," Selene sobbed. "I don't know where he is. Oh God."

"What are you doing in the house?"

She had to ask the question twice before the real estate agent answered.

"The new owners are arriving today. I wanted to check that everything was okay."

"So it's a house being sold by Friberg Properties?"

"Yes."

"Are you still in the house?"

"No, it was horrible. I couldn't handle—"

"Stay outside," said Hanna. "The police are on their way."

The minute she hung up, Hanna called Ove to get a patrol car and technicians out there as soon as possible. Her immediate instinct was to go straight to the address Selene had given her, but Ove asked her to come inside for a quick debrief first. The fact that Thomas had been found dead turned the entire investigation on its head, and something else had come up that he didn't want to discuss over the phone.

When Hanna got to the investigation room, everyone but Carina was already waiting inside. Judging by their dogged faces, she knew that Ove had just briefed them on the call from Selene.

"What's going on?" she asked.

She lingered in the doorway, still keen to get away.

"Yeah, so, I was asked to take a closer look at Thomas Ahlström's daughter, Lykke Henriksen," said Daniel. "She finished her degree in biology in Uppsala this spring, and I called them and spoke to the man in charge of the program. It seems there was some kind of dispute between her and one of the professors."

"Over what?" asked Hanna.

Ove pulled out a seat for her, and she walked over and sat down.

"Well, he wasn't exactly thrilled to talk about it," said Daniel, "but apparently she went over to the professor's house and assaulted him."

"She went to his house?" Amer blurted out.

"Yeah, I asked that question, too. According to the man I spoke to, this wasn't the first incident. He didn't explicitly say it, but he definitely painted her as a stalker. I'm going to call the professor she hit, too."

"Good work," said Ove. "Keep it up."

Daniel squirmed at the praise, but Ove had already moved on.

"We've received Thomas's phone records," he said, "and I've tasked an analyst with going through them. The last call his wife claims to have had with him seems to fit, at least in terms of timing."

"What about the location?" asked Erik.

"The last tower it connected to was in Södra Möckleby," said Ove. "So hopefully we'll recover the phone at the crime scene. We've also got access to his bank records now. Another analyst is working on those."

"Have you spoken to Hektor?" Hanna asked Erik.

He shook his head. Considering Thomas had been found in a house being sold by Friberg Properties, they needed to get ahold of Hektor as soon as possible. And they would have to talk to Selene, too. Jenny Ahlström thought she was the one her husband had fallen out with, after all.

"We've received quite a few tips," said Ove. "But the only confirmed sighting so far is a woman who saw Thomas and Hugo at the playground in Skogsby on Sunday. Hugo almost choked on something in the sandpit."

"Almost?" asked Hanna.

"Yes, the woman remembered it because it was so dramatic.

Thomas managed to dislodge whatever was stuck and then Hugo kept playing. They left the playground just after eleven."

Hanna's mind raced back to their first conversation with Thomas's wife.

"Jenny Ahlström told us that Thomas and Hugo were in Skogsby when she last spoke to them, but that was around half past two in the afternoon."

"Strange," said Amer. "Did he go there twice, or was he lying?"

"I'll request a more detailed trace on his phone," said Ove.

"What are we doing to find Hugo?" asked Daniel.

His mother and Thomas Ahlström's were second cousins, but what did that make him and Hugo? There was probably a name for it, but Hanna couldn't remember what it was. Ove shifted in his chair.

"I've sent three units over to Södra Möckleby," he said. "One of them will search the house and the others the area around about. With a bit of luck, we'll find his car there. And if not . . ."

Ove gave a deep sigh. His granddaughter Penny had to be around the same age as Hugo.

"My grandpa got in touch with Thomas Ahlström's dad, by the way," said Daniel. "His cousin."

"Did he find out anything?" asked Ove.

"Thomas's dad said, and I quote: *That boy has always been trouble. And now this.* But that was when he thought his son was just missing."

Trouble was the same word Ingrid had used.

"Can I go over to Södra Möckleby now?" asked Hanna.

She was sick of sitting there, listening. She wanted to see Thomas. That was the first step in understanding what might have happened. In finding Hugo.

"Yes, you and Erik go. Stop off at the crime scene, but then I need you to break the news to Jenny Ahlström. I'll call Växjö and ask them to inform Thomas's parents once we've confirmed it's definitely him. They'll have to question the father about what he said, too. The first interview with them didn't contain anything like that."

Ove's phone rang, and after a quick glance at the number he hurried to answer. The crease between his brows deepened as he listened to the voice on the other end.

"That was the first unit on the scene. It looks like Thomas Ahlström was murdered," said Ove. "They've done a search of the house, and unfortunately there's no sign of Hugo."

16

Erik gazed out through the windshield at the lampposts and railings racing by. Until now it had been possible to hope that Thomas and Hugo would still turn up, that their disappearance had been voluntary. Even though there was nothing but the missing car to suggest as much. But on the other hand, there hadn't been anything to suggest that a crime had been committed, either—child abduction notwithstanding. He pushed back the image of a dead young boy. Children and death didn't belong together, it was as simple as that. There was every chance they would find Hugo alive and well.

His phone buzzed in his pocket, and he dug it out. It was Supriya, who had sent him a picture taken outside Lilavati Hospital in Mumbai. She and Nila were standing either side of Aavika.

Everything was fine, she wrote.

Great.

Erik was just about to hit send when Hanna pulled out to overtake a Saab, quickly swinging back to the right to avoid another car coming up fast behind them.

"Relax. I'm in control."

"I didn't say anything."

"No, but you were thinking it."

Erik shook his head. Hanna was back in the left-hand lane

again, but she didn't make any attempt to catch up with the speeding car.

"What did you get up to last night?" she asked.

"I video-called Nila and Supriya," he said, finally sending the message. "Then I ate, did a couple of guitar lessons, and went out for a beer."

It had been a good evening, largely thanks to the video call. The time difference occasionally made it tricky, but Nila had been allowed to stay up. She had spent a large part of their conversation talking about a monkey that had stolen her sunglasses.

Erik had then gone for a beer at Slipkajen, which was currently the only restaurant in the neighborhood. The staff there knew him, and he liked to show his face from time to time. He'd also had a long chat with his older brother, who was thinking about quitting his job as a police officer—he'd even been to an interview for a temporary PE teacher role. Their father was a retired policeman, just like his father before him. Their sister was an officer, too. Her twin brother was the only one who had chosen a different career path, as a graphic designer. Erik glanced down at his phone. Supriya hadn't sent any more messages.

"What about you?" he asked.

Hanna tensed slightly, as though it were a sensitive subject. But if that was the case, why had she brought it up?

"I went over to my neighbor Ingrid's for a while," she said.

"And then?"

"Then I called Kristoffer."

When they spoke yesterday, Hanna had mentioned both the investigation into her father and a meeting with his friend Gunnar, and the fact that she was voluntarily sharing this information with him made Erik realize just how far they had come. He wanted to take better care of the trust she was putting in him than he had yesterday.

"How did it go?" he asked.

"I made him cry and hang up on me."

Hanna turned south onto the 136, and Erik glanced over at her to check whether she was joking.

"What did you say?"

"Just what Gunnar told me."

Erik studied Hanna again. Was she more hunched over the wheel than usual? He desperately wanted to say something sensible, something that would make her feel better, but even he knew that there was nothing he could say. Everything that raced through his mind sounded so stupid and inadequate.

"Honestly, I don't know what to say," he said.

Hanna laughed and leaned back in her seat.

"That was hard to admit, huh?"

"Yeah."

Erik forced himself to keep quiet for the rest of the drive to Sö-dra Möckleby. He could sense that that was what Hanna needed right now.

THE HOUSE WHERE THOMAS had been found dead was on the bend of a long street. The adjacent plot of land hadn't been built on, and beyond the house the fields opened out into the distance. From the road, Erik could see the silhouette of a windmill. Hanna parked behind one of the patrol cars, and an officer came over to them as they got out.

"Still no sign of either the child or the car, I'm afraid," he said.

"How far out have you searched?" asked Erik.

"We've only managed to check the closest streets so far, but we're still looking. And we're going to start knocking on doors as soon as possible."

"Where is Selene Friberg?" asked Hanna.

"She's on the swinging seat behind—"

That was as far as he got before Selene appeared around the

corner of the house. Erik glanced along the street. One of the neighbors quickly stepped back behind his hedge, but others seemed less concerned by how they came across. An old man had come out onto the road to get a better look, but at least he wasn't filming. Erik realized they were going to have to work quickly here; Thomas's wife, Jenny, needed to know.

They walked over to Selene and led her in the direction of the field beside the house in order to put more distance between themselves and the nosy neighbors. Erik wanted to talk to Selene before they went inside. The technicians were already on the scene, and needed to be left to work in peace as much as possible.

"Why did you come over here?" asked Hanna.

"What do you mean?"

Selene's lower lip was trembling, her face puffy. She had swapped the smart trousers she was wearing yesterday for a skirt, but her white blouse looked the same—if a little more crumpled.

"You said you wanted to make sure everything was okay," said Hanna. "Is that something you usually do?"

Selene turned to the house with a sob, and Hanna reached out and touched her arm. Directed her attention back to them.

"Sometimes. It depends."

"On what?"

"Every sale is different. These sellers live in Spain, and the buyers are from Oskarshamn. Most of the paperwork was done remotely."

Selene glanced at the house again, then back at them. She seemed surprised, as though they had materialized out of nowhere and she had no idea what they could want.

"Were you worried the house might be a mess?" Hanna continued.

"No, but . . ."

She pressed her hands to her face, mumbling into her palms: "What have I done?"

"Selene," said Erik, his voice sharp.

She looked up at him, her face frozen in fear.

"I was afraid I might not be able to get in."

"Didn't you have the keys?" he asked.

Selene lowered her hands, pausing at the waistband of her skirt to straighten her shirt.

"No, I should have handed them over to the buyers by now, but . . ."

Yet again, she turned to the house.

"What happened to the keys?" Erik pressed her.

Selene's head snapped back to them.

"What time is it?"

"What happened to the keys?" Erik asked again.

"I . . . I gave them to Thomas."

As the words left her mouth, a large white moving van turned onto the street.

17

The water pressure in the shower was terrible, but Lykke hadn't had the energy to do anything about it. She didn't even know whether anything could be done. She closed her eyes and raised her face to the jets of cold water, trying to enjoy the feeling of last night's sweat being washed away. Her body was protesting against the way she was treating it right now. She hadn't managed to fall asleep until the early hours, and had dozed fitfully until late morning.

Lykke turned off the shower and grabbed her towel, casting a quick glance out at the sea through the small window. Today was the first day since she had come to the island that she hadn't started with a dip. Once she had pulled on her thin silk robe, she went through to the kitchen and filled the coffee machine. Deep down, she knew she had to stop this before it went too far. Before it became impossible to drag herself back. But she didn't deserve to feel well right now. As she waited for the coffee to filter through, she sat down at the kitchen table.

What she needed was a future. Something to long for. The same way she had longed for a father. A family.

Lykke looked down at the laptop on the kitchen table. With a sigh, she reached for it. Having a reason to get up in the morning was enough for now. She logged in to the Public Employment Service website and scrolled through the job ads.

Shop assistant. Why not? Lykke clicked on the listing for the job in a clothes shop in Kalmar, but the negative thoughts immediately reared their heads. It was too far from Grönhögen. And the job required experience, which she didn't have. She knew all about butterflies, but not how to work a till.

"I'm a quick learner," she said aloud.

She pictured herself being interviewed by a stylish woman with a condescending smile. Casting a judgmental eye over her ripped jeans and filthy T-shirt. The load of washing she had done yesterday was still in the machine. Lykke closed the ad and kept scrolling. The home help service in Mörbylånga was looking for staff, but she probably wouldn't be able to handle being around people who were old and dying. What she really wanted was to do something that at least touched upon what she had spent so many years studying at university.

The knot in her gut grew. The memory of his sudden anger. He had pushed her up against the wall, and she had reached for whatever she could find to defend herself with.

He was the one who had done something wrong, not her.

Lykke got up and filled one of the cups on the draining rack with fresh coffee. There was a dishwasher, but she never used it while she was here alone.

She looked down at her cup and then over at the kitchen table. Carrying it all the way over there seemed impossible. She hated feeling like this. Everything was a battle. Sitting still. Doing something. Her eyes moved over to the pantry, a voice begging her to eat one of the salted crackers. She hadn't eaten a thing since a clementine on Sunday evening.

Lykke took a cautious sip of her coffee. Then another. It helped to dampen her hunger a little.

No, she wasn't going to eat. Not yet. Everything would come crashing down on her if she did.

The voice that kept droning on and on about how she needed to eat also seemed to think there was only one thing that could really help.

You need to talk to the police.

"Shut up!" Lykke shouted, hurling the mug at the wall.

18

The moving van braked sharply and gave a long, angry blast of the horn. Hanna swore to herself. No one could miss that something was happening now. A car pulled out from behind the van, blocking the street as it came to a halt. The driver leaped out.

"That's the buyer," said Selene. "I need to talk to him."

"No," said Hanna, grabbing Selene's arm as Erik hurried over to the man. "This is a crime scene. We'll handle all contact with the buyer."

Selene tried to pull free.

"What time is it?" she asked again. "They weren't meant to be here until ten."

The real estate agent was clearly in shock, and Hanna ignored her question about the time. All that mattered now was to keep working. To do everything they could to find Hugo.

"I need to talk to him," Selene repeated, trying again to pull her arm free. Hanna maintained a tight grip.

She scanned around for a colleague. The officer who had come over when they first arrived was now nowhere to be seen. Worst-case scenario, she could always call to Erik for help.

"Selene," she said. "Look at me."

The real estate agent turned to face her.

"I know it must have been awful to find your colleague dead," Hanna continued. "But right now I need your help."

"With what?"

"Answering my questions. If you didn't have the keys, how did you get inside?"

"The door wasn't locked. At first I was really annoyed with him, but then I went inside and he was just lying there."

"Why did you give the keys to Thomas?"

Selene couldn't manage to stay focused, her gaze drifting away.

"Is it really ten o'clock already?" she asked. "They weren't meant to be here until then."

Her eyes latched onto the new owner again. He was talking to Erik over by the moving van. The driver of the van had also climbed out now. Hanna let go of Selene's arm and took a step to one side, blocking them from view.

"Why did you give the keys to Thomas?" she repeated.

"Because he asked me to."

"Did he say why he needed them?"

"No. I tried to make him tell me, but he said he couldn't. If he had, then . . ."

Selene couldn't manage to say what difference it might have made, and trailed off.

"Have you given him keys before?"

Selene shook her head. The drivers got back into their vehicles, and her focus vanished again. The car engine started first, and the buyer chose to drive farther down the street rather than backing away. There was a young girl in the back seat, her palms pressed to the window. She was holding a threadbare rabbit in one hand. The woman sitting beside her had an enormous pregnant belly. Erik came back over.

"What are they going to do?" asked Selene.

"Find somewhere to store their furniture and then check in to a hotel."

The driver of the van had no choice but to reverse down the street, unable to get past the police cars. The van slowly made its way back to the main road, managed to swing around the corner, and pulled away.

"I've ruined everything," Selene sobbed. "This is going to crush Dad."

Her eyes darted over the house and then continued out across the fields. The wind was tugging at the rye, which would probably need to be harvested soon. The sky was a gloomy shade of pale gray.

"Had you and Thomas fallen out?" asked Hanna.

Selene firmly shook her head. "Absolutely not."

"Your father told us that the Fribergs are a tight-knit family, but what are things really like?"

Selene let out another sob. "So-so."

"In what way aren't things good?"

"Hektor and Dad struggle to talk, I don't know why. Dad has always supported me. Sometimes I . . ."

She straightened her blouse for at least the third time.

"Sometimes you what?" asked Hanna, managing to keep the impatience from her voice.

"Haven't been so well," said Selene.

"It can't have been easy for Thomas," said Erik. "Being the only non-family member in the office."

"No," said Selene. "I know you're not meant to say things like this about your own brother, but Hektor wasn't always so nice to Thomas."

"So it was Hektor and Thomas who didn't get on?" asked Hanna.

Selene gave them a pleading look, as though she actually believed they might tell her it was okay not to reply.

"We need to know," said Erik.

"Yes," she whispered.

"Why did they fall out?"

"Thomas owed him money."

"How much?"

"I've got no idea. But I was so mad at Hektor. It felt like the only reason he lent Thomas the money was so he'd have a hold over him."

"How did Thomas behave toward Hektor?" asked Hanna.

"He tried to ignore him, but once when I got to the office they were arguing so much I thought they might start fighting."

"Was Karl there at the time?"

"No, neither of them wanted him to know what was going on."

Selene shivered, though she didn't seem to notice it herself.

"Please, can I go now? I don't want to be here."

"Soon," said Erik. "Do you know where Hektor is?"

"What do you mean?"

"We can't get ahold of him, so we're wondering if you know where he might be."

"No, how would I know that?" Selene took a deep breath. "Do I have to tell Dad?"

"No," said Hanna. "We'll do that. But first we need to break the news to Thomas's wife."

"What should I do now?" asked Selene. It sounded as though she meant with the rest of her life.

"Go home," said Hanna. "And if anyone calls, don't pick up. That applies to your family in particular."

Since Selene was so shaken up by what had happened, Hanna offered her a ride. She turned them down, and they couldn't exactly force her. Hanna watched her drive away and then turned to Erik:

"What did the guy who was supposed to be moving in have to say?"

"Not much. They didn't have the keys, so they were banking on getting them from the agent here." He sighed. "He wanted to know if we could give them to him instead."

Hanna nodded to the house.

"Shall we . . ."

They walked over in silence. The first thing Hanna saw as she stepped inside was a large white stone fireplace. It was directly opposite the hallway, at the end of what must be the living room. A technician had set out a series of step plates, and they followed them in the other direction, into the kitchen.

Thomas Ahlström was lying on his side on the brown cork floor, just inside the doorway. One arm was covering his face. There was a children's bandage around his index finger, but it was barely visible for all of the blood. His throat had been slit, and it looked like he had pressed his hands to the wound. The blood had pooled beneath his head, and there was a dark red splatter on the fridge door. The fridge was the only thing in the room that looked remotely new. The rest was all drab and dated, likely from the seventies.

"Well, you don't exactly need to be Einstein to see that the wound to his throat is probably what killed him," said a technician in full protective clothing. "And judging by the amount of blood, he died here."

"What caused the wound?"

"No idea. We haven't found anything resembling a murder weapon yet, but they must have used something."

Hanna's eyes moved over Thomas's body. He was wearing linen trousers and a gray T-shirt. Looked slightly dressed up. Maybe Jenny was right after all. Maybe he really had made an effort because he was planning on picking her up from the station. Hanna couldn't see his eyes, and his arm was bent at a strange angle. She wondered if that was how he had fallen or whether his arm had been moved later. If so, why?

"Could you lift his arm?" she asked the technician.

He did as she said, and Thomas's wide eyes stared up at them. The whites were dull, his pupils huge. Hanna knew that had nothing to do with what he had experienced in the moment of death—the body simply began to change postmortem—but that was how it felt. He looked scared. Resigned.

"Look at this," said the technician.

Hanna turned her attention to where the technician was pointing. There was a long gash running along Thomas's forearm. Hanna had seen enough knife wounds to know that this had been caused by something else. She asked the technician to hold his arm, and leaned in close. There was some kind of black powder in the wound. Hanna closed her eyes to think. She forced back all images of the dead man and thought about where she had seen that kind of powder before.

It was soot, she realized. Ash. Her grandmother had had a tiled stove in her kitchen, and Hanna had loved sitting beside it, listening to her tell stories about Öland.

Hanna opened her eyes and walked back out into the hallway. The white stone hearth was covered in the same fine black powder. She glanced around the room. Beside the hearth was an iron stand holding a poker and a brush. She had occasionally helped her grandmother to rake out and light the tiled stove and knew there should be a shovel on the rack, too.

19

They left the house less than ten minutes later. Erik came out onto the front step and looked up at the sky, where the clouds seemed to be fighting for the best view. This was now a murder investigation, and it had been over thirty-six hours since Hugo was reported missing.

"Where's the kid?"

He must have asked the question out loud, because Hanna replied:

"Uff, I know."

He was impressed that she had spotted the ash in Thomas's wound. The technicians would go over the hearth and the floor around it with a fine-tooth comb, taking in the rack for examination. There was every chance that the missing shovel was the murder weapon. Erik would contact the previous owner for more information, so that they knew exactly what they were looking for.

"What do you think about Thomas?" he asked.

"Either he was involved in something criminal or he was having an affair," said Hanna. "I can't see what else he could have needed the keys for."

Erik called to update Ove as they walked toward the car. Their number-one priority now was to tell Jenny that her husband was dead. All sorts of thoughts were racing through Erik's mind, but he kept them to himself. He couldn't talk his way out of what lay ahead. Breaking the news of a death was always one of the hardest parts of their job, but this was more than that. Jenny would have so many questions, and they didn't have any answers.

Where was Hugo? Erik stared out across the alvar, but all he could see was Thomas lying dead on the kitchen floor. How had he ended up being separated from his son? Erik took out his phone and sent a heart to Supriya. He watched the three little dots turn into line after line of faces and animals. His wife had clearly let Nila reply. It felt good to know that they were there, even if the physical distance between them was huge. But why hadn't Supriya written anything herself?

Hanna pulled up outside the Ahlströms' house, and Jenny came rushing out as she had on their first visit. She was wearing the same clothes, her top still inside out, but her body language seemed more guarded this time. All the hours of anxiety and not knowing had taken their toll on her. She paused on the steps and pulled her cardigan tight around her body, like she could sense that they had bad news. It must have been visible in the way they moved slowly toward her.

"Just tell me," Jenny begged them.

"Let's go in and sit down," said Erik.

"No, I want to know now."

Erik turned to his colleague for support.

"Come on," said Hanna.

She led Jenny through to the living room, where she slumped into the same seat on the sofa as she had last time. Nothing in the room seemed to have moved, the pieces of the train set still scattered across the floor. Their positions in the room were the same, but the mood was completely different.

"Tell me," said Jenny.

Hanna, sitting in the armchair closest to her, had had the most contact with Jenny, but she couldn't bring herself to say it. The words came from Erik.

"I'm sorry to have to tell you that Thomas is dead."

Jenny closed her eyes. Silent tears spilled down her cheeks.

"And Hugo?"

"We haven't found him yet," said Hanna. "He wasn't there."

Jenny's eyes snapped open again.

"What do you mean, he wasn't there? Where did you find Thomas?"

"In a house in Södra Möckleby."

"So where is Hugo?"

"We don't know," said Erik.

Those three words were too much for Jenny, and she slumped forward and let out a howl. Erik struggled against the impulse to cover his ears. Her loud, shrill scream cut right to the heart of him. Hanna hurried over to the sofa and put her hand on Jenny's back. She met Erik's eye through the despair that filled the room.

Doctor? mouthed Erik.

Hanna shook her head. It might be better to wait awhile, until they knew how bad it was. Jenny's scream faded into tears, and the minute she was somewhat responsive again Erik explained that they were putting every possible resource into finding Hugo. That didn't take away from what he had already said: that they still didn't know where her son was. All they could do for Jenny in that moment was pass her a roll of paper towels and water. She pressed the paper to her eyes and sat that way for some time, her upper body rocking back and forth.

"Is there anyone we can call?" asked Hanna.

"No."

"A psychologist or a priest?" Erik clarified.

He knew that Jenny needed more than they could provide.

But Jenny shook her head and lowered the paper from her eyes.

"What was Thomas doing in Södra Möckleby?"

"I'm afraid we can't say," said Hanna. She made it sound like they knew the answer, when in truth they had no idea.

"Does he have any links to the area?" asked Erik.

"No. Or, I don't know."

Jenny pressed the paper to her eyes again, then used it to blow her nose.

"A woman saw Thomas and Hugo in the playground in Skogsby on Sunday morning," Erik continued. "And according to her Hugo almost choked on something."

He wanted Jenny to hear it from them, in case the woman's story was picked up by the press.

"What do you mean, he nearly choked?"

"He put something into his mouth and couldn't breathe, but Thomas managed to dislodge it."

"Couldn't breathe?" Jenny echoed. "Why didn't Thomas mention any of this?"

"Thomas and Hugo kept playing afterward, according to the woman," said Erik.

He wanted to tone down the event, to make it easier for her to process. Every fiber of his being remembered the panic he had felt when Nila staggered over to him one day, her face blue. A piece of apple was lodged in her throat, but he had managed to get it out.

"But Thomas told me they were there in the afternoon?"

Jenny gave them both an accusatory glance, but she would never get any answers to her question. Thomas was dead. Their silence irritated her.

"I'd like you to go now."

"Soon," said Hanna. "Why did you think that Thomas and Selene had fallen out?"

"Because she's weird," said Jenny.

"In what way?"

"It's hard to explain, but there's something about her that just doesn't seem right."

"What about Hektor?"

"Please, I can't do this right now. You need to go."

"Are you sure you don't want us to call anyone?" asked Erik.

"Yes. The only thing I want you to do is find Hugo."

THE LAST DAY

Hugo's screaming in the back seat feels like a knife to the gut. It's physically painful. Their lunch with Selene dragged on and on. She had needed to talk, telling him she was afraid that her parents might get a divorce—like it really matters; they're all adults. Still, considering what she is doing for him, it hadn't felt right to leave her. In the end Thomas had no choice but to tell her that he had to go. He let Selene hold Hugo while he went to the toilet, and when he came back out she had managed to get the boy to settle down. Thomas hopes everything works out for her, that she meets some-one, too.

"Don't you want a nap?" Thomas asks in an affected voice, glancing back in the rearview mirror.

All he can see is Hugo's wriggling head. They have him in a backward-facing child seat—it's safest that way. Jenny sometimes jokes about the way he talks to their son, but Thomas just can't help himself. Hugo really has changed him.

"Come on, buddy, what's up?"

For a split second the boy grows quiet, but only to catch his breath. The scream that follows is even louder than before, and Thomas realizes that he can't keep driving. He slams on the brakes to pull into the bus stop at the side of the road. The car behind blasts its horn, and he raises a hand in apology. As soon as it has passed, he gets out and hurries around to his angry, overtired son.

Thomas unfastens the belt and lifts him out of the seat. He holds Hugo's sweaty red head to his body.

"Shh, shh," he whispers. "We're almost home."

But that isn't quite true. They have made it only as far as Kleva.

Hugo stops screaming as Thomas hushes him and rocks back and forth. He gives his son a gentle kiss on the forehead. Could the boy be coming down with something? No, he doesn't have a fever, he's just hot and tired. Thomas reaches into the car for the changing bag and pulls out a bottle of water. He manages to get Hugo to take a couple of sips, but then the boy bats the bottle away. A car tears by, and Hugo's eyes follow it. He whines as Thomas lowers him back into the child seat, but this time he doesn't start howling.

"Get some sleep," Thomas tells him in his baby voice, laughing at himself.

Hugo doesn't go to sleep, but the screaming has been replaced by soft whimpering, which is much easier to take than his piercing cries. Thomas turns off toward Resmo, between the fields that will soon be harvested, and past the church. He heard somewhere that this is the oldest medieval church still in use in Sweden, but he doesn't know whether or not that's true. He knows every single bend in the road, every windmill and ancient monument. Before long he swings east, across the alvar, stepping on the accelerator.

"Almost home," says Thomas.

This time he is telling the truth.

After pulling up into the driveway, Thomas unfastens a still-sweaty Hugo from the car seat. He takes out a plastic cup in the kitchen and fills it with a few ice cubes. He doesn't want his son to start screaming again, so he holds him in his arms. The boy seems happy now; he knows what's coming.

Thomas lowers Hugo into his high chair and sets down the mug in front of him. Hugo immediately reaches into the cup, laughing as the ice cubes rattle around inside. He smiles happily as he pops one into his mouth. Thomas feels a stab of anxiety. Should he have broken the ice into smaller pieces? No, Hugo has had ice cubes before, and nothing bad has ever happened.

"Are you hungry?" asks Thomas.

"Not food."

The boy is only fourteen months old, but he can already manage two-word sentences. Thomas's chest swells with pride. It really is incredible to be able to experience all this. As he strokes his son's curls, it occurs to him that Lykke was around the same age the last time he saw her. A year or so after he broke up with her mother Natalie, they met up at a restaurant in Färjestaden. It had been her idea. Looking back now, he can see that she must have been hoping the meeting would spur him to take an interest in his daughter's life, but he hadn't realized that at the time. Thomas is ashamed of the man he was back then. Sure, he had thought Lykke was cute, but he and Mille had plans to watch the soccer game and drink beer in Kalmar later that day. In his mind, he was already there.

A piece of ice slips out of Hugo's hand onto the floor. Thomas gets up and rinses it off before passing it back to him.

Should he call Lykke again? If she doesn't get in touch with him, he'll have to. Almost three weeks have now passed since their last conversation. She told him she needed time to think, but maybe what she really wants is for him to prove that he is serious? To show that he is no longer the kind of man who'll let her down and disappear from her life. Now that he has been given a second chance, one he doesn't really deserve, he is so keen to do the right thing.

Hugo is trying to climb out of his high chair, and Thomas lowers him to the floor. Their lunch with Selene has upset the schedule, and he really does need to try to put him down for a nap.

Thomas changes Hugo's diaper and walks around the house with him in his arms. Jenny doesn't like it when he does that, but it's one of the only things that works when Hugo is overtired. Besides, Thomas enjoys it.

Jenny saved me.

The thought has crossed his mind before, but never as strongly as it does now—with Hugo's heavy head against his shoulder. Their son. Ever since that day when Jenny came over to him in Krögers nightclub in Kalmar six years ago, he has tried his best to become a better person, but it was only once Hugo was born that he really began to think differently. Yes, he still enjoys soccer and grabbing a beer with Mille, but all of that pales in comparison with this.

Thomas lowers Hugo into his crib and tiptoes through to the living room. He sits down on the sofa and swings his legs up onto the coffee table, then reaches for the remote control. Hugo usually naps for about an hour, so with a bit of luck he'll have time to fit in another episode of *Vikings*.

Seven minutes, that is how long his break lasts, because someone rings the doorbell. Muttering to himself, Thomas jumps up from the sofa and hurries toward the front door before they have time to ring the bell again.

Who the hell could it be?

20

The drive to Friberg Properties was just over thirty kilometers, and Hanna grew restless behind the wheel. *We'll find him*, she had told Jenny. It was the kind of promise she knew she shouldn't make, but saying that they would do their best just hadn't seemed like enough. Pushing on with their work was what mattered now, and from the seat beside her Erik was using his phone to do just that. She listened as he talked to the previous owner of the house in Södra Möckleby.

"They left the shovel on the fireside rack," he said once he hung up. "And they told me where they bought it, so I'll pass on all the info to Ove."

Hanna pulled up outside the real estate agency. The lights were on inside, but there was a note on the door. *Closed*.

"Seriously, what are they up to?" she muttered, trying the handle.

The door was locked. She called Hektor's number, but he didn't pick up, and Erik reported that Karl had switched off his phone. A man in his thirties appeared, tugging at the door. He was wearing jeans and a polo shirt, and he swore when he spotted the note.

"You know where they are?" he asked.

"No idea," Erik replied.

Hanna was already on her way back to the car, but she heard the man say something about a job interview. She called Ove to explain what was happening. As Erik climbed into the car and closed the door, she switched her phone to loudspeaker to avoid wasting time on recapping what he said.

"Go over to Hektor's place," said Ove. "Priority number one right now is to track him down. He did six months for embezzlement."

"Any news from the house?" asked Erik.

"No, no sign of Hugo yet," Ove replied. He knew exactly what they wanted to know. "But we need to find him ASAP. The press has already started calling. I've spoken to Missing People, and they're going to launch a search in and around Södra Möckleby while we keep knocking on doors."

Hanna realized that she had never followed up on her promise to call Freya Amundsdottir, the contact person for Missing People. She apologized, but Ove kept talking.

"An official search-and-rescue operation has also been launched. The Armed Forces are sending a helicopter, and we'll bring in some dog handlers, too. We're also going to ask everyone in Södra Möckleby to search their properties, to check their sheds and anywhere else Hugo might be hiding."

Every available resource would be thrown into the search for the toddler. If only they had found Thomas sooner. Hanna batted back that thought. It wouldn't do any good right now.

"Did forensics find Thomas Ahlström's phone in the house?" she asked.

"Afraid not, but the IT technicians had no trouble getting into his laptop, so we'll see what that throws up. Good work with the fireplace, by the way."

Ove was quiet for a moment, then turned back to what was weighing on them.

"Any thoughts about Hugo?"

"Either the killer took him," said Erik, "or he wandered off from the house. Or he could still be in the car somewhere."

"But if the killer didn't take him, surely he should have been found by now?" said Ove.

"Not necessarily, no. It depends where the car is, or where Hugo wandered off to."

"This could actually be about him," said Hanna.

"What are you thinking?" asked Ove.

Hanna didn't quite know why she had said it, but the image of Hugo had just popped into her head. The one in which he and his mother were playing with building blocks. The joy on his little face was wonderful. Who wouldn't want that?

"Someone might have wanted to snatch him."

Neither of the others spoke.

"It was just a thought," said Hanna. "But it would explain why we've only found Thomas."

"Okay," said Ove. "Keep that on the back burner while you continue to focus on Thomas as the main victim. Find Hektor and talk to Karl about the keys. Don't leave Öland until you've done it."

He was probably only half joking about that last part. Hanna ended the call.

"Do you really think this could be about Hugo?" asked Erik.

"I don't know," said Hanna. "Honestly, it was just a thought."

She looked up Hektor's address online and realized that he lived only a few blocks from the office. Erik took a deep breath, and Hanna knew what was coming.

"You got any plans this evening?"

It was the same question he asked virtually every day. It had almost become a kind of ritual.

"Working, I guess."

"Yeah, but after that."

"We can get something to eat somewhere," said Hanna. "But I'm not promising anything."

"Thanks," Erik said with a grin. "That'll do."

Hanna's phone began ringing just as they pulled up on Hektor's street, and she swallowed when she saw the number. It was the care home where her grandmother lived. Her grandmother was no longer capable of making calls herself—it had been several years since the dementia robbed her of the ability to speak—and whenever the home called, Hanna was always convinced that she must have died.

"Iris has a nasty fever," said the nurse. "If it doesn't break soon, we'll have to send her to the hospital."

21

"D o you want to go over there?" Erik asked the minute he heard about Hanna's grandmother.

"Not now. They promised they would call if she got any worse."

Erik didn't argue; they needed to track down Hektor as soon as possible. They crossed the street and entered the pale brown three-story building. According to the list of names by the entrance, Hektor lived on the ground floor, and to Erik's surprise he opened the door right away. Hektor looked more like his sister than his father. His strawberry-blond hair was longish, and his cheeks were dotted with freckles. He was wearing sweatpants and a T-shirt.

"What do you want?" he asked.

"We're from the police," said Hanna, holding up her ID. "We've tried calling you a few times. Why haven't you been answering your phone?"

Hektor shrugged and took a step back.

"I heard about Thomas," he said. "And where he was found. It's really horrible."

"Who told you?" asked Erik.

"Dad."

Erik exchanged a quick glance with Hanna.

"And how did he know?"

"The guy buying the house called him in a total panic. It's

understandable, really. What a fucking shock, you know? And my poor sis."

"Is there somewhere we can sit down?" asked Hanna.

Hektor showed them through to a small living room that smelled faintly of cigarette smoke. The only thing on the wall was a huge TV, a set of dumbbells on the bench beneath. The impression Hektor and his apartment gave was more bachelor than real estate agent, though Erik's only real experience of real estate agents was in Malmö, and there was probably a big difference between working there and on Öland.

Hektor slumped into the armchair, leaving the black leather sofa free for them. It was so old and tired that Erik tipped back when he sat down. His body was still upset about what he had put it through during the weekend, and wouldn't quite do what he wanted. Hektor smirked.

"You okay?" he asked.

"I did the Ironman last weekend."

"Oh shit. I really want to try that. Was it tough?"

Erik opened his mouth to reply, but Hanna got in before him.

"How was your relationship with Thomas?"

Hektor reluctantly forgot about the Ironman and turned his attention to her.

"Not great," he said. "But since you're here I'm guessing you already know that."

"We're speaking to everyone who was close to Thomas," said Erik. "But you're right, we heard that the two of you had fallen out. What was that about?"

He didn't want to help Hektor by revealing what anyone else had said.

"He owed me money."

"How much?"

"Fourteen thousand kronor."

Neither officer said anything, which seemed to trigger Hektor.

"Sure, I was pissed with Thomas," he snapped, "but I'd never fucking kill anyone over such a stupid amount."

Erik had once worked on a case in which a man was stabbed to death for two hundred kronor. Just a few weeks prior to his death, the victim and his killer had celebrated Christmas together. Both had lost their families. There may well have been alcohol involved, but booze was rarely the only reason.

It was clear that Hektor was temperamental, and judging by the look on his face he knew he had lashed out.

"Sorry," he said. "But I'm guessing you also know about the time I did inside? It's just really annoying that people can't forget about that."

Erik remained quiet, and Hanna did the same. That seemed like the best way to make Hektor talk. The real estate agent gestured irritably.

"Prison changed me," he said. "That's why I lent the money to Thomas. I wanted to be nice, you know? Everything's easier if we help one another."

He stared at them for a long moment, as though he were challenging them to question what he had just said.

"Why did Thomas need the money?" asked Erik.

"No idea," said Hektor. "But he was always short of it. Look, I know I can blow my top sometimes, but I never cross the line. Thomas was the exact opposite. Everyone thought he was so charming, but he could really lose it. I mean, you've got to wonder why he changed jobs so often."

Hektor was talking so fast that Erik struggled to keep up.

"What do you mean when you say he could lose it?"

"One time he started shouting at me like a fucking madman for being late with an ad. Another day he was really pissed off with me for missing a meeting with a client. It was lucky Selene came in, otherwise he probably would've hit me."

"Why did your father hire him?" asked Hanna.

"You'll have to ask him. He likes to think of himself as a bit of a white knight. I don't know how many stray cats he's taken in over the years."

The armchair creaked as Hektor shifted in it. His tone sounded slightly mocking, which Erik found strange considering he had just tried to convince them that he had lent Thomas money out of kindness.

"How well do you and your dad get on?" Hanna continued.

"Are you a therapist or a detective?" Hektor laughed at his own joke.

"Just answer the question," said Erik.

"I don't get what that's got to do with anything, but fine. We get on well. Sure, I'd imagined doing something other than working for his company, but if it wasn't for him I'd be unemployed right now. I'd already studied economics and tax law, but he helped me with the other courses I needed to take."

Hektor used the crook of his arm to stifle a yawn.

"Sorry," he said, "but I'm going to need to go lie down soon."

"We just have a few more questions," said Erik. "Do you know what Thomas was doing in the house?"

"Nope. It's totally crazy that he was found there, I just don't understand it. I mean, I have wondered why he never managed to hold on to a job before. . . . Whether, you know, he was up to something dodgy. But the job seemed really important to him, and I honestly don't think he'd put the company at risk."

They still didn't know exactly when Thomas had died, but the rigor mortis had relaxed by the time the technician lifted his arm, which meant it had likely happened sometime Sunday evening.

"Where were you Sunday evening?" asked Erik.

"I had dinner here," said Hektor. "Then I watched a film. I felt a bit rough, so I couldn't be bothered doing anything else. I usually go over to my folks' place to eat on Sundays."

Yet again, he seemed to take their silence as doubting.

"I'm ill," he said. "That's why I'm not at work. And that's why I might seem a bit insensitive. I really do feel like crap. I didn't like Thomas, but no one deserves to die. And it sucks about the little guy. I really hope you find him. If I was feeling better, I'd help you look myself."

"You were working yesterday, weren't you?" said Erik.

"Yeah. Sometimes it's tricky to stay at home. Surely you must know that, as police officers?"

22

H e was almost as chatty as you," Hanna said as they left the apartment building.

"Thanks for that," Erik said with a grin.

She had no doubt that Hektor's anger had caused him to cross the line in the past. The only question was when. Hanna turned around and looked up at what should be his window, but she couldn't see anyone. On the floor above, a gray-haired woman was watering her plants. The sight reminded Hanna about the call from her grandmother's care home. The elderly woman caught her eye and nodded in greeting. Hanna smiled and raised her hand.

"Have you changed your mind about going to see your grand-mother?" asked Erik.

"No. She wouldn't even know I was there. I'll go after work."

"So no dinner with me, then?"

Erik made the corners of his mouth curl downward.

"Sorry. You'll have to convince someone else."

Hanna got behind the wheel for the short drive back to Friberg Properties. She asked Erik to send a message to Ove saying that someone should contact Thomas's previous employers. Not just because of what Hektor had told them, but because Thomas had been using one of the houses the firm had sold. Even if he wasn't doing anything illegal there, it was definitely inappropriate behavior.

The lights in the office were now out, and a Saab was in the process of reversing out of one of the parking spaces. Hanna quickly pulled in and blocked the exit, but the man driving the car wasn't Karl Friberg. He blasted the horn, and she hurried to get out of his way.

"There's another note," said Erik.

Hanna drove right up to the door so that he could read what it said.

"It says they're out on an errand, and there's a number."

Erik used his phone to dial the number.

"No answer." He sighed. "What do we do now?"

Hanna didn't want to drive back to Kalmar without first having spoken to Karl.

"Guess we'll have to pay him a visit at home, too."

Karl and his wife, Madeleine, lived in a villa in the Svamp area of eastern Färjestaden. A few young boys had set up a floorball goal on the street, and were practicing penalties. The minute they saw the car, two of them ran over and, in a well-oiled routine, moved the goal out of the way.

The Fribergs' house was at the far end of the street. A single-story wooden villa, painted blue. The garden was simple but well tended, with a couple of fruit trees out front and a flower bed running along the side of the house. By the steps up to the front door there was a stone sculpture of a dog. Hanna rang the bell, but nothing happened. She waited a few seconds and then tried again.

"I'm coming!" a voice called inside.

A woman opened the door. She was wearing a flour-streaked apron and wasn't far off Hanna's height. Her thin hair was cropped short.

"Are you Madeleine?"

"Yes, and I suppose you must be from the police?"

Hanna and Erik nodded.

"Is Karl here?" asked Erik.

"I'm afraid not."

She turned around, and Hanna noticed a slender, furless cat poking its head out from behind a chest of drawers. It got ready to make a leap, but Madeleine prevented it from slipping outside by holding out her leg. The cat darted back beneath the chest of drawers with a hiss.

"When did you last speak to him?" Erik continued.

"Half an hour ago," said his wife. "But only briefly. The way he's been running around, he'll have a heart attack any minute now."

Madeleine glanced down at her dusty apron.

"Everything is upside down," she said. "What happened is so awful. I like to bake when I'm stressed."

"Could you call Karl for us?" asked Hanna.

"Yes, but you'll have to come in and close the door so the damn cat doesn't get out."

They did as they were told as Madeleine went off to get her phone. The seconds ticked away, but she didn't come back. Minutes passed. The house was completely silent. The cat glared up at them. Hanna took a few steps down the hallway and saw Madeleine leaning back against the kitchen worktop. It was covered in mixing bowls, measuring spoons, and ingredients. She was clutching her phone to her ear.

"He's not picking up," she said.

"Tell him to give us a ring whenever he calls you back," said Hanna.

She noticed a cat curled up on one of the kitchen chairs. It had long gray fur and seemed to be fast asleep.

"I will," said Madeleine, putting down her phone. "Have you found that poor little boy yet?"

"We can't comment on an ongoing investigation."

"No, of course. It's just so awful that he's still missing. Do you have any idea what happened?"

"We can't comment on an ongoing investigation," Hanna repeated.

"Did you have dinner together on Sunday?" asked Erik, who had followed Hanna deeper into the house.

A crease appeared between Madeleine's grayish black brows.

"Why are you asking me that?"

"Just answer the question."

"Both kids usually come over to eat, but Hektor wasn't well on Sunday and Selene didn't feel up to it."

"But you and Karl ate together?"

"Yes, around five thirty. Since it was just the two of us I heated up some leftovers. Then I watched TV while Karl went out to his work shed."

"What does he do in there?"

"He's building a canoe. I went to bed just before ten, right after he came back in."

"So he spent all evening in the shed?" asked Erik.

Madeleine took a couple of sips from a glass of water on the counter.

"Yes, he did," she said. "I would have noticed if he'd left."

"Did you know Thomas?" Erik continued.

"I've only really met him once, when Karl threw a little staff party here. We didn't talk much, but he seemed nice."

Hanna's phone started ringing, and when she saw Daniel's name on the screen she thanked Madeleine and hurried out of the house.

"Ove wants you to interview Lykke Henriksen again," he said.

Hanna turned around. The kitchen window was empty.

"Why?"

"Because I've just spoken to her old professor, Roger Wasselius, and he confirmed that she was stalking him. She got it into her head that they were in some kind of relationship, and when he tried to talk to her about it, she slashed his tires. Then she turned up at his house. He let her in so that he could convince her to stop, but she wouldn't listen, and when he tried to make her leave she grabbed a candlestick and hit him over the head with it."

"Is there anything to suggest he's lying?" Hanna asked, getting behind the wheel. "That they did actually have a relationship?"

"I spoke to his wife, too. She claims she saw Lykke outside their house on several occasions, just standing there. The wife found it unsettling. She wanted her husband to file a police report, but he didn't dare."

"Didn't dare? Why?" asked Hanna.

"He was afraid it would ruin his career if anyone believed Lykke."

"Okay, we'll head over to Grönhögen now."

23

As Hanna pulled up outside Lykke Henriksen's house forty minutes later, Erik peered over toward the garden. The weather was cooler today, and she wasn't digging in the flower beds. During their first meeting with Lykke it had been obvious that something wasn't quite right. What her professor and his wife had now told the police could well be true, but that didn't automatically make her a killer. Erik realized that they would also have to inform her that Thomas Ahlström had been found dead. She may not have had any real relationship with him, but he was still her father.

The wind tugged at Erik as he got out of the car. The house was in a beautiful location, but it was also a little too exposed to the elements. Hanna's phone started ringing, and after listening for a few seconds she ended the call with the words, "You'll have to call the press spokesperson."

"How much do they know?" asked Erik.

"Most of it, but given the whole circus in Södra Möckleby and the search for the boy that's planned, it doesn't exactly take a genius to work out roughly what's going on."

Erik raised his hand to knock, but the door opened before he had time. Lykke must have spotted them through the window. The dogged look on her face revealed just how little she wanted them there.

"We need to talk to you again," said Erik.

"I'm busy."

"It won't take long," said Hanna, taking another step toward the front door.

Lykke moved to one side with a sigh, letting them into the cramped hallway. She was moving slowly, as though she might fall apart otherwise. The house stank of coffee. Erik glanced into the kitchen as he passed and saw that there was a large coffee stain on the wall, shards of china scattered across the floor.

They sat down in the living room, where the two sofas took up most of the space. It was cramped but cozy. The open hearth looked like it was still used, and there was a TV leaning against the wall on the floor. Erik's gaze landed on a basket of toys. From the quick background check they had run on Lykke, he knew that she didn't have any children or siblings, but perhaps she looked after her friends' kids from time to time.

"I rent the house out quite a bit," she said, clearly following his eye. "A lot of families with kids book to stay here, and they appreciate the toys."

Erik didn't think the press had managed to release the news of Thomas Ahlström's death yet, but information about the Missing People search for Hugo had already begun to circulate.

"I'm sorry to say that your father was found dead this morning."

Lykke's body tensed, but her head was still turned toward the toys, so he couldn't see the reaction on her face. She slowly turned back to them.

"Where?"

"We can't say," said Erik.

They wouldn't be able to keep that detail quiet for long. Far too many people knew. All the neighbors had seen what was going on.

They had told Jenny the truth, but with Lykke things were more complicated. She hadn't actually known her father, and there were certain circumstances that made her a potential suspect. Erik expected her to ask more questions, but she remained quiet. Shouldn't she at least ask about her half brother? Lykke felt strangely absent somehow. He checked her eyes but couldn't see any sign of her being high on anything.

"We spoke to your old university," he said. "Could you tell us what happened between you and your professor?"

Lykke closed her eyes on hearing the word *professor*.

"Who did you talk to?" she asked.

"Does it matter?" Erik replied. "That shouldn't have any bearing on your version of events."

Lykke pulled her feet up onto the sofa and rested her chin on her knees. Her eyes were open again, but she wasn't looking at either officer.

"I hit him on the head with a candlestick," she said.

"By 'him' I assume you mean Roger Wasselius?"

Lykke nodded.

"Why did you hit him with a candlestick?" asked Hanna.

"It was the closest thing at hand."

"Okay, but why did you hit him at all?"

Lykke turned to face the window. All Erik could see through it was the wall of the building outside.

"I thought he was going to strangle me," she said. "He pushed me up against the wall with his arm on my throat."

"What were you doing at his house?" asked Erik.

Lykke didn't reply, just continued to stare out the window.

"It's important that you tell us," said Hanna.

Lykke's only reaction was to hug her knees more tightly.

"From what the university told us, it wasn't the first incident," said Erik.

When Lykke turned to look at him, her face was still blank.

"What do you mean?"

"They said you'd been stalking your professor."

For a moment Erik thought she hadn't heard him, but then Lykke leaped up from the sofa and rushed out of the room.

24

The porcelain felt cool beneath her palms. Lykke was so upset she was shaking, and though she knew she should let go, she just couldn't bring herself to do it. The basin wasn't made for this, and the pipes were creaking ominously.

Yes, she had hit Roger, but she hadn't had any choice. The anger inside her merged with the look she had seen on his face. Maybe they were better suited for each other than either of them had realized.

There was a knock on the bathroom door.

"Is everything okay in there?" the police officer asked.

He had come running after her like he seriously thought she was planning to take off.

"I'll be out soon," Lykke stuttered.

The moment the officers came into her house, it was like she had stepped out of herself. *Tell them*, the observant, rational part of her had screamed. *Tell them everything.* But she couldn't.

Thomas was dead. No, don't go there. Not now. It was too much.

Why hadn't she reported Roger to the police? She knew the answer: It would have been her word against his, and all the times she had been with him voluntarily would have been used against her. Besides, she wasn't the one with injuries, he was. Roger had let go of her, clamping his hand to his temple in shock. The same hand that had just grabbed her between the legs as he pushed her up against the wall and practically suffocated her with his other arm. The look of rage on his face and all the horrible things he had shouted at her had made her run away.

Lykke finally managed to let go of the sink. She splashed her face with icy water and stared at herself in the mirror. Tried to mimic Roger's voice: *You're insane.* But it came out more as a croak than anything.

The officer knocked again.

"Yes," she said. "Just a minute."

Lykke had gone to see her faculty program director the Monday after it happened, and she guessed that must be who the police had spoken to. She really had thought he was on her side. She had told him all about their relationship and said that Roger had become violent when she confronted him over his lies. The program director had asked whether she wanted to file a police report, and when she said no he had said that it was good that she had come to him. That #metoo had forced the university to get better at dealing with this kind of issue. He had promised to talk to Roger, to make him understand that his behavior was *unacceptable.* Lykke sneered at her reflection when she remembered that word. She and Roger had barely spoken since.

Stalked, seriously?

Yes, she had hung around outside his house a few times, but that was only because he suddenly stopped taking her calls. She had been worried, looked up his address, and gone over there. Through the window she had seen the woman and child and realized what an asshole he really was. She had slashed his tires in the parking lot outside the Evolutionary Biology Center the next day. And the day after that, she'd had to go over to his house again. It was like she couldn't quite trust what she had seen.

Another memory came back to her, making her lose her breath.

They had gone out to the archipelago together, to Vaxholm, one weekend. Just the two of them. They had checked in to a hotel, eaten well, walked around the island. . . . That was when Roger told her that he'd never met anyone like her before. That she was funny and smart. Beautiful. That he wanted them to be together forever. And for the first time in a long while, Lykke had felt happy.

There was something wrong with her. It wasn't normal to behave the way she had. Slashing tires, tracking down Roger, and imagining that it might solve anything. Believing that it would help if she stopped eating. Thomas was dead. No, don't go there. Lykke slammed her palms down on the basin and left the bathroom. The police officer was still standing in the corridor outside, and she avoided his eye. Just followed him back through to the living room.

Tell them, nagged the voice in her head. She knew she at least had to try.

"We spoke to Roger Wasselius, too," said the man.

"And I'm guessing he told you I was a stalker?"

"More or less. Is he wrong?"

"Yes."

"Roger's wife claims she saw you outside their house on several occasions," he continued.

"Yes," said Lykke.

She couldn't manage another word. There was so much she was ashamed of.

"How would you describe your relationship with Roger?" asked the female officer.

All these questions about Roger were bothering Lykke, but she knew what they were getting at. The police wanted to know what kind of person she was.

There's something wrong with me.

Lykke forced back that thought.

"I was so in love," she said. "And obviously I noticed that we were always at my place, but I just thought that was because he was my professor. I wanted to surprise him one evening, so I went over to his house. And that's when I discovered that he had a wife and a child. That he'd been lying to me. And no, I didn't take it very well."

"What did you do?"

"I slashed his tires. He was really pissed off, threatened to report me."

"And the other times you were there?"

"It was like I couldn't believe what I'd seen, and then . . ."

Lykke stared down at the Persian rug. She was nearing the most difficult part of the story and couldn't bring herself to meet their eyes. Her stomach was aching and her head pounding. And Thomas was dead.

"Go on," said the woman.

"I went over to Roger's place because his wife deserved to know what a bastard he was, but she wasn't home. He pushed me up against the wall and I thought he was going to kill me. That's why I hit him."

"Do you have anything that proves the two of you had a relationship?" asked the man.

Lykke kept her eyes locked on the rug. Being questioned like this hurt so much.

"Like what?" she asked.

"Love letters, text messages, receipts. Anything, really."

"We sent a lot of messages, but he always just signed them *R*."

Lykke reeled off Roger's number when they asked for it.

"Do you have any pictures of the two of you together?"

"No, Roger claimed he hated having his picture taken."

She knew just how distant she sounded. She was so exhausted she thought she would probably fall asleep if she lay down on the sofa. How many times had Roger reached for her phone when she tried to take a picture of him? Told her she was a much prettier subject. Naïve as she was, she had been flattered. No, not naïve. Starved. The only relationship she had ever had before was with a spotty, insecure high school student who had dumped her after just a few months because he thought she was impossible to get close to.

The realization hit her like a stab to the gut. *They think I'm lying, and they're going to think that about Thomas, too.*

"What happened in the kitchen?" asked the man.

At first Lykke didn't know what he meant, but then he began talking about the coffee.

"An accident," she said.

Why hadn't she cleaned it up? She hated herself for being so useless. She bit the inside of her lip until the taste of blood filled her mouth.

"Is what you said about Thomas true?" asked the female officer.

"What do you mean?"

"That the only contact you had with him was one phone call?"

Tell them, the voice urged her, but all Lykke could do was nod.

25

Hanna called Daniel from the car to bring him up to speed on what Lykke Henriksen had told them. He said he would investigate the phone number she had given them. They needed a better understanding of what really happened between Lykke and her professor, because if what Roger Wasselius had said was true, then they would also have to take a closer look at her relationship with Thomas. The impression Hanna had gotten during their first meeting with Lykke had only grown stronger. The girl wasn't well.

"Can we stop off in Södra Möckleby?" asked Hanna.

"Why?"

"Because I need to introduce myself to Freya Amundsdottir from Missing People," she said. "And I want to check on the search party. We can try to track down Karl Friberg again afterward."

Erik didn't ask any more questions, and Hanna was grateful for that. She could always just call Freya, but she knew she had messed up by not getting in touch right away. Going over there was one way of making up for that. Missing People's help was vital, and they needed to take care of that relationship. Hanna also wanted to see how many people were taking part—and who they were. After Joel Forslund was found dead at the rest area in Möckelmossen, she had gone out there every day to photograph the people visiting the scene. It had helped them find the killer. Whoever was responsible for Thomas's death might be taking part in the search party. Or whoever who had taken Hugo, if that was what it was all about after all.

There were cars parked down both sides of the road, but Hanna kept going until she reached the church in Södra Möckleby. The village had been built around the church, with farms and fields on the outskirts. She found a pocket of space outside the small library, which didn't currently seem to be open. On the grass slope by the church, a woman in a red vest had climbed up onto an overturned crate and was giving instructions through a megaphone. It had to be Freya Amundsdottir, which meant she and Erik had no choice but to wait.

"Hi," said a quiet voice nearby.

Isak.

He was standing right by her side. Hanna had never been this close to him before, and she could smell lemon. His shower gel. She swallowed.

"Hi," she said. "What are you doing here?"

She blushed at the ridiculous question. The color of her cheeks deepened as she realized it was the very same question she had asked in Gårdby. But did he really have to stand so close? She couldn't focus.

"I wanted to help with the search," said Isak.

"Good."

Good? What the hell did she mean by that? And particularly in this context. Hanna glanced over at him, but she couldn't see any sign that he was offended. He smiled, and Hanna came a hair's breadth from pushing him away—anything to regain control. He was wearing a knitted Icelandic sweater, and the wind had ruffled both his hair and his beard. There was something about men with beards. Fabian had had one when they first met, but he'd had it trimmed at one of the trendy salons he visited, eventually getting sick of it and shaving it off entirely.

"Do you have any idea what—"

"I can't talk about the investigation, I'm afraid."

"Understood," said Isak. "I suppose I knew that already. It's just so awful."

Why had she interrupted him? Isak turned to look at her, and Hanna realized that she hadn't responded to his comment.

"Yeah, it's awful."

She wanted to say something else, but she couldn't think of anything that sounded even remotely sensible. She leaned away from him, but it didn't help. Freya finished what she was saying, and Hanna nodded in her direction.

"I need to talk to her."

"Of course," said Isak.

He sounded slightly hesitant, like he didn't really want to let her go. Perhaps he had something he wanted to say.

"Did you know Thomas Ahlström?" she asked.

"No, but I always try to help out whenever anything like this happens."

From the corner of one eye Hanna realized that Freya was walking away, so she excused herself and hurried after her. The air immediately grew easier to breathe.

"Hi. I'm Hanna Duncker, from the Kalmar police."

"I'm so glad you could come," Freya said with a smile. "Do you have any updates?"

"Afraid not."

"Would you like to join the search?"

Hanna scanned the area for Erik. He was still standing by the car, gazing longingly toward the small café. She saw a journalist from Barometern making her way over to him.

"No, I . . . I really just wanted to introduce myself," said Hanna. "And to apologize for not calling you."

"Hey, don't worry about it. I know you have a lot on your plate right now."

Hanna nodded. She really did. And not just because of the investigation.

"Could I have a list of everyone who has volunteered for the search?" she asked.

"Yes, I can email it to you," said Freya. "A couple of hundred people have registered so far, but there'll probably be a lot more joining us later on. We thought it was important to get going as quickly as possible."

"Thank you."

Hanna's eye briefly met Isak's before she looked away, taking in the mix of people milling around. Many were well past pension age, while others seemed to be only just eighteen—the minimum age required to take part. It was early afternoon, and those volunteers with jobs likely wouldn't arrive until later.

Why had she insisted on coming here? As the thought crossed her mind, Hanna noticed a woman staring straight at her, like she was trying to make contact. The woman's behavior seemed too hesitant for a journalist, and Hanna decided to go over. Even if she wasn't the killer, she might have joined the search party because she knew something.

"Hi," said Hanna. "What brings you here today?"

"To help out."

A helicopter swung low overhead, and Hanna waited until the dull whir of its rotor blades had faded away.

"Are you a friend of the family?" she asked.

"You don't recognize me, do you?"

Hanna didn't know what to say.

"I'm Klara," said the woman. "My little brother Robin was friends with Kristoffer."

Since Klara was older than Robin and Hanna younger than Kristoffer, the two women's social circles had never overlapped, but Gårdby was a small community and Hanna was ashamed that she hadn't recognized her. Her long brown hair and small upturned nose were the same as ever, though it was clear that the past sixteen years had left their mark on her. Her posture seemed different somehow, and she had dark circles beneath her eyes. Hanna knew she should make small talk, ask Klara how she was these days, how Robin was. But that would mean talking about herself. And, worse: talking about Kristoffer.

Klara continued to study her with the same intense, searching gaze. What was she looking for? A trace of Lars the killer, perhaps.

"It's good to see you," said Hanna. "But I should get back to work."

She walked over to Erik without so much as glancing in Isak's direction. The journalist had moved on, and was now interviewing a woman who had volunteered to take part in the search. Hanna saw a flicker of interest on the journalist's face as she passed. She always received far more requests than any of her colleagues. Nothing was as powerful as a comment from Detective Hanna Duncker, the murderer's daughter. The journalist broke off the interview and hurried after her.

"Let's go back to Färjestaden," Hanna told Erik, getting in behind the wheel before the journalist managed to reach her.

26

"Are you dating anyone?" asked Erik.

Hanna lost her concentration on the road for a moment. She had noticed the flock of starlings out in the fields, but suddenly the car was surrounded by them. Erik gasped. The starlings sounded like a flock of angry sopranos bickering over what tempo they should be following. She eased off the accelerator.

"Relax," said Hanna. "They're just birds. And no, I'm not dating anyone."

In complete control of their airspace, the starlings banked around the car and away. For someone who wanted to live in the countryside, Erik really was clueless—not that she said anything. She remembered he had dropped that idea and taken up the guitar instead.

"Daniel hooked up with some guy on Saturday," said Erik. "After the Ironman."

"How do you know?"

"He vanished so suddenly that I got in touch to make sure he was okay."

"Very considerate of you."

"It was."

Hanna guessed that Daniel must have spent his Sunday with the man, too. That he was the reason Daniel had ended up getting sunburned. Isak's smile popped into her head, and she stepped on the gas. She didn't have time for either him or Kristoffer right now. The meeting with Robin's sister Klara had brought up a new memory. Kristoffer and Robin had spent a lot of time together that last spring before everything fell apart, and when she got home from Rebecka's one evening, she had found them playing poker in the kitchen. They had asked if she wanted to join in. Kristoffer had seemed happy, for once, and she had thought that everything might be okay after all. Lars was elsewhere, probably drunk like usual, but right there and then things had felt good, like an echo of an earlier life. But just a month or so later, the police had shown up and arrested their father.

THE TRIP DOWN to Grönhögen and Södra Möckleby had taken almost two hours, but the same note about running an errand was still hanging on the door of Friberg Properties. This time, however, Karl Friberg picked up when Hanna called.

"I'm just a few minutes away," he said. "Maybe you could wait outside?"

They found a bench in a bus shelter not far from the office. Sitting there was more pleasant than in the car.

"There's a grill restaurant over there," said Hanna, nodding down toward the harbor. "I'm sure they do something vegetarian, too."

"Thanks, but I can hold out awhile longer."

A few minutes turned out to be more like fifteen. Karl Friberg's Saab came racing around the corner and into the small parking lot outside the office.

"He drives like you," said Erik.

Hanna snorted and got to her feet, hurrying over to him. There was so much she could say about how Karl had been ducking their calls, but right now all she wanted was answers. Karl unlocked the door and let them inside. After removing the note from the door, he turned around.

"Sorry," he said. "I know I should have picked up, but everything is just so damn stressful right now. Hektor is ill and Selene isn't in any fit state to work, either. I had to take her to the emergency psychiatric clinic. Maybe I'm focusing on the wrong thing, given what happened, but I'm just so disappointed in her."

"So she told you about the keys?" asked Hanna.

"Yes, I called her right after the new owner got in touch. I've been a real estate agent for over thirty years, and this . . . I really can't understand what Thomas could have wanted the keys for."

Karl gave a resigned shake of his head, turned in to the small pantry, and reappeared a moment later with a cup of coffee.

"Maybe you'd like one, too?"

"We're fine, thanks," said Erik.

"Sorry," said Karl. "I just can't think straight."

They sat down in the same room they had on their first visit. It was much cooler this time, and Karl didn't need to turn on any fans. Only a day had passed since they'd first met him, but he seemed to have aged by several years.

"Do you know whether Thomas took the keys on any other occasions?" asked Hanna. "Himself, I mean. Before he went on paternity leave."

"No," said Karl. "He would've been out of a job if I'd ever caught him doing it."

"He might have had a good excuse," said Hanna. "That he forgot to put them back, for example."

"No."

Karl reached for his coffee cup, almost knocking it over in the process.

"Uff, I'm just really struggling to take all this in," he continued. "Poor Jenny. And it's so terrible about the boy. You still don't know what happened to him?"

Hanna shook her head.

"I was so happy to finally have both kids involved in the firm," said Karl. "But now . . . it's probably egotistical of me to be thinking about myself right now, but I don't know whether we'll survive this. Our clients have already started to jump ship."

Karl was as chatty as his son, though Hanna thought he came across as much more likable. Despite what he had just said about being egotistical, it was clear that he cared about the Ahlström family.

"Where do you keep the keys?" asked Erik.

"In a locked cash box in that cupboard over there."

Karl nodded to a gray metal cabinet on the other side of the glass wall. Hanna found herself wondering what it was about real estate agents and glass walls. Did they just want as many people as possible to witness the happy moment when the buyer signed the contract?

"Who has keys to the box?" she asked.

"Everyone in the office. But Thomas gave his back when he went on paternity leave."

"And you really can't think of any reason he might have needed the keys?"

"I'm sorry," said Karl. "Maybe he just wanted to get out of the house for a while."

He smiled, embarrassed. It was obvious he didn't believe that himself.

"Did you know that Thomas owed Hektor money?" asked Erik.

"No."

His answer came a little too quickly, and Hanna was fairly sure he wasn't being entirely truthful.

"Did Thomas know that Hektor had been to jail?"

Karl studied them for a long moment before he answered.

"No, we kept that in the family."

He sipped his coffee.

"And I keep a close watch over the company's finances," he continued. "Hektor was young and dumb back then. He'd never do anything like that now. He's finally calmed down."

"I'm sure you can understand that we need to ask where you were on Sunday evening," said Erik.

"Of course. I was at home. We were supposed to be having dinner with the kids, but we canceled because neither of them felt up to it. It was just Madeleine and me in the end. And after dinner I went out to my work shed, it must've been around sixish. Madeleine can confirm that."

The main door to the office opened and closed. It was the same man they had bumped into by the note earlier.

"If there's nothing else, I need to get back to work," said Karl. "And do what I can to save the firm."

"That's everything for now," said Hanna.

Hanna's and Erik's phones beeped in unison, and they hurried out. Hanna desperately hoped it was about Hugo, that he had been found.

The image of Hugo in his red T-shirt was all over the news, and Missing People had switched to using that picture in their new search—one focused solely on the boy. They had received a huge number of tips, and one seemed so trustworthy that Ove thought it should be looked into. He had forwarded a photograph someone had snapped of their neighbor's garden. According to the woman who took it, her neighbor had mental health issues and no children. But she was playing with a young boy in a red T-shirt.

THE LAST DAY

Thomas only makes it a few meters toward the front door before he hears Hugo howling in the bedroom. For a brief, indecisive moment he pauses, then hurries through to the crib. Hugo is sitting bolt upright, staring straight ahead in terror. He doesn't seem to have any idea where he is. Thomas picks him up and holds him tight, whispering calming words in his ear. The boy settles down, but when the doorbell rings for a second time he immediately starts crying again.

Hugo hates the noise it makes, and Thomas can understand why. It sounds like a baby being let loose on a xylophone. If he has time this week, he'll drive over to Kalmar and try to find a replacement that isn't so damn loud. He's sure Jenny would appreciate that, too.

"Okay, okay, I'm coming," Thomas mutters, making his way to the front door.

Karl is standing on the porch outside.

"Hi," says Thomas, surprised.

A sense of panic surges through him. Has Selene blabbed about the keys? Karl says hello, his eyes on Hugo. He probably thinks that Thomas is the world's worst father, because the boy is howling. But it's all his fault. Thomas reluctantly steps aside to make room for his boss. Gazing around the room, Karl starts talking about the viewing he had that day, a villa right down by the water in Sandvik. There are building blocks and plastic cars scattered across the floor. The two toys Hugo plays with most often right now.

Karl seems nervous. But why?

"So, how's the paternity leave going?" he asks.

"Good."

Karl once told him that he regrets not spending more time at home with Hektor and Selene. His wife, Madeleine, seems to do most things around the house. She has been on sick leave for almost a year now, but she used to work as a teacher. Hugo settles down. Thomas knows he should tell Karl to take a seat, but he doesn't.

"I don't want to bother you," Karl tells him.

"It's no problem."

But he doubts he will be able to get Hugo to go back to sleep.

"It's just I didn't want to do this over the phone," the boss continues.

"Do what?"

Karl has paused in front of the small box on the bookshelf where he had put the letter from Lykke. The reminder that he had failed so spectacularly the first time he became a parent. Hugo is starting to get heavy, and he moves him over to his other hip.

"I'm afraid we can't keep you on."

Thomas's immediate reaction is that this must be a joke. It has to be. But Karl is avoiding his eye, beads of sweat glistening on his forehead. A tidal wave of anger surges through Thomas. He feels like letting it take over, unleashing it on Karl, but for Hugo's sake he holds back.

"Why not?" he asks.

Karl sighs. "Now that you're a parent yourself, maybe you can understand why I need to put Hektor first."

So this is about his conflict with Hektor, not the keys. Thomas didn't think that Karl had noticed anything, but maybe Hektor has been talking crap about him.

"What has Hektor said?"

"I have eyes, you know," says Karl. "But he did mention the debt."

Karl takes a step forward and holds out a hand to Hugo, but Thomas pulls back. There is nothing he wouldn't do for his son, but Hektor isn't a child anymore. He's an idiot, and so is Karl for letting Hektor ruin things for him. For the company. Hektor gets away with the exact same things Thomas lost his previous job over. Sometimes, after a night out, he doesn't show up at the office until lunchtime, and he forgets important meetings. Yes, Thomas owes him money, but he also does his job much better than that stuck-up ass.

"Too much has happened," Karl continues. "And I don't just mean this thing with Hektor. It's not working anymore, simple as that."

Yet another wave of anger courses through Thomas. What isn't working? The whole thing is so unfair, and he is *this* close to being swept up in his emotions. To shouting exactly what he thinks of Karl.

"I'd like you to go now," he snarls.

The boss studies him. Gives him an uncertain smile. Probably just nerves, but it's provocative all the same. Karl likes to talk about how important it is to support one another and how everyone deserves a second chance, but clearly that applies only to his own offspring. Thomas is on the verge of throwing Hektor's prison sentence back in Karl's face, but he stops himself. Does he really think that Thomas has no idea his son was in the slammer?

"I know this—"

"Just go."

"If there's anything I can do, then . . ."

"No."

Karl finally turns to leave, and as the front door swings shut Thomas hugs Hugo. When the boy starts crying, Thomas does, too. Why does everything have to be so damn hard? He should have made more of an effort with regard to Hektor, but everything about the man irritates him: his superficiality, the way he doesn't give a damn about his family. Possibly because he reminds Thomas of how he once was. He should have known that he couldn't take money from him, but he was naïve enough to believe that Hektor had changed. The idiot has used the debt to dump work on him several times.

Hugo has settled down, and is looking up at Thomas in surprise. Thomas wipes his own tears away, but they are immediately replaced by new ones. He should have made more of an effort with Lykke, too. Who has she become? Thomas has no idea, and he realizes that he can't afford to give her any more time. He was the one who let her down, and he needs to show her just how much he regrets that. To make her see how happy he was to read her letter. That he wants nothing more than to be a part of her life.

"Dada," says Hugo, patting him on the cheek.

"Daddy's just a bit sad. It'll be okay."

But it feels like Karl has pulled the rug out from beneath his feet. Shredded it, more like. He needs this job. He needs the income and the stability. He needs Jenny.

27

The picture wasn't particularly sharp. The boy was standing in the middle of a lawn, his eyes on something out of shot. Erik zoomed in on his face, but that just made his features even blurrier. His expression was hard to read, but it seemed more surprised than upset. He had blond hair and looked to be around the right age, but above all he was wearing a red T-shirt—as they were fairly sure Hugo had been when he went missing.

"What do you think?" he asked.

"Hard to say," said Hanna. "But it feels right to take the tip seriously."

"I agree, I—"

A call came through from Ove before Erik managed to get any further.

"I want you to go over there," he said. "And don't get in touch with the woman in advance. If it really is Hugo, we can't take the risk of forewarning her."

"Sounds sensible. Have you had time to look into her?"

"All we know is that her name is Olivia Sandén. She's not in any of our registers, and it's not clear how she makes a living. I'll send you the address. And in case you haven't already heard, the press knows both the address where Thomas was found and the fact that the company he worked for was handling its sale."

A voice in the background called for Ove.

"I've got to go," he said. "The media is putting a lot of pressure on us regarding the boy."

Erik was glad he didn't have Ove's job. He rarely felt under pressure at work, but he definitely did right now. Both his father and sister had been in touch to ask if he was working on the case— though the brother who was thinking about quitting the force hadn't. Young Hugo had been missing for over forty hours, and they simply had to find him. Erik brought up the message containing the address.

"The house is in Gårdstorp," he said.

"South again, then."

Erik peered up at the sky as they rolled out of Färjestaden. The swarm of birds had unsettled him, but the only flock he could now see was in the distance. There were a lot more clouds in the sky, though if the forecast was to be believed, the stormy weather wasn't due to arrive until tomorrow. He really hoped Hugo would have been found by then. The temperature had already started dropping as low as fifty degrees overnight.

Just under thirty minutes later, they drove past a sign reading GÅRDSTORP.

"How close are we to Södra Möckleby?" asked Erik.

"It's the next village over."

Hanna braked as they approached the edge of the community, did a U-turn, and parked on a strip of grass outside a small red wooden house.

"Should we talk to the neighbor first?" she asked.

"I don't think so. She could hardly have missed us pulling up out here, and we're visible from the house. We need to check whether Hugo is here right away."

They got out of the car and opened the metal gate to the empty yard. Erik couldn't hear any children's voices. There was a patio, but no sign of any toys. A woman in her fifties opened the door in the next house over, and Erik gestured for her to go back inside.

They made their way up to the front door, and since there wasn't a bell, they knocked. The woman who answered was in her thirties, wearing a vest top and a long patterned skirt. Her hair was tied up in a loose plait. Erik had met several Westerners dressed like her during his time in India. From inside the house, they could hear the TV. The voices were shrill, slightly hysterical. It sounded like a cartoon. They introduced themselves as being from the police.

"What's going on?" asked the woman.

"Are you Olivia Sandén?"

"Yes."

"Are you alone?"

"No . . ."

Her face twisted, likely reflecting all the thoughts swirling around her head. But what was she afraid of? That someone close to her had died, or that she was about to lose the boy she had snatched?

"Could we come in?" asked Erik.

"Of course, but what is this about?"

"Who else is here?"

Olivia hesitated, her eyes drifting around as though she were searching for an escape route. Or a weapon. There was an umbrella and a long metal shoehorn in a wicker basket by the door.

"Noah," she said.

"And who is that?" Erik continued.

"My nephew."

"Why is he here?"

"Because . . . Sorry, what exactly do you think I've done?"

The fear in her voice and on her face mixed with something else. A hint of anger, perhaps. They still hadn't made it any farther than the hallway.

"We'll explain," said Hanna. "But first we'd like to say hello to Noah."

They went into the living room, and the boy sitting inside turned his attention from the screen to them. He looked older than he had in the picture. Erik guessed he must be at least two. In all likelihood this wasn't Hugo, but they had only ever seen him in photographs.

"Hi," said Erik. "What's your name?"

"Noah."

"How old are you, Noah?"

The boy thought for a moment and then held up his index finger and thumb.

"Would someone please tell me what's going on here?" said Olivia.

"We will," said Erik. "But it would be better if we could sit down somewhere else."

Olivia led them through to the kitchen and they sat down at a pale blue wooden table. There was a vase of handpicked flowers in the middle. The décor in the room was a mix of old and new. She had net curtains over the windows, but the sill was full of abstract metal sculptures. On the other side of the glass, the horizon was a straight line in the distance. Perhaps it was just because the birds were still on his mind, but Erik thought the desolate landscape looked like something out of a horror film.

"We're here because of the missing boy," he said.

Olivia stared at them with a blank face.

"Someone thought—"

"My damn neighbor," Olivia interrupted him.

Erik didn't want to add fuel to the fire by confirming her suspicions, so he simply explained that he couldn't say where the tip had come from.

"I saw her skulking around outside," Olivia muttered, as though she hadn't heard him. "And I shouted for Noah, told him we were going inside."

Erik suspected that must have been the moment the neighbor captured on her mobile phone.

"Don't tell me, she also expressed concern for my mental health?" Olivia continued.

"How are you?" asked Erik.

They had to be confident she was in a fit state before they left, though she was hardly going to admit it if she wasn't.

"Great, thanks. Noah, too. You can ask him if you don't believe me."

"No need," said Erik.

The young boy had come across as a perfectly ordinary two-year-old.

"Why would anyone think you weren't well?" asked Hanna.

"Well, I like being alone," said Olivia, nodding her head toward the neighbor's house. "And some people just can't wrap their heads around that. I'm also writing a book set in India. I studied film there."

Erik couldn't help but smile at the Indian connection, at the fact that he had spotted it, but Olivia seemed to think that his reaction was about the book. She smiled back.

"I know. Crazy to want to isolate myself and write a book, huh? Preferring to be in an imaginary world than the real one."

28

When they left Olivia Sandén's house, the neighbor was standing by the low stone wall separating the two properties. Hanna walked over, eager for her to leave Olivia and Noah in peace. On the neighbor's side of the wall, the grass was neat and the flower beds tidy. Olivia's garden was much wilder, and most of the plants she grew were edible.

"The boy is her nephew," said Hanna.

The woman was unable to stop the corners of her mouth from drooping.

"Are you sure?"

"Yes."

"Maybe you should take the boy with you anyway," the neighbor continued. "I don't think Olivia is the least bit suited to be looking after a child. Do you know what—"

"He's fine."

The woman attempted to argue, and Hanna kindly but firmly told her to go back inside. She waited by the wall until she did as she was told. Erik had already walked over to the car.

"I'm glad I don't have any neighbors like that," Hanna muttered once she was back behind the wheel.

"Me, too," said Erik. "Our closest neighbors are really nice. We have dinner with them sometimes. Speaking of which, I'm getting hungry. There's nowhere to eat around here, is there?"

"No," said Hanna. "The closest place is probably the pizzeria in Degerhamn."

"Degerhamn?"

"Södra Möckleby, then. They're basically the same."

Erik shook his head.

"But Prästgårdens Café in Smedby is better," Hanna continued. "It's north of here."

After her meeting with Gunnar on Sunday, pizza was the last thing she felt like eating. She knew she would have to speak to him again, but not yet. She wanted to try to find another way forward first. But how? Pushing Kristoffer for answers felt about as unappealing as getting in touch with Ester Jensen's daughter Maria. Right now Hanna felt like she was completely stuck, but that could just be down to the investigation taking so much out of her. Focusing on anything other than Hugo was near-impossible.

Fifteen minutes later they sat down in the garden outside the café with two bowls of bean stew. Hanna had been to the café a few weeks earlier, with Ingrid. Göran Shröder, a classical guitarist, was playing a show there, and her neighbor had wanted to see it. It had been high summer at the time, the nights tropical, but now it was a little too cold to sit outside—largely because of the wind.

"This is great," said Erik, wolfing down his food in no time at all.

He probably would have said the same about almost anything. It was nearly three in the afternoon, but their days were sometimes so intense that they didn't really have time to stop and eat.

"Back to the station?" he asked.

"Yeah, there's not much else for us to do here."

Hanna had just gotten to her feet when her phone started ringing. It was Freya from Missing People, and she felt a flicker of hope. The fact that Hugo was still missing was weighing on the investigation. No, on everything.

"We've found the car," said Freya, sounding short of breath. "It's empty."

Hanna shook her head at Erik, who was watching her closely.

"Where is it?" she asked.

"On the gravel track leading down to the quarry. There's some kind of trash dump here."

"How far is that from the house in Södra Möckleby?"

"I'm not sure," said Freya. "No more than a few minutes by car. But on foot? Uff, I don't know. Where could the boy be?"

"We'll be there in a few minutes," said Hanna. "Don't touch anything."

As Hanna sped toward Södra Möckleby, Erik called Ove. They needed forensic technicians to examine the car, and both the helicopter and the dog handlers would have to be diverted.

At the turnoff to the gravel track, there was a sign announcing that only authorized vehicles were permitted. Hanna ignored it and drove a few hundred meters before she spotted Freya.

There were three other people there, and one of them was Isak. Hanna's eyes briefly touched upon him before darting away. She didn't want him to be there. Not right now. The only person she had space for was Hugo.

"I'm glad you could come so quickly," said Freya.

"We were in the area," Hanna explained.

She and Erik made their way over to the car. It was clear it had been parked there so that it wouldn't be visible from the village. The pile of flammable material, most of it branches and such, was obscuring it from view. It was also set back from the gravel track, making it easy to pass without noticing. Anyone who did spot it would assume it belonged to whoever owned the land, or to someone out on a walk. Hanna didn't know exactly how far they were from the quarry, but it had to be a kilometer or two.

As they approached the car, she realized that one of the rear doors was ajar. The window had been wound down a few centimeters, as had the one by the driver's side. There was a child seat in the back, an empty gruel bottle in the footwell. Could Hugo have gotten out himself? Or had Thomas taken him with him after all? Could the car have been moved after the event? Hanna still didn't know what had happened.

"Do you want to do it, or should I?" asked Erik.

Hanna replied by walking over to the trunk and gripping the lid. She slowly opened it. Swallowed and tried to steel herself.

Other than a folded buggy and a tote bag of beach toys, it was empty.

She and Erik walked back over to the others. Hanna was still finding it difficult to look at Isak, and made sure to keep her distance from him.

"Who found the car?" she asked.

"It was us," said Isak, nodding to the two women beside him.

"Who was the first to reach it?"

"Me," said Isak.

"Did you touch anything?"

"No, I just looked in through the window."

She felt his piercing gaze, but avoided making eye contact.

"I think we should continue our search," said Freya. "Taking the car as our starting point."

"That sounds like a good idea," said Hanna. "But you'll have to wait until the technicians are here, so they can secure any possible evidence first."

Erik had grabbed a roll of tape from their car and started cordoning off the road. The small group backed up to give him room to work.

"What if we go in the other direction?" asked Freya. "We could drive over to the quarry and start from there."

It hadn't occurred to Hanna that there was, of course, another way in. Cementa had been using the quarry to make cement, but production there had been shut down a few months ago.

"Okay, do that," she said.

Her words were drowned out by the approaching helicopter, which swung over the car and continued toward the quarry.

"We can start from the house in Södra Möckleby, too," said Freya. "We've already done it once, but we can search again. We might have missed something the first time."

Hanna nodded. The gratitude she felt toward this woman and everyone else who had volunteered so much of their time to look for Hugo was enormous. They simply had to find him. There was no other option. But at the same time, she knew that the odds of finding him alive had to be vanishingly small. No, she couldn't allow herself to think like that.

She also couldn't avoid Isak any longer. Hanna glanced over at him, and he smiled when he noticed. His brown eyes seemed to flash. Hanna forced her mouth into a smile and looked away.

Freya and the group began making their way back toward the village, but Hanna and Erik had to stay with the car until the technicians arrived.

"I'll call Jenny," said Hanna.

"Don't you think we should go over there?"

"It'll take too long," she said. "You know what people are like. News of the car will leak any minute now, and if Jenny hears it from someone other than us, she'll panic."

Jenny picked up on the first ring, a strange mix of hope and fear in her voice.

"We haven't found Hugo," Hanna began. "But we have found the car."

She heard Jenny inhale, and the call dropped. When Hanna tried to phone her back, she got the engaged tone.

"What's going on?" asked Erik.

"I'm not sure."

She forced herself to be patient, and Jenny called her back a few minutes later.

"Sorry," said Jenny. "I hugged the phone to my chest."

Her voice sounded thick, and it was hard to hear what she was saying.

"You don't have anything to apologize for."

"Where was the car?"

"On a gravel track not far from the house where Thomas was found."

"But what does that mean?"

"We don't know yet." Hanna was honest with her. "But Missing People have adjusted their search area. Everyone is working flat-out to find Hugo right now."

The silence that followed was heavy with questions and fears.

"Do you want us to come over?" Hanna asked.

"No, just keep working. My parents are on their way over."

Hanna ended the call and followed after Erik, who had started walking toward the quarry.

"Hugo!" she shouted.

Quietly, to herself, she asked: *Where are you?* All she could hear was the wind rustling the grass and the low bushes along the edge of the trail. Beyond that, the fields spread out into the distance. Hanna stared at the black dot slowly moving toward her.

A combine harvester.

29

The Coast Guard was approaching the sailing boat that had run aground outside of Grönhögen harbor. Lykke had been following the drama from her garden, and would have gone inside to fetch a pair of binoculars if she'd had the energy. It was blustery, but no more than around four or five meters per second, and she could make out the nervous movements on deck. Some kind of rope was thrown up to them. The Coast Guard managed to pull the boat free on their second attempt, and she quickly lost interest.

She had slumped onto the sofa the minute the two officers left, but she had also managed to clean up the coffee and the pieces of broken cup. She had even emptied the washing machine, where her clean laundry had been sitting for over twenty-four hours. It was now hanging on the line, and she hoped the breeze would help get rid of the musty smell.

Lykke knew she should keep looking for jobs, but she was too tired. Thinking about the future felt impossible right now.

She glanced out at the strait again. The boat swung around, approaching the inlet much too fast, but this time it managed to get into the harbor.

A sudden gust of wind made Lykke shiver. The sun had disappeared behind a thick bank of cloud. She was always cold these days. She got up to grab a cardigan from inside.

Her phone started ringing, and after hesitating for a moment she accepted the call. The number felt vaguely familiar. It could be the police, and she didn't dare duck a call from them. But the moment she heard the voice on the other end of the line, she regretted picking up. It was Jenny.

Jenny seemed so different from her own mother, so hard. Lykke couldn't help but wonder what Thomas had seen in her. She knew that was unfair of her. Jenny's child was missing, after all. And her husband had just died.

No, Lykke's father had died.

But she couldn't feel sad.

"Why did you reach out to Thomas?" Jenny demanded to know.

"Because he's my dad."

"You've ruined everything!"

"I haven't—"

"Yes, if you hadn't written that letter then . . . I wouldn't . . ."

She broke down in tears. Lykke made another attempt to explain, but Jenny had already hung up. It was just as well. Lykke knew she had ruined things, but that had never been her intention. She had just wanted to fill the void. To have someone she could call family.

She finally began to cry, her body trembling with everything that needed to come out. The pressure was unbearable, and Lykke screamed. She realized that someone might hear her and call the police, and managed to calm herself down, slumping into a chair. For a few minutes she sat quietly, letting the tears flow. Gasping for air. After a while, her tears dried.

The image of the chocolate bar in the fridge flickered before her eyes. The sensible part of her wanted to give up and wolf it down, but she was so scared. If she did that, she wouldn't have anything left. Right now she was good at one thing and one thing only: not eating.

Lykke got to her feet again, slowly. The damn chocolate meant she didn't dare go any farther inside, so she headed back toward the strait instead. Her thoughts turned to her mother. To all the arguments they'd had during her teens. About her friends. About food. About her clothes. And how all of that had stopped when Lykke told her she had gotten accepted by the university.

During her first trip home after she moved to Uppsala, they sat face-to-face like two grown adults. When Lykke asked about Thomas, her mother had actually been willing to talk about him. She said that he was a charming idiot. That he was funny and sociable, handsome—the kind of man all the girls liked—but that he didn't know how to take responsibility for anything. She said he was always hanging around with a guy called Mille, who was, if possible, even worse. And at some point she had called Thomas a selfish bastard. Right there and then, Lykke finally understood why her mother had imposed so many rules on her when she was younger. She wanted to guide her in a different direction than Thomas. Than herself.

But at some point along the way Thomas had clearly pulled himself together, because he had managed to get this Jenny woman to want to live with him—to have a kid with him. Lykke had read that he was working as an assistant real estate agent when he died. It probably wasn't so strange that things hadn't worked out between him and her mother. They were only teenagers when they met.

Lykke hadn't had time to form her own impression of Thomas. All contact between them had been so hesitant, so full of his betrayal. And now she would never get to know him.

Tell them. The voice was back again. But what would happen if she called the police and said, *I'm sorry, but I lied to you. I did actually meet Thomas.*

No, there was no way.

30

The combine harvester continued its relentless march forward. Hanna sped up in an attempt to ward off the image of a child's body being mangled. Before she ran off, she had told Erik to call Ove, to try to reach the landowner that way, though she suspected her approach would be the quickest. The wheat whipped against her legs. It came up to her thighs, and for once she was grateful for her height, that it wasn't corn or one of the other crops grown on the island.

"Hugo!" Hanna shouted.

It was more a way to keep her anxiety in check than anything. She tried to keep an eye out for him on either side, but her focus right now was on reaching the combine harvester. On making it stop. When she was only fifty or so meters away from it, she began waving her arms. It was coming straight toward her. The man in the cab was wearing a cap and a pair of big yellow ear protectors, and she couldn't see his face.

The machine finally came to a standstill, and the driver opened the door and jumped out, pulling off his ear protectors.

"What are you doing?" he shouted.

He was younger than she had expected, roughly her own age. Hanna held up her ID and breathlessly explained that they had found the car belonging to the murdered Thomas Ahlström. That she wanted them to pause the harvest until they had scoured the fields, because his son was still missing.

"Of course," he said. "My mom and dad are both involved in the search."

"Are there any other landowners around here?"

"Yeah, but we're the only ones harvesting right now."

Hanna took his phone number so that she could contact him once they had completed their search. The man returned to his combine harvester and locked the cab, then trudged away over the field. She turned back to Erik, who was talking to two dog handlers. Their Alsatians were both sitting patiently. With a quick nod in Hanna's direction, the handlers hurried out into the field. One of the dogs let out an eager bark.

Erik told Hanna that he had searched the trash heap and the area around Ahlström's car, but that he hadn't found anything. Neither of them could bear doing nothing while they waited, so they began walking along the gravel track toward the quarry again. Had Hugo wandered off on his own? Could someone his age really open a car door from the inside? She asked Erik.

"Doubt it," he said. "Though it could've been left ajar."

Hanna peered around in frustration. There were so many places for a person to disappear here. The walls flanking the lane were full of openings. She had no idea what the road was like up ahead, how many forks there were. She had walked along it once, but that was seventeen years ago now. And what about wells? They would have to check whether there were any in the area. Hanna turned around. Ahlström's car was almost out of sight, meaning they couldn't go any farther. The chain of evidence had to be preserved.

"We can't hold off on searching around here," she said.

Erik agreed, and they called Freya to say that they could allow a team to search the area between the car and the quarry. Hanna explained that they had stopped the harvest, that the dogs were currently scouring the fields closest to the car. Just a few minutes later, a group of five people appeared—none of them Isak. Hanna felt a mix of disappointment and relief. They led the group through the cordon, all eyes on the car as they passed.

Erik walked back over to the vehicle, moving slowly around it as though looking for something.

"What is it?" she asked.

"The diaper bag isn't here."

"What does that mean?"

"I don't know, but it makes you wonder where it could've gone."

The bag hadn't been in the house in Södra Möckleby, either, though it could easily have vanished before Thomas died there. They still had no idea what he had done after going to the playground in Skogsby that morning.

Hanna's phone started ringing. It wasn't a number she recognized, but she had no choice but to answer in case it was linked to the investigation.

"Hello, my name is Veronika Krans, I'm a reporter with *Expressen*. What can you tell me about the car? Was there any sign of Hugo in it?"

"No comment," said Hanna, ending the call.

When the reporter tried to get through again, she didn't pick up.

The forensics technicians arrived after half an hour, and they immediately got to work. There was no longer any reason for Hanna and Erik to stay at the scene; other people were far better equipped to continue the search than they were. She told the technicians that they had allowed a group from Missing People past the cordon, but that she wasn't sure they would come back the same way.

Ever since Thomas Ahlström had been found dead, one task had followed another, and they hadn't had time to stop and think. It was already four o'clock, but as things stood they couldn't call it a day yet.

"Should we go and talk to Thomas's friend Mille?" asked Hanna.

"Sure," said Erik.

His voice mirrored the way she felt. Tired. Anxious. It was always difficult when a small child went missing, and likely all the more so for him, who knew what it meant to be a parent. Hanna felt a stab of longing, a desire to experience that for herself.

Jenny had said that Mille was the only one of Thomas's friends she had called when she discovered her husband was missing. The only person he talked to. Yet Mille hadn't replied to the message Hanna had left with him. He lived in Skogsby, and ran a small tobacconist in Färjestaden. Since he was still ignoring Hanna's calls, they swung by his house first, but he wasn't home.

Outside the tobacconist, there were a couple of tabloid billboards. Both were asking the same question, in large black letters: WHERE IS HUGO?

It bothered Hanna that Mille was displaying them outside his shop, though she knew her attitude toward the tabloid press had been shaped by everything that had happened sixteen years ago. After her father was arrested, the photographers had started prowling around their house, searching for good camera angles. Outside her school, too. And the journalists had called and called, harassing both her and Kristoffer. Strictly speaking she was an adult at the time, nineteen years of age, but she hadn't known how to handle it.

Erik gave her a questioning glance, but she just shook her head.

The young man behind the counter in the tobacconist didn't look much older than twenty.

"We're trying to find Mille Bergman," said Hanna. "Is he here?"

"Mille!" he shouted to the doorway behind him.

The man who came out looked familiar somehow, and he paused when he spotted Hanna and Erik, his gaze wandering. Probably because he realized they were from the police. Hanna finally remembered where she had seen him before.

"You were at Friberg Properties," she said. "Fixing the AC."

He had swapped his soccer jersey for a white shirt, and no longer stank of booze.

"Yup," said Mille. "I try my hand at all sorts."

"But air-conditioning?"

"I can fix most things that stop working, though I'm not great at relationships."

He sounded serious as he said it, and probably hadn't meant it as a joke.

"We'd like to talk to you about Thomas Ahlström," said Erik.

"Yeah, I figured as much," said Mille. "It'd be better if we went outside. It's so cramped in here."

They left the shop, and Mille led them around the corner to a small cluster of trees. The ground was strewn with cigarette butts. A crumpled potato chip bag had been dropped by a pine tree.

"I'm still in shock over this whole thing," he said. "It's like I can't wrap my head around Thomas being dead."

"How long have you known each other?" asked Hanna.

"Since we started school," said Mille. "We both grew up in Färjestaden, and he's the only person from grade school I still hang out with."

"What did he tell you about his job?"

"The only person he liked there was Selene, if you can believe that. He thought Hektor was an idiot and Karl a loser."

"Is that so?"

"Yeah, but Thomas never spoke his mind. That was probably the main difference between him and me. He's always been too nice, whereas I've never had any problem telling people what I think."

"What do you have against Selene?"

"We were together a few years back. Do you know what happened to Thomas?"

Hanna ignored his question and asked one of her own:

"What can you tell me about Thomas and Hektor's dispute?"

"Thomas owed him money. His car was on the blink and he didn't dare tell Jenny that he'd forgotten to pay the insurance. Hektor overheard him talking to someone from the garage and offered to lend him the money for the repairs."

Mille looked around at the cigarette butts, clearly irritated.

"The kids come back here to smoke . . . Though obviously I only sell to over-eighteens."

"Obviously," said Hanna. "Couldn't you have fixed the car for him?"

"Cars aren't really my thing. AC systems, photocopiers, computers . . . I can fix stuff like that."

"How was Thomas's relationship with Jenny?" asked Erik.

"Good, I guess."

Mille was still staring down at the cigarette butts, and seemed to be on the verge of attacking them with his feet.

"But . . . ?" Erik pressed him.

"Jenny's really bossy, and Thomas wasn't always so happy about that. Like I said, he wasn't the best at speaking up."

"Were either of them unfaithful?"

"I don't think so, though that's probably the only thing he'd keep from me. Sorry, but I really need to get back to the shop."

"It'll have to wait," said Hanna. "Thomas took keys from the real estate agency. Do you have any idea why he might have wanted them?"

"So it's true, he was found in a house the agency had sold?"

"The keys," Hanna reminded him.

"No, I've got no idea what he could've wanted them for."

"Where were you on Sunday evening?" asked Erik.

"I was at the gym until about five, then I went home, took a shower, had something to eat, and crashed on the sofa. I work more than I should, so I never have much energy left over in the evenings."

"Do you live with anyone?"

"Nope, sorry."

"Why were you drinking on Sunday evening?" asked Hanna.

Mille folded his arms and looked up at the treetops.

"I was lonely."

After making Mille promise to pick up if they called, Hanna and Erik let him go. Hanna sighed.

"It feels like we're moving forward at a snail's pace."

"What have I told you about that?"

"What?"

"You need to think positive."

Hanna swatted at him. Her grandmother always used to say the same thing.

"I should probably go and see my grandmother after all," she said.

"Sounds like a good idea," said Erik. "I can drop you off at the home after the debrief with Ove."

They got back into the car and Erik called Ove on speakerphone, giving him a quick recap of their chat with Mille.

"The door-knocking brought up an interesting lead," said Ove. "The immediate neighbor saw a van parked on the street outside on Sunday evening. He was pretty sure it was just after seven. Unfortunately, he couldn't tell us much about the van other than the fact that it was white and said something about construction on the side. I've got Amer looking into it."

"Did anything come out of calling Thomas's previous employers?" asked Hanna.

"No," said Ove. "Thomas was only fired from one place, and that was for being forgetful and showing up late. He quit all the others himself. Hold on, I've got someone on the other line."

Ove ended the call, but called back less than a minute later.

"The dog handlers have found a comfort blanket that looks like a rabbit. Blue. It was at the edge of a field, close to the road to the quarry. I need you to check with Jenny whether Hugo had anything like that."

This time it was Erik who ended the call, and he turned to Hanna.

"Let me deal with this," he said. "After I've dropped you off at the home."

Hanna hesitated, but the urge she felt was stronger than it had been in a long while. She needed to see her grandmother.

"Okay," she said.

The care home was only a kilometer or so away, but right now that felt too far to walk. She would have to take the bus in the morning, because her own car was still parked outside the station in Kalmar.

Erik pulled up by the entrance, but Hanna wasn't ready to leave him yet. Thoughts about what might have happened to Hugo were still churning away at the back of her mind.

"Imagine Hugo was in the car or walked away from the house on his own, and someone found him. Anyone in their right mind would call the police. But what if whoever found him wasn't in their right mind?"

"Yeah, the thought did occur to me, sadly," said Erik. "Maybe Hugo was so unlucky that the first person he bumped into was a pedophile."

Hanna wanted to find an argument against the word Erik had used, but she knew that, statistically speaking, people who abused children were more common than murderers.

"Go in," said Erik. "I'll bring this up with Ove once I've checked the blanket thing."

Hanna got out and rang the bell to be let in.

"I'm so glad you could come," said Besma.

Besma had been a carer for a long time, and Hanna remembered meeting her during one of her very first visits to the home. Her name meant smile in Arabic, and though Besma didn't smile particularly often, she was pleasant.

"Your grandmother is doing better," she said. "Her fever has gone down, and we've managed to get some liquid into her."

Besma followed Hanna to her room.

"You're a police officer, aren't you?"

"Yes."

"I hope you find that little boy."

"I do, too."

Hanna paused before she stepped into the room, trying to let go of the investigation and any hopes that her grandmother might suddenly be her old self again. Her grandmother was lying on her back, staring up at the ceiling. Hanna sat down by her side. Other than the bed, the room also contained a toilet, a seating area, and a small pantry. It was cozy, full of photographs, cushions, and trinkets from her old home. From a life that no longer existed. In one of the images, Hanna's mother and grandmother were sitting outside a café in St. Mark's Square in Venice. It was the early eighties, her grandmother's first trip abroad. Probably her mother's, too, though Hanna wasn't sure, and that made her sad.

Her phone buzzed, and Hanna brought up the message from Erik: *Hugo has one of those comfort blankets, but his is speckled and has a cow's head.*

Hanna squeezed her grandmother's hand, but she didn't seem to notice. She looked so small and fragile, and a small part of Hanna thought that it would be best if she was just allowed to die. That enough was enough. Another part of her never wanted to let go. She wanted her old grandmother back. The one she could talk to. The one who knew who Hanna was. The one she could take on a trip to Italy.

Hanna thought back to how it had felt the first time her grandmother didn't recognize her. Happily surprised, she had looked up from her knitting and called her Kristina. Her daughter, Hanna's mother, who had been dead for over a decade. On another occasion she had thought Hanna was a childhood friend. Toward the end, before she disappeared into herself and stopped speaking entirely, she had often thought that Hanna was one of the carers. The only thing that occasionally made her stir to life was children. Once, while they were sitting in the dayroom together, someone had come in with a young boy, and her grandmother had raised her head and smiled at him.

Hanna's phone started ringing, but there was still no reaction from her grandmother. She got up and moved over to the window to answer. Thought her grandmother might find the sound of her voice calming.

"Hi, this is Klara Svensson. We met earlier today."

"Robin's sister," Hanna replied, showing that she remembered.

"I wanted to say something at the time, but it didn't really feel like the right moment."

"Say something about what?"

"Kristoffer called me."

"Okay . . . ," said Hanna.

She couldn't understand why Kristoffer had called Klara when he was still refusing to speak to her.

"We need to talk," said Klara.

"About what?"

"I can't say over the phone."

WEDNESDAY, AUGUST 21

31

As we suspected, Thomas Ahlström was killed with the shovel from the hearth," said Ove. "The wounds on his throat and arm both contained ash. The medical examiner . . ."

Hanna gripped her coffee cup and tried to focus on Ove's mouth, on the words coming out of it. The medical examiner thought that Thomas had died on Sunday evening sometime between five and ten p.m. Thanks to the previous owner of the house, they now knew exactly what the murder weapon looked like, but unfortunately it was still missing. No matter how hard Hanna tried, she just couldn't stop her mind from drifting out of the room, away from the investigation. Her focus kept shifting to the question that was running riot inside her.

What did Robin's sister Klara want? Hanna wouldn't find out until lunch, when she drove over to Lindsdal to see her. Klara had wanted to meet that evening instead, but Hanna knew she wouldn't be able to wait that long. She had found herself scrolling down to Kristoffer's number several times, but had never actually made the call. A soft hand on her arm brought her back to the station. She saw the anxious look in Daniel's eyes and realized she must have been rubbing her tattoo. She gave him a quick shake of the head.

"The house had been cleaned ahead of the new owners arriving," said Ove. "But the damper on the fireplace had been left open, meaning some ash had blown into the room. Forensics found a half shoe print in the ash, and considering it was right in front of the rack of tools, it likely belongs to our killer."

Ove brought up an image of the print, and Hanna studied it closely. The shoe print consisted of three rectangles, the middle one thinner than the others. The soles of boots and trainers were generally much busier in design.

"Since we only have half a print, it's difficult to determine the size," Ove continued. "But it's probably closer to a forty-two than a thirty-eight. Forensics are working to establish the brand. The print doesn't match the shoes either Thomas or Selene were wearing."

"What kind of shoes did Selene have on when she found Thomas?" asked Erik.

"A pair of pumps, size thirty-nine."

Ove grew quiet and studied the image himself. Having a partial print was obviously a good thing, but its evidential value would depend on what the technicians could come up with. He paused for so long that Amer jokingly called for the boss. Ove turned to Hanna.

"Good thinking with the pedophile angle," he said. "Or not good, but you know what I mean . . . Unfortunately, no one in Södra Möckleby or the villages around about has been convicted or suspected of it. Or maybe not unfortunately, exactly, but . . ."

He sighed, and it struck Hanna just how drained he seemed. How tired they all were. She studied Daniel more closely. He looked weary, too, didn't he? Though perhaps not quite as resigned. Things were probably going well with his new guy.

"Considering the time frame of Thomas's death, the tip about the van is particularly interesting," Ove went on. "Have you managed to track it down, Amer?"

"I've called every single construction firm on Öland, but none of them were in Södra Möckleby on Sunday evening. My guess is that the logo was stuck on the side of the van to avoid raising any suspicions. It was parked outside a house that was just about to get new owners, after all."

"Shame, but keep looking," said Ove. "Our colleagues in Växjö have spoken to Thomas's parents again, and they painted a slightly different picture of their son this time. It seems he struggled to stick with all kinds of things—his studies, jobs, girlfriends . . . Or he did until he met Jenny, anyway."

"Anything criminal?" asked Erik.

"Other than crashing into a cyclist while he was driving a moped under the influence, no. He also stole some money from his parents, but only small sums."

Ove took off his round black glasses and used his shirt to clean the lenses.

"How are things going with Lykke Henriksen?" he asked, turning to Daniel. "Have you found anyone who can confirm her relationship with the professor?"

"The phone number she gave us is for an unregistered pay-as-you-go SIM, so there's no way of linking it to Roger Wasselius."

"Okay, forget the phone number for now," said Ove. "Try to find someone who can give a statement about Lykke and the professor. Or just Lykke."

Daniel nodded, and Ove turned to Carina instead.

"Could you take us through the Ahlströms' finances?"

"Sure. It's Jenny's income that keeps them afloat. The position with Friberg Properties is the longest Thomas has ever held down a job. Before that, he worked a lot of odd jobs and had a few long periods of unemployment. Their biggest debt is the mortgage. They bought the house less than a year ago."

"Is there anything to suggest he was a criminal?" asked Ove.

"Possibly," said Carina. "A number of smallish deposits of between two and five thousand kronor. We're looking at twenty-eight thousand in total."

"Who made them?"

"Thomas. The analysts are digging deeper into that."

"Good. And what about his call lists, Daniel?"

"The person Thomas communicated with most is his wife," said Daniel. "And this Mille Bergman guy. Other than them, he had a few—"

"What's the communication with his wife like?" Erik interrupted.

"There's nothing to suggest they were having any problems," said Daniel. "Short phone calls, mostly. Almost no texts. I guess they used WhatsApp or something."

"Okay, sorry, go on. . . ."

"Yeah, so, what sticks out is his communication with Hektor. They messaged each other quite a bit over the past few weeks, and the tone gets angrier and angrier. It seems to be over Hektor wanting his money back."

"How threatening does he get?" asked Ove.

"*I'll trash your car if you don't pay up,*" Daniel read aloud.

"Okay," said Ove. "We'll have to confront Hektor with this. Anything else?"

"Thomas had lunch with Selene on Sunday. There are a couple of messages about it. And—"

"Selene said it had been two weeks since she last saw Thomas," Hanna interjected.

"Okay, talk to her, too," said Ove.

The working day had barely begun, but the list of tasks relating to the investigation was already getting long. Still, they had to do everything they could. Missing People hadn't found any sign of Hugo either by the quarry or on the gravel track where the car had been recovered. And other than the comforter someone had dropped, the search dogs hadn't made any more finds. Södra Möckleby had been searched, as had the fields, and the police had knocked on doors throughout the village. They would continue their door-knocking today. It often took time to get ahold of every-one. Some people simply weren't home the first time around, others refused to open the door. The search efforts would also continue, with the groups planning to increase the distance from Södra Möckleby, in case Hugo had wandered off.

"Did anything come up when we looked into the people who volunteered to help Missing People?" asked Hanna.

"An analyst is still going through the list," said Ove. "So far there's only one name that needs to be followed up. A woman with a record for abduction in the criminal suspect register. I want you and Erik to go and talk to her."

Hanna nodded. If someone had taken Hugo, either because it was planned or because an opportunity had presented itself, then they stood a much better chance of finding him alive.

32

The woman from the register of suspects was called Linda Claesson, and she lived on Trollbackevägen in the Berga district of north Kalmar. The street was also home to the woman whose six-year-old daughter she was accused of having abducted. Any leads connected to Hugo had to be prioritized, and they had decided to come out and see her before doing anything else. Over sixty hours had now passed since he had vanished.

"Do you think we'll find Hugo there?" asked Erik, pulling out onto the main road heading north.

Hanna shrugged.

Erik had dreamed about dead children last night. He was standing by the abandoned car, staring out toward the combine harvester, and the leaden gray sky was full of shadowy birds. The driver of the combine harvester had come running, shouting that he was dead. Somewhere around that point, Erik had realized it was a nightmare, but he hadn't been able to drag himself out of it. He had walked back to his own car and found Nila's bloody body in the back seat. That was when he finally woke up, and once he managed to calm himself down he hadn't been able to resist video-calling his wife and daughter. The moment he saw Nila on the shaky screen, the dream had lost its grip over him. She and Supriya were just fine.

"It's a pretty long way between Berga and Södra Möckleby," he continued.

"Yeah," said Hanna. "But she could have found him during the search."

"Don't they work in teams?"

"Yes, but it's still possible to sneak off," said Hanna. "Or to say that you can't manage another round of searching and then hang back."

Her words came out quickly, irritably, as though she wanted to put him in his place.

"What's up?" he asked.

Perhaps she had had nightmares, too. Nightmares she hadn't managed to break free from.

"What do you mean?"

"You're acting weird."

"Weirder than usual?" asked Hanna.

Her joke grated, and she must have realized, because she went on.

"Something happened, but I don't have the energy to talk about it. Not right now."

"Okay," said Erik, forcing himself to keep quiet.

They couldn't drive right up to the door, so he pulled into the parking lot. They rounded the barrier and walked the short distance over to the dirty yellow apartment building. Linda Claesson was on sick leave, which meant she should be home. In the large inner courtyard, Erik could see grass, trees, and a playground in which a mother was pushing her child on a swing. There were likely a number of families with children in the area. Erik held the door for a woman who had just negotiated the stairs with a buggy. The building didn't have an elevator, but he was in luck: Linda Claesson's apartment was on the first floor. His legs still found stairs difficult, but the aches had finally started to fade. Linda

Claesson didn't open the door until he rang the buzzer a second time. She was wearing an old pale pink dressing gown.

Erik introduced himself and Hanna as police officers, but his words didn't have the usual effect. No stress. No fear. This was a woman who didn't have anything left to lose.

"Could we come in?" he asked.

"Rather you didn't. I was sleeping, and I'd like to keep doing that."

"Rough night?" asked Hanna.

The prickliness was gone. Whatever had happened, she had put it out of her mind. Linda nodded.

"We only need a few minutes of your time," said Erik.

They had to get into the apartment and take a look around.

"What's this about?" asked Linda.

"Hugo," said Hanna. "The missing boy."

Linda's hand dropped from the door handle, and she took a few steps back into the apartment. They followed her in. Erik found it strange that she hadn't asked why they wanted to talk to her about him. She led them through to a small kitchen. There was a deep plate full of what looked like dried-on soured milk in the sink. Erik asked if he could look around, and her only reaction was a nod.

The apartment was a one-bedroom, furnished with only the bare necessities. It looked neat and tidy at first glance, but that was largely because there was no clutter, and Erik noticed that the baseboards were dusty. He opened every closet door and checked the bathroom. There was no sign of a child. On a chest of drawers in the living room, he spotted a framed photograph of a man in his thirties. It had been taken in the park outside Kalmar Castle, and he was smiling. Erik paused to study the image for a few seconds before heading back to the kitchen. Both Linda and the apartment filled him with a sense of unease. He hadn't been able to resist discussing the case with his father yesterday, and the old man seemed to agree with Hanna's theory that someone had taken the boy.

"Tell us about what happened last month," said Hanna.

"I've already told the police everything."

"Take us through it, too."

"It was a misunderstanding. The girl was out in the yard on her own, and she was bored. I just took her to the convenience store and bought her an ice cream."

"The two of you were gone for over three hours," said Hanna.

Linda shrugged, clearly reluctant to say any more. Several weeks had now passed, and the prosecutor still hadn't decided whether to bring charges against her. Erik hoped they would, but he wasn't here because of the six-year-old girl. He was here for Hugo's sake.

"What made you volunteer to take part in the Missing People search?" he asked.

"I wanted to help."

She turned her head toward the window. Toward the playground in the yard. After eating dinner at home yesterday evening, Erik had gone for a walk to loosen up his legs. When he reached the Kattrumpan swimming area, he had sat down on a bench and watched the people taking an evening dip and playing in the playground. His longing for Nila was like an iron weight on his chest. Kattrumpan was one of her favorite places. She had thought he was joking when he first told her its name—Cat's Bum. It had been too late to call her, and he was sure that had contributed to his awful dreams.

"Why aren't you joining the search today?" asked Erik.

"It got to be too much."

"Did you find Hugo during the search?" asked Hanna.

Linda shook her head, the only response she seemed capable of. She still hadn't queried why they wanted to talk to her about any of this, even though Hanna's question implied that she had found Hugo and then hidden him somewhere.

"Do you wish you had kids?" Hanna pressed her.

"There's something wrong with my fallopian tubes. I can't get pregnant."

Every single word was dripping with longing.

When Nila was just a couple of years old, Erik and Supriya had decided to try for a sibling, but after three failed rounds of insemination they had given up. Supriya was now too old for IVF. How would it have felt if they didn't already have Nila? Though they never managed to have a second child, they were still a family of three.

Erik could sympathize with Linda's longing, but that didn't excuse what she had done. Another woman had been left with no idea what had happened to her child for several hours. The six-year-old had described the incident as fun at first, but said that when she wanted to go home to her mom, Linda had refused. Demanded that they play happy families together. Threatened to lock her inside otherwise. And she had also described her as cuddly.

"Who's the man in the picture in the living room?" asked Erik.

"My ex. He left me because of the problem with my fallopian tubes."

Linda was still staring out the window. The two women out in the yard seemed to know each other, and were chatting as they pushed their children on the swings.

"Do you have any family nearby?" asked Erik.

"My parents. Why?"

"It's good to have a support network," he said. "Do you have a good relationship with your parents?"

Linda shook her head. The real reason he had asked was because he wanted to find out who she might be close to. Whether she could have left Hugo with anyone else.

"What about good friends, then?" he continued. "Someone you can share this with?"

"No one can be bothered with me anymore," said Linda.

Erik turned to Hanna, who had been unusually quiet so far. Her eyes were fixed on the narrow corner cabinet by the window. It was full of plates, but on one of the shelves he could see a pair of black binoculars. Linda craned her neck to see what they were looking at.

"I'd like you to go now," she said.

33

There was a crack in the living room ceiling. Lykke had never noticed it before, despite it being about twenty centimeters long. She should fill it in and paint over it, but what if it was a sign that there was something wrong with the house?

Lykke rolled onto her side to avoid having to look at the crack. She hadn't had the energy to climb the stairs to her bedroom last night, and had slept on the sofa. The memories of Roger were everywhere. The way they had lain in her bed, listening to Kris Kristofferson together. She hadn't been especially keen on the music, but she had liked listening to Roger talk about it. About his longing to get out and away. Right there and then, she had wanted to run to Nashville with him. They had gone to Vaxholm together a few weeks later, at least.

She reached for her mobile from the coffee table and scrolled through the thread of messages from Roger.

I love you. /R

He had written all kinds of declarations of love to her, and it hurt so much that he hadn't meant a single one of them. How could she have been so easily duped? The anger inside her was starting to build again. The same anger she had felt when she slashed his tires. When she knocked on his door to tell his wife what a bastard he was.

What would have happened if Roger's wife had been home that day? Lykke didn't even want to think about it. Even if the wife had left him, he would hardly have wanted Lykke afterward. The person who suffered most would've been their young child, just a few months older than her little brother.

Hugo.

Lykke saw him in front of her. Climbing up the slide and getting onto his stomach. That was the moment when she first realized she had a brother. It had looked dangerous, and she had jumped the fence and rushed over to him, but then Thomas had come running.

Fucking Roger. It was all his fault.

Though she knew she shouldn't, Lykke sent him a message.

You've ruined my life.

It was probably Roger's fault she hadn't been accepted into the research program. Not that he had any say in the matter, but her program director did.

Lykke lay perfectly still for a few minutes, staring at her phone screen, but he didn't reply. Roger probably didn't even have the phone anymore. She tossed her own mobile onto the sofa, but it bounced onto the floor. Damn it, she'd probably broken that now, too. Lykke picked it up. Ran a finger over the screen, searching for cracks.

How was it possible that she still missed him? After everything he'd done.

She got up and went through to the kitchen on shaky legs. Opened the fridge and stared at the bar of chocolate inside. Closed it and reached for the coffeepot.

Her hunger was a monster that had to be subdued. One sip, that was all she could manage. Her stomach didn't want any more coffee, it wanted food. Lykke hurried back to the fridge and grabbed the chocolate, tearing open the wrapper and pushing piece after piece into her mouth. Barely bothering to chew before she swallowed.

Anxiety was the monster now. It launched itself at her with its razor-sharp claws, tearing her to shreds. She was worthless. What she had done was unforgivable. She rushed through to the bathroom and dropped to her knees by the toilet, pushed her fingers down her throat, and threw up.

34

"What are the binoculars for?" asked Hanna.

Linda Claesson was still facing the corner cabinet.

"I like looking out at the yard," she said.

"Why?"

"I'm lonely."

She turned her head to the window.

"I'd like you to go now," she said again.

Linda may have answered their questions, but she still wasn't quite present. She was likely on some form of medication. There was a darkness inside her, and Hanna suspected it was down to more than just her longing for children. Feeling a certain hesitation, she got up.

Hugo wasn't here, but leaving still felt like a failure. Her thoughts drifted to Robin's sister Klara, but Hanna forced them back to the present. That darkness would have to wait.

"I think I should call her parents," Hanna said the minute she and Erik were outside.

"Yeah, the thought crossed my mind, too," said Erik.

Hanna managed to find their number. Linda's parents still had a landline phone.

A man picked up. "You've reached the Claessons."

Hanna introduced herself and explained that she and a colleague had just been to see his daughter and were wondering when he had last seen her.

"What's she done now?" Linda's father asked.

"What do you mean?"

"I thought it must be about the neighbor's boy again," he said, his voice suddenly much more defensive.

"Why would it be about the neighbor's boy?"

The child Linda was accused of having abducted was a six-year-old girl. The man whispered to someone in the background, likely her mother, but the words *police* and *Linda* were the only ones Hanna caught.

"She got into an argument with one of her neighbors last week," said the man.

"About what?"

"The neighbor's son. They thought she was getting too close and threatened to call the police."

"What did Linda do to the boy?"

"I don't know," he said. "The way Linda explained it, she was just watching him in the playground. But, well . . . it was probably more than that. You probably noticed that she's not well."

"This is about Hugo," said Hanna. "The boy who . . ."

A muted gasp made her trail off. There were now two people listening to everything she said.

"As you can hear, we know who he is."

"Has Linda mentioned him to you?"

"No, not at all. But why did you go to see her about him?"

"She took part in the search."

"Aha," said her father. "She barely talks to us these days. Seems to think we're just a nuisance."

"When did you last see her?" Hanna asked again. He hadn't answered her the first time.

"Saturday."

The man said they would go over to their daughter's place.

Hanna was convinced they didn't know anything about Hugo, but after hanging up she felt a powerful anxiety. As Linda's father had pointed out, it was clear that she was struggling mentally, and the abduction she was suspected of clearly wasn't the only time she had behaved oddly around children. What if she had snatched Hugo after all? What could she have done with him, if so? It was hardly likely to be anything good. Robin's sister Klara raced through her mind again. It was as though Hanna were constantly prepared for catastrophe.

"Shall we head over to Öland?" asked Erik.

Hanna checked the time: almost ten thirty. It would take them a while to get over to the island and track down both Hektor and Selene. She briefly considered getting in touch with Klara to say that she didn't have time to meet at lunch, but decided against it; she needed to do this now. It was getting in the way of her job.

"Could we grab an early lunch first?" asked Hanna. "I need to stop off in Lindsdal."

"Does this have something to do with whatever you didn't want to talk about earlier?"

Hanna hesitated, then decided to tell Erik about the call she had received yesterday, explaining that she was going to meet the sister of one of her brother's old friends.

"Want me to tag along?"

Hanna stared at him in surprise.

"It's not that weird a question, is it?" asked Erik. "I think we've been getting along really well lately."

She felt herself blushing, unsure whether he was being serious or not. Maybe it was just a joke.

"Yeah," she said. "We have."

For the most part she really did believe that, but Hanna knew that this was something she needed to do alone. For the sake of the investigation, if nothing else. And Erik didn't insist. He said he would discuss Linda Claesson with Ove in the meantime. They would have to comb through her movements and find out what she had been up to over the past few days.

As they walked back to the car, Hanna called Freya from Missing People. It went straight to voice mail, so she left a message asking her to call back—without mentioning why. She wanted to know whether Linda Claesson had stuck out in any way.

After dropping Erik off at the police station, Hanna drove north. She had been planning to buy something to eat along the way, but when she reached the turnoff to Lindsdal the only restaurant was a pizzeria, something she still didn't feel like eating. She might have been able to buy something from the small shop next door, but she realized that she wouldn't manage to eat anything anyway. She had to see Klara Svensson, and she had to see her right now. She had to find out what she had to say. The only part that made sense to her was that Kristoffer had called Klara at some point after Hanna spoke to him on Monday evening. But why?

THE LAST DAY

Karl fucking Friberg. The resignation Thomas felt earlier has swung back around to fury. He is so angry with his boss that he doesn't know which way to turn. Where does he get the nerve to come over here and give him the boot, and all while pretending to be his buddy and care about him? Selene can't have told him about the keys, can she? Surely Karl would have asked for them back if she had. Right?

The smart move would probably be to cancel, but no matter how much Thomas wants to, he knows he can't.

He walks back through to the bedroom and lowers Hugo into his crib, but the boy seems to feel how tense he is and he can't get him to doze off again. Hugo is crying and keeps getting to his feet, even when Thomas sits down on the floor with his hand between the railings. After a while Thomas lifts Hugo out of the crib and lies down beside him on the bed, but not even that works. Hugo refuses to stay still. He doesn't even relax when Thomas wraps his arms around him. In the end the only thing Thomas can think of is to carry him through to the kitchen and give him an ice pop.

Jenny doesn't like it when Thomas gives their son sweet things to eat. But the ice pop is basically just half a glass of frozen juice. It's hardly the end of the world.

Besides, it's the weekend.

Thomas watches with fascination as Hugo laughs at the frozen treat. The boy loves putting cold things in his mouth, possibly because he is teething again. He has only four teeth so far. His red cheeks are the only sign that he was upset earlier.

Thomas takes a picture and sends it to Jenny, only realizing what he has done once it's already too late.

Cutie! she replies, ignoring the ice pop.

We can't wait to see you, Thomas writes back.

It's true, more than he thought physically possible, but he isn't looking forward to telling her that Karl has fired him. Just a few weeks ago, Jenny started talking about how nice it was that he finally had a regular income. She'll almost certainly demand that he report Karl—you can't fire someone for going on paternity leave. But that isn't the reason. Is it really just because of Hektor, or is it because of the keys, too? Thomas struggles to shake off the suspicion that Karl knows. Though, if he does, he should also have reported him to the police. Or maybe not. Karl would never do anything to risk the firm.

As Thomas watches his son, a wave of self-pity rises inside him. Jenny is going to think he's even more of a loser now. She might be able to live with him losing his job, but not the rest of it. The fact that he hasn't stood up to Mille. She'll throw him out, and that realization leaves him panicked. He doesn't want to mess things up with Jenny. Doesn't want to go back to how things were before he met her.

"More," says Hugo.

Thomas ignores his son's pleading and picks him up from the high chair. He needs to turn things around. To become the father Hugo deserves.

"Shall we play trains?" asks Thomas.

"Trains!" Hugo parrots.

They bought him a Brio train set for his first birthday. He's probably still a bit too young for it, but he likes spinning the wheels.

Hugo runs over to the box containing the train set, and Thomas helps him tip its contents onto the floor. He quickly tidies away some of the building blocks and other toys, then starts piecing together the tracks as his son happily rolls an engine back and forth. The risk of no longer playing a part in the boy's life is more than Thomas can handle. He can't just lie back and let Karl walk right over him. He needs to track down his boss and make him change his mind.

35

Hanna pulled into the empty driveway outside the white brick villa where Klara Svensson lived. She peered in through the kitchen window. The lights were off inside. What if Klara wasn't home? It was still almost an hour until they were due to meet, but she hadn't wanted to get in touch again in case Klara used it as an excuse not to see her at all.

Hanna rejected a call from a journalist from *Barometern*. He had first phoned her the evening before, but she had ended the call and saved his number to her contacts list the minute he introduced himself. She got out of the car and made her way over to the front door. This area felt so different from the one in which she had grown up. The houses were much more tightly packed together, and the countryside surrounding them consisted largely of hillocks, fields, and trees.

Hanna's heart skipped a beat as she reached for the bell. She both wanted and didn't want to be there. She heard footsteps inside and cast a quick glance back at her car, but it was too late to run. Klara opened the door with a young child in her arms, another clinging to her leg.

"I know I'm early," said Hanna. "I hope that's okay."

"It's fine," said Klara. "But the house is in a bit of a state. I'm on maternity leave with the little one, but my eldest has a cold. I'd been planning to tidy."

"I'm just glad we could meet so soon."

The child Klara had referred to as her eldest was a girl of around four. Her eyes were glossy and feverish, her nose running. Hanna smiled down at her, and the girl moved behind her mother.

"I'll get the entertainment started," said Klara. "You go through to the kitchen."

Klara disappeared down the stairs with the kids, and Hanna kicked off her shoes, immediately treading on a piece of Lego. She managed to stop herself from swearing and bent down to pick up the brick, putting it on the kitchen counter. She had known the sound of the TV was coming, but it was so loud that it made her jump. When Klara returned, she was still carrying the youngest child.

"She's only five months old," she explained. "So it's not like she can understand what we're saying."

Hanna gave the baby a smile, and this time she got one back.

"Who was looking after the kids yesterday while you were helping with the search?"

"Their dad's mother usually takes them on Tuesday afternoons," said Klara. "My eldest was already a bit snotty then, but nowhere near as bad as today. I just really wanted to help look for Hugo."

Hanna nodded. There was no faulting that desire. It really was touching to see just how many people had volunteered for the search. According to the local radio, almost a thousand people had shown up yesterday evening.

"Like I said on the phone, I got a call from Kristoffer on Monday," said Klara.

She paused, as though the mere mention of Hanna's brother should be enough for her to understand, but she didn't. Hanna suspected it was in some way linked to her conversation with Gunnar, of course, but why would Kristoffer call Klara of all people about that? She thought he had cut all ties with Sweden.

"What did he want?" she asked.

"To talk to Robin. He was hoping he could reach him through me."

From the way Klara said it, Hanna understood that Robin was no longer reachable, but she still wasn't prepared.

"Robin is dead," said Klara.

She gazed down at her daughter as she said it. The daughter sitting in her lap, chewing her own hand and gurgling happily. From the basement, they heard a shrill laugh from the TV.

When? Where? How? There were so many questions Hanna wanted to ask, but she began by paying her condolences. When Klara failed to go on, Hanna asked what had happened.

"It was a car accident," said Klara. "Five years ago."

Hanna felt the weight of everything she had left out.

"Why did Kristoffer want to talk to Robin?"

"I don't know."

"Okay," said Hanna, unable to fully hide her disappointment. "So why did you want to talk to me?"

"Robin was struggling," said Klara. "He got a job at the supermarket right after graduating from high school, but after a year of that it was like he lost his spark. He never really got going again. From the little he told me, I'm pretty sure it had something to do with Kristoffer."

"In what way?"

"I think they did something stupid together."

Hanna didn't know what to say. Both women were watching the young girl, who was now tugging on her mother's top. Perhaps she was hungry. Hanna's mind was racing. Something stupid. Together. The memory of that evening when she had found the two of them playing poker in the kitchen came back to her again. She remembered how spirited they had both been.

"What did Robin say to make you think that?" Hanna eventually asked.

"That he shouldn't have listened to him," said Klara. "They also stopped hanging out pretty much from one day to the next. Robin lived with me for a while, and I remember suggesting that he call Kristoffer once—I thought it would do him good to get off his computer."

"What did he say to that?"

"Nothing. He just stared at me like I'd lost my mind." Klara looked Hanna straight in the eye. "Do you know what it could have been?" she asked. "That they did, I mean."

"Did Kristoffer say anything?"

"No, but his reaction was really strange when I told him Robin was dead. He hung up on me."

Hanna's mind was back on her own phone call with her brother. The one that had ended in the exact same way. But before he hung up, he had started to cry.

"Ever since Robin died, I've wanted to know what was bothering him," Klara continued. "And when I spotted you and realized what you did for a living, I thought maybe you could help. Or that we could help each other. Is Kristoffer okay? He honestly didn't sound so great."

36

Erik brought up a picture of Hugo on his computer. The one in which he was playing with building blocks on the floor. As though to remind himself of what was at stake.

Forensics had just sent the report from their examination of the car, and it would take time before they had any answers to the leads that had come up. Unfortunately, Thomas Ahlström's phone hadn't been found in the vehicle. Missing People's searches were still ongoing, but the distances were growing greater and greater. Wells had been checked, as had any abandoned buildings Hugo might have made his way into. It was starting to feel much more likely that someone had taken the toddler, either before or after Thomas was killed.

But who? And why? Erik hoped it wasn't Linda Claesson or someone like her. He had spoken to her ex, who claimed her inability to have kids wasn't the reason he had broken up with her at all. The real reason was how handsy she was around his nieces and nephews. Ove had tasked Daniel with digging up as much information as he could on her.

Interpol had also put out an alert for Hugo. Thousands of people went missing in Sweden every year, and around ten percent of them were children. The vast majority reappeared within a few hours, and when the police launched a search operation, as they now had, a full ninety-seven percent were eventually found. Erik wasn't sure whether the same statistics also applied to the children, but he couldn't think of a single case in which the child hadn't been recovered—though what difference did that make when Hugo was still missing and the search operation was moving into its second full day?

He closed the image of Hugo and brought up a photograph of Nila instead, from when she was four. It had been taken in summer, but she was fast asleep in bed wearing a Santa hat and a pair of pink earmuffs. They'd had guests at the time, and though Nila had told them to be quiet, they hadn't managed to lower their voices enough. The girl was so imaginative and funny and . . . Erik reached for his phone to get in touch with Supriya, but a call came through from Ove before he had time.

"I need you and Hanna to look into another of the volunteers from the Missing People search."

"Who?"

"Isak Aulin."

It took Erik a moment to put a face to the name. Isak Aulin was part of the group that had found the car. He worked as a teacher at Gårdby School, and Erik had first met him during the investigation into Joel Forslund's death.

"Why is he of interest?"

"He's also in the register of suspects. For assault."

"Assault?" asked Erik.

That didn't fit with the impression he had of Isak, though people weren't always who they appeared to be.

"Yes, it seems that while he was working at a kids' camp last summer, he grabbed one of the boys so hard he was left with bruises. He also lost his partner seven years ago."

"In what way is that—"

"She was eight months pregnant."

"How did she die?"

"It just says natural causes."

"Okay, Hanna and I will talk to him."

It wasn't until Erik hung up that he realized that might be a problem. He had the sense that Hanna might have feelings for Isak. Should he ask her? No, that was a bad idea. She would only deny it. Instead, Erik called Isak to find out where he was, pretending it was something to do with the recovered car. Once he ended the call, he paused, gazing down at the phone in his hand.

"Penny for your thoughts," said Hanna.

She had just come into the room.

"I was about to call you and track you down," said Erik. "Shall we head over to Öland?"

"Can I quickly check my emails first?"

"Sure."

He took the opportunity to call Selene and Hektor. Selene didn't pick up, but Hektor was at the office and promised to stay put there. Erik waited until they were in the car and had pulled away from the station before he revealed that there was another interview they needed to conduct.

"With who?"

"Isak Aulin."

Erik sensed Hanna turn to look at him, but he was too busy making a left turn to have time to see her face.

"Why?" she asked.

Erik told her about the assault and his pregnant partner who had died.

"Isn't it a bit of a leap to think he might have Hugo because of that?"

"You're the one who suggested that someone might have taken him, remember."

"Yes, but . . . do we even know where he is? Isak, I mean."

"He's at the school. He said he'd wait for us there. Given it could be linked to Hugo, I think we should start with him."

"Did you say what you wanted to talk to him about?"

"The Ahlströms' car."

The sky grew darker the farther east they drove. It had felt like a storm was brewing for the past day, and now it was close. Even the air in the car felt oppressive. Hanna was staring stubbornly through the windshield, and Erik wanted to ask whether she wanted him to do the interview alone, but he knew she would only reply with an irritated no. However hard she found it, he didn't doubt for a second that she would manage to do her job. He had seen her carry out plenty of difficult interrogations before, though probably never involving feelings of this kind.

Erik pulled up outside Gårdby School beneath a leaden sky, and a few drops of rain hit him as he got out. A small group of children were playing what looked like tag in the yard. Isak hurried over to greet the two officers, and Erik's eyes darted between him and Hanna. There was definitely some kind of tension in the way they kept stealing glances at each other.

"Why don't we sit down in the staff room?" suggested Isak.

"Don't you need to watch the kids?"

"I finish early on Wednesdays, so they're not my responsibility anymore. I'd been planning to join today's search, but that can wait. Is there any news?"

"No," said Hanna. "Sadly not."

"Lots of the parents here are anxious," said Isak. "They've started picking up and dropping off their kids, and they're keeping them in in the evenings."

A young teacher was reading the *Ölandsbladet* in one of the armchairs in the staff room, but she got up and left when Isak asked her to. He offered Hanna and Erik coffee, but both said no. They sat down around the small table.

"Why did you want to talk to me about the car?" asked Isak.

"We're following up on the fact that it was you who found it," said Erik.

"Not just me."

"No, but you said you were the first to reach it."

"Yes."

"What exactly did you do next?"

"I checked the registration plates to make sure it was the right car, then I looked through the window to see if Hugo was inside. When I saw that he wasn't, I went to get the others."

Isak's words seemed to be coming out increasingly slowly, as though he needed time to think.

"And then I called Freya."

Erik nodded.

"Could you tell us what happened in Mörbylånga last summer?"

"At the camp, you mean?" asked Isak, sounding surprised.

"Yes."

"A twelve-year-old boy locked a nine-year-old in a cupboard and called him a fag. When I told him to open the door, he just laughed. So I pulled him away. I don't regret what I did, even if it leads to charges."

The tempo of his speech was increasing with every word. The issue clearly upset Isak. Erik swallowed. He didn't like what he had to do now, but it was part of the job.

"You lost your pregnant partner seven years ago," he began.

"Yes . . ."

Everything about Isak seemed to slump: his shoulders, his mouth, his eyebrows. He glanced over at Hanna, who hadn't said a word since they began talking about the search.

"I don't know what my partner has to do with this," he continued.

Isak gave Erik a pleading look, and then his anger flared up.

"Do you think I took Hugo?"

37

On the wall behind Isak was a bulletin board full of drawings and postcards. Hanna was sitting too far away to be able to read them, but she guessed they must be from the students. She knew she should say something, or at least make herself look at Isak, but instead she was staring at a yellow square that was probably supposed to represent the school building. It was flanked by two straggly black trees.

"Why would I take Hugo?"

"Relax," said Erik. "We're just doing our job."

"It doesn't seem like it."

His words were quivering with barely repressed rage.

"All we want is to find Hugo," Erik continued. "And to do that, we have to investigate every possible lead."

"How can . . ."

Isak didn't get any further. Hanna cast a quick glance at him. She felt so much sympathy for him, for his pregnant partner, for everything that he had lost. That kind of trauma could be incredibly damaging to a person, mentally. But Isak didn't give that impression. Not at all. He seemed to be in complete control of himself, and yet he had been physically rough with a twelve-year-old. Could they really trust his version of events? There were so many conflicting thoughts and emotions tugging at Hanna, the strongest of which was an urge to apologize for barging in and asking questions about his partner. But Erik was right, this was something they had to do. Hugo had been missing for three days, his father had been found dead, and it felt like they were still fumbling in the dark.

"If you don't have any other questions, I think you should leave now," said Isak. "I'd like to keep looking for Hugo."

"We will, soon," said Erik. "What did you do after you found the car?"

"I went home," said Isak. "I didn't have the energy to keep looking."

"Did anyone see you leave?"

"I told the others I was going home. Someone must have seen me."

Hanna just wanted the questions to stop, and when Erik got to his feet, she did the same. All she could think as she stepped out of the staff room was that she had destroyed something she didn't want to destroy. In the corridor outside, she almost walked straight into the teacher who had been reading the paper earlier. She was making her way back into the staff room with an empty mug. The woman was small and pretty, and Hanna found herself speeding up again. The moment she pushed open the door and came out onto the steps, she filled her lungs with the damp, heavy air. It felt like the storm would be here any moment.

"We have to follow every lead," said Erik.

"I know. I don't know why I'm reacting like this."

Erik smiled, and she glared back at him. They walked toward the car.

"Shit," she said. "Is it that obvious?"

"Yeah, but at least this one probably isn't gay."

Erik had noticed her longing for Daniel that spring, and in the end he had explained why she would never stand a chance with their colleague. A feeling of self-pity welled up inside her. There were so few people she could really talk to—just Ingrid and, to an extent, Rebecka and Erik—and that made her longing all the more powerful. Hanna didn't want to be alone anymore.

"I'll contact the other members of Isak's search group," said Erik.

They got into the car and drove away in silence.

"It just feels so fucking unfair sometimes," Hanna said with a sigh.

"What does?"

"The way life turns out."

"Yeah."

The weather turned when they were halfway to Färjestaden, the rain pelting down against the car and the tarmac. Hanna had been referring to both Isak and herself. There were times when she couldn't help but wonder what life would have been like if her mother hadn't died, if her father hadn't . . . But what exactly had he done? Her thoughts drifted back to Klara, to what she had told her. Hanna had wanted to talk to her about Ester Jensen, but she had stopped herself. Klara would have put two and two together, and Hanna needed to get ahold of Kristoffer first. She couldn't call him right now, because she wasn't alone, so she sent him a message instead:

I spoke to Robin's sister. What did you want to talk to Robin about?

Kristoffer didn't reply. She hadn't expected him to, but she knew she needed to start working on him.

Erik pulled up right in front of the door to the real estate agency, and though they ran inside, they both got soaked.

"God, this weather," said Erik.

Hektor ignored his attempt at small talk. He was alone in the office and didn't bother to get up from his desk. They walked over to him, and Hanna looked down at his feet. He was wearing a pair of shiny black leather shoes.

"What size shoes do you wear?"

"Forty-two," said Hektor. "What do you want now? Because I'm assuming you're not just here to talk about my feet?"

Hanna knew the soles probably weren't right, but she asked to see them anyway. They were almost smooth.

"You threatened Thomas Ahlström," she continued.

"Did I?"

Hanna read his message back to him: *I'll trash your car if you don't pay up.*

"But you found the car," said Hektor. "Was it trashed?"

"No," Hanna replied after a moment's hesitation. "But that doesn't change what you wrote. You could have decided to go after him instead."

"That was just talk," said Hektor. "Besides, I wasn't even at home on Sunday evening. Or Monday morning."

"Where were you, then?" asked Erik.

"At some girl's place."

Hanna sighed. "Why didn't you tell us that from the start?"

"I didn't think it was anyone else's business," said Hektor. "It was the first time she'd let me stay over. I didn't want to mess things up by having the cops call to ask her if I'd been there."

"Name and number," said Erik.

Hektor scribbled down her details and handed the scrap of paper to him.

"Feel free to give her a call," he said. "I don't think she's the one for me after all."

They ran back out to the car without another word. The rain was now drumming down. An image of Hugo popped into Hanna's head. Huddled up in the middle of a wheat field, freezing cold, hungry, and afraid. That was better than several of the alternatives, at least. Hanna cranked up the heat in the car. She was just about to bring up Selene's number when a call came through from Ove. He explained that the forensics technician who had been examining Thomas Ahlström's clothing had been in touch.

"They found traces of toad lily pollen on his shoes. It's a—"

"A flower, I know. His daughter Lykke has them in her garden."

THE LAST DAY

His T-shirt feels tight around his throat. Thomas lowers the train track to the floor and tugs at the fabric. He can't breathe. He looks desperately at Hugo, who is busy pushing the engine back and forth across the parquet. It isn't like the young boy can help him. Thomas wants to get up and go out into the kitchen, but he makes it only as far as the armchair. Gasping for air, he slumps into it. His mouth is bone-dry, and he can feel a tingling sensation in his left arm.

I'm having a heart attack. I'm about to die.

His field of vision narrows to a thin line. He frantically tries to keep his eyes locked on Hugo on the floor. How will the boy survive until Jenny gets home? What if he runs out onto the road? No, that just can't happen. Thomas needs to call an ambulance somehow. Where did he leave his phone? All he can see are shadows jumping around him, and he lets out a sob.

"Dada," says Hugo.

Thomas focuses on the direction of the sound. And there, on the floor in front of his son, he can see a black shape. That must be it.

It isn't a heart attack. You're just panicking.

The moment Thomas realizes that, the pressure on his chest eases and he takes a few quick breaths. He smiles at Hugo, who turns his attention back to his playing. Thomas focuses on his son and forces his lungs to slowly inflate and deflate. He eventually manages to get up and stagger through to the kitchen, where he fills a glass with cold water and drinks it down in one go. He leans back against the counter for a few seconds, until his heart stops racing, then returns to the living room.

"Choo-choo train," the boy says happily.

Thomas sits down on the floor beside Hugo. He knows what set off the attack. It was the thought of tracking down Karl, begging him to change his mind. Thomas needs his job. He needs to continue to prove to Jenny that he deserves to be with her. The fear of losing his family gets his heart pounding again, but this time he manages to ward off the panic.

"You have a sister," he tells his son. Saying it aloud feels so good.

Hugo has a sister, and no one can take that away from him. Thomas has often wished he had a sibling of his own. Someone else for his parents to project their hopes and dreams onto. They have always made him feel like such a failure. Nothing he ever does is good enough. Hugo might be the exception, though the last time he visited his parents his mother said something about the boy being lucky to have at least one real parent. Thomas had snapped that he was a good parent, and his mother had tried to claim she was only joking.

Thomas was too young when Lykke was born. Everything was different back then. He knows he needs to track her down. That can't wait. Yes, he's afraid of what he might say when he sees her. That he'll get caught up in excuses that aren't true. But he can't let that stop him. Tracking her down feels easier than begging Karl.

"You and I are going for a drive," says Thomas.

With a hoot of joy, Hugo gets up and runs over to the door. He already seems to have forgotten that he cried all the way back from Färjestaden earlier. Thomas had been planning to stay home all afternoon, but that feels impossible right now. He needs to go to

Grönhögen. He needs to show Lykke that he was serious when he said he wanted to be her dad. And if the meeting goes well, it'll be easier for him to talk to Karl.

Hugo is laughing in the back seat, chatting to everything racing by outside. The houses and the sky and the cows. Hugo loves cows. They often walk down to the shore, where a herd of cattle grazes freely. His comforter has a cow's head, and he holds it up and lets it talk to its friends outside.

Thomas can still feel the sense of panic lurking behind his every breath. He can't be unemployed, not again. He was fired from his last job before Friberg Properties, and prior to that he always quit whenever he got bored, which never took much longer than a few months. How could he have been so childish and selfish? A car swings out in front of them, and Thomas has to slam on the brakes to avoid running into the back of it. He glances in the rearview mirror and realizes his son has dozed off.

It's good that Hugo is finally getting some rest. He is still asleep when Thomas pulls up outside Lykke's house in Grönhögen, and Thomas winds the window right down and leaves him in the car. The sun is shining, but it's as breezy as ever, and he'll never be so far from the car that he can't hear if Hugo starts crying.

How will Lykke react to the news that she has a little brother? To Thomas showing up like this? During their brief phone call, she made it clear that she needed time to think. But ever since he received her letter, Thomas has been carrying her words with him like a kind of sorrow. He made a mistake by abandoning his child, though he knows he didn't really have a choice. But how can he make her understand that?

He had looked her up right after her letter arrived, and had been surprised to see that she was registered at an address in Uppsala. In her letter she wrote that she was in Grönhögen, in her mother's house. But that was probably just for the summer.

Natalie lived in Grönhögen when they first met. With her

parents, in this very house. Did that mean she had stayed put? He
knows that she died a few years ago. Mille told him after he saw
the notice in the paper.

Thomas looks up at the pale yellow façade and remembers
sneaking over one night, throwing pebbles at her window. Coax-
ing her out and away.

Hugo whimpers, and Thomas turns back to the car. Just a
dream. The boy's eyes are still closed, his lids twitching. Part of
him wants to wake his son and protect him from the nastiness of
his bad dream, but Thomas starts walking over the lawn toward
the house instead. He sticks close to the neighbor's property, still
unsure whether or not he should be doing this. Natalie was funny,
easy to convince to tag along. But, Christ, her mood swings. She
could throw things across the room if she didn't get her own way.

I wasn't ready.

The thought is like a stab to the heart. Thomas didn't want to
become a parent at nineteen, but what about now? Why is he hesitating? Because he is afraid of Lykke's reaction. And of what Jenny
will think about all of this. Unemployed and with an adult daughter. Everything was supposed to work out this time around. In some
ways, Jenny is similar to Natalie, particularly when it comes to her
moods.

There is a patio at the front of the house, surrounded by bushes
and flowers, a low stone wall. He is fairly sure it wasn't there when
he used to come here with Natalie. Thomas pauses by the apple
tree, which he definitely remembers. He and Natalie once had an
apple war with the fallen, rotting fruit. He makes his way over to
the stone wall. It's time to make up his mind. Is he going to do this
or not?

38

We need to go back over to Grönhögen to speak to Lykke again," said Hanna, explaining that Thomas had traces of toad lily pollen on his shoes.

They were in the car outside Friberg Properties, and the rumbling of the storm was forcing them to raise their voices. The windshield wipers were running at top speed, but they were still no match for the rain. The pavements were deserted, the cars moving along the roads at a crawl.

"So he was there," said Erik.

"Looks that way. But that doesn't necessarily mean they met."

For her own sake, Hanna hoped they hadn't. She was so sick of people lying to them, deliberately making their job harder. But considering how used she was to those lies, and considering how Lykke had behaved so far, she suspected they had met. An elderly woman was taking shelter beneath an overhanging roof nearby, pressed up against the wall. Hanna felt an urge to tell her to get into the warm car, but she knew they had to get going. Her phone started ringing.

"You tried to reach me," said Selene.

"How are you feeling?" asked Hanna.

The moment the question left her mouth, she remembered that Karl had driven his daughter to the emergency psychiatric clinic.

"So-so, but I'm back home now. Dad said he'd told you that . . . Though I'm guessing that's not what you wanted to talk about?"

"You had lunch with Thomas on Sunday."

"Yes."

"Why didn't you mention it?"

The question was followed by silence, and Hanna waited it out. She mouthed to Erik to set off for Grönhögen. It would take some time in this weather.

"I didn't want to," said Selene.

"Why not?"

"For Jenny's sake."

"Were you and Thomas having an affair?"

"No, but Jenny gets really jealous. She didn't like us seeing each other outside of work."

"Is that something you often did?"

"No, but it happened from time to time. Thomas was so easy to talk to."

Selene took a deep breath. Hanna didn't want her to start talking about how fantastic Thomas was, how much she missed him.

"Why did the two of you meet on Sunday?" she asked.

"That was when I gave him the keys."

"How did Thomas seem?"

"Stressed. He had to rush off."

"Why did he want the keys?"

"He wouldn't say."

Yet again Hanna made use of the silence. She looked out at the rain, which showed no sign of letting up. In fact, it was now coming down so heavily that it was like a wall of water. Erik had switched the headlights to full beam, but they couldn't quite compete with the sudden darkness.

"I'm sorry I didn't tell you about the lunch from the start," said Selene. "But I wasn't lying about the keys."

Hanna ended the call, summarizing it for Erik, though she could see he was struggling to focus on anything but the road. In the villages they passed, the buildings seemed to be leaning in to them to escape the rain. The world had shrunk. She felt sorry for the poor people taking part in the search. No, she felt sorry for Hugo—if he was still out there somewhere, cold and wet.

The rain eased off as they drove through Södra Möckleby, and the clouds broke up just before they reached the turnoff to Grönhögen, letting through just enough sunlight to make it feel like daytime again. Now that she was almost dry, Hanna was glad she didn't have to go out in the rain again. Her feet were the only part of her that got wet, because the ground hadn't had time to soak up all the standing water.

There was no answer when Erik knocked on the door, so Hanna walked around the side of the house. The clothesline was full of dripping wet clothes. Through the living room window, she saw Lykke trying to hide behind the fireplace. Hanna told Erik, who knocked again, leaning in to the door.

"We know you're in there," he said. "But if you refuse to talk to us here, we'll have to take you back to the station."

Lykke opened the door and led them through to the living room without a word. She was barefoot, and her feet were small. Likely no bigger than a thirty-six or thirty-seven. But wearing a pair of shoes that were too big was much easier than the other way around.

"Did Thomas come here?" asked Hanna.

Lykke stared down at the coffee table. Her cheeks were sunken, and she was wearing an oversized woolen sweater. Perhaps she was under the weather somehow.

"Yes," she whispered.

"When?" asked Erik.

"Sunday afternoon."

"What happened?"

Lykke's eyes were still locked on the table. She kept clawing at her left forearm, but didn't seem to realize she was doing it.

"You really need to talk to us," Hanna told her.

"I cycled to the supermarket to buy some fruit and other things," said Lykke. "And when I got back he was in the garden."

Another pause, though this time she managed to pull back from it herself.

"I don't have any memories of him, obviously, but I immediately knew who he was. And it was so weird to see him. I wasn't prepared for how it would make me feel."

"Which was?"

"Confused. I mean, I know I wrote to him, but then I wasn't sure whether I actually wanted any contact."

"Why not?"

Lykke looked up at Hanna as though it were the most ridiculous question she had ever heard, and perhaps it was. She demonstratively turned toward the open fireplace.

"Did the two of you talk?" asked Erik.

"Not really."

"What did you say?"

"I asked if he was Thomas, and he nodded."

The words came out slowly, as though she were carefully choosing every one. Hanna felt herself getting irritated. They didn't have time for this; they needed to find Hugo. Erik gave her a reassuring glance.

"Anything else?" he asked.

"I told him I didn't feel up to talking. That I needed more time to think. And that he had to accept that."

"Did he have Hugo with him?"

"No. I don't know. I think he was in the car."

"What makes you think that?" asked Hanna.

"Thomas kept turning back to check on it."

Her fingernails started scratching her arm again, up by her shoulder this time.

"What else happened?"

"Nothing," said Lykke. "I went inside."

Hanna felt like taking a step forward and giving the girl a shake, making sure she was telling the truth. The look Erik gave her seemed slightly more warning than before.

"How did Thomas react to that?" he asked.

"He shouted after me."

Lykke stopped scratching her arm and studied her nails. Maybe she was expecting to see blood. Hanna said her name, and she looked up.

"It's important that you tell us everything."

Lykke nodded.

"Was Thomas angry when he shouted after you?" Hanna continued.

"I don't think so. He was probably more sad than anything."

"How long did he stay outside the house?"

"I don't know. When I looked out fifteen minutes later he was gone."

39

The two officers eventually left. Lykke leaned forward with her forehead against the door. Her heart was beating so hard that she felt sick.

Why hadn't she jumped at the chance to tell them? That was what she had decided to do when she first let them in. And she had tried. But she didn't seem to be able to do anything at the moment.

Self-hatred welled up inside her, and Lykke hit her head against the door. The truth was too awful, too ugly. She hadn't felt confused at all when she saw Thomas in her garden. She had been furious. When they spoke on the phone she had told him that she needed time to think, but he had ignored her. Her mother had been right: he was an egotistical bastard who never thought of anyone but himself.

Lykke had felt like rushing over and hitting him, but there was no way she could admit to that. The police would have taken it the wrong way. With everything that had happened in Uppsala, they already thought she was a crazy stalker. And if they found out now? It would make it all so much worse.

She waited until she heard the car pull away before she went through to the kitchen. Her hand was shaking as she reached for the kettle. She filled it with water and put it back on the stove. Dropped a bag of mint tea into her cup, then sat down at the table to wait for the water to boil.

For so much of her life she had hated Thomas for what he had done to her mother. To her. And she had wanted to shake off that hate. To shake off the crushing, aching longing in her chest. The feeling had always been there, but Roger had pried it open into a huge black hole. That was why she had written the letter.

But when she heard Thomas's voice over the phone, she had realized that she might not be able to forgive him for the things he had done.

And when she saw him in the garden, standing in the middle of the toad lilies, completely oblivious to the fact that he was trampling them, it was like something inside her snapped. All that darkness had come spilling out. And in that moment she had hated herself more than she hated him. She had betrayed her mother by making contact with him. Her mother had loved those flowers, her shadow lilies, as much as Lykke did. No, more. *Even beautiful things can grow in the shade*, she had often said. *Never forget that.*

Lykke felt her cheeks grow hot when she remembered the things she had screamed at Thomas. That was when he had turned back to the car, but she hadn't realized he had a child in there. She had been convinced he was about to run again. Lykke didn't think the neighbors had heard her outburst. The police would have asked different questions if they had.

The kettle began to whistle, and she forced herself to get up. She could live with herself for having told Thomas she hated him, but not for what happened later.

Lykke was afraid of herself, because she knew what she was capable of.

She pictured Hugo again, his face beaming with happiness as he got ready to plunge headfirst down the slide on his belly. She wanted to go back to that moment. Wished she had never run over. And more than anything, she wished she had managed to restrain herself when Thomas came out of the house.

40

Making the time pass at the station was like wading through deep water with seaweed tangled around your legs. Hanna moved the cursor across the screen and clicked on yet another tip report. She was frustrated that they still hadn't made any progress, and had decided to go through all of the tips that had been deemed irrelevant. There was a chance they had missed something there. In this particular tip, a woman was convinced she had seen Thomas and Hugo at a gas station on the outskirts of Kiruna, some sixteen hundred kilometers to the north. Hanna didn't get any further than the first sentence before closing the document. At the time the observation was made, Thomas was already lying dead in Södra Möckleby.

But where was Hugo?

The clock was ticking, and their chances of finding him alive grew smaller with every minute that passed—assuming it wasn't already too late. Yet another day was drawing to a close. Almost seventy hours had now passed since Jenny arrived home to find her husband and son missing.

Ove and their press spokesperson had held a press conference just under an hour ago, sharing what little they could about the case and appealing for information once again—though it would be someone else's job to go through any new tips that came in. The official search-and-rescue operation had been wound up, but Missing People would continue their searches. Ove had been peppered with questions: *Is there a killer on the loose? What should parents do to protect their children? Who killed Thomas Ahlström? What are you doing to find the boy? Have you stopped looking?*

His replies had been calm and clear: *We are doing everything we can to find the boy, but we didn't deem it reasonable to continue to deploy the helicopter and the search dogs.*

Just one question had left him noticeably stressed and irritated: *Do you think Hugo is dead?*

Hanna tried to ignore that question; she didn't even want to think about the answer. All she could do was keep going. If they continued to work on the basis that Thomas was the primary victim, that left them with two main theories. One was that he had been involved in something illegal, and that was why he had needed the keys to the house. Hanna had called Jenny to ask about the deposits made into his account, but she claimed to have no knowledge of them. The other theory was that his daughter Lykke had killed him. It no longer seemed likely that Thomas's death was linked to his dispute with Hektor. The woman he had spent the night with had confirmed his alibi, giving a slightly too detailed account of their time together: dinner, conversation, and sex. And despite what Hektor had been hoping, the call from the police actually seemed to have piqued the woman's interest.

But what if Hugo was the intended victim? If someone had killed Thomas just to get at his son. That might mean that their perpetrator was someone who was mentally ill or desperate for children—or both. Hugo could also have been taken by someone even if it wasn't all about him. Someone who spotted him and seized the opportunity. If that was the case, they were looking for two perpetrators, not one. Hanna massaged her temples. She could feel a tension headache building from her shoulders.

She sighed and called Freya, who still hadn't returned her previous call. The search leader picked up on the first ring.

"Sorry I never got back to you. Had a bit of a crisis in my day job."

Hanna knew that the people who led Missing People's operations were volunteers, just like the other searchers, but it was easy to forget.

"Does the name Linda Claesson mean anything to you?" she asked.

"Yes. Is she okay?"

"What makes you ask that?"

"She joined the search on Tuesday, but she disappeared so suddenly that the other volunteers were worried."

Hanna had another call incoming, so she wrapped things up with Freya. When she realized that it was the same journalist from *Barometern* who had phoned earlier, she hurried to reject the call. He probably wasn't satisfied with what he had found out from the press conference.

Daniel was still busy digging up as much information as he could on Linda Claesson, so Hanna sent him a message with the information from Freya and asked him to look into it. She then continued to wade through the many tips that had been called in. A woman in Södra Möckleby had phoned on Monday to say that she had seen an old man with a young boy who looked like Hugo. Hanna reread the tip to make sure she had understood it correctly. Why hadn't this been followed up? The answer quickly dawned on her: at the time of the call, Thomas's body still hadn't been found, and they were looking for him and his son together. Hanna called the woman and introduced herself.

"Do you know who the man was?" she asked.

"Sorry, no," the woman replied. "I don't actually live on Öland. I was just visiting my sister."

"Could you take me through what you saw, in detail?"

"I was looking out the window when the man and the boy walked by. He was carrying the boy, and he had a diaper bag on his other shoulder. The sight cheered me up. I assumed he was an older relative giving the boy's parents a break."

"What time was this?"

"Early, around five in the morning. I couldn't sleep, so I got up."

"Did you see what the boy was wearing?"

"No, I'm sorry. It was windy, and the man had sort of tucked him inside his jacket. But when I saw the pictures of the boy and his dad, I thought maybe it was him, though to be perfectly honest I'm not sure."

"Could you describe the man?"

"He had his hood up, so I didn't see his face."

"In that case, how can you be sure it was a man and that he was older?"

"From the way he was moving. And I could see a lock of bright white hair poking out."

"Did you mention any of this to your sister? Did she know who the man might have been?"

"She's never up that early, so she doesn't know who's usually out and about at that time of day."

Hanna thanked her and phoned Ove. He said he would task someone with preparing a list of elderly men in Södra Möckleby. It didn't feel like too much of a stretch to think that an older person on a morning walk might have found Hugo in the back of the car and taken him home. But if that was the case, why hadn't they also called the police?

Hanna eventually reached the stage where she couldn't bear to be in the station any longer. It was just after five, and she had worked a lot of long days recently. She needed to head home. Perhaps she could swing by the Missing People search that was making its way away from Södra Möckleby. Help out for a few hours.

Her mind was back on Hugo again. Where could he be?

Not with Isak, in any case. There was just no way. Hanna pushed aside all thoughts of him. Of how upset and hurt he had looked after they'd confronted him about the assault. How sad the questions about his dead partner had made him. She started the engine and began the drive back to Öland. It wasn't until she was up on the bridge that she felt a real sense of calm. It never failed. Coming home always did her good. As she drove across the bridge, she decided to keep going to Kleva. There were so many volunteers taking part in the search that her being there wouldn't make any difference. She needed to get some rest. To be at work early tomorrow.

As Hanna pulled into her driveway, she noticed something on the step by the front door. She got out and slowly made her way over. It was a gas can, made of translucent white plastic, and it was empty. Why had someone left a gas can on her step? Her mind started racing, searching for a reasonable explanation. Had she lent it to someone who now wanted to give it back? Did someone think she wanted to borrow it? Deep down, she knew neither of those were the answer. Someone wanted to make her think about fire. About Ester Jensen.

The gas can was a threat.

Hanna closed her eyes. She didn't know what to do with this threat. It bothered her on so many different levels. The fear was more powerful than ever; someone genuinely wanted to hurt her. She sniffed the air, but couldn't smell any gas. She opened her eyes and forced her body to keep moving.

After checking that the front door was locked, Hanna went back to the car for a pair of plastic gloves and a paper evidence bag. She pulled on the gloves and put the can into the bag, pausing for a moment before she took it over to the small garden shed. She knew she should hand it in to forensics, but the moment she did that she would have to tell someone what was happening.

Hanna went through to the kitchen and heated up a frozen

lasagna for dinner. She had worked so many late nights recently that she hadn't managed to do much cooking. It wasn't even that late, but she still didn't have the energy. She was too wound up to cook.

She ate the lasagna on the sofa in front of an episode of *Call the Midwife*, but she just couldn't make sense of the images on-screen. Hanna knew she should call Kristoffer and confront him over what Robin's sister had said. He still hadn't replied to the message she had sent him earlier that day. But Hanna didn't want anyone else to be upset with her right now. Particularly not Kristoffer. Before she had time to think too much, she wrote him another message.

We need to talk. About Robin and what you wanted from him. You can't keep ignoring me forever.

The minute Hanna hit send she regretted it so much that she had to get up. She had started something she wasn't sure she wanted to finish. Kristoffer knew more about what had happened to Ester Jensen than he had let on, she was convinced of that. What if he was actually involved in the murder itself? It was as though she had just opened herself up to that possibility. That Gunnar really had been telling the truth. Why else would Kristoffer have reacted the way he had? Both when she spoke to him and when Klara told him that Robin was dead.

Hanna couldn't handle being home alone, and hurried over to Ingrid's place. She knew the older woman's schedule by heart, and the only day she wasn't home in the evening was Thursday, when she went over to a friend's for dinner. Her sewing group met on Sunday afternoons.

"What is it?" Ingrid asked the moment she laid eyes on her.

Hanna's fears came spilling out of her. That someone wanted her gone. That her conversation with Klara Svensson meant she could no longer ignore the possibility that Kristoffer was involved in Ester's death. That they wouldn't find Hugo alive. That she had decided the whole case might be about him and accused a poor man who had lost his pregnant partner of snatching him.

Without even asking whether she wanted one, Ingrid poured them each a whiskey. Hanna welcomed its warmth in her chest.

"Were you talking about Isak Aulin just now?" asked Ingrid.

"How did you know?"

"I know his mother a little," she said. "It was awful when his partner died."

"What happened?"

"She had a stroke. He found her dead in bed."

Hanna took another sip of her whiskey.

"He's a nice man," Ingrid continued. "And handsome."

Hanna felt herself blush, and she batted the thought away.

"It's not the right time for anything like that. A child is missing."

Ingrid studied her with a slight smile.

"It's always the right time for something like that."

"My grandmother is ill, too," Hanna continued. "I went to the care home to see her yesterday."

The minute the words left her mouth, the memory of how her grandmother had been at the start of her illness came rushing back to her. The way she mixed things up from time to time, mistaking Hanna for her own daughter, turning up at school late. Perhaps there was another possible explanation as to why an older person might have taken Hugo and not called the police. One that felt much more appealing than them being a pedophile. She grabbed her phone and scrolled down to Ove's name, sent him a quick message:

I think we should be focusing on older men with dementia.

THURSDAY, AUGUST 22

41

Hanna stood beside the upside-down rowboat and gazed out across the Kalmar Strait. She had needed her walk down to the water that morning. It was overcast and breezy, but as she walked past her house Ingrid had called over to say that they would escape the rain today—and if there was one thing Ingrid knew about, it was the weather.

The lookout spot, little more than an opening between the trees, was just south of the swimming area in Kleva. The footpath continued all the way down to Ottenby, but Hanna was in a hurry to get to the station today. She filled her lungs with sea air one last time and then turned around to walk back up to the parking lot. There was a gray Volvo parked there now, the blond man behind the wheel checking something on his phone.

Hanna followed the long, straight gravel track back toward the small community. There was a field of corn on one side, and the crop on the other had recently been harvested. The weeds on the shoulder of the road were so tall that the low stone walls were almost entirely hidden from view. Hanna reached out and brushed a hand through the long grass. She thought back to her childhood, to all the times she had walked along roads just like this.

She heard the rumble of an engine approaching from behind

and moved toward the cornfield to let the car pass. The gray Volvo couldn't have been in the parking lot for long. Perhaps the blond man had taken a wrong turn and just pulled over to check the map.

The engine switched up a gear, gravel clattering against the underside of the car. Hanna was annoyed by how fast he was driving and began to turn her head, but as she got halfway it was as though time came to a standstill. A whole host of realizations hit her: how close the car was, that it was accelerating to mow her down, that she needed to act—and now. Time sped up again, and she threw herself over the stone wall, felt the breeze from the Volvo as it tore by.

Hanna landed on her elbow in the cornfield, but the adrenaline pumping through her veins numbed any pain. Her training was like second nature, and she leaped up, ready to face the driver if he pulled over. The corn was almost two meters high, and she could see only small slivers of the road, but she could still hear the engine revving. Hanna jumped out over the wall. By the crossroads up ahead, the car swung right and disappeared to the south.

Hanna felt all her strength vanish, and she slumped onto the road and lay panting as the adrenaline ebbed.

"Fuck!" she shouted.

If she had continued the movement and kept turning her head, it would have been too late. The Volvo would have hit her, tossing her into the wall, and she would have been left with much worse injuries than a sore elbow.

I could have died.

Hanna let out another scream, releasing her fears. First the gas can, and now this. Why was this happening?

She slowly got to her feet and began making her way along the road, gingerly flexing her elbow. Nothing seemed broken, at least. She pulled out her phone and jotted down everything she could recall about the car, which wasn't much other than the make and color. She remembered even less about the man. His hair color, a possible age. She had thought he looked around twenty, though she didn't quite know why; she had seen only one side of his face.

Should she call Ove? Hanna had no trouble imagining how that conversation would go.

Hi, some fucking madman just tried to mow me down.

Stay there, I'll send a unit right now.

It would only divert time and resources away from the ongoing investigation, and this was about her father, not Hugo. She was getting close to something, though she still didn't know exactly what that something was. She wanted to find out, now more than ever, because she couldn't go on like this. Hanna knew all that, but she still had to wait. Hugo was more important than her damn family.

Hanna reached the crossroads, and the sound of an engine made her heart race, but it was just a dark green Renault slowing down for the turnoff to the swimming area. She automatically raised her hand in greeting to the man behind the wheel.

Hanna tried to spot Ingrid as she passed her house, but her neighbor had gone back inside. Her elbow was now throbbing. Once she got back, she cleaned herself up and took a couple of painkillers. She had just made it back out when she realized she would also need to change her jacket; the sleeve of the one she was wearing was ripped. Her shirt beneath had survived unscathed, and she didn't even want to look at her elbow. Hanna grabbed the paper bag containing the gas can and dropped it into the trunk of her car. Before she got in behind the wheel, she couldn't help but give her surroundings one last once-over.

HANNA WAS LATE getting to the station, and she went straight up to the meeting room. To her surprise, Ove wasn't yet there. She popped her head out into the corridor and saw him hurrying toward her with a cup of coffee in one hand and his phone clamped to his ear. Hanna turned back and sat down. All she caught of his call was the *love you* before he hung up. She still hadn't met his wife, only his youngest daughter, who hadn't yet flown the nest. She had come to the office after forgetting her keys one day, with her pink hair and black clothes. The Rebel, Ove had called her, his voice dripping with warmth. She was in the ninth grade, and was considerably younger than her sisters.

Ove began the meeting by saying that they should ignore everything they read in the papers. Hanna hadn't seen the headlines that morning, but it seemed a number of journalists were claiming the police had given up, despite the fact that a large proportion of the officers in the building were still working on the case. It was just that the things they were doing simply weren't quite so visible anymore. Once Ove was done with his pep talk, he moved on to the tip about the old man with the child who had walked through Södra Möckleby early on Monday morning.

"It was Hanna who found the tip, and she thinks we should start by focusing on any men with dementia in the area."

"Why dementia?" asked Carina.

Hanna's cheeks flushed with irritation, but then she glanced around the room. Amer was absentmindedly scratching his neat beard, the way he often did when there was something on his mind. Daniel was focused on Ove. Erik was giving her a strange look. Was she overreacting? Was she the only one who had noticed the sting in Carina's question? Ove took a sip of coffee.

"Because, as we've already discussed, any sensible person would call the police if they found an unaccompanied toddler," said Hanna.

"Okay," said Carina.

It didn't sound like she meant it. Hanna closed her eyes to prevent herself from snapping at her, and felt the breeze from the Volvo again. Once she realized that it was just the car driving her irritation, any desire to say anything to Carina faded away.

"I contacted the home help service—it's all council-run on the island," said Ove. "And I have a few names that might be interesting. One in particular."

He grabbed his phone and read from the screen.

"Ragnar Hagfors. He's fifty-two and has Alzheimer's."

Fifty-two. So young to be suffering from such a terrible disease. When her grandmother was fifty-two, Hanna had only just begun to string words together. Her world hadn't started to crumble until Hanna was already grown up. Without her grandmother, she never would have survived her mother's death and everything that came later, with her father.

"Where does he live?" asked Hanna.

"One street down from where Thomas Ahlström was found," said Ove. "He didn't pick up when one of the uniforms tried to reach him, and we haven't managed to speak to his kids, either."

Hanna had checked a map to see where the witness lived, and it was roughly halfway between the house where Thomas was killed and the car.

"What color hair does he have?" she asked, remembering that the witness had seen a lock of white hair.

"Unclear."

"Did anyone speak to him during the door-knocking?" asked Amer.

"No," said Ove. "Hanna and Erik will have to pay him a visit."

Hanna pushed back her chair.

"Hold on a minute," said Ove. "There are a few other things to go through first. Daniel?"

"I think we can probably rule out Linda Claesson," he said. "At least from snatching Hugo during the search. The reason she vanished so suddenly was that she'd booked an emergency appointment with her therapist. He didn't want to tell me exactly what they talked about, but in his view it's completely unthinkable that she might be guilty of this. But I contacted the detective in charge of the abduction case and told them about the latest incident and what her ex said. They'll definitely be pressing charges now."

Once Daniel was done, Ove talked about where they were in terms of forensics. The technicians hadn't yet finished their analysis of the shoe print, and nor had they found anything of interest on Thomas's computer—nothing in his emails, search history, or documents. His mobile phone was still missing. According to the trace, he had done quite a bit of driving on Sunday. He had probably gone to Färjestaden after leaving Grönhögen, though the cell towers on Öland were so few and far between that using cell data was a fairly blunt tool.

Hanna found herself struggling to focus, images of the Volvo still lingering in her mind. She wanted to get up and leave. There was a chance Ragnar Hagfors had found Hugo and was looking after him. The boy might have been with his father, wandering off only after Thomas was killed. Lost and alone, he could have bumped into Ragnar, who thought he was helping by taking him home.

42

One more day, then Erik would finally get to hug Nila and Supriya. He had called his wife the moment he woke up that morning. She was on her way to lunch with her parents, then they were planning to head back to the apartment to finish packing. Her parents had invited a huge number of friends and relatives over for a farewell dinner that evening. *The last supper*, Supriya had called it, a hint of sadness in her voice. Their plane left early the next morning, the middle of the night for Erik. The journey would take them sixteen hours, with a stopover in Frankfurt.

"One more day," said Hanna, taking her eyes off the road for a split second.

"Yup," said Erik. "Got any plans this evening?"

Hanna smiled and shook her head.

"I might be able to grab a beer," she said. "But I'm not making any promises. It all depends on work."

Should he say something? The real reason Erik had asked was that he was curious to see whether Hanna had any plans. Isak Aulin had called him yesterday, wanting to apologize for losing his temper. Erik had brushed it off, but when Isak seemed reluctant to hang up he had asked whether there was anything else. That was when Isak had asked for Hanna's private number. Two of the women from the search group had confirmed that they saw Isak

get into his car and drive away, but Erik still hadn't wanted to give
out her details—not that her number would be difficult to get ahold
of. Isak might already have been in touch with Hanna. The vibes
Erik was getting from her told him that something had happened.

In order to stop himself from saying anything, Erik turned to
look out over the side of the bridge. The mottled sky almost seemed
to be caressing the surface of the water. It was impossible to get
sick of this view, but then he remembered where they were going.
Work, right. It would likely keep him busy for much of the day.
Stop him from thinking about his family. If he couldn't convince
anyone to go out with him that evening, he could always work
late. Eat somewhere near the station and then head home to do a
few guitar lessons. Erik had almost managed to learn "Hakuna
Matata" from *The Lion King*, and it was the first tune he planned
to play for Nila, who loved the film.

The cordon was still up around the house where Thomas Ahlström had been found dead. The new owner had called Erik yesterday, wanting to know how the investigation was going. He had
sounded far more resigned than he had when they spoke at the
crime scene. Back then, the man had gone on and on about needing the keys. The family was staying in a hotel for the time being,
and were no longer sure whether they actually wanted to move in.

How are you supposed to sell a house where someone died? the
man had asked him, as though he seriously thought Erik might
have the answer.

Right now the police cordon was the only physical indication of
what had happened in the small community. Missing People would
be searching the area again today, moving farther north and south.
The eastern area toward the quarry had already been thoroughly
scoured, as had the land to the west, out toward the Kalmar Strait.

There were no more than eight houses between the crime scene
and the house where Ragnar Hagfors lived. Perhaps Hugo had
been in the house when his father died after all. There was a chance

that whoever murdered Thomas hadn't been able to kill a child
and had put their faith in the fact that someone so young wouldn't
be able to identify or testify against them. But if that was the case,
the diaper bag should have been found in the house. Unless, of
course, the door had been left open, and Ragnar had wandered in
and picked up both Hugo and the bag.

Erik realized that there was yet another possibility they hadn't
considered.

"Maybe the killer moved the car."

"Yeah," said Hanna. "They could have. But what would that
mean?"

She pulled up outside Ragnar Hagfors's house, and a face immediately appeared in one of the windows in the house opposite.
A wrinkled old face, surrounded by straggly gray hair. Erik raised
his hand in greeting and the face disappeared. They rang the bell,
and a dark-haired man in his thirties opened the door. He was
wearing jeans, a patterned shirt, and a pair of yellow rubber
gloves, and he had a sponge in his hand. His eyes were wide with
stress.

"Can I help you?" he asked.

"We're from the police," said Erik, holding up his ID.

"Can I help you?" the man repeated.

"We need to talk to Ragnar Hagfors," said Hanna.

"I'm his son. Why do you want to talk to him?"

"Is he here?" asked Erik.

"No, but you know he's not well, don't you? I mean, you can
talk to him, but what he says isn't exactly reliable." The man gave
a resigned shrug.

"Where is he?" Erik pressed him.

"In the hospital."

"Since when?"

"Yesterday. I came over because I couldn't get ahold of him. I
heard about the murder on the next street over and was really

worried. He was just lying on the floor, and at first I thought he . . ." The man swallowed. "It was horrible. He'd probably been lying there for a whole day."

If his son had found him on Wednesday, that meant he had been on the floor since sometime on Tuesday—though obviously they couldn't know for sure.

"Doesn't he have home help?" asked Erik.

"Yeah, but not every day. They help with the shopping, showering, that kind of thing. I've applied for more support, but they haven't made a decision yet."

"Could we come in and have a look around?" asked Hanna.

"I'd like to know why."

"We're looking for the missing boy," said Erik. "Hugo. His father was found dead not far from here, and we've received a tip about an older man who was seen with a young boy matching Hugo's description. Considering your father's illness, he could have decided to help the boy by taking him home."

The man sighed and stepped to one side to let them in. While he returned to his cleaning in the bathroom, Erik and Hanna began searching the house. They opened wardrobes and checked beneath beds, just to be on the safe side. The house was full of oil paintings, balls of wool, and dust. Hugo definitely wasn't there, and there was no sign he ever had been. They had just thanked the man and opened the front door when a piercing scream reached them from the street.

43

The image of Hugo on his belly on the slide kept coming back to her. The joy and expectation on his chubby little face. Lykke left the house in an attempt to shake off the memory.

She had been planning to go for a swim, but she felt far too cold. She wasn't sure her skin would be able to handle it. Her upper body was itching like crazy all over.

You need to eat, the voice pleaded with her. It had finally stopped nagging her to tell the truth.

Lykke glanced over to the washing on the line. It had been hanging there during the storm yesterday, and she would definitely have to rewash everything. For a few seconds she managed to entertain the idea of doing it right now, but just touching a stiff pair of jeans was enough to make her change her mind. Moving slowly, she left her property and wandered down toward the harbor. She liked walking along the curved stone breakwater, letting the spray wash over her.

I shouldn't have run toward him.

The regret was like a knife to her gut, and she pressed her hands to her abdomen. If she hadn't run over to him, their meeting might have ended differently.

A family with a daughter who looked to be around ten were busy pulling their motorboat out of the water, likely leaving the island for the season. She had seen them there quite often that summer, but didn't know exactly where they lived.

Lykke paused halfway along the breakwater. She didn't have the energy to go any farther. The wind was pushing the waves into the side of the structure, throwing white foam up into the air. It wasn't quite strong enough to blow it over the top.

She and Roger had gone for a walk among the boats in Vaxholm, because she had wanted to. The guest harbor there was much bigger than this. It was early spring, and the sun had been shining. Four months and an entire lifetime ago. She had been happy then. When she suggested that they get a boat of their own, Roger had nodded and taken her hand. Squeezed it tenderly. Lykke had always wanted a boat as a girl, but her mother got seasick easily and didn't like being on the water. Besides, they'd never had enough money.

Everything with Roger had been a lie.

Lykke turned around and began walking back, the hatred like a pulsing mass inside her.

"Go to hell!" she shouted.

A head popped up from a windswept fishing boat, but she pretended not to have noticed. The man in the boat had lived in Grönhögen all his life, and his garden was full of apples. He had a sign on his fence telling people to help themselves. He was one of the many people who had stepped in to babysit Lykke when her mother had to work evenings. She hadn't been able to finish high school because of her pregnancy. Or hadn't wanted to, more like. Instead she had gotten by working various odd jobs. Cleaning, in a shop, on the checkout in ICA, as a personal assistant, and so on. And she had been so happy when Lykke told her that she had gotten into the university in Uppsala.

What was she doing? She was letting Roger win by destroying her future. The very thing her mother had always warned her about. She had practically forbidden Lykke from hanging out with boys. The sensible part of her wanted to give in and go to the grocery store, buy several bags of food. But she was also terrified of what would happen if she did. Terrified that she would no longer be in control. The image came back to her again, the image of the joy on Hugo's face. The look that had quickly turned to terror.

44

A young boy had fallen off his bike. Hanna was quicker than Erik, and got to him first. The boy's father soon came running, carrying a much younger child in a sling.

"You need to listen when I tell you not to ride off like that!" he scolded him, though the boy was crying too much to be able to hear.

The baby in the sling stared down at their older sibling with wide eyes. Hanna placed a reassuring hand on the father's arm and then turned her attention to the boy. He had a few nasty scrapes on his elbows and knees, but there was no sign of any protruding bones. Once he managed to get up, she left him with his father and turned back to Erik.

"So, what now?" he asked.

"I'll call Ove," said Hanna. "Check whether there's anyone else we need to look into."

She waited until they were back in the car before she made the call.

"Ragnar Hagfors didn't take Hugo," she said.

"How sure are we?" asked Ove.

"Pretty sure. He's in the hospital. Granted, he wasn't admitted until after the murder, but there's nothing in his house that suggests Hugo was ever there. Do you have any other names for us?"

"Yes, there was a man not far from where the car was found, hold on. . . ."

Hanna pulled a face at Erik in the passenger seat. He knew exactly what she meant. Ove had a tendency to lose focus from time to time.

"He's been ruled out, unfortunately," Ove said once he came back on the line. "Amer spoke to his wife. He's moving into a home this coming weekend, and she's been there for several days now, helping him pack."

"Anyone else?"

"Yes, there was one Bror Erlander, but . . ."

"But what?"

Hanna could no longer hide her irritation.

"He lives farther from both the house where Thomas was killed and the spot where the car was parked," Ove replied, sounding weary. "And one of the uniforms spoke to him the day after Thomas was found. I'll send you the interview notes."

Once she had been given the address, Hanna ended the call and told Erik to read through the interview. The witness had raised her hopes. Her tip was their only concrete lead for Hugo, but perhaps the woman's first instinct had been right after all, and what she saw was nothing but an elderly relative helping the child's exhausted parents. Still, they had no alternative but to keep working. Hanna gripped the wheel and fought back all thoughts of the gray Volvo. Her elbow was aching, but that didn't stop her from driving. Over eighty-five hours had now passed since Jenny had come home to find both Thomas and Hugo missing. Eighty-five hours. It was becoming increasingly difficult to cling to the belief that they would find the toddler alive.

Bror Erlander's house was directly opposite the church in Södra Möckleby, not far from where the volunteers had gathered during the first day of the search. It was a large white structure surrounded by a tall hedge, and Hanna parked the car on the street outside.

They weren't so far from the gravel track to the quarry, but there were a number of houses in between. A single witness. Shouldn't someone else have noticed if Bror had walked past with a young child? If not at the time of the event, then later—once the photograph of Hugo was released? The early hour was the obvious explanation. They were lucky that even one person had happened to look out the window.

"What did Bror Erlander have to say?" asked Hanna.

"He was chopping wood in his garden and claimed not to have seen anything."

They got out of the car and walked toward the house. There was no car in the drive, and the lights inside were off. Considering what an overcast day it was, it didn't look like there was anyone home.

They followed the gravel path up to the stone steps. Like many older houses on Öland, there was a small overhanging roof above the front door.

"Don't you find it strange that there are so many people with dementia around here?" asked Erik.

"The average age is really high in southern Öland," said Hanna. "And I think something like twenty percent of all over-eighties have some form of dementia. How old is he?"

"Eighty-three."

Hanna rang the bell. When no one answered, she tried again. She turned around. On both Tuesday and Wednesday the community had been full of people, but the tall hedge blocked almost all views of the property.

"Let's do a loop around the house," said Erik.

There was a shed full of neatly stacked wood to one side of the main building, an ax and a chopping block beside it. The blade of the ax was buried deep in a piece of wood that had split only halfway. The sight bothered Hanna. Should Bror Erlander really have something like that? Her grandmother's diagnosis had shepherded in a whole host of restrictions. One of the first things she had lost was her driving license.

The lawn was overgrown, and there was a broken umbrella clothesline standing behind the house. The only furniture on the wooden veranda was a table and a couple of chairs. Hanna stepped up onto the veranda and tried to peer in through one of the windows, but the thin net curtains blocked her view. She knocked firmly on the windowpane and shouted hello. Bror Erlander could have problems with his hearing.

The curtain moved to one side and a child's face peered out. A face with bright blue eyes, surrounded by curly blond hair. And below it: a dirty red T-shirt. Hanna got such a shock that she jumped back and hit her hand on one of the chairs, sending a jolt of pain up to her injured elbow, where it seemed to explode outward. She swore.

A moment later, the face was gone.

THE LAST DAY

The car door slams shut, and Hugo whimpers. Thomas braces himself for the scream, but the boy remains quiet. He knows that if he doesn't want to increase the chances of Hugo waking, he should start the engine and drive away. It's already afternoon, and all his earlier attempts to get him to nap have been disrupted. On the other hand, maybe it's just as well that he doesn't sleep now, because it will make him more likely to go down easily that evening. Thomas pushes the key into the ignition, but he can't bring himself to turn it. Lykke's words are still searing through him.

I hate you!

She screamed those three words and then stormed away.

Why did she make contact with him if that's how she feels? No matter how much Thomas detests it, he can't blame Lykke. He is a worthless deserter, and what he did to Natalie was terrible. He left her alone with sole responsibility for a baby, and all because he didn't feel like taking any himself. There might not have been any love left between them, but he never should have abandoned Lykke like that. It hurt so much to see the pain and anger on her face. All her life she must have felt like she had been rejected. By him. He has to make amends for that somehow.

Thomas wants to reach back and place a hand on his son's chest, but he decides against it. *I'll never leave you*, he thinks.

He looks out at the house, but there is no sign of Lykke. Should he wait awhile and then knock on the door? With a bit of luck she might have calmed down by then. Maybe he could take Hugo with him once he wakes up. Thomas doubts Lykke knows that she has a little brother. And if Hugo is with him, she probably won't start shouting and screaming. He might be able to make her listen.

All the things Thomas should be doing are pulling him in different directions.

The sound of his phone ringing bounces around the cramped space inside the car. Damn it, why didn't he switch it to silent? Hugo wakes up, howling.

It's Jenny.

"Sorry," she says when she hears her son crying.

"He'd just gone down for his nap," says Thomas.

That isn't exactly true, but he wants to off-load some of his guilty conscience.

"I just wanted to see how you were doing," says Jenny.

Her voice is soft, swaddling his heart and diluting his guilt.

"We're fine," says Thomas, glancing out at Lykke's house again.

He could tell her now. But how? He tests out the words in his mind: *I have a daughter.* Those words are impossible, because he has no idea how Jenny might react. Maybe he no longer needs to tell her at all, because it seems like Lykke wasn't serious about wanting any contact. But he was. He can't let her vanish from his life again.

"We're in the car," he says instead.

"Why?"

Thomas tries to detect any suspicion in her voice, but he can't find any.

"We went over to the playground in Skogsby."

"Cool," says Jenny.

And they did, that was just several hours ago now. When did he become someone who lies so often?

"I was just about to start driving," he says. "Maybe he'll nod off again."

"Go for it," says Jenny. She pauses briefly: "I can't wait to see you both."

"It's going to be so nice having you home," says Thomas.

That isn't a lie. They end the call with a couple of *I love you*s. The words make Hugo settle down. Thomas closes his eyes. His heart feels like it no longer quite fits in his chest. Jenny is everywhere around him. Inside him. He needs to try to get his job back before she comes home. He can't handle looking her in the eye and telling her that he has lost it. Jenny makes him want to be a better person. Mille jokes about her sometimes, saying that she keeps Thomas on a tight leash, but he has no idea. Or maybe he's just jealous. He bought that little house in Skogsby because he was hoping for the same thing Thomas has: a lasting relationship. It was him who first took them to the playground there.

"Your mom is incredible," says Thomas, glancing in the rear-view mirror.

Yes, Jenny has opinions on a lot of things, but she isn't demanding or mean. And he likes that about her, that she really knows what she wants. He has never doubted that she loves him. The next time Mille makes a joke, he'll stand his ground.

After giving Hugo a quick pat on the head, Thomas starts the engine and pulls away. He has realized several things. One is how much he wants to get to know Lykke, and that it's his responsibility to make sure it happens. Another is that he is done helping Mille. If that means cutting all ties to him, so be it, though it'll be much harder if he doesn't have a job. He needs to talk to Karl as soon as possible. He needs to make him change his mind before Jenny gets home.

45

S hit," Hanna muttered, turning to Erik. "Did you see that?"

But Erik was already by the porch door, trying to open it. It was locked. He pressed his forehead and palm to the glass. Hugo was clearly nowhere to be seen inside, because he turned around in frustration. Hanna called Ove to tell him what was happening, and hurried back around to the front of the house after Erik. The front door was also locked.

"Are you sure it was Hugo?" asked Ove.

"Yes," said Hanna.

"How did he seem?"

"Fine, but it's hard to know what's happening here."

Hanna stared at the front door, panic fluttering in her chest. She was trained to deal with stressful situations, but the adrenaline from that morning was still lingering in her veins, and she had never experienced anything like this before. She had once been called out to a shooting at a gas station in Stockholm, but another unit had taken over the minute it developed into a hostage situation. People with specialist training in the area. In this instance, they were dealing with a young child and an elderly man with dementia. Was it even possible to prepare for something like that?

Where was Bror? If he had left Hugo alone, they would have to try to break in right away. Perhaps he was sleeping. He might be injured or unwell. Before Hanna got any further, a booming man's voice told them to clear off. It was followed by the sound of metal on metal, something being pulled back. That it sounded like a gun being loaded and taken off safety was all Hanna had time to think before the curtain on the front door moved to one side and they saw the barrel pointing straight at them. She and Erik took a few quick steps back from the house.

"What's going on?" Ove's anxious voice asked down the line.

"That was Bror shouting at us," said Hanna. "He's not happy that we're here. And he's armed."

She heard Ove's fingers clattering against his keyboard.

"Bror had a firearms license," he said. "But he was stripped of it after his doctor deemed him unfit. I'll send backup. And an ambulance. We need a negotiator out there, too."

Hanna wasn't sure it would help to have any more officers surrounding the house. The man may well have a gun, but he was also unwell and likely wouldn't respond well to pressure.

"I'm not sure we'll be able to negotiate with him," she said.

"I'll call the home help again," said Ove. "And ask about him specifically."

Hanna made Ove promise to keep any reinforcements at a distance for the time being, and she walked back over to the car and motioned for Erik to follow her. Once they were on the other side of the hedge, she scanned the street around them. Perhaps there was a neighbor Bror was in regular contact with. What they needed right now was someone he recognized.

"Does Bror have any children living nearby?" she asked.

"I'll check," said Ove, the sound of fingers on keys filling her ear again. "A daughter in Färjestaden."

"Give me her number."

Hanna had Bror's daughter Beatrice on the line less than a minute later. She summarized what was happening as quickly as she could.

"Oh God," Beatrice gasped. "Hang on . . ."

Hanna heard her tell someone that they would have to start without her.

"I was just going into a meeting," she explained. "Are you saying my dad has the little boy in his house? And that he's got a gun?"

"Yes," said Hanna.

The worst of her panic had subsided. Though the situation was new, Hanna had a certain self-confidence when it came to her work. It was everything else, linked to her father and to Kristoffer, that was so much hazier and more difficult.

"Dad was so angry when they took his license away," said Beatrice. "He swore he'd sold his gun. I searched the house for it, but I couldn't see it anywhere. I should've—"

"Have you been to see your father this week?" Hanna interrupted her.

"I haven't had time," said Beatrice. "Things have been so busy at work. I usually visit him on the weekend. The home help did actually call me on Tuesday afternoon. He wouldn't let them in."

"Does that happen often?"

"No, they thought he must be stressed out by everything going on in the village. With the search and so on."

Her voice trembled as she said that last part.

"How advanced is his dementia?" asked Hanna.

"He has good days and bad days, but he can generally still look after himself. It's his mood swings that are the tricky thing. He gets so angry sometimes."

"Does he know who you are?"

"Yes," said Beatrice. "I've often wondered whether he should move, but we've both struggled with the idea. I grew up in that house."

Hanna knew from her own experience with her grandmother that people could deteriorate rapidly. She also knew that anger was a common reaction to a worsening grip on reality.

"How bad are his outbursts?"

"He seems fine with things, for the most part. He even jokes about the dementia sometimes. But occasionally . . ."

"He seems to see us as a threat."

Beatrice didn't speak, and Hanna wasn't quite sure what to make of her silence. A woman with a Labrador paused to peer through the opening in the hedge. Hanna held up her ID and gestured for her to move on, and she did so without a word. They were fortunate the house was so secluded.

"What are you going to do?" asked Beatrice.

Her voice sounded much harder now, and Hanna suspected her use of the word *threat* hadn't gone down too well.

"In all honesty, we don't know yet," said Hanna.

"You can't force your way in," said Beatrice. "Especially not if he has a gun."

She was becoming increasingly agitated, and Hanna wanted to distract her.

"Do you have any siblings?" she asked.

"No. I mean, I had a brother, but he died in an accident when he was only two."

46

Erik's eyes darted between the house and Hanna's face. Her features seemed to have hardened, and it was clear that whatever Bror's daughter was telling her wasn't good news. Hanna said that she needed to speak to her boss and ended the call.

"What is it?" he asked.

"Bror had a child who died, so there's a possibility he might think Hugo is his son."

"In that case he's going to protect him," said Erik.

"Yeah. We've got backup on the way, including a negotiator, but it's going to be a while before they get here. I'm not sure they'll even be able to get through to him. And breaking in is hardly a solution, considering he has a gun. His daughter said he has angry outbursts sometimes. What do you think we should do?"

Erik turned to look at the house again. It bothered him that the lights were off inside. What had the past few days been like for Hugo? And what was going on in the old man's head right now? One way or another, they needed to bring him back to reality.

"We could ask his daughter to come over, or Hugo's mother."

"Not the mother," said Hanna. "It wouldn't look good if something happened. And there's a risk she'd make things worse for Bror."

Erik agreed, unsure why he had even suggested it. But they had to consider every option. He called Ove, who agreed that they should ask Bror's daughter to come over. The minute they had his blessing, he nodded to Hanna to let her know she could call Beatrice again. Erik promised Ove that he wouldn't let the daughter contact her father until backup was in place. According to the home help, Bror had come rushing out onto the porch, shouting at them the minute they pulled up outside. Ove had asked them to hold off on their scheduled visit that afternoon.

The wait was awful, but right now all they could do was keep an eye on the house. Hanna slowly flexed her arm, wincing in pain.

"Are you hurt?" he asked.

"I fell over while I was out running this morning," she said. "Landed right on my elbow."

There was a joke about just how dangerous running could be on the tip of Erik's tongue, but he swallowed it when he noticed a movement in one of the windows.

"Did you see what that was?" he asked.

"No," said Hanna. "But he's not going to hurt him."

"I don't think so, either, but . . ."

"I know."

The tall hedge ran right around the garden, meaning there was only one way in. Erik took another few steps toward the car, and Hanna followed him. If Bror looked out, it would probably be best if they weren't standing right at the edge of his property, gawking up at his house. They weren't visible from where they were now standing, but that also meant they couldn't see what was going on inside, and that made Erik nervous.

"Why do people have such high hedges around here?" he asked.

Hanna studied him, one eyebrow slightly raised.

"Because of the wind," she explained when he failed to understand what she meant.

Erik could only feel a slight breeze, and he realized that was because the houses and hedges around him were providing shelter. The same woman who had walked by with her dog earlier passed the house again. Her eyes shone with curiosity, but she didn't dare ask the questions she so clearly wanted to ask. Erik felt a sudden, overwhelming need for Supriya, and he wrote a quick message to say that he was thinking of her, followed by a heart. He stared down at his screen for several minutes, but she didn't reply. In the end he put his phone away.

It took another fifteen minutes for Bror's daughter to arrive. She pulled up behind their car and hurried out, stumbling in her heels. She was wearing black trousers and a white blouse, and her hands were flecked with red paint.

"He sent me a message about him," she said.

"What do you mean?"

"I didn't understand it at the time, I thought he was just confused. But on Monday he sent me a message saying that Jesper was back. Oh God. What should I do?"

"Nothing yet," said Erik, because she seemed to be making her way toward the house.

Beatrice's face twisted, and Hanna reached out and touched her upper arm.

"We need to wait for backup from Kalmar," she said.

"Backup?"

"There's every chance it won't be necessary," she explained. "But we need more people here. Just in case."

"And then what? You can't break in. He'll . . ."

Beatrice folded her arms and peered toward the opening in the hedge. *Shoot you?* Was that what she was going to say?

"When did you last see your dad?" asked Erik.

"I popped in on Sunday, but he got annoyed on Monday when I didn't take the whole Jesper thing seriously. I'd heard about the missing boy, but even then I didn't—"

"It would probably be best if you started by calling him. Try to make your dad think that it's just you out here. That might calm him down."

She nodded, though she seemed far from convinced. Beatrice was so agitated that Erik was no longer sure any of this was a good idea.

"How is your relationship with Bror?" he asked.

"Good. I'm worried he'll be able to tell how stressed I am."

"You can come up with an excuse, if you like," said Hanna.

"Yeah, but what?" said Beatrice, trying to scratch off a fleck of paint with her nails. "I'm useless at lying."

"What do you do for a living?" asked Erik.

"I run an advertising agency with a friend."

"How's it going?"

"So-so," said Beatrice. "I just ran out of an important meeting with a new client."

"And that?"

Erik nodded to her paint-spattered hands. Only then did Beatrice seem to realize what she was doing.

"I've been decorating the house in my spare time. It's a much bigger job than I thought."

"Stick to talking about the house and your agency if he notices your stress," said Erik. "About how hard it is to find time for everything."

"Do you have children?" asked Hanna.

"A son. But he doesn't live at home anymore."

Beatrice scratched even harder at the fleck of paint.

"What am I supposed to say when I speak to him? What's the aim here?"

"The best outcome would be if you could get the boy outside," said Hanna. "Or your dad."

"Okay, but how?"

"It depends. You know Bror best. If he still thinks that Hugo is your little brother, maybe you could suggest letting him out to play. But if he no longer believes that, then you could try to convince him to let Hugo go home to his mom."

"You can't hurt him," said Beatrice.

"That's the last thing we want," said Hanna.

Erik's phone started ringing, and he hurried to answer.

"The backup's here."

Beatrice swallowed and went back to her car to get her phone. She scrolled down to her father's number and closed her eyes as it rang. Erik could hear it, too. After eight rings, she opened her eyes and gave them a slightly confused look. There was a click on the other end of the line.

"Hi, Dad," Beatrice said in a bright voice. "I'm outside."

"What are you standing out there for? Come in!"

"Could you—" she began.

But she didn't get any further before the line went dead.

47

S orry," said Beatrice. "I couldn't get him to talk to me."

Her lower lip began to tremble, and she stared at them. It was almost as though she expected a telling-off.

"Try again," said Hanna.

Bror picked up after just one ring this time, his loud muttering audible to all three of them.

"Stop calling me," he snapped. "You're stressing him out. Come in!"

"Dad—"

But he had already hung up. Beatrice swore. Hanna tried to catch Erik's eye, but he was focused on the hedge obscuring the house.

"I want to go in," said Beatrice. "I think there's a much better chance of this ending well if I do."

Hanna agreed, though she wasn't sure whether they could really expose Beatrice to that kind of risk—particularly given that her father was armed. The problem was that none of the alternatives seemed sensible. They had walked around the house. The curtains were drawn and the lights were off, and Bror was hardly going to open the door if an officer rang the bell, no matter how well trained in negotiation they were.

Beatrice's phone buzzed, and she held it up to them:

Hurry! Jesper is so excited!

The message contained a picture of Hugo. It was blurry, taken from much too close, and his eyes were wide.

"Please, you have to let me do this," said Beatrice.

"I need to call our boss first," said Erik.

Beatrice nodded, and Erik moved over to one side. His face was so dogged that Hanna couldn't work out what Ove must be saying, but after a few minutes he came back.

"What do you say about one of us coming in with you?" he suggested. "We could pretend to be a colleague."

"Dad knows the people I work with," said Beatrice. "And I'm sorry, but you both look like cops."

There was no arguing with that. Hanna was wearing jeans, a button-down, and a bomber jacket, Erik jeans and a T-shirt. They were both fit and tall. And Bror had already seen them.

"You could go in with someone other than us," Hanna suggested.

Beatrice shook her head.

"Do you understand the risk you're taking?"

"He's not going to shoot me," Beatrice snapped.

She sounded incredibly like her father when she was agitated. If they thought there was a chance of her getting hurt, they would never let her in. But the truth was that sometimes things just happened. *I didn't mean to.* Hanna forced back all thoughts of her own father.

"Go in alone," said Hanna. "But call us immediately if you need any help. You have my number."

Hanna watched as Beatrice stepped into the garden and began walking slowly toward the house. She was carrying a huge weight on her shoulders, but they needed to separate Bror and Hugo, and the fact of the matter was that if Hanna, Erik, or any other officer went inside, they would only be putting Bror under more stress. Saving Hugo was their primary concern right now. Beatrice quickly vanished from view.

She rang the bell.

"It's me, Dad," she called. "Open the door."

Her cheery tone felt grating, and Hanna hated that she couldn't see what was going on, but she had no choice but to stay put. After a few seconds, the door opened. Hanna leaned forward as it swung shut. Bror had let his daughter inside.

The wait this time was possibly even worse than before. A message came through after a few minutes.

He's convinced the boy is my little brother.

Good, Hanna replied. *That means he won't hurt him.*

She wanted to reassure Beatrice, to provide her with a sense of calm she could pass on to her father, and *hurt* probably wasn't the right word to have used. She quickly wrote another message:

Just relax. Don't stress.

Unfortunately, it had the opposite effect.

I can't do this, Beatrice wrote.

Of course you can, Hanna replied. *Where's the gun?*

I asked him to put it down.

Hanna showed the message to Erik.

"Should we go in?" she asked.

"I think we should wait."

Hanna leaned back against the car hood. When Erik reached out and touched her, she realized just how hard she had been gripping her tattoo. She let go of her arm and rubbed her palms on her trousers instead. If anything went wrong now, the consequences for them would be severe, but right now she cared most about the young boy. That he was okay. That he would continue to be okay once this was all over.

A man with a Labrador was approaching along the street. Hanna smiled at him, hoping he would continue on his way, but he paused. The dog looked suspiciously similar to the one the woman had been walking earlier.

"Who are you?" he asked.

Hanna responded by holding up her ID.

"What are you doing here?"

"I'm afraid we can't say."

The man wasn't satisfied with her answer, and demanded to know whether something had happened to Bror.

"I'm afraid we can't say," Hanna repeated.

The man tugged irritably on the leash. The Labrador had been making its way over to a lamppost, but it raised its leg and peed on the hedge instead.

"Has the killer struck again? It's appalling that we no longer feel safe around here."

It was only once Erik took a step forward and told the man to keep moving that he reluctantly walked away. He glanced back over his shoulder several times, and after twenty or so meters he dug out his phone and made a call.

Hanna took out her own phone, but there were no new messages from Beatrice. A sizable part of her felt like sending a question mark, but she managed to refrain. They had to let her do this at her own pace.

Just as she was about to put her phone away, a message came through from Ove. The same question mark she had wanted to send to Beatrice.

Nothing yet, she wrote.

Hanna leaned forward again. There was now a light on in one of the windows at the front of the house, and she found herself hoping that was a good sign.

Sixteen minutes. That was how much time passed before the front door opened. Hanna and Erik moved forward. Beatrice was standing on the front step with Hugo in her arms. His face was turned back to the house. As the door swung shut behind her, Beatrice staggered toward them.

THE LAST DAY

Thomas is so worked up over his decision to put Karl up against the wall and demand his job back that he accelerates a little too hard. When he realizes just how fast he is driving, he slows down. He'll have to talk to Mille, too, he decides, after he has been to see Karl. Given that he'll be in Färjestaden anyway. They've been friends since the first grade, and Thomas needs to make him understand that he is serious when he says that tonight is the last time.

"Sorry," says Thomas, glancing in the rearview mirror.

Hugo's head moves. The boy is neither asleep nor unhappy, but Thomas still feels guilty for running around with him like this. Maybe he should phone Karl to check where he is, but he doesn't want to give him a chance to sneak away.

The majority of weekend viewings take place on Saturdays, but Thomas still swings by the office in case Karl is there. The lights are out, so he makes his way over to Karl's house on Kantarellgatan. He has been here once before, when Karl hosted a barbecue in his garden, inviting both Thomas and the other assistant at the time.

Karl's wife, Madeleine, is in the garden, raking the cut grass. Thomas's only memory of her from the barbecue is that she was pale and quiet. Selene had told him the next day that Madeleine had cancer. A brain tumor she had undergone surgery to remove, and radiation. She has recently been given the all-clear, according to Selene. Madeleine looks up and raises her hand to shield her eyes as he parks the car on the street in front of the house. Looking at her now, you would never know she had been unwell. Thomas is glad to see that. Selene often talks about how difficult her illness was for the family.

"Is Karl home?" he asks.

"Yes," says Madeleine, putting down the rake. "Hold on, I'll get him."

She seems troubled to see Thomas. Maybe she knows that Karl has fired him. Thomas unclips Hugo and lifts him out of the car seat. The boy is awake, and he hates being left alone in the car. Karl comes out onto the step, his wife just behind him. Thomas can't help but wonder if there is any truth to Selene's fears that they are getting a divorce. She claims that Madeleine is sick of Karl for working so much—he didn't even cut back when she was ill. He actually worked more than ever.

"What are you doing here?" asks Karl.

It's obvious that Thomas isn't welcome, but he won't give in that easily. He has to fight for his job. For his family and his future. He clings to the determination he felt on the drive over.

"We need to talk," he says.

Karl turns to his wife.

"It'd be best if you went inside."

With a brief nod, she does as he says.

"I've done a good job," Thomas says once Madeleine closes the door behind her.

"You have," Karl concedes.

It strikes Thomas just how uncomfortable Karl is with all of this, which gives him a glimmer of hope that he might be able to change his mind after all.

"No, I've done more than that. I've never said no to overtime, and I've covered for both Hektor and Selene on several occasions."

Thomas is proud of how well he has done in the job, despite his issues with Hektor. Hektor completely ignores anything he doesn't feel like doing. Selene is absent fairly often, too, but Thomas has more understanding for that. She has periods when she isn't well, and at least she tries her best. In his previous jobs Thomas always gave in at the first hint of any problems, choosing the easy way out.

"I know." Karl sighs.

It might not have been the best idea to mention his children; Karl can never quite see clearly, where they're concerned. Still, what's done is done.

"So I really don't understand why I can't keep my job," Thomas says as gently as he can.

If he wants to stand a chance here, he knows he needs to keep his rage at bay.

"Why did you have to borrow so much from Hektor?"

"I'll be able to pay him back this week."

"With what money?"

"Is that important?"

The look Karl gives him makes Thomas realize that it was the wrong thing to say.

"Sorry, of course it is," he apologizes. "I'm doing some work for a friend. For Mille."

Hugo starts squirming, and Thomas lowers him to the ground. There is a fence around the garden, but the boy isn't interested in the road beyond. He runs over to the rake and lifts it up. Karl smiles down at him.

"You've got a wonderful son."

"I know," says Thomas. "And I really need this job, for his sake. For Jenny's."

Something shifts in Karl's eye, and Thomas doesn't like it.

"I've finally managed to straighten my life out," Thomas pleads with him. "Please, don't ruin that."

Karl is quiet for quite some time; Thomas, too. He doesn't know what else to say. Thomas notices a movement in the window be-hind Karl, and he looks up. Madeleine is standing on the other side of the glass, watching them. A second later, she disappears.

"Hektor might be the main reason, but he's not the only one," Karl eventually says. "It's because of Selene, too."

"Okay . . ."

Damn it. Did she tell him about the keys after all?

"I didn't want to bring it up before, because it's a sensitive sub-ject for her. But she finds it difficult to be around you."

Thomas stares blankly at his boss. Why would Selene find it hard to be around him?

"She has feelings for you," Karl explains, clearly noticing the confusion on his face.

48

Beatrice's heel gave way beneath her, and she stumbled down the steps with Hugo in her arms. Hanna hurried toward her while Erik called the reinforcements. It really did look like she was going to fall, but somehow she managed to maintain both her balance and her grip on the boy.

"Take him," she panted.

She tried to pry Hugo's arms from around her neck, but he didn't want to let go. Beatrice eventually managed to pass him over to Hanna, who felt the boy's squirming body against hers.

"Choccit!" he said.

"Dad has been giving him all kinds of sweets," said Beatrice, immediately understanding what he meant.

Hanna made her way over to Erik, keen not to stay too close to the house. An ambulance and a patrol car turned off onto the street. Hugo began wriggling to be let down, but Hanna held him tight. She had a terrible vision of the boy being run over, of having to explain it to his mother, and she felt a huge wave of relief as she handed him over to the paramedics.

"Has anyone called Jenny?" she asked Erik.

"Ove wants you to do it. We've got a car on the way to pick her up and take her to the hospital."

Jenny answered on the first ring.

"Have you found him?"

"Yes. And he's alive," Hanna added on hearing Jenny's sharp intake of breath.

They would never break the news of a death over the phone, but Jenny couldn't know that, and Hanna's words made her burst into tears. A completely different kind of tears than after she found out about Thomas's death.

"Where?" she asked.

Her voice was thick with emotion.

"Södra Möckleby. A man with dementia has been looking after him."

Hanna turned toward Beatrice as she said it, but Beatrice was busy staring at the house.

"How is . . ." Jenny couldn't bring herself to go on.

"Hugo is fine," said Hanna. "But he's being taken to the hospital just to be on the safe side."

"Thank you, thank you, thank you," said Jenny. "My parents took my car to the supermarket, but I'll leave the minute they get back."

"Don't worry, we've got a car coming to pick you up."

"Thank you," Jenny said again, ending the call.

The joy in her voice made Hanna feel warm all over. Beatrice turned back to them.

"Can I go back inside?" she asked.

"Not yet," said Erik. "We need to talk to him first."

"Won't it be easier if I'm there?"

"Maybe," said Erik. "But I think it would be best if we start by trying ourselves."

"But I don't want you to question him without me there."

"Stay here," Erik told her, much more firmly this time.

For a moment it looked like Beatrice was going to argue, but then she nodded. Hanna and Erik made their way over to the front door. The gun was still in the house, and Bror could have picked it

up again once Beatrice and Hugo had left. Both Hanna and Erik
unsecured their weapons before they stepped inside.

They found Bror sitting at the kitchen table, stirring a small pot
of yogurt with a teaspoon. The gun was nowhere to be seen, so
they holstered their own weapons. The tabletop was messy, strewn
with the bag from a loaf of bread, a few discarded crusts, a melted
pack of butter, some banana skins, and a huge number of candy
wrappers. There was also a wooden bus, likely a relic from his
own childhood, and some paper and pens. It didn't look like Hugo
had wanted for anything.

"Where's Jesper?" asked Bror. "Beatrice said she was taking
him out to play."

"They'll be back later," said Hanna.

She knew from experience that it was often best to play along.
Her grandmother had occasionally had outbursts, and they typi-
cally occurred whenever someone questioned her version of reality.
She had once been furious when Hanna told her that her daughter
Kristina was no longer alive, throwing a cushion at her and scream-
ing: *Don't you think I would know if my own daughter was dead?*

"Who are you?" asked Bror.

"We're from the police."

"Ah."

Bror looked up but didn't ask any more questions. His pupils
were huge, and Hanna suspected he hadn't slept in some time.

"Where is your gun?" she asked.

Bror nodded to the cleaning cupboard, and Hanna opened the
door and took it out. Made sure the safety catch was on.

"Where did you find Jesper?" asked Erik.

"In the car."

"What were you doing over there?"

Bror's eyelids lowered, and he leaned heavily against the table.
He looked up when Hanna said his name, and he asked again who
they were.

"We're from the police," said Hanna. "What were you doing by the car where you found Jesper?"

"I was out walking," said Bror. "I like getting out and about. It's important to stay active."

"We can see you're in good shape," said Erik.

Bror smiled. "It was lucky I found the car," he said. "Jesper was screaming with hunger. But he settled down as soon as I picked him up."

"What did you do then?" asked Erik.

"We came home."

"Did you see anyone else around the car?" asked Hanna.

"No. Most people are asleep then."

"What time was it?"

"The sun was coming up."

In late August, that meant sometime around five thirty in the morning. It fit with what the witness had told them. She had seen Bror and Hugo, which meant that Hugo had only had to spend one night alone in the car. Bror yawned, his mouth opening so wide that his jaw clicked. A waft of sour yogurt hit them.

"Is Jesper coming soon?"

"Sorry," said Beatrice, stepping into the kitchen. "I couldn't stay outside."

One of their colleagues should have prevented her from coming in, though Hanna and Erik hadn't actually told them to. Hanna thought Bror had given a surprisingly clear account of finding Hugo, and it wasn't like he could really tell them much more. She nodded to Beatrice that it was okay.

"How are you doing, Dad?"

"I'm fine," said Bror. "But I'm very tired. What have you done with Jesper?"

"He's still playing outside. He'll be here later. What do you say about having a bit of a nap now?"

Beatrice gave them a pleading look.

"He really should go to the hospital to be checked over," said Erik.

Bror had likely been so busy taking care of Hugo that he hadn't been looking after himself. They also had no idea about any other illnesses or health issues he might have.

"I'll see if the paramedics can check him over here instead," said Hanna, turning back to the door.

"Thank you," said Beatrice.

Hanna stepped outside and felt herself come close to collapsing the same way she had that morning, after she leaped out from the cornfield and realized that the Volvo had raced away. The threat had passed. They had found Hugo alive. But Hanna wasn't alone here. Several of her colleagues were gazing toward the house, and with her weariness like a couple of concrete blocks around her legs, she forced herself to keep moving.

49

He doesn't need to go to the hospital," the paramedic who had just left the kitchen told Hanna. "His daughter has said that she'll stay with him and make sure he eats and gets some sleep."

Hanna thanked them and did a quick loop of the house. The trash can in the bathroom was overflowing with diapers, and the stench made her hold her breath. She grabbed the changing bag and hurried back out. She found Hugo's comforter with the cow head in the bedroom. The last hour had been so hectic that it wasn't until she was out on the steps that she realized Missing People probably hadn't been informed.

"Thank you, but I already knew," said Freya Amundsdottir. "Ove phoned me, and we've called off the search. We're all so thrilled he was found. Please pass that on to his mom."

"Absolutely, I will," said Hanna, walking over to the car where Erik was waiting.

The seized gun was in the trunk, but Hanna kept the diaper bag on her lap as she climbed into the passenger seat. She didn't want to forget to give it back to Jenny. They were on their way to the hospital in Kalmar to talk to her now. Hanna tipped her head back and closed her eyes.

She gave up after just a few minutes and stared out at the road instead. She had never been able to sleep upright, and there were too many thoughts swirling around in her head. Now that Hugo had been found, it was clear that Thomas's murder hadn't been about his son. So why was he killed? The evidence so far pointed in several different directions.

"Shall we stop off at the cafeteria and grab a coffee?" asked Erik.

"Sure," said Hanna. "I could do with something to eat, too."

It could only be a good thing for them to give Jenny time. Now that her son had been found safe and well, they might be able to coax out more information about her husband. Hanna looked down at the small cow's head peeping out of the bag and couldn't help but stroke it.

"What do you think?" asked Erik.

"About the murder, you mean?"

"Yeah."

Erik drove up onto the bridge, and Hanna gazed out the window as she tried to make her mind stop racing. The sky was a mosaic of different grays, and she thought she could make out the shape of a sumo wrestler in the clouds.

"Given the keys and the deposits into his account, it seems likely he was involved in something illegal," she said. "Then there's the tip about the van parked outside, too. My guess is that it has something to do with that, or maybe it was someone from the real estate agents."

"He could've been having an affair," said Erik. "And that's why he wanted to borrow the house."

"Possibly, but we haven't found any evidence of that."

"What about his daughter?"

"I don't know," said Hanna.

A more truthful answer would have been that she didn't want to know. She had seen plenty of cases involving one family member killing another, and the act in itself was no different than any other murder. To Hanna, there was nothing worse than taking another person's life, but perhaps the guilt afterward was even darker. Once the consequences sank in. Particularly if the person who died had once meant something to their killer.

Fucking Kristoffer. The thought came out of nowhere. Hanna could just imagine hitting him with something hard. What if he had kept the truth from her all these years, allowing her to believe that their father was a murderer when he was nothing of the sort? The idea was still too big and prickly for her to take in. But if it was true, what could have happened? And why? She just couldn't imagine any reason why Kristoffer would kick someone to death. Or Robin Svensson, for that matter. She should probably try to dig up more information about him, she realized.

"Maybe it was all just a coincidence," said Erik.

"What?"

Hanna was so deep in thought about the murder of Ester Jensen that she couldn't come back from it. She had been beaten so badly. Someone, whether on their own or as part of a group, had kicked her until nineteen bones were broken. As she lay on the floor, bleeding. Did she plead with them at first, while she was still able?

"Maybe someone bumped into Thomas while they were trying to rob the house."

"But the house was empty," said Hanna.

"Sure, though the robber might not have known that. The van could have belonged to them."

Hanna didn't bother to reply. Erik occasionally said things he didn't believe himself, purely because his mind couldn't keep up with his mouth. Either way, they needed to get to the bottom of why Thomas had needed the keys. That was the crucial question right now. Hanna glanced down at the cow's head again. Thomas would never get to see his son grow up, but it would be Jenny and Hugo who suffered most.

Erik parked outside the hospital, and they went straight to the cafeteria. Hanna didn't feel comfortable carrying the changing bag on her shoulder, but she didn't know what else to do with it. If she tried to pass it to Erik, he would just make some kind of stupid joke.

After a moment of indecision, Hanna chose a plastic-wrapped prawn sandwich to go with her coffee. Erik managed to wolf down his entire avocado sandwich in the time it took her to eat half, so he called to find out where Jenny and Hugo were.

They followed the signs up to the right floor. Jenny and Hugo were still on the emergency children's ward, and as they stepped into the examination room Jenny was deep in discussion with a gray-haired doctor wearing square glasses. He turned to them with a look of irritation, and Hanna held up her ID.

"We need to talk to Jenny, if that's okay."

"Of course," said the doctor. "You can do that now. I'll be back in a little while."

"He wants Hugo to stay in overnight," Jenny told them the moment he had gone.

She sat down on the bed with her son in her arms. Hugo leaned his head against her chest. His bright blue eyes were wide, but he was smiling happily.

"Won't that be nice?" Hanna asked.

She put down the changing bag on a chair, took out the comforter, and held it out to Hugo.

"Moo!" he said, hugging the cow to his face.

"No, why would it be nice?" asked Jenny. "He's his usual self. A bit clingier than normal, maybe. And he keeps nagging me for sweets."

"It'll be easier for you to get some peace and quiet here," said Hanna.

"Peace and quiet?"

"From the journalists."

"I'd forgotten about them."

Both the local press and the tabloids had written countless

articles about the disappearance and murder, as well as the search for Hugo. Many no doubt already knew that he had been found, and the news would spread quickly. The journalists would be desperate for a statement from Jenny.

Erik recapped everything Bror had said, telling Jenny that Hugo had spent only one night in the car and that he seemed to have been given an abundance of care. Both food and games. And sweets. Jenny hugged her son tight when she heard that.

"So the man has dementia?"

"Yes," said Hanna. "And he had a son who died when he was around Hugo's age."

"I know I should probably be grateful," said Jenny. "But I'm really struggling. The past few days have been awful. I honestly thought I'd lost him, too."

Hugo looked up at her in surprise as she started to cry.

"I miss Thomas so much I don't know which way to turn," she said, hugging the boy even tighter. "And it hurts so much to know that Hugo won't . . ."

Her son whimpered, not because his father was dead but because his mother was squeezing him too hard. Jenny loosened her grip.

"I know this is a terrible situation," said Hanna, "but I'm afraid we need to ask a few difficult questions."

Jenny rubbed her eyes with her sleeve and gave Hanna a defiant look.

"I loved Thomas, but he had a real problem. He was way too gullible."

"What do you mean?"

"I've suspected Thomas had been dragged into something for a while now. And I know I should have told you that right away, but my brain wasn't working properly. I wanted to protect him because I couldn't accept that he was never coming back."

"Do you know what it was?" asked Erik.

"I'm pretty sure it was all about helping Mille."

Hanna repeated Erik's question.

"Not really," said Jenny. "But I think it had something to do with cigarettes."

"What are you basing that on?"

"I heard him and Mille whispering about a shipment once. They were watching soccer at our place and probably thought I was too busy with Hugo to hear. I'm guessing that was where the money came from."

"Did you bring it up with Thomas?" asked Hanna.

"No," said Jenny. "But I did try to talk to Mille about it after Thomas was found."

"What did he say?"

"He went crazy, started shouting that I'd imagined the whole thing."

THE LAST DAY

She has feelings for you.

Karl's words poke holes in Thomas's determination. What exactly has Selene said? He puts the question to his boss, but Karl just shakes his head. Madeleine appears fleetingly in the window again, probably wondering what is going on. Thomas walks over to Hugo, who is struggling to get the rake to do what he wants it to do.

"No," he says as Thomas pries his fingers loose and carries him over to the car.

"Thomas," Karl pleads.

But Thomas ignores him. With fumbling hands, he manages to fasten Hugo into the car seat, then sits down behind the wheel and starts the engine. He needs to get out of here. He turns the car around in the turning circle and glances back at the house, but Karl has already gone inside.

Thomas only just makes it around the corner before pulling over to the side of the road. *She finds it difficult to be around you.* The question is right there again: What exactly has Selene said? They get along well together. If she finds his company so difficult, why hasn't she said anything? Her feelings for him must be much stronger than he realized. But would she really bring it up with Karl? Possibly. They seem to have a good relationship.

Maybe he could talk to Selene. And Hektor. Get them to help save his job. Karl isn't usually this impossible. He could offer Hektor more money, but how should he deal with Selene?

Thomas starts the engine again with a sigh. He knows he should give Mille a call to check where he is, but his friend is usually in the shop in the late afternoon and early evening—the man almost never stops working. Thomas sometimes wishes he had Mille's energy, or rather his perseverance. His chest feels tight when he thinks about everything they have done together.

He was with Mille when they smoked their first cigarettes. When they drank their first beers. They once wound toilet paper around a handsy teacher's car. But by the time they got to high school, they started to drift apart. Some of the things Mille came up with frightened Thomas. He wanted to celebrate getting his driver's license by stealing a car. After they graduated they had virtually no contact at all for a few years, but they eventually found their way back to each other. Mille has helped him out so many times. He was the one who lined up the job at the real estate agency, for example. Karl Friberg is friends with his old man, and Mille fixes things for them from time to time. He was there to fix the photocopier one day and heard that they were looking for a new assistant. This was around the same time Mille and Selene got together, though that lasted only a few months.

"I've managed to lose that job, too, haven't I?" Thomas says into the rearview mirror, using his baby voice again.

He knows he should think about the things he says to Hugo. That's probably a bigger issue than the voice he uses. How much does a child really understand at that age? It's hard to know for sure.

"Your daddy has got himself mixed up in something silly," he chirps. "But that's over now."

"Moo!" Hugo shouts, hitting the window.

But there are no cows out there, only houses. His son is probably engaging in a bit of wishful thinking, just like him. Mille's shop isn't far from Karl's house.

"Moo!" Hugo shouts again.

"Your big sister's name is Lykke," says Thomas.

No reaction from the back seat.

Thomas spots Mille the minute he pulls up outside the tobacconist, and since Hugo is awake he has no choice but to take the boy inside. Not that it matters. Mille is great with Hugo, and Thomas knows he would love to have kids of his own one day. Hopefully he will before too long. It would really help him reassess his priorities in life.

"Hey, little man," Mille says as Thomas and Hugo step into the shop.

He was busy flicking through a folder on the counter, but he closes it with a thud that makes Hugo blink and laugh. Thomas keeps hold of his son, doesn't want him to start pulling things from the shelves—or putting them in his mouth; he still can't quite process the fact that Hugo almost choked at the playground that morning—though like always on Sundays, there isn't much left on the shelves.

"Everything ready for tonight?" asks Mille.

They are alone in the shop, but Thomas still doesn't appreciate him asking about it so openly.

"Yeah," he says. "I've got the keys. But just so you know, this is the last time."

Mille rounds the counter and comes over to them. He grips Hugo's chubby little hand, lifts it to his mouth, and blows a raspberry.

"What's this rubbish your daddy's spouting, huh? Of course he's not going to stop."

"I'm serious," says Thomas, resisting the urge to snatch Hugo away from him. "I really need to stop. It just doesn't work now that I'm on paternity leave."

"So get Selene to help."

"No, I don't want to."

"Come on, man. She's already shown how keen she is."

"That doesn't matter," says Thomas. "Enough is enough."

He sounds like a stubborn child, and Mille takes a step back and studies him closely.

"You can't stop," he says. "They won't let you."

Thomas has always known that there must be someone above Mille. The first time his friend asked him to borrow a set of keys from the office, he was afraid of something bad happening if he didn't get the help he needed. All he said was that he had something that needed to be kept safe overnight, and though Thomas knew it must be illegal, he hadn't asked any questions. He couldn't let Mille down. But he has to think of himself now. Of Jenny and Hugo.

"Who are 'they'?" he asks.

"It's better you don't know."

The fear is back, the same fear Thomas saw when Mille first begged for help. But this time it seems much worse, mixed with something else. Sorrow. It's as though he is convinced this will end badly.

50

Why was she here? Lykke stared at the information board at the entrance to the hospital. After reading in the Öland group on Facebook that Hugo had been found, she had jumped straight in the Škoda and driven over here. But even if she managed to work out which ward he was on, she probably wouldn't be allowed to see him. They didn't have the same surname. She had no way of proving they were related, and Jenny was hardly going to admit it.

Lykke tried to find her way back to the feeling that had filled her as she read the news about Hugo. Relief and longing. Maybe even happiness. It had been so long since she last felt it that she had forgotten what it was like. The news had made her imagine that she might stand a chance after all.

A man came over and stood beside her, much too close. His white shirt stank of aftershave, and he was clutching a bunch of red roses in his veiny, liver-spotted hands. Lykke closed her eyes and thought back to the moment when she first saw her little brother in the garden outside Thomas and Jenny's house. She had immediately known who he was. He had the same hair she'd had at that age. Blond, slightly curly. It wasn't until she was older that it had darkened, turning a shade of light brown. Right there and then, as she studied the curls clinging to his forehead, she had realized that Thomas had another child. A child whose life he had chosen to be a part of. She was only a few months old when Thomas had abandoned her.

That same child must have been in the car when Thomas appeared out of nowhere, trudging among the toad lilies in her garden. If she had known she had a sibling then, she might have been able to control her anger better. Or not, considering how she behaved once she did actually realize. When Hugo got onto his belly to go down the slide, when Thomas came rushing out of the house.

What about now? Lykke was no longer angry, nor was she happy. She was sad and afraid. But the longing was still there.

"Is everything okay?"

Lykke's eyelids snapped open, and she met the pair of pale blue eyes gazing anxiously at her. They belonged to the old man who had also been studying the map.

"Do you need any help?" he asked when she failed to respond.

She shook her head, quickly realizing that wouldn't be enough. "I'm fine, thank you."

Only once she managed to mumble those few words and force a smile onto her face did the man turn around and walk toward the elevators. Coming here had been idiotic. She wanted to meet Hugo, but Jenny would never allow it. Yes, Lykke needed help. She needed help knowing what to do when the anger surged through her. And she needed help eating.

Though she knew there was no way she would be able to manage anything here—among all the people staring at her—she gazed over at the cafeteria. Lykke turned to leave, glancing back at the man, who had now reached the elevators. One of the doors opened and the two police officers stepped out. The same ones who had come to visit her twice. Panic wiped their names from her memory. Her eyes desperately tried to find a hiding place, but the woman had already spotted her.

Hanna, that was it.

"Wait!" she shouted as Lykke hurried back toward the main doors.

51

Erik caught sight of himself in the mirror in the elevator and ran a quick hand through his hair. It was getting long, but he wouldn't have time to get it cut before Supriya and Nila came home tomorrow. His daughter was more appreciative of the curls than his wife was. He didn't have much of an opinion himself, but he didn't like it when his hair got in his eyes.

"Do you think Thomas could have been mixed up in cigarette smuggling?" asked Hanna.

"Yeah, sounds like the most likely explanation."

Erik's phone beeped, and he found himself hoping it was Supriya. He hadn't felt calm enough to let her know that Hugo had been found until he was sitting down in the hospital cafeteria. They shared all major events with each other, and the thought of going through life without her was hard to imagine. According to the clock on his phone their plane would be landing in twenty-six hours.

But the message wasn't from Supriya. It was from one of their neighbors, a man he had stopped to chat with in the stairwell recently. He wanted to know if Erik was interested in going to a beer-tasting with him. Why wasn't Supriya replying? He could see that she had read his first message, the one that said he was thinking about her.

"Wait!" Hanna shouted. Erik looked up.

He saw Lykke Henriksen hurrying toward the exit. It was obvious she had spotted them and didn't want to talk. The sudden burst of movement made Erik's leg muscles scream in protest, but he silenced them by taking another step. Lykke glanced back, and when she saw that they were following her, she broke into a run.

"Stop!" Erik shouted.

All eyes turned to the two detectives. Even the woman with the walker he had to swerve around. It was only once Erik had darted past her that he realized she probably thought he'd been yelling at her. They caught up with Lykke just outside the building, but she didn't stop until he physically grabbed her.

"Why did you run?" asked Erik.

Lykke looked over at the parking lot without a word. He repeated the question and let go of her arm, but she still didn't react.

"What are you doing here?" asked Hanna.

The sound Lykke made was somewhere between a sigh and a sob.

"I wanted to see Hugo."

"Why?"

"Because he's my little brother."

There was a bench a few meters away from them, and Erik nodded over to it. "Let's sit down and talk."

"I want to go home," said Lykke.

"Either you sit down and talk to us here," said Erik, "or we take you down to the station."

Lykke stood still for a moment, her eyes still fixed on the parking lot. Erik knew he might have been slightly too hard on her, but he was sick of her being so evasive. He just hoped she wouldn't try to run again. Not because she stood a chance, but because they had already drawn enough attention to themselves. Erik was fairly sure the man hovering behind them had followed them out. He held up his ID, and the man nodded and headed back inside.

"I just wanted to see Hugo," said Lykke.

"Come on," said Hanna, taking a step toward the bench.

This time Lykke did as they wanted, and they sat down on either side of her. She pushed her hands between her knees as though she needed to prevent them from doing something.

"Is there anything else you haven't told us?" asked Erik.

"What do you mean?"

"Exactly what I said. You've consistently told us that you never met Thomas, but that isn't true, is it?"

Lykke shook her head.

"So now I'm wondering if there's anything else we should know."

She shook her head again, then leaned forward and pressed her palms to her temples, as though she needed to hold her head in place. Hanna put a hand on her back.

"Are you okay?" she asked.

Lykke stood up, reeled forward, and collapsed.

52

Lykke hit the pavement with a dull thud. Hanna threw herself toward her, shaking Lykke's upper body and saying her name, but there was no reaction. Her chest heaved, and Hanna pressed two fingers to her throat. Lykke's pulse was fast and irregular. This was more than just a fainting. Hanna looked up to tell Erik to run for help, but he had already gone. She got Lykke into the recovery position and then sat down beside her, one hand on her upper arm.

What was taking them so long? They were right outside the hospital. As Hanna turned to look back at the main entrance, she saw a stretcher being wheeled out of the ER. The doctors lifted Lykke onto it. Erik seemed to have explained the situation, because they didn't ask any questions, just hurried away.

"I told them to call me once they know how she is," he said.

"Good."

They needed to speak to Lykke as soon as she was feeling up to it. Every single meeting with Thomas's daughter so far had only served to reinforce the feeling that she was hiding something.

"Have you been in touch with Ove?" asked Hanna.

Erik shook his head, so Hanna called the boss to brief him on what had just happened. She also told him what Jenny had said about Mille Bergman and that they suspected Thomas might have been smuggling cigarettes with him.

"Ove is going to get someone to contact Customs about the smuggling," she said when she hung up.

"Good."

There was a screech of brakes, and a car swung into the parking lot. Hanna saw the *Barometern* logo on one side. She was just grateful they hadn't arrived while she was sitting with Lykke on the pavement.

"We'd better hurry," she said, nodding to the car.

But it was too late. The car came to a halt and the reporter jumped out, running over to them.

"Hanna Duncker," he said. "I really need to talk to you."

He reached out and touched her arm, but Hanna shook him off. Probably a little too forcefully, but he just made her so damn angry.

"Hey, take it easy," he said.

"You'll have to call the press spokesperson."

"I have, but I actually wanted to talk to you about something else."

Hanna glared at him.

"About your father."

If Erik hadn't been there to grab her arm, she probably would have hit the journalist. Hanna couldn't bear to look at him any longer; she needed to get out of there. She hurried toward their car.

"I have a theory about what really happened to Ester Jensen," he called after her.

Hanna stopped, but she didn't turn around. She couldn't cope with this. Not right now. Erik was still standing by the journalist's side. Why wasn't he coming?

"Erik," she barked, marching the last few meters to the car.

She got behind the wheel and waited for him to catch up, pulling out of the space the minute he closed the door. In the rearview mirror she saw the reporter watching them. His photographer raised his camera and took a couple of pictures.

"Shouldn't you have talked to him?" asked Erik.

Mind your own business, Hanna felt like screaming, but she took a deep breath and waited a few seconds.

"I can do it later. We need to focus on the investigation right now."

"Okay," said Erik. "Wasn't there some kind of raid up Stockholm way a month or so ago? Where they seized a whole load of smuggled cigarettes?"

"I think so," said Hanna.

In truth, Hanna hadn't been following the news at all a month ago. She had been far too busy renovating her little house in Kleva and trying to ward off all thoughts of Ester Jensen. What kind of theory could the journalist have? She would contact him the minute they found Thomas Ahlström's murderer. But before that, she wanted to have a better understanding of everything herself. Erik took out his phone.

"Yeah, one-point-five million cigarettes were found on a sailing boat from one of the Baltic states," he said, putting his phone down again. "But I haven't heard of any similar cases around here."

"There's a harbor in Degerhamn," said Hanna. "Which isn't far from the house in Södra Möckleby. The entire Öland coast is full of tiny harbors like that."

Hanna's grandmother had once told her about the widespread alcohol smuggling that used to take place across the Baltic Sea a hundred years ago, but cigarettes were probably far more common now. There was a lot of money in it, and the penalty for being caught was considerably less severe than for smuggling drugs. Still, she didn't know much about it; the police weren't usually involved in investigating it, after all.

Once Hanna had parked in the garage at the station, they went straight to Ove's office.

"Mille Bergman's name doesn't come up in any of the registers," he said. "But there were a couple of Russians and a Swede convicted of smuggling cigarettes into Grönhögen a few years back. The Customs officer in charge of the case is going to check the files for names and speak to the Swede who was sent down. They also found a van full of cigarettes outside of Bläsinge last autumn. There was plenty of physical evidence, but they didn't manage to tie it to anyone."

"Should we bring in Mille Bergman?" asked Hanna.

"I think you should hold off until tomorrow at least," said Ove. "Until we know more."

"Okay."

Erik headed off somewhere, but Hanna paused in the doorway.

"Was there anything else?" asked Ove.

There was, but she had no idea where to start. Nor how much she should reveal. Her elbow was throbbing, and she knew she should probably tell him about both the gas can and the Volvo.

"Is it to do with your dad?"

Hanna nodded and took a seat by his desk.

"Does the name Robin Svensson ring any bells?" she asked.

Ove shook his head.

"He drove his car into a tree a few years ago. I spoke to his sister yesterday, because Kristoffer called her. She's convinced he and Robin did something stupid."

"And you think it could be linked to Ester Jensen?"

"Maybe."

Hanna couldn't bring herself to say yes.

"What exactly do you want?" asked Ove.

"I want to look into both Robin Svensson and the accident that killed him."

Hanna needed Ove's blessing before she took any investigative measures. What she really wanted was to look into Gunnar, too, though she knew that was completely irrational. There was no real reason for him to have lied, other than the fact that he clearly didn't like Kristoffer—and that wasn't enough.

"Have you spoken to your brother?" asked Ove.

"Yes, but it didn't exactly go well."

Ove's focus shifted to his computer, his eyes darting back and forth. After a moment or so, he turned back to her.

"Okay, do it," he said. "But you need to keep me updated if you find out anything at all about Ester Jensen."

"I will," said Hanna, getting to her feet.

Perhaps she should call the journalist from *Barometern* after all, to hear what he had to say, at least. But no, she didn't want to do that before she had spoken to Kristoffer.

"I got another email today," said Ove. Hanna took a seat again. "And this time it wasn't anonymous. A woman claims you flew off the handle with her at ICA Kvantum in Färjestaden."

That was the supermarket where Hanna did most of her shopping, where she stopped off on the way home from work. It was unsettling that the emailer had chosen that particular branch. Someone was clearly keeping tabs on her, that was the only explanation. For both this and the Volvo—she walked down to the shore almost every morning.

"Why would I do that?"

"You called her a bald old bitch."

A bald old bitch? Hanna stifled a laugh. Couldn't they have come up with something slightly worse?

"Who is this woman?" she asked.

"Her name is Kristina Persson."

Hanna was so shocked that she couldn't manage a single word. Ove watched her with an anxious look on his face.

"You know, I understand that you—"

"Kristina Persson was my mom's name."

"Oof," he said. "That never crossed my mind."

Ove knew that her mother had died of cancer. Lars had talked about Kristina in almost every interview, about the shock of her

suddenly becoming ill and dying. How everything had felt so hope-
less and dark afterward. Being unable to find meaning in anything. That was exactly how he had sounded whenever Hanna
tried to get him up off the sofa or out of bed, during all those years
before everything with Ester. While she was struggling to manage
her schoolwork alongside all the cooking and cleaning.

"This is linked to my father," she said.

"Possibly, but it could just as easily—"

"No."

That it was connected to Lars was the only thing that made
sense. Why else use her mother's name and allude to the cancer
that had killed her? She had lost all her hair toward the end, become a completely different person in both appearance and man-
ner. But who could have sent the email? Kristoffer would never do
something like this to her—assuming he was even in Sweden and
therefore physically capable of it. Was Ester's daughter Maria trying to make her suffer like she had? Or Carina? But how did that
tally with what happened this morning? It was a man behind the
wheel of the car that tried to run her down.

"Has anyone tried to trace the previous email?" she asked.

"Yes, but unfortunately it was impossible."

This was the moment for Hanna to bring up the gas can left
outside her house. To have it dusted for prints. To mention the
Volvo that had tried to run her down. But if she did, she would no
longer be able to keep her fear in check. She tried to drum up an
argument against telling Ove. Considering the email had been impossible to trace, she doubted the gas can would give anything,
either. And they would hardly be able to find the Volvo. But most
important of all: she didn't want Ove to change his mind about
Robin Svensson.

Hanna got up and left Ove's office. She would get to the truth,
somehow.

53

L ykke . . ."
     It was so dark, and the voice was coming from somewhere
beyond the darkness. Was she locked up? She was falling, and for
a long time she couldn't hear a thing. There was nothing but a
quiet, black embrace. Suddenly her mother was there. The summer
sun was spilling in through the dusty kitchen window in Grönhögen. They each had a mug of coffee in front of them, and for once
her mother didn't shake her head in irritation when Lykke asked
about Thomas. She opened her mouth to tell her about him, but
then that voice was back again, the one calmly and clearly saying
Lykke's name. The voice dragged her upward, away from her
mother. But she didn't want to go, she wanted to hear about
Thomas. About her dad.

"Lykke . . ."

Shut up, she tried to scream, but it came out as a grunt.

She opened her eyes, stared straight into the light. It was so
bright that she had to blink. An unfamiliar face in the glare. A
kind face surrounded by short black hair, and Lykke forgot what
she had wanted to say. White clothing beneath the face, a blurry
name badge. A nurse.

"You're in Kalmar General Hospital," he said. "You collapsed."

Lykke closed her eyes and tried to let herself fall through the darkness again, but the darkness didn't want her. At first all she could remember was the old man by the information board. The scent of his roses was so powerful that it made her queasy. But then she remembered the police officers and how she had tried to run when they pressed her about Thomas. Why hadn't she just told them the truth? She knew the answer: because she was afraid.

"Lykke." The voice was firm. "I can see that you're awake. You've been given a drip."

Lykke opened her eyes and stared down at her arm, at the needle forcing nutrients into her body. At the tape holding it in place. The shock made it difficult to process, but she soon pulled herself out of it. She writhed desperately in an attempt to dislodge the needle, but the nurse held her down.

"We've read your medical records," he said. "Your body collapsed in protest at the way you've been treating it. I'll let go if you promise not to touch the needle."

The nurse was studying her, waiting for her reaction. When Lykke nodded, he let go of her arms. She glared down at the cannula. If she was quick enough she might manage it. But no, there was no point. Lykke turned her head to avoid having to look at it.

"Are the police still out there?" she asked.

"No, why would they be?"

Lykke caught the look on his face before he managed to compose himself. The frown that quickly disappeared. The slight lean back. The question made her someone else in his eyes. Someone he had to be on his guard around.

"I don't know," said Lykke. "They helped me."

"When did you last eat?"

"I had a clementine on Sunday evening," said Lykke. "But I've been drinking plenty of liquids."

"That's not nearly enough, as I'm sure you know. When did your problems start coming back?"

"Spring," she whispered.

Lykke knew the exact moment. It was as she stood outside Roger's house and realized that he had a wife and child. But she didn't say that, because she was ashamed of how she had dealt with it. Of how she dealt with everything. She could feel that shame and still look around for some way to escape. She didn't want to be here.

"I know this is hard," said the nurse, placing a hand on her shoulder. "What happened on Sunday to make you stop eating again?"

Words were the only thing that could help her get out of this. She couldn't bear the thought of having to spend the night taped to the needle.

"Nothing particular. It's all just been a bit much lately."

Lykke knew her words weren't enough to make the nurse leave her in peace. To walk away and not force her to stay. Those weeks in the hospital had been awful. The complete lack of control. Everything had hinged on the impression she gave, rather than how she actually felt. She remembered why she had defied her reluctance and come to the hospital today.

"The boy who went missing is my little brother," she said. "Or half brother."

The nurse's eyes widened, but not with compassion. His guardedness was back.

"Can I see him?" asked Lykke.

"I don't know," said the nurse. "But I'll speak to his mom."

54

Hanna paused as she left Ove's office. She hadn't needed to convince him to let her look into Robin Svensson. She had gotten what she wanted, yet somehow it still felt like a failure. She didn't like that she had been so open with her suspicions, but there was no turning back now. And what about the Volvo? The gas can? It might have felt good to off-load that onto someone else.

Hanna noticed a movement behind her and made her way into the investigation room. Everyone but Erik was there.

"I've booked a table at Kött and Bar tonight," said Amer. "So now it's your job to get him there."

"Don't they mostly serve steaks and burgers? You know Erik is a vegetarian, don't you?"

Amer laughed. "Yeah, I thought it was a nice gesture. But relax: they've got rabbit food on the menu, too."

"Good," said Hanna. "Erik asked if I wanted to grab a beer tonight, so I'll let him drag me out and make sure we end up in the right place."

Hanna sat down at her desk and took out the files from the investigation that was carried out after Robin Svensson's fatal crash. It didn't take her long to read through everything. The forensics analysis of his car hadn't flagged any mechanical faults. There was a trace of alcohol in his blood, but the witness in the car behind his hadn't seen him brake or swerve; he had simply left the road and plowed straight into the tree. All things considered, it certainly sounded like suicide. Hanna flicked through the documents, but she couldn't find an autopsy report. The only other explanation she could think of was that Robin had taken ill somehow. Though, if that was the case, the car should have swerved.

The investigating officer had concluded that it was likely a suicide, but he hadn't wanted to rule out an accident. That was just it: no one could know what was going on in Robin's head in the moments before he died. Did it really make any difference? Robin was dead and no one else had been physically harmed. For his family, it surely did matter. For Klara. Perhaps that was why the investigating officer had chosen to be so vague in his conclusions.

Hanna leaned back in her chair, making it creak beneath her. Klara had said that Robin had started struggling a year after graduating from high school, that he hadn't been able to hold down any of the few jobs he managed to get, always either quitting or being fired. He bore a certain resemblance to Thomas Ahlström on that front. The list of positions Thomas had held over the years was considerably longer, but he hadn't managed to stick with any of them.

Robin had been admitted to the emergency psychiatric ward a few times, and his sister was convinced he was troubled by something he had done with Kristoffer—though that didn't seem to be based on anything other than the fact that they had abruptly cut off all contact and that Robin had lost his temper at the mere mention of Kristoffer's name.

But the time frame . . . One year after Robin and Kristoffer graduated from high school, just a few weeks before Hanna herself would do the same, Ester Jensen had been murdered.

Hanna massaged her temples. Robin had seemed like he was in good spirits when they played poker in the kitchen, but she searched further back, away from that moment. Her overriding memory of Robin was his shyness. The DIY haircut, and the acne he tried to draw attention from with designer clothes he had almost certainly shoplifted. For a while he had probably been interested in her. He had occasionally sought out Hanna when they ended up at the same parties, anyway—though that might have been down to nothing other than a lack of anyone else to hang out with. Hanna had Rebecka back then, but Rebecka was friends with everyone and often went off with other people. The same was probably true with Robin and Kristoffer. Something else came back to Hanna: Robin's family were Jehovah's Witnesses, and he was actually forbidden from going out to parties. That was probably where his desperate desire to fit in had come from. She had never known Klara, and had only a vague memory of their parents.

Hanna called Robin's sister.

"Hi," said Klara. "Have you spoken to Kristoffer yet?"

"I've tried," said Hanna. "But he's avoiding me right now."

Kristoffer still hadn't replied to any of her text messages. She heard a child crying in the background. Likely the older girl, since Klara told her to be quiet. A little too firmly. That was probably her disappointment speaking. The command was followed by a shocked silence.

"I promise I'll keep trying," said Hanna.

"Good. I think Robin's death would be easier to take if I just knew more about why. Hold on. . . ."

She whispered an apology to her daughter, but Hanna couldn't tell whether it got through.

"Do you remember anything else?" she asked.

"Sorry, no."

"Are you still a Jehovah's Witness?"

"Is that relevant?"

There was a bang in the background, and Klara told the girl to be quiet again. She sounded much calmer this time.

"I don't know," said Hanna.

"No, I'm not." Klara sighed. "And Robin had jumped ship, too. That's why I miss him so much. We only had each other, you know?"

Hanna wondered whether Klara lived with the father of her children, but she didn't ask. The girls' paternal grandmother was involved in their lives, at the very least.

Erik reappeared and came over to Hanna's desk. It was obvious he wanted to say something.

"I'm sorry, but I've got to go," she said. "I'll call you again once I've spoken to Kristoffer."

"Thanks."

"We just got a phone call from one of Thomas Ahlström's neighbors," Erik said once she hung up. "She saw him with a woman on Sunday afternoon. And from the description she gave, it sounds like Lykke."

"Where did she see him?"

"In the garden outside his house. And it seemed like they'd had a real falling-out. The neighbor thought they were arguing about Hugo."

Lykke had initially told them that she had never met Thomas, and then that it had happened only the once—when he showed up in her garden. But they had now caught her in yet another lie.

"Why didn't the neighbor get in touch before now?"

Hanna was venting her frustration more than anything, but Erik answered her question:

"She went in for elective surgery on Monday."

"When are we going to bring this up with Lykke?" asked Hanna.

"She was just discharged. She and her lawyer are coming in to-morrow morning."

"Did you speak to the hospital, too?"

"Yes. At first the nurse didn't want to say anything other than that she has a history of eating disorders, but when I pressed him he told me that she hadn't eaten since Sunday."

"Sunday?"

"I know."

THE LAST DAY

How could Mille do this to him, after everything they've been through? Thomas is so angry that he genuinely feels like his blood is boiling. He sacrificed himself to avoid letting Mille down, and this is the thanks he gets?

The traffic has built up behind an enormous German camper van, and Thomas steps on the brake. Most people realize that over-taking it is impossible on this particular stretch of road, but the car behind him swings out into the other lane, and Thomas blasts his horn. The driver only just makes it back into the right-hand lane in time to avoid the approaching vehicle.

Mille refused to say who "they" are, and when Thomas de-manded to talk to them he said no. In the end he agreed to have a word with them himself, though he claimed it wouldn't change anything. That they need the houses to stash their cigarettes. They lost an entire shipment last autumn after leaving it in a van. Mille also tried to play down the whole thing, claiming the risks are minimal, and the extra money great. The risk might well be small for him; he doesn't have a family.

Thomas grips the wheel and casts a quick glance back in the rearview mirror. Hugo seems happy enough, and the car behind is staying put. He tried to give Mille the keys to the house, but his friend refused to take them. Said that since Thomas works for the real estate agent, he needs to be there in case anyone sees them and starts asking questions. Nothing like that has ever happened before. Why would anyone bat an eyelid at the sight of men carrying boxes in and out of a house in the process of being sold?

Why is Mille doing this? Thomas realizes it must be down to fear, and his grip tightens on the wheel. He can feel a panic attack building, but manages to breathe it away. He is stuck, and every attempt to break free just drags him deeper and deeper. Imagine if the other people show up.

The camper van turns off, and Thomas steps on the accelerator again. The car behind him turns, too. When he sees the sign for Hulterstad his pulse begins to slow to its usual rate, but he doesn't feel truly calm until he pulls up outside the house and lifts Hugo out of the car seat. The boy almost always has that effect on Thomas. Just holding him makes everything else seem less important. He has to go over to Södra Möckleby this evening, he has no other choice, but tonight will be the last time. Mille can say whatever he wants. It's hardly like he and the others can report Thomas for it—they'd be incriminating themselves if they did.

But they could kill me.

The thought sends a wave of nausea through him. No, Mille would never do that. But what about the others? He doesn't know. They could be afraid of him giving them away. Though if that's the case, they should be threatening him, or beating him up. It dawns on Thomas that he won't be able to help them with any more houses even if he wanted to, because he no longer has a job. But if he tells them that, there's no guarantee they'll actually believe him. Besides, Selene still works for the firm.

Thomas strokes Hugo's blond curls, but his son squirms out of his grip. The minute he is down on the ground he runs over to the small plastic slide. Thomas spotted it during a trip to Biltema, and he hadn't been able to resist. Jenny thinks he spoils Hugo, but Thomas struggles to see that as a problem.

Hugo climbs up to the top, but he can't quite manage to bring his legs around beneath him and slides back down on his stomach. The sound of his laugh as he tumbles onto the grass seems to bubble through Thomas. He picks up his son and tries to help him slide properly, but Hugo refuses to sit down and Thomas decides just to let him keep sliding on his belly.

He takes a picture next time Hugo reaches the top of the slide and sends it off to Jenny. *Cutie*, she replies, followed by a smiley face. And then: *I'm getting on the train soon.*

It's going to be so good to see you, Thomas writes back, adding a pulsing heart.

The thought rears its head again: that he should forget all about going to Södra Möckleby that evening. But it's as impossible as ever. He can't do that to Mille. A shipment of cigarettes is on its way, and there is no good place to stash them down by the harbor. Besides, he needs the money to pay off Hektor and get him to talk to Karl. Maybe he should take Selene for a nice lunch and clear the air with her once and for all. He just needs to get his job back first.

Somehow he needs to convince Mille that this is the last time. Thomas feels a flutter of fear. What if his visit to Mille has set something in motion? What if the others show up instead?

"Thirsty," says Hugo.

"Come inside with me, then."

"No."

Thomas doesn't like leaving Hugo alone outside. Yes, they have a fence around the garden, and the house isn't exactly on the main road, but the gate is broken and Hugo might be able to get it open himself. Then again, he seems so absorbed by his game right now. Thomas takes the jug of water out of the fridge, grabs two mugs and a pack of rice cakes. The sound of a car engine makes him glance outside.

A rusty car has pulled up on the other side of the fence. A series of nightmare scenarios race through Thomas's mind. He should never have left Hugo alone.

"Hugo!" he shouts, but the boy can't hear him through the glass.

He has just gotten onto his stomach to race down the slide again. In his world, all that exists is the sloping yellow plastic and the grass down below.

The car door opens, and Thomas springs into action. He runs out of the house, clearing the step in a single bound. He won't let them take Hugo.

55

W hy don't we go to Lilla Puben instead?" asked Erik. "They've got better beer."

Hanna agreed, but she couldn't tell him that. The others were already waiting in Kött & Bar, and were starting to get impatient. *Hungry* was the word Amer had used in the message he sent to ask how long they would be.

"Let me pick the place," said Hanna. "Before I change my mind."

"It was just a suggestion."

Erik was in a bad mood. Supriya didn't seem to be replying to his texts, and it was now the middle of the night in India. Since they were already running late, Hanna sped up.

"You in a hurry or something?"

"No, but I walk the same way I drive. Haven't you noticed?"

He actually laughed at that.

As they cut over the cobblestones in Larmtorget, she saw the others in the outdoor seating area. Everyone was there—even Carina and Ove. Amer was saying something, and Daniel seemed to be disagreeing. They were at a crucial stage of the investigation, but there was no denying that some of the pressure had eased once Hugo was found. They were exhausted and needed to recharge their batteries before they got back to work in the morning.

Erik wouldn't have noticed them if it weren't for Hanna nudging him in the side. He strode over to the railing.

"What are you guys doing here?" He sounded pleasantly surprised.

"Come in and sit down," said Amer.

The minute they did as he said, he handed them each a beer.

"I was planning to drive home later," said Hanna.

Amer turned the bottle so that she could see the label. It was alcohol-free. Erik's eyes were darting around the group. He seemed to be struggling to understand how the entire team could have ended up at the same table, and he turned to Hanna.

"Did you know about this?"

Hanna nodded, struggling not to laugh.

"So this whole thing was planned?"

"Yes, genius," said Amer, raising his glass. "Your last evening with the gang."

"Thanks," said Erik, holding up his own beer. "I'm getting all emotional. You won't have to put up with any more of my whining from tomorrow on."

His bad mood seemed to have completely evaporated. The waiter came over and took their orders. Aside from Erik, everyone wanted the burger. He ordered the Halloumi version.

Once the waiter had left, Ove raised his glass in another toast.

"Damn good work, everyone," he said. "Keep it up, because we're not done yet."

He and the press spokesperson had held a press conference that afternoon. Hanna hadn't watched it, but she could just imagine the headlines it might generate. "Hugo is Alive" and "Hugo Saved." Hanna hoped the journalists would leave Jenny and her son in peace. Bror and his daughter, too. The journalist from *Barometern* had tried calling her again, but she wanted to wait until she had managed to speak to Kristoffer before she got in touch.

Hugo was alive. Hanna lingered on that thought for a moment.

It was almost unbelievable, considering how long he had been missing. Everyone felt the same way—even Carina was smiling at her. Hanna's phone buzzed in her pocket, and she fished it out. Had Kristoffer finally responded?

You're not still in Kalmar, are you? I'd really like to see you.

Hanna didn't recognize the number, but the three bouncing dots below the message told her that another was on the way. She felt her phone vibrate.

Best wishes, Isak Aulin.

His message raised so many questions. Did this mean Isak knew she lived on Öland? Hanna didn't remember having told him that. And why did he want to see her?

"What's up?" Erik whispered.

"Nothing," she said, feeling the familiar infuriating redness spread across her cheeks.

She turned her attention to Daniel, who was busy ducking questions about the guy he was seeing. He didn't even want to share the man's name. Hanna pretended to need the toilet, in order to write back to Isak in peace. The restaurant was part of a hotel, so she paused not far from reception.

What is this about? she asked.

Just say yes, he wrote. *I'll explain when we meet.*

Hanna lowered her phone and watched as a dark-haired woman bought a beer from the bar and then made her way toward the stairs. She looked tired. Probably wanted to wind down alone in her room after a long day. Hanna couldn't say no, she realized. She needed to know what Isak wanted.

We can meet at Pipes in an hour.

Hanna had chosen a bar that was nowhere near the one she was currently in so that none of her colleagues would see her with Isak.

Thanks!

She went back out to join the others, but struggled to focus on either the food or the company. No one seemed to notice that she wasn't saying much. They had enough to talk about as it was. The conversation moved from Ove's grandchildren to the new roof Carina needed on her house and the fact that Amer's son had to wear glasses despite being only four. The minute Hanna finished her food, she excused herself and said her goodbyes. She noticed Erik watching her anxiously as she left.

HANNA SPOTTED ISAK the minute she stepped into Pipes. He was sitting with a half-empty glass in front of him, running his finger around the rim. He looked up and smiled, possibly relieved. Hanna felt butterflies in her stomach. She swallowed and made her way over to him.

"Thanks for coming," said Isak. "What would you like?"

"I'll get it."

Hanna turned around and walked the short distance to the bar, where she bought a non-alcoholic beer. Her car was parked down by the old bus station, and she wanted to be able to drive home. She did occasionally take the bus to the station, but she had an important interview with Lykke in the morning.

"Why did you want to see me?" she asked once she was sitting opposite Isak with her beer.

He gave her a tentative smile, and perhaps it was her lack of a reaction that made him turn to look out the window. She was so nervous she felt queasy, and had absolutely no idea how to behave. Hanna studied him in profile. His beard was shorter than she remembered it, and though he was only a few years older than her, she could see a smattering of gray in his hair. He was wearing a button-down.

"I'm glad you found the boy," he said, his eyes still fixed on the window.

"Me, too."

Did he just want to talk about Hugo? About how awful it had

been to feel like a suspect? But he never had been, not really. He was just a lead they had to follow up. Every investigation was full of them. Hanna took a deep breath, drawing in his scent. She could still smell his lemon shower gel, but he was also wearing aftershave, and it definitely contained nutmeg.

"It was tough when you came to the school and asked me all those questions," said Isak. "Especially the ones about my partner."

Hanna didn't know what to say. She slowly raised her glass to her mouth and took a sip.

"But I understand why you did it," he continued.

"So why did you want to see me?" she asked again.

Isak turned back to her and smiled. He was as nervous as she was, she realized.

"Because I can't stop thinking about you."

"Okay."

Okay? What kind of pathetic response was that? Her cheeks grew hot.

"I've been thinking about you, too," she hurried to add.

Hanna's mind felt utterly blank, so she took another sip of her beer. One part of her wanted to get up and leave. This was too much. It might actually have been easier if he'd started shouting at her.

"I never normally do this kind of thing," said Isak.

The word *okay* was on the tip of Hanna's tongue again, but she managed to hold back.

"Me, neither," she said instead.

"And I'm not violent. I really lost my temper with that boy, but all I did was grab his arm."

Hanna often heard that kind of excuse in interviews, but she couldn't work out how to react now. She desperately wanted to believe Isak.

The door opened, and a loud group of men in their mid-twenties came into the bar. It sounded like they were talking about a fight they had seen in the square. Isak waited until they sat down at a table toward the rear before he went on.

"That wasn't how I wanted you to find out about what happened to my partner. And the baby we were supposed to have."

The grief on his face made Hanna's throat tighten, and she wasn't sure whether she would be able to say anything.

"It must have been awful," she forced out.

"Yes, it was. And I know who you are. Or rather who your dad is."

Yet again, Hanna felt a powerful urge to get up and leave. She had been nervous with Fabian, of course, but never like this. The pleading look in Isak's eye was all that was keeping her there. She didn't want to leave, not really. What she wanted was to lean forward and run her fingers through his hair.

"I knew when we first met in the spring," Isak continued. "And I realized that you might be someone who understood."

"Understood what?"

"How shitty life can be sometimes."

Hanna stared at him. That was almost exactly what she had said to Erik after they spoke to Isak.

"Sorry for being so forward," he said. "I don't know what's got into me. Did I say that I can't stop thinking about you?"

"Yeah, you mentioned that," said Hanna.

This time she was the one who smiled. A small part of her still wanted to run, because she didn't know how to talk to Isak without coming across like an idiot. But she was so sick of always running, and she refused to let that part of her win out. Hanna leaned forward and breathed in his scent again.

FRIDAY, AUGUST 23

56

Hanna turned toward the morning sun that was seeping into the room. Her bedroom had a sloping ceiling, and the blind didn't quite fit. The light formed long, slender arms that seemed to be groping for her along the wall. Something was different, and it took her a moment to realize what it was. An absence, a lack. There was no longer any anxiety in her body.

The previous evening slowly came back to her. Isak's smile. His scent. His intense gaze, never leaving her. Once her initial nerves had faded she had found him so easy to talk to. She had been herself for once. Not taking a step back, watching and observing, like usual.

Toilet, shower, clothes, breakfast—that was her morning routine. She skipped the walk down to the water today. Neither her head nor her body needed to be cleansed of anything, and she didn't want to subject herself to the gravel track where the gray Volvo had almost mowed her down. Casting a sweeping glance all around her was the only precaution Hanna took as she stepped out of the house. In some strange way, yesterday's morning walk no longer felt real. Not in the same way as Isak's aftershave or his arms around her body as they hugged goodbye outside Pipes.

· · ·

IT WASN'T UNTIL HANNA parked outside the station in Kalmar that
her thoughts turned back to the investigation. To their imminent
interview with Lykke Henriksen. Who had killed Thomas Ahlström, and why? Hanna refused to give in until she knew. When
she stepped into the investigation room, Erik was the only person
there.

"Morning," she said. "Get much sleep last night?"

"A bit. You?"

"Why wouldn't I have?"

Erik had such a strange look on his face that Hanna wondered
if he had walked past Pipes on his way home to Varvsholmen. She
and Isak had stayed in the bar until it closed at eleven. But walking
quietly by didn't feel like Erik's thing; he was much more likely to
have knocked on the window and waved.

"I spoke to Isak."

Hanna sat down at her desk and switched on her computer
without a word. What did he mean, spoke to? Afterward? Hanna
hadn't thought the two men knew each other.

"Didn't he say?" asked Erik.

"No."

Hanna stared at the box where she was supposed to enter her
password. She couldn't remember a single letter or digit of it. If
they had spoken afterward, she wanted to know what Isak had
said about her, but how could she ask without sounding paranoid?

"He called me the day before yesterday," Erik explained. "He
was embarrassed about the way he reacted at the school. He also
asked me for your number, but I didn't give it to him."

"Why not?"

"We still hadn't found Hugo, it didn't feel like a good idea."

Hanna closed her eyes in frustration, but when she opened them
again she managed to enter her password and log in.

"So, how was it?" Erik continued.

"Nice."

Now that she had admitted who she was with, Hanna wanted to say more, but that desire vanished as Carina came into the room. Hanna clicked on the first unread email, but she couldn't take in a single word of it. Isak's arms were around her again, his beard tickling her chin. Their goodbye hug had lasted only a few seconds, but she hadn't wanted to let go. After one last deep breath, they had drifted apart. Each heading back to their own car.

And now? They hadn't made any plans, and Hanna didn't know if she dared get in touch.

Amer came into the room just behind Carina, walking straight over to his standing desk beside Erik's.

"Did I miss something?" he asked, his eyes darting between them.

"No." Erik smiled. "Thanks for last night."

"Thanks yourself," said Amer. "What time do they land again?"

"Four thirty this afternoon."

Hanna grabbed her phone and brought up the first message from Isak. The one in which he had written that he really wanted to see her and she hadn't known why. It really wasn't any more complicated than that, simply saying what you wanted to say. Erik studied her with a smile.

"What?" she asked, though she already knew.

"Nothing."

Amer's curious gaze flitted between them. Hanna put her phone screen-down on the desk and tried to focus on her emails. She deleted the alerts from HR about the ongoing recruitment of both officers and civilian support staff in the Southern Police District.

Just before eight thirty, they all went through to the meeting room. Lykke was due to arrive for her interview at nine.

"Just a quick meeting today," said Ove. "Mille Bergman's name cropped up in the investigation into cigarette smuggling."

"Cropped up how?" asked Daniel.

"He owned the fishing hut the cigarettes were stashed in once they came ashore, but he claimed the smugglers had broken in. The examination of the hut backed up that claim. There was no real evidence he was involved, so his name was quickly eliminated."

"What should we do?" asked Hanna.

"Let's hold off on making a decision until the Swede who was convicted of smuggling has been re-interviewed." Ove straightened his glasses before he brought up an image of the shoe print. "The technicians say that the shoe that made this print likely has some damage to the sole. You see the pale line toward the top right? Unfortunately, they haven't managed to identify the make yet."

"Could that be because the shoe isn't Swedish?" asked Erik.

"Interesting thought," said Ove. "I'll pass that on to the technicians."

"I have one more thing to add about Lykke Henriksen," said Daniel. "I called around among her teachers and the people she studied with. Everyone at the university described her as reserved and ambitious, but the head teacher of her high school said that she was suspended for two weeks during her second year there."

"What happened?" asked Hanna.

"She assaulted another student."

57

The reception desk called up at ten to nine to let them know that Lykke Henriksen had arrived. Erik left the morning meeting to bring her up while Hanna got the interview room ready. He found himself smiling at the thought of how embarrassed she had seemed earlier, but it could only be a good thing if she met someone, and Isak was probably a good guy after all.

Less than eight hours to go, then Erik would finally be able to hug Supriya and Nila. He had been so anxious that the night had been a write-off, relaxing only enough to get some sleep once he saw Supriya's message saying that she and Nila were at the airport, about to board the plane. Despite the lack of sleep, he didn't feel tired. Erik glanced at his watch. They should have landed in Frankfurt by now. Why hadn't Supriya been in touch? She hadn't given him any kind of explanation for her earlier silence, just that it was great news that Hugo had been found.

Erik repressed his longing and opened the door to reception. Lykke clearly hadn't managed to get much sleep, either. The dark circles beneath her eyes were enormous. Her lawyer held out a hand to support her as she got up, but Lykke ignored it. Erik had met the lawyer on several occasions, and he liked her—though he knew that was partly because she was from Finland, and he had a special fondness for her accent.

Lykke almost seemed to be hugging herself as she walked down the corridor, and Erik tried not to talk to her. He could tell it would be pointless. And though he knew he shouldn't, he opened the flight tracker app he had downloaded onto his phone and saw that the plane his wife and daughter had hopefully boarded was still in the sky above Austria.

Hanna was waiting for them in the interview room. She said hello, but Lykke slumped into the other armchair without responding. After asking whether they would like anything to drink—both said no, the lawyer verbally and Lykke with a shake of her head—Hanna started the tape recorder and introduced everyone present.

"You took the natural sciences line at Lars Kagg School here in Kalmar," said Erik.

Lykke nodded, only adding a "Yes" when she was asked to speak up. She kept rubbing her arm, where there was some sort of stain on her sleeve. She and her clothes both looked like they could do with a good wash.

"How did you get on with your classmates?"

Lykke glanced at her lawyer, possibly because she was confused by the question. The lawyer gave her an encouraging smile.

"Most of them were nice," said Lykke.

She turned to her lawyer again, and this time the woman decided to interject.

"Why are you asking about this?"

Erik ignored her question and maintained his focus on Lykke.

"You were suspended from school for two weeks in the spring term of your second year there. Could you tell us about that?"

Lykke shuffled forward in her armchair. It looked like she wanted to keep going onto the floor.

"I don't want to talk about that," she said. "It's got nothing to do with this."

"We'll be the judge of that," said Hanna. "Go on."

"There was a girl in my class who was always annoying me.

Eventually I got sick of it and threw a tray of food at her. I didn't mean for it to hit her so badly."

"What happened to the girl?" asked Erik.

"She had to have a couple of stitches on her forehead."

"Do you often have trouble restraining yourself like that?"

Lykke didn't answer, though her silence spoke volumes.

"Tell the detectives about Vaxholm," said her lawyer.

Lykke peered up at Erik, as though she were seeking his permission. He gave it to her. They could always return to her suspension later, if necessary.

"Yeah, so, when we spoke before you asked if I had any evidence. Of my relationship with Roger, I mean," said Lykke. "We spent a weekend together in Vaxholm."

Erik thought Lykke seemed tired and stressed, but she was also more present than she had been in any of their previous interviews.

"Go on," said Hanna.

"We stayed at Waxholms Hotell from the nineteenth to the twentieth of April. He paid for everything. And on the Saturday we went on a long walk and ate at Hamnkrogen. Someone must have seen us."

"Thank you," said Hanna. "We'll look into it."

"Let's talk about your father, Thomas," said Erik. "Tell us about the second time you met him."

Lykke's eyes widened, and she almost seemed to be radiating panic. The reaction gave Erik hope.

"We have a witness who saw you in his garden," he continued.

The way her lawyer's mouth twitched suggested that this was news to her. Lykke shrank back in the armchair, covering her eyes with her hands.

"You need to tell us what happened," said Hanna.

"I know," Lykke mumbled from behind her hands. "It's just so hard."

She let her hands drop to her knees after a moment or two.

Raised her eyes, though they didn't seem to get any higher than her questioners' chins.

"I went over there to talk to him."

Both her voice and her hands were trembling.

"Why?" asked Erik.

"Because I wasn't very nice to him when he showed up at my house in Grönhögen. I wanted to apologize."

"And did you?"

"No."

"Why not?" asked Hanna.

"I never got that far."

The lawyer glanced at her client, but didn't interject. Lykke seemed to take the look as a sign of support.

"I saw Hugo in the garden," she said. "And that was when I realized Thomas had another child that he'd chosen not to abandon. Hugo was alone, and I went over to him. But then Thomas came running, screaming at me like I was an intruder."

"Did the two of you fight?"

"I guess I shouted a few things back."

"Like what?" asked Hanna.

"I can't remember. I was so angry. It felt like I didn't mean a thing to him, but that little boy . . . you could tell just how much Thomas loved him."

Lykke bit her lower lip.

"You know what?" said Hanna. "I think you know exactly what you said, and that's why you're finding this so hard."

Lykke buried her face in her hands again.

"What did you shout?" Hanna asked calmly.

"You and your stupid kid can go to hell," Lykke sobbed. "And that I wished it was him who died, not Mom."

Her hands dropped to her lap, and she stared down at them.

"What happened then?" asked Erik.

"I couldn't stay there. I ran off, but Thomas came after me. He started shouting again, but I didn't hear what he said. I honestly didn't."

Those last words were clearly aimed at Hanna.

"Did you see him again after that?" Erik pressed her.

"No."

"Did you kill Thomas?" asked Hanna.

"No."

Lykke forced herself to meet their eyes.

"No, I didn't kill him, but I did more than just shout. I raised my hand to Hugo, in that moment when I was so angry. Thomas probably thought I was about to hit him, because he tried to grab me. I pushed Thomas, really hard. And he fell over backward."

58

The female detective brought the interview to a close, but despite hearing every word she said, Lykke didn't quite dare believe her. She remained seated, waiting for the next question. For them to tell her she was under arrest or whatever it was called, because they thought she had killed her father. To be locked in a cell for nights on end. She had been so nervous ahead of the interview that she couldn't sleep, but she had managed to eat a bowl of soured milk for breakfast. Before they discharged her from the hospital yesterday they had made her speak to a psychiatrist, and she had another appointment scheduled for next week. If she hadn't started eating by then, she risked being admitted again.

The weeks Lykke had spent on a psychiatric ward had been awful, and she didn't want to go back there. Or to a cell. She hated being locked up. Not being in control. She could no longer influence what the police thought of her, but she had managed to get over her aversion to food once before, and she knew she had to do it again.

Lykke could still remember the day she got home from the hospital as a teenager as though it were yesterday. She had sat down in the garden with a woolen blanket wrapped around her shoulders, shivering though it was the middle of July. A common brimstone fluttered by, and its movements fascinated her. The strange mix of determination and randomness. The butterfly landed on one of the toad lilies for a few seconds before lifting off again. It left her convinced that she wanted to become a biologist.

The others got up, so Lykke did the same. They really did seem to be letting her go, because the male detective accompanied them back out to reception. The lawyer stopped her once they got outside.

"Do you have any questions?"

Lykke shook her head.

"Give me a call if you do."

Lykke nodded. She couldn't talk right now. The lawyer squeezed her arm and headed off to her car. Lykke did the same, but the minute she sat down behind the wheel she began to cry. Her tears were for everything she had failed to do. Making Roger love her. Thomas, too. Being accepted into the research program. Knowing what to do with her life. But most of all: getting to meet Hugo. The nurse who had said he would check with Jenny had never come back. Maybe he had decided not to bother. If Lykke got in touch with Jenny herself, Jenny would probably accuse her of being a stalker.

She just couldn't shake the guilt. Everything might have been different if Lykke had stayed and talked to Thomas outside his house. If she hadn't been such a damn idiot.

I wish it was you who'd died!

How could a person say something like that to their own father? She had only just found him when she lost him again. Her last memory of Thomas was of him shouting and running toward her car. Trying to tear the door open. The need to see Hugo had overpowered her. That tiny boy who shared so many of her genes. Lykke lowered her head to the steering wheel. Why had she raised her hand to him like that?

The lawyer had said she could help Lykke sue the university. That they likely hadn't handled her application for the research program properly. But Lykke was no longer sure she even wanted to do it, nor that she wanted to return to Uppsala.

It would be hard to avoid Roger there.

She raised her head and met her eye in the rearview mirror. Rubbed at the mark the wheel had left behind. The lawyer had been hesitant when it came to reporting Roger to the police.

If you hadn't hit him . . .

If she hadn't hit him, then she might have stood a chance. But what was she supposed to do? Let him strangle her? Rape her? That was the only part she hadn't mentioned to the police: that Roger had forced his hand inside her trousers, groping between her legs and saying that he should fuck her one last time.

He had apologized for that part, though that was probably more out of fear than anything.

The lawyer had told her to hold on to the messages from Roger in case she did ever decide to report him. And until the investigation into Thomas's death was over. She had tried to reassure Lykke, told her that the police were fumbling in the dark, that it was obvious they didn't have anything to connect her to the murder. Lykke took out her phone and scrolled down to one of Roger's messages.

Sorry, I can't. Got loads of exams to mark.

He had sent that a month or so after Vaxholm, when Lykke suggested going away for the weekend again, longing for the bubble they had been in while they were together. Largely because she had noticed the difference in the way he looked at her and touched her. The noes came increasingly often, and on some level she had known that he no longer wanted her, though she hadn't been able to accept that. But when she saw his wife and child, she had realized that it was all just a game to him. Right there and then, she honestly could have killed him, and that insight terrified her.

Lykke was convinced the police had understood that. And though she had told them the truth, she wasn't sure it would help. She had pushed Thomas. Sometimes that was all it took for a person to die.

Lykke was back in Vaxholm. Walking along its picturesque

streets. Eating a three-course dinner at Hamnkrogen. She saw the way Roger looked her in the eye and told her that he loved her. Remembered how that had made her feel. And she didn't know how she would ever be able to trust anyone again.

Lykke started the engine and drove away. She wanted to get back to Grönhögen. To her toad lilies and butterflies. To the sea.

The minute she got home, she changed into her swimsuit. The soured milk from breakfast and the nutrients they had forced into her in the hospital had staved off the worst of the chill. She felt dirty, like she needed to burn off some stress, and with a towel wrapped around her body, she made her way down to the rocky beach close to the house. She felt more like jumping into the depths of the old limestone quarry, but the water was colder there, and she didn't want to bump into anyone else.

She dropped her towel to the ground and picked her way across the slippery stones. As soon as the water was deep enough, she began to swim. Straight out. She dipped beneath the surface and took several powerful strokes. Held her breath until it felt like her lungs might burst.

When she finally broke the surface, she realized she wasn't alone. On a rock around a hundred meters away, she saw a seal lying with its head toward her. When it spotted her, it slipped back into the water and disappeared.

Lykke paused, treading water. She felt the pull of the darkness, the depths, but she didn't want to go down there. She turned around and swam back to the shore.

THE LAST DAY

"Hugo!" Thomas shouts.

From the corner of his eye, he sees the driver of the car climb over the fence into the garden. He feels the same sheer terror he did back at the playground that morning. The fear that he is about to lose Hugo and have to answer to Jenny. Hugo turns to look at him, but he doesn't move.

"No!" Thomas roars at the driver. "Damn it!"

When he looks up, he realizes that it is Lykke. She stops dead and stares at him without saying anything. Her face has crumpled at his reaction.

"Sorry," he says.

The panic pumping through his veins means the word comes out as a croak. He can't make sense of her. She was the one who wrote to him, but when he called her she didn't want to speak, and when he went over to see her she shouted at him for the way he treated Natalie. Screamed that she hated him.

And yet: She is his daughter. This is all his fault. Things ended up this way because he betrayed her. He wants nothing more than to walk over to her and give her a hug.

Lykke takes a few steps toward Hugo on the slide, and the objection that comes out of his mouth is a sheer reflex. The look his daughter gives him is full of such rage that Thomas is shocked. He can't manage to speak.

"Fuck you!" she shouts. "You didn't give a shit about me, but him . . . You and your stupid kid can go to hell."

She takes another few steps forward and raises her arm. What the hell is she doing? Is she going to hit Hugo? The boy looks terrified.

"Stop it," Thomas hisses.

"I hate you," Lykke sobs.

Thomas hurries over to comfort her, but Lykke gives him a shove in the chest.

"I wish it was you who'd died!" she shouts. "Not Mom."

She shoves him so hard that Thomas loses his balance and lands on his backside, the air knocked out of him.

Lykke turns around and rushes back toward the fence.

"Stop!" Thomas shouts.

He sounds more irritable than he intended, and Lykke doesn't listen, of course. She climbs over the fence. Thomas's shock fades and he gets back onto his feet and starts running, but she is already in the car. He reaches for the handle, but the metal jolts backward beneath his hand, and he has to jump to one side. The Škoda swings around the corner and speeds away.

Thomas swears in frustration, and Hugo mimics him. It'll be just his luck if the first words the boy says after they pick up Jenny from the station are *fucking hell*. Should he go after Lykke? No, that's a terrible idea. Thomas returns to the garden and picks up Hugo instead. Buries his nose in his hair. Lykke just wanted to provoke him with her outburst toward Hugo, and as ever he let her down.

"Fucking hell," the boy says, and giggles.

He already seems to have forgotten the raised voices that were just swirling around him.

"Yes," says Thomas. "Fucking shitty hell. But those are very bad words."

Thomas carries Hugo over to the porch and sets him down there. He goes back into the kitchen to fetch the tray and hands his son one of the rice cakes. He isn't hungry, but he takes one for himself, too.

The meeting with Lykke feels like a dull ache in his gut. How should he deal with her? Perhaps the best approach would be to wait until she contacts him again, to give her time, though there is no guarantee she ever will. Thomas wonders if he should write her a letter and try to explain himself, but writing has never been his strong suit. He doesn't regret leaving Natalie, but he should have made more of an effort to keep Lykke in his life.

But how would that have worked? In the years after he and Natalie broke up, he wasn't fit to be anyone's father. For the first time, he really understands what he put Natalie through. She was younger than him, and she likely had dreams of doing something other than taking care of an infant. She sometimes talked about moving to New York and working in a bar. She once mentioned going to Berlin. Thomas uses Natalie's parents to push back some of his guilt. They helped her, in a way his own parents never would have.

"Full!" says Hugo, getting to his feet.

He sways as he tries to make his way down the step, and Thomas reaches out and grabs him.

"I do it," his son protests.

"I know you can do it."

Thomas checks the time on his phone. He needs to be in Södra Möckleby in just over three hours, and he has no choice but to take Hugo with him. Their neighbor could probably watch him, but he doesn't want to have to come up with an excuse. Besides, he wants Hugo with him when he picks up Jenny from the station.

Maybe he could tell her about Lykke on the way home? It'll be

far worse if she finds out some other way. A sudden, terrible suspicion hits him: Lykke has already been in touch with Jenny. But
why would she do that? To tell her what an asshole he is?

Hugo is on his way toward the gate in the fence.

"Wait," says Thomas, hurrying after him. "Where are you
going?"

"Cows!"

"No, not today."

Hugo's little face crumples.

"Do you want a bath?" asks Thomas. During the heat wave last
week, he took Hugo down to the beach to splash around in the
shallows, but there is no time for that today.

The boy's features smooth out, and he runs back toward the
house. Hugo can just about reach the door handle, but he can't
quite manage to open the door himself.

"I'm coming," says Thomas.

Right then, his phone starts ringing. It's Karl. Thomas stares
down at the name on the screen, unsure what to do. His anger over
how Karl has treated him immediately flares up again, but he
doesn't want to let it out while he is with Hugo. Not again. It's bad
enough that Hugo had to see what happened between him and
Lykke.

"Dada!"

Thomas opens the door as he accepts the call.

"Sorry," says Karl.

Thomas hadn't been expecting to hear that, and he is stunned
into silence.

"I was an idiot earlier," his boss continues. "I know how hard
you've been trying at work."

Thomas still doesn't speak. Hugo tears off his clothes on the way
through to the bathroom, and Thomas kicks them toward the
washing basket. He turns on the taps, holding his fingers in the
water to make sure the temperature is okay. Karl starts talking

about how worried he and Madeleine are about Selene, and Thomas can't work out where the conversation is going.

"I don't want to burden you with Selene's depression," Karl eventually says. "But I've also realized that it's not fair to punish you for something that isn't your fault. So what I wanted to say is that I've changed my mind."

"What do you mean?"

He hears Karl's words, but it's as though he can't quite process them.

"It wasn't right of me to say that you couldn't keep working for us. So I've decided to give you another chance."

"You mean I haven't lost my job?"

"No, you haven't."

Neither man speaks for a few seconds as the news sinks in. Thomas wonders what made Karl change his mind, but he is too worked up to dig any deeper. He wants his boss to keep groveling, to admit how weak and pathetic what he did was, but his anger quickly fades and a sense of relief takes over.

"Thank you," he says. "I promise you won't regret it."

Thomas clamps the phone between his ear and his shoulder and lifts Hugo into the tub.

"I hope not," says Karl. "I'll talk to the kids. We can work this out. We still have a few months before your paternity leave ends anyway."

"Thank you," Thomas says again.

He hangs up and feels the sense of relief spread through him, turning into a bubbling joy. He laughs. This is almost too good to be true, and he has to check his call list to make sure Karl really did just phone him. He has a job to go back to. He no longer needs to tell Jenny that he was fired. Hugo laughs, too, reaching for the plastic ducks and pulling them into the water.

Thomas grabs one of the ducks and makes it swim toward Hugo, quacking. It's crazy how well his life seems to have turned out despite everything. He really wouldn't have thought it possible just a few years ago. When he picks Jenny up that evening, he'll tell her that he loves her. If he starts with that, he is sure she can handle him telling her that he has a daughter. Thomas knows that Lykke needs to rage against him, but this time he isn't going to give up on her.

59

Hanna turned her phone over to check the screen for what was probably the tenth time. There were no new messages, so she put it down again. She had started writing a message to Isak earlier, but quickly deleted it. What could she say that didn't sound like way too much or way too little?

She turned her attention back to the summary she was busy writing instead. Waxholms Hotell had confirmed that Roger Wasselius had spent the night there on April 19, but hadn't been able to provide the team with any information about his guest. They now knew that Roger had lied to his wife about that weekend, however. She had thought he was attending a conference, but according to the university there was no such event that weekend. Lykke Henriksen had likely been telling the truth about their affair.

Ove popped his head into the investigation room.

"It's time to put some pressure on Mille Bergman," he said. "Where's Erik?"

"He isn't back from lunch yet."

After realizing that he didn't have any of Supriya's favorite wine at home, Erik had leaped up and hurried off. Their plane from Mumbai was delayed, but that just meant they had less of a layover in Frankfurt. Hanna knew far more about their travel plans than she cared to.

"Head over there as soon as he gets back."

"Has something come up?" asked Hanna.

"The investigator from Customs spoke to the Swede who was convicted of smuggling cigarettes," said Ove. "And this time he admitted to playing five-a-side soccer with Mille."

"Five-a-side?"

"Yes, but that's not the important part," said Ove. "During the last investigation he claimed not to know who Mille was. I've got the green light to put Mille under surveillance for a few days, starting tomorrow."

Hanna called Mille Bergman as soon as Ove left the room, but he didn't pick up. She tried his shop instead, but got a busy tone. Ten minutes later, she got the same result. Erik reappeared with two shopping bags, one from the liquor store and another from Gerda's Tea and Coffee.

"Chocolate," he explained when he saw Hanna looking at them. "I realized I needed to get something for Nila, too."

"Ove wants us to go over to Öland to track Mille Bergman down," she said, recapping what the boss had told her.

Erik nodded. "Sure, that's better than watching the clock here."

Hanna glanced at the time on her computer: 13:08. Supriya and Nila would be landing in Kalmar in just over three hours. She grabbed her phone and, though she knew there were no new messages from Isak—she had turned up the volume—she couldn't help but feel a flash of hope as she turned it over. Erik yawned, his mouth opening so wide that his jaw clicked.

"Sorry," he said. "The lack of sleep is really catching up with me."

"I'll drive," said Hanna.

"Works for me."

"You can get some sleep in the car."

"Pff, you just want me to be quiet."

When they got into the car, Erik opened the app he had downloaded to track the flight from Germany.

"They're in Swedish airspace now," he said with a smile. "I can't believe I get to see them soon. Six weeks. It's crazy how long they've been gone."

He gazed out through the windshield, as though he thought he might be able to see the plane. Supriya and Nila first had to fly to Stockholm before the final leg to Kalmar.

"Have you spoken to your brother yet, by the way?"

"No."

Hanna hadn't sent any more text messages. If Kristoffer continued to ignore her, she would have to take some time off and go over to London to force him to talk to her. Right now she couldn't see any other way forward. Ingrid had suggested she talk to Ester's daughter again, but that was the last thing Hanna felt like doing.

"What about Isak, then?"

Hanna shook her head.

There were no free parking spaces outside the tobacconist, so she pulled over in the cycle lane. The same young man was behind the counter as on their previous visit. He was on the phone, and it sounded like he was planning a party.

"It's my bro's twentieth," he explained once he hung up.

"Is Mille Bergman here?" asked Hanna.

"He just nipped out."

"Where did he go?"

"Friberg Properties."

Hanna and Erik headed over to the real estate agency, but Karl was the only person there. He glanced up as they came in, but didn't get up from his desk.

"We heard Mille was coming over here," said Hanna.

"He and Selene stepped out."

"Why?"

"I don't know," Karl said with a sigh, jabbing at his keyboard with his index fingers. "They probably wanted to talk about something they didn't want me to hear."

"What size shoes do you wear?"

"Forty-three," said Karl, still not taking his eyes off the screen. He was wearing the same kind of polished black leather shoes as his son. Hanna and Erik went back outside, but she couldn't see any sign of Mille and Selene. It felt like they had no choice but to wait. They really did need to get ahold of Mille Bergman so that they could confront him with the latest information.

"Should we sit down somewhere?" asked Erik.

"Are you hungry already?"

"A bit. Just had a sandwich for lunch."

Hanna went back into Friberg Properties and grabbed a few sweets from the bowl. All she got from Karl was a stressed glance. Hektor must have been in the toilet earlier, because he was now back in the office, and the look he gave her was considerably more searching. By the time Hanna came back out onto the street, Erik was gone. She dropped the sweets into her pocket and set off looking for him. Her phone beeped, and she assumed it must be him, but it was Isak.

Thanks for a great evening yesterday. At the risk of seeming forward: would you like to do something again tonight?

Yes, Hanna wrote back before she had time to think.

Great! Färjestaden? I can book a table at Seasalt for 7.

Hanna sent him a thumbs-up. The rush once it was done made her grin from cheek to cheek. For a few seconds, she was back in his arms, his beard against her cheek. She would get to see Isak again that evening.

As Hanna rounded the corner, she spotted Erik's back. She was just about to say something when the sound of raised voices stopped her in her tracks. Erik turned to her and nodded.

The voices belonged to a man and a woman, and judging by their tone, they were arguing. Hanna couldn't quite make out what they were saying. She and Erik moved closer.

"Stop lying," said the man.

"I'm not."

"Yeah, you are, I fucking know you."

"And I know you."

They were so close now, and Hanna almost walked straight into them as she stepped forward.

"Hi," she said.

Both were equally shocked.

"We need to talk to you," she said to Mille, before turning to Selene: "And from the sounds of it, we need to talk to you, too. Go and wait for us in the office for the time being."

Selene did as she was told without another word.

"Why do you want to talk to me?" asked Mille.

"Your name popped up in an old investigation," said Erik. "Into cigarette smuggling. Are you still involved in that kind of thing?"

"I've never smuggled anything," said Mille. "They broke into my fishing hut."

"Was Thomas involved?"

"Not as far as I know."

"How often do you play five-a-side?" asked Hanna.

"Once or twice a week. Why?"

"I've been thinking about taking it up. Seems like you can make all kinds of interesting friends there."

Mille glared at her. It was obvious their questions were making him uncomfortable. He didn't deny playing soccer with the convicted Swede, though he insisted it was a coincidence. Hanna hadn't been expecting a confession, but she now knew that the people investigating Thomas Ahlström's murder had found a link to the cigarette smuggling. Perhaps he would give himself away once they started tailing him.

"What size are your feet?"

"Forty-four, why?"

It was a shame they didn't know much more about the shoe than that it was probably around a forty-two—though even with an exact size, they wouldn't be able to rule anyone out. They needed to find the actual shoes that had left the print by the fireplace. Hanna looked around and saw a flower bed nearby.

"I want you to step on the soil over there," she said.

Mille's eyes widened, and she thought he was about to refuse, but he walked slowly over to the flower bed and pressed his foot down on the soil. The pattern of the sole was completely different than the one left in the house.

"What is Selene lying about?" asked Erik.

"Everything."

"Could you be more specific?"

"She was in love with Thomas, and believe me, I know how she gets. After I dumped her she threw a rock through my kitchen window, and she kept calling and harassing me. Selene killed him, I'm telling you."

60

They watched Mille Bergman hurry back to his shop as though he couldn't get away from them quickly enough. The man was behaving like he had something to hide, Erik was sure of it.

"What do you think?" asked Hanna.

"That he's guilty. He was trying to get us to turn our focus elsewhere with all his talk about Selene."

"Maybe," Hanna conceded. "It'll be interesting to see what she has to say."

Selene was at her desk when they got back to the office, but unlike Karl she immediately got to her feet.

"It'd be better if we did this outside," she said.

Karl cast a quick glance in their direction and then turned his attention back to the computer screen. Hektor appeared from the pantry, much more smartly dressed than he had been when they went over to his house. He was wearing suit trousers and a shirt rather than jogging bottoms and a T-shirt, but his clothing couldn't hide just how tired he looked. Perhaps he wasn't quite back to full health yet. He marched over to them.

"Why do you want to talk to Selene?" he asked.

Selene put a hand on her brother's arm and shook her head, and that was enough to make him back off.

"What were you and Mille talking about?" Erik asked her once they were out on the street.

Selene glanced anxiously around.

"He's gone," said Hanna. "But we can talk in the car if you'd prefer."

The thought of getting into a police car seemed to make Selene even more nervous.

"We were talking about Thomas," she said.

"What about him?"

"How it's so sad that he's dead. We were probably the two people who knew him best. Well, other than Jenny. . . ."

"What do you think happened?" asked Erik.

"How am I supposed to know?"

"Why did Thomas want the keys?" asked Hanna.

Selene took another step away from the office and shook her head in despair.

"You need to tell us the truth," said Erik. "This is a murder investigation."

"But I've told you I don't know."

Erik reached out to her.

"Okay!" Selene shouted, turning toward the office. When she next spoke, her voice was much lower: "I think Thomas was hiding some kind of stolen goods in the house."

"Was that what you were talking about with Mille?"

"Yes, but he got really angry. Said I was lying."

"What made you think it was stolen goods?" asked Hanna.

"I've been going over and over everything in my head and that's the only thing that makes sense. That Mille made him do it. He'd never do anything like that otherwise."

Selene glanced toward the office again, but her eyes bounced back when she realized Hektor was looking out at them.

"Go on," said Erik. "What were you going to say?"

"I think Mille used to do that kind of thing when we were together," said Selene. "That's why it didn't work out."

"You think?" Hanna pressed her.

A couple in their forties walked by a few meters away, heading for the harbor. The good weather was on its way back, and there were more people out and about. All three watched the couple pass. Selene waited until they were out of earshot before she went on.

"Yeah, he used to get these phone calls, and he always went outside to answer. At first I thought he was cheating on me, and he totally lost it when I confronted him. A guy paid him a visit once, too. He spoke English with an accent and he looked like . . . like some kind of Eastern European criminal, which I'm probably not meant to say."

"When was this?" asked Erik.

"Last autumn. November, I think. It was before the snow."

"What did they talk about?"

"I don't know. Mille told me to get out."

"Did you see anything else?"

"There was a car outside."

"What kind of car?"

"A really small one, dark blue. I don't know what make it was, but the registration plate started with XL. That's all I saw. I was in such a hurry to leave."

"How can you remember all this?" Hanna wanted to know. "It was almost a year ago."

"Because I knew something wasn't right, and I remember that the letters XL made me think extra-large."

Erik was annoyed that Selene hadn't mentioned any of this earlier, but there was no denying it was a breakthrough in the investigation. They now had it confirmed from a second source that Mille—and likely also Thomas—was involved in something illegal, and Selene had also shared details that they hadn't heard before.

"I'm scared," said Selene, sensing his irritation. "That's why I didn't say anything. Imagine if something happens to me now."

"It's good that you've told us," said Erik.

"Can I go?"

"Soon," said Hanna. "Mille told us you were in love with Thomas. Is that true?"

"Yes. I don't know if *love* is the right word, but I definitely had feelings for him. I didn't do anything about it, though. He was married."

"According to Mille you didn't take it very well when the two of you broke up."

"What do you mean?" Selene's cheeks turned an angry shade of red.

"Is it true that you put a rock through his kitchen window?"

"Yes," said Selene.

"He also claimed you killed Thomas," Hanna continued.

"What? No! He's lying."

The redness spread to the rest of her face, and her breathing grew labored. For a moment Erik was worried she might be about to collapse like Lykke had, but she managed to compose herself.

"He's lying," she said, her voice slightly calmer this time.

They let Selene go on the condition that she remained available in case they had any further questions. Erik glanced at his watch.

"We need to question Mille again," he said. "But maybe it can wait until tomorrow? It would be good if we looked into the blue car first. Plus I don't want to be late to the airport."

"Are you really planning to work tomorrow?"

"I'm guessing they'll both be jet-lagged anyway," said Erik. "So I can come in for a while in the morning. Monday feels like too long to wait."

"I can handle it on my own otherwise."

"That's hardly a good idea."

"I'm a big girl."

Erik hesitated.

"I'll drive," said Hanna. "And you can discuss it with Ove."

Erik brought Ove up to speed on the latest developments: that Mille and Selene were essentially blaming each other. Their boss said he would task someone with looking into the car right away, and someone else with digging deeper into Selene's background.

"Hold off on the interview until tomorrow," he said. "We won't have him under surveillance until then anyway."

As soon as they ended the call, Erik phoned Mille. He didn't pick up on his mobile, but the man behind the counter in the tobacconist handed the phone over to him.

"What do you want now?" he asked once he realized who it was.

"Some new information has come to light," said Erik. "So I'd like you to be at the station at ten a.m. tomorrow for another interview."

"What information?"

"We can go over that in the morning."

"And if I refuse?"

"We'll pick you up."

Mille slammed down the phone.

"We don't have enough evidence," said Hanna.

"I know. But getting him to talk is our best shot. Either that or the car leading somewhere. Or that we manage to put enough pressure on him that he gives himself away."

"Do you really think he's our killer?"

"Yeah, it seems pretty likely. Or whoever they were working for. I don't think he's right about Selene."

"What about Lykke?"

"No," said Erik. "It feels like she finally told us the truth in that last interview, and we've got no evidence to suggest that she saw Thomas again after the argument in his garden."

Erik needed to pick up his own car, so he went back to the station with Hanna. He got to the airport with half an hour to spare, and sat down to wait on a bench. In an attempt to make the wait somewhat bearable, he opened the Tetris app on his phone, but he couldn't concentrate on the colorful blocks. After just a few minutes he gave up and walked over to the window.

"Who are you waiting for?" the woman beside him asked.

"My wife and daughter."

"I'm finally going to meet my grandson."

The plane from Stockholm eventually began making its approach, and Erik held his palms to the glass. He had to make a real effort not to press his whole body up against it. Right then he remembered he had left both the wine and the chocolate at the station, and the realization made him feel like sobbing.

The passengers began to disembark and make their way toward the arrivals hall. What if they hadn't boarded the plane in Stockholm after all? Just as the pressure began to build, he spotted her. Nila came down the steps and waved.

She knew he was waiting for her there.

"Is that your daughter?" asked the woman.

"Yes."

He saw Nila speed up. Could see she was excited too. Supriya didn't seem to be in quite as much of a rush, though she was likely tired.

They finally came inside, and he wrapped his arms around his wife and daughter. From the corner of one eye, he saw the woman beside him standing in front of a young boy of around five. She tentatively held her arms out to him, and the boy hesitated. There was a story there, but right now Erik didn't care.

"God, I've missed you both."

61

Once she got back to the station, Hanna started going through the interview transcripts and forensics reports that had come in. She didn't really need to look for the blue car—that was someone else's job—but she did it anyway, in the notes from the door-knocking and other witness statements. More than anything she wanted to take a step back and get an overview of the case, to look at everything they knew with a fresh pair of eyes. Like Erik, she didn't believe that Lykke had killed Thomas, but she wasn't quite as convinced that his death had anything to do with the smuggling ring.

Her thoughts drifted back to what Mille had said about Selene. It bothered her that she had only just now brought up the car and her suspicions.

Hanna called Madeleine Friberg. She wanted to hear what she had to say about her daughter.

"Are you trying to get ahold of Karl again?" Madeleine asked. "He promised he'd answer his phone, but he's working like a madman right now."

"It was actually you I wanted to talk to," said Hanna.

"Me?" Madeleine laughed nervously. "Why?"

"What did you make of your daughter's relationship with Mille Bergman?"

Madeleine was quiet for a moment or two.

"You should probably talk to Selene about that."

"I already have," said Hanna. "Now I'm asking you."

"Selene has always struggled with relationships."

"Why?"

"Because she has periods when she isn't well."

"Does she have an official diagnosis?"

"Recurrent depressive disorder."

"Did she ever talk to you about Thomas Ahlström?"

"They didn't have a relationship," Madeleine said firmly.

"That's not what I said. I was just wondering if she ever talked to you about him."

"I'm not comfortable with this conversation anymore," said Madeleine. "I want to know why you're asking all these questions."

"I can't say," said Hanna.

Madeleine spat out a "Goodbye" and hung up.

Hanna debated briefly with herself and then decided to leave her be for now. Her phone beeped. It was Erik, sending a selfie of himself and his family at the airport.

Supriya and Nila appreciate you guys taking care of me.

You guys? Hanna realized he had sent the message to the entire group.

Just after five, she decided to give up for the day. She was meeting Isak in Färjestaden at seven, and wanted to go home and get changed. The thought of sitting opposite him made her feel queasy. What would they talk about? There was a part of her that wanted to apologize and say she couldn't come. Maybe she could blame the investigation. Hanna turned on the radio in the car to drown out her swirling thoughts.

As she pulled into Kleva, she saw Ingrid out on one of her walks. Hanna pulled over and wound down the window. She realized just how loud the radio was, and turned it off.

"What's wrong?" asked Ingrid. "You look like you've seen a ghost."

"Do I?"

"Yes. Has something happened with your brother?"

"No." Hanna hesitated. "I'm actually going on a date."

"Who with?"

"I'd rather not say."

"I think it's with that Isak Aulin chap."

"How did you know?"

Hanna was genuinely shocked, but then she remembered that Ingrid had talked about how kind and handsome he was. The older woman laughed and shook her head.

"He's a good boy," she called after the car as Hanna drove on.

When Hanna got back to the house, she took a shower in the tiny bathroom on the ground floor and then went upstairs and opened her closet. Why hadn't she stopped off to buy a top at the shopping center on the way home? She had absolutely nothing to wear. Hanna pulled out one of the few dresses she owned, but after catching sight of herself in the mirror she quickly took it off. Her body just wasn't made for dresses. She was a little over six feet tall and in decent enough shape, but hardly what you might call slim. Jeans and a blouse it was. But what about makeup? Hanna found her small makeup bag in the bathroom cabinet. The mascara had dried up, but she applied a little lipstick. As she stared at her pale pink lips, the thought came back to her again: that she should cancel.

"Stop it," Hanna hissed at herself.

She decided to take the bus to Färjestaden, because she wanted a glass of wine. She felt like she needed it to calm her nerves. The bus wasn't due for another twenty minutes, but she put on her shoes and walked up to the stop. It showed up early every now and again.

The wind had died down and there was just one cloud in the

sky, but Hanna regretted not taking a jacket. The temperature might well be over sixty-eight now, but it would hardly be that warm on the way home.

Hanna was alone at the bus shelter, and for once that made her uncomfortable. There was a red wooden shed on the other side of the road, likely belonging to the stables nearby, and behind her the fields opened out into the distance. She heard a car approaching and instinctively took a few steps back, trying to calm her racing heart. But the car neither sped up nor drove toward her. The driver gave her a confused look as he passed. How long would this fear last? Probably until she found whoever had tried to kill her.

Just a few minutes before the scheduled departure time, a teenage girl came running along the road. Hanna couldn't remember her name, though she knew who her parents were. They nodded to each other, but the girl was preoccupied by whatever was coming out of her huge headphones.

The departure time came and went, but there was no sign of the bus. Hanna peered south along the road. Maybe she should call for a taxi, though it would have to drive all the way over here—she didn't know where it would be coming from. She felt like going home, hiding behind an imaginary stomach bug. Hanna stared down at her phone and couldn't make up her mind. When she next looked up, she saw the bus headlights on the horizon.

ISAK WAS ALREADY at the table when Hanna arrived, her cheeks flushed with stress, and he got up and gave her a hug. He was wearing the same aftershave as yesterday, and Hanna felt some of the tension fade as she breathed in his nutmeg scent.

"It's good to see you again."

"You, too."

Hanna took in her surroundings as they sat down. The people, above all. The only ones she recognized were a woman who worked in reception at the station and a man she occasionally saw at the supermarket in Färjestaden.

"How's the investigation going?" asked Isak.

"I'd love to talk about absolutely anything else."

"Of course."

Hanna opened her menu and skimmed through the options.

"I think I'll have the char," said Isak.

He seemed much more bubbly than he had last time, so much so that he almost reminded her of Erik once he got started talking about the other main courses. Was he as nervous as she was? Or had he been anxious yesterday, and this was just what he was like when he was relaxed? Hanna wasn't sure how she felt about that. She had grown used to Erik—come to like him, even—but he was just a colleague.

"I'll have the same," she said, closing her menu.

They each ordered a glass of white wine to go with the fish.

"So, what made you become a police officer?" asked Isak. "Or maybe you'd rather not talk about that, either?"

"It's okay," said Hanna.

They hadn't touched upon their jobs at all yesterday. Without going into any detail about what had happened over the past few weeks since reading through the investigation, she told him that it was because of her father. That she had wanted to be on the other side of the law. That she had thought her experiences would mean she could do good as an officer.

"And do you?"

"Yes, I'd say so. But what about you? Why did you become a teacher?"

Hanna wanted to steer the conversation away from herself. The truth was that the basis for her decision had begun to falter.

"I like kids," said Isak.

The flicker of grief that passed over his face was plain to see.

"Sorry," she said. "I didn't mean to . . ."

"Hey, it's okay."

The silence between them grew and grew, eventually breaking into her and wreaking havoc. The waiter arrived with their fish a few minutes later.

"This is delicious," said Isak. Hanna could only agree.

The anxiety was tying her in knots. Had they already run out of things to talk about? Hanna glanced over at the couple at the next table. She watched their quiet, weary movements as they ate. The woman was in her fifties, the man a little older. She turned back to Isak, to his brown eyes and the beard that had tickled her cheek yesterday. Aside from his tragic past, she knew so little about him. He returned her gaze with a smile, and she discovered that he had a dimple on his left cheek.

Three hours later, Hanna couldn't understand what she had ever been worried about. Something seemed to have come unstuck, and their conversation flowed from one topic to another: TV series, walking trails across the alvar, the perfect Parmesan grater, how irritating know-it-alls were.

Isak's hand crept over the table toward hers. Their fingers found one another, seeking out the spaces in between, gripping. His touch sent a shock wave through her body.

"This might be me being forward again," he said. "But would you like to come home with me?"

THE LAST DAY

Once Hugo has finished his bath, Thomas puts him down in front of the TV and goes through to the kitchen to make dinner. From the clock on the microwave he realizes that time has run away from him. Leftover mashed potato and sausages it is. The stress makes him clumsy, and the knife slips as he starts cutting the sausages.

"Shit," he mutters, pushing his finger into his mouth.

Thomas tears off a piece of paper towel and wraps it around his finger as he goes through to the bathroom for one of Hugo's cartoon bandages. He tosses the bloody paper into the trash and sticks the bandage over the cut. The sausage has survived, so he slices another couple and then begins frying them.

Thomas hears a wail from the living room and rushes through to check on Hugo, but the sound is from the TV, not his son. The boy is transfixed by the colorful characters on-screen, and the towel he was wrapped up in has slipped down. Thomas finds himself gazing down at him until he notices the smell of burned sausage from the kitchen. The slices are almost black on one side, and he has to start again. This time he stays by the stove, leaving it only to set the table. Once everything is ready, he returns to the living room for Hugo.

"Time to eat," says Thomas, turning off the TV.

Hugo protests as Thomas lifts him from the floor, and he struggles as he tries to get him into his high chair.

"What's wrong?" Thomas asks.

He sounds annoyed, and Hugo flinches.

"Sorry," Thomas whispers, hugging the boy to him. "Sorry."

His phone starts ringing, and Thomas carries Hugo over to the counter to see who it is. Jenny could be calling to say that her train is late. But it's Selene. Why? No matter how much he wants to know, he can't pick up. What if she asks him for the keys? Thomas no longer needs to talk to her to get his job back, but he still plans to take her out for a nice lunch sometime. They need to find a way of being colleagues that works for them both.

Thomas sits down at the kitchen table with Hugo on his lap. He manages to get him to eat all of the mashed potato and almost all of the thinly sliced sausage that he dotted with ketchup, though he can't manage a single bite himself. One of the pieces of sausage falls onto his leg, leaving a mark on his jeans.

Thomas gets up with Hugo and carries him over to the sink. He wets a paper towel and cleans him up as best he can. He then grabs some clean clothes from the closet and gets Hugo into the red T-shirt he loves. He refuses to wear his leggings, and Thomas shoves them into the diaper bag instead. After changing his own trousers, he quickly gives himself a once-over in the mirror. Jenny will appreciate that he is wearing linen trousers.

With a jolt, Thomas realizes just how late it is. He needs to leave right now, and doesn't have time to tidy up in the kitchen. He isn't happy about it, but he knows that Jenny will want to spend time with Hugo once she gets back, so he can do the washing-up then. And if Hugo is asleep, she can sit down with a glass of wine in the kitchen and keep him company while he tidies. Thomas takes the bottle of gruel he prepared earlier out of the fridge and puts it into the changing bag, then carries Hugo out to the car and straps him into the child seat.

"We're going to get Mommy," he says. "I just need to do one little thing first."

"Mommy!" Hugo says cheerily, looking around as though he expects her to show up in the car.

"She's on the train," says Thomas.

"Train," Hugo echoes.

Jenny and Hugo took the train down to Malmö to see her parents a few months ago, but Thomas doesn't know whether he remembers that. He can see just how tired his son is, and wants nothing more than for him to doze off. For him to sleep through their visit to Södra Möckleby. Today has been a strange day, for both him and his son. Karl's call helped to dispel some of his anxiety, at the very least. He has a job to go back to once his paternity leave is over.

Thomas reverses out of the driveway and casts one last look back at the house. They really are lucky to have found it; it's perfect for them. He can't wait until tomorrow, when his new life begins. Tonight he just wants to enjoy being with Jenny again, spoiling her and telling her how much he loves her. And once Hugo is asleep in his crib, he will tell her about Lykke and Mille, about what he has been helping him with. He'll promise never to break a single law again, and Jenny will stand by him. She has this far, so why would she stop now?

Ten minutes, that's all it takes for Hugo to doze off, and Thomas decides that the wind is still in his sails.

Everything is going to be fine. It has to be.

Thomas doesn't want to drive right up to the house in Södra Möckleby, doesn't want his son nearby in case anything goes wrong, but he knows the perfect place to park. On the gravel track leading to the old quarry there is some kind of trash heap. From there he can walk back to the house in just a few minutes.

Before Thomas pulls off onto the gravel track, he scans the street around him, but the only other living creature he can see is a tabby cat. Everyone is probably still busy having dinner.

He parks as close to the trash heap as he can get. A bird soars over the wheat field to one side. It must be a bird of prey, but he doesn't know what kind. As he turns off the engine, he can feel his heartbeat in his mouth. There is a certain risk that someone might walk past the car while he is gone, but he hopes he has left it far enough from the gravel track that they won't react. The biggest risk isn't here, after all. It's in the house.

Thomas takes the bottle of gruel out of the changing bag and carefully places it in Hugo's lap. Just in case he wakes up hungry. Right now the boy is sleeping soundly. The heat has already faded outside, but Thomas winds down a couple of the windows to allow a soft breeze through the car. He then closes the door without a sound and pauses for a few seconds, watching the sleeping boy through the window. He reaches out and presses his fingertips to the glass.

"Daddy will be back soon," he whispers.

62

It was as though Hanna lost the ability to speak as they climbed into the taxi. Isak was quiet, too. The driver studied them with a look of amusement in the rearview mirror, but for once Hanna didn't care. She lowered her hand to the seat, palm up, and Isak's hand was immediately there.

Their fingers weaved together, and the rush that sent through her body felt—if possible—even more powerful than his first touch at the restaurant.

Isak lived in Södra Näsby, not far from Gårdby. As the taxi drove through the small community, all Hanna could feel was Isak's hand in hers, the warmth of his skin. She gazed out through the window in an attempt to stop that warmth from overwhelming her.

Her childhood home was one of a handful with the lights on, but there was room for only one thought in her head right now: she would soon be at Isak's place.

As the taxi left the main road, the darkness seemed to come rushing up on them. The car turned again and again, eventually pulling up in a small gravel yard. Its headlights were the only source of illumination, shining on a red barn wall.

"Must've forgotten to leave the light on," said Isak.

They stumbled out of the car, and Isak switched on the

flashlight on his phone. Led them through an opening between the side buildings into the pitch-black garden. A trail of limestone slabs snaked across the lawn, where the bush crickets were singing. Hanna could make out a few outbuildings and fruit trees. A dark branch reached out to her, and she felt her fears flare up. Isak dropped the key as he reached to unlock the door, quickly bending down to retrieve it.

"Can I get you anything?" he asked once they were inside. "A glass of wine? A cup of tea?"

Hanna shook her head. She still hadn't regained the ability to speak, and she knew she wouldn't be able to manage to drink anything. Isak's house was in better shape than her own, despite her efforts over the summer, and he showed her around. The wooden daybed in the kitchen reminded her of the one her grandmother had had. People had once slept on those things. He had a dining room and a living room and two bedrooms. Hanna wondered if this was where he had lived with his partner, though she didn't ask. There was a photograph of her on the wall in the living room. She was pretty and blond and probably around four or five months pregnant. Hanna couldn't quite tell.

"Maybe I should have taken it down."

"No," said Hanna.

It was the first and only word she could manage. Isak moved over to her. Touched the woman's belly in the photograph.

"I felt him kicking, and it hurts so much that I never got to meet him. In some ways grieving her is easier, but in others . . ."

Hanna didn't know what to say, and she felt a strong urge to turn around and run. What was she doing here? She wasn't made for this kind of thing.

"Come on," said Isak, leading her away from the picture, toward his bedroom.

When she felt his hand on hers, the urge to run died away. His warmth spread through her. It struck her how little she had thought of Fabian over the past few days, but she brushed him aside. She wouldn't let him ruin this moment for her.

Isak reached up and pushed back her hair from her eyes. *This is it*, she thought. *This is when it happens.* Hanna took a step forward and their lips met, parted. All her fears and anxiety drained away, until all that was left was expectation. Hanna pressed herself against him. She felt like her body was on fire. She wanted more. She wanted everything. And she wanted it now. Her hands danced over his body, exploring every inch of him.

Right then, her phone started ringing. The special ringtone she had set for Ove, so that she never missed his calls.

"Shit," she said, letting her hands drop to her sides. "That's my boss."

Hanna was close to tears. Because this was how it was and because Isak would realize just how difficult being with a police officer could be. It would be over before they even had time to give it a chance.

"Answer it," said Isak, as though she had a choice.

"Am I interrupting?" asked Ove.

"No," said Hanna, struggling to hide the disappointment from her voice.

"One of Selene's neighbors reported an argument spiraling out of control; they heard a series of loud thuds. We've got a unit on the way, but you and Erik should probably get over there, too."

Hanna wanted to refuse, but she couldn't. Selene had been afraid, and she hadn't taken those fears seriously enough.

"Of course."

Isak studied her with his kind brown eyes.

"You have to go, don't you?" he said, cocking his head slightly.

"Yes, I'm sorry."

Hanna felt like crying again, and Isak reached out and touched her cheek. She turned away from his hand.

"Where to?" he asked.

"Färjestaden."

"I'll give you a ride."

Hanna checked her watch. Almost three hours had passed since they were drinking wine, so it should be okay—at least for him. Still, she hesitated. It would feel strange to have Isak drop her off at a possible crime scene, but calling a taxi wasn't really an option. It would take far too long.

"Thanks," she said. "That's kind of you."

Was this life's way of punishing her for trying to be happy? If she were in Kleva, it would have taken her only ten minutes to get to Färjestaden, but the drive from Isak's place took over twice as long.

"It's okay," Isak said once they were in the car. "We can pick up where we left off another time."

"Yes," she said, though she didn't dare believe that he really meant it.

"Tomorrow?"

This time she couldn't help but smile. Maybe this wasn't the end after all.

When Isak turned off onto Rylgatan in Färjestaden, the patrol car was already on the scene. As was Erik. Hanna squeezed Isak's hand before getting out of the car, but she was too worked up to be able to feel his warmth. Erik studied her in surprise. "I thought you'd already be here."

He turned to look at the car reversing down the street. "Supriya and I had just put Nila to bed. Hope you two got further than us."

Hanna shook her head, too embarrassed to answer.

"What do we know?" she asked.

"I spoke to the responding officers on my way over," said Erik. "Selene took a nasty blow to the head. The ambulance will be here any minute now."

"How bad is it?"

"Hard to say, but she could talk. She claims Mille attacked her."

Hanna and Erik went into the apartment, which was accessible from the street. Selene was lying on the floor and one of the officers was helping her press a tea towel to her head. It was drenched in blood.

"How serious is it?" Hanna asked.

The police officer gave a dogged shake of the head. The corner of the chest of drawers nearby was bloody, and Hanna assumed that must be what Selene's head had struck.

"And the perpetrator?"

"My colleague is searching the area."

Selene turned her head to them, but the movement made her sob. Her face was pale and clammy. She closed her eyes for a few seconds and then looked straight at Hanna with a pair of blood-shot eyes. Forced out the words:

"It was Mille who killed Thomas."

63

Hanna dropped to her knees beside Selene and placed a hand on her shoulder.

"What happened?"

Selene's breathing was now irregular, and she closed her eyes again.

"Call my dad," she panted. "I want him to come."

"What happened?" Hanna repeated, giving her a gentle shake. But Selene's body had gone limp. She had lost consciousness.

"You should probably go," said the young officer who was still pressing a towel to her head. He too was pale and clammy. He probably hadn't even turned thirty yet.

"Do you want us to take over?" asked Erik.

"No. Help my colleague find whoever did this instead."

But Hanna didn't want to leave Selene. She wanted to stay until she knew exactly what had happened and why.

"Come on, Hanna," Erik told her when she failed to get up.

With one last glance at Selene's face, Hanna did as she was told. Once she was outside, she called Ove to give him an update. She gazed out into the night. Lights had begun to break up the darkness, people wondering what was going on. A blue door opened on the walkway up above, and a man in a dressing gown came out. Hanna gestured for him to go back inside, and after hesitating for a few seconds he did as he was told. Yet another patrol car was only a few minutes away, but Ove had called for further reinforcements and sent a car for Selene's parents. Mille Bergman had to be found.

"Should we start looking?" asked Erik.

"Yeah, but not here. Ove wants us to go over to Mille's place. He might not have realized that Selene would be able to point the finger at him and gone home."

Erik walked toward the unmarked car he had picked up from the station. "I should probably drive."

Hanna ignored his teasing tone.

Erik managed to keep quiet for almost an entire minute.

"So, did you have a good time, you and Isak?"

"Yes," said Hanna. "But could we please just focus on the job right now?"

The drive to Skogsby never usually took any more than ten minutes, but Erik stayed well beneath the speed limit. They couldn't be sure Mille had driven to Selene's apartment, and both scanned the roadside as they drove. A shadow emerged from between the trees.

"Stop!" Hanna shouted.

Erik braked, but the shadow had already been illuminated by a streetlight. The cyclist who turned off into the residential area was a woman.

The lights were out in Mille Bergman's house. There was no answer when they knocked on the door, so they did a loop around the low brick building. His car was nowhere to be seen. Hanna reported back to Ove.

"I think you should wait in Skogsby for a while," he said. "There's a good chance he'll head home."

"Okay, we'll stay as far out of sight as we can," said Hanna.

They had parked the car in the small parking lot above the row of houses, and they got back into it, slumping down as low as they could in the seats with the lights out. Mille's street was accessible from two directions, and they needed to keep watch over both to make sure they didn't miss him. Hanna had spent many an hour on surveillance jobs during her career, but there hadn't been much call for it since she transferred to Kalmar.

A movement on the other side of the windshield made them both tense and keep quiet, but it was just an old man walking along the road beyond the parking lot, and he didn't even glance in their direction. After thirty minutes, there was still no sign of Mille. Hanna's phone buzzed in her pocket. A message from Isak.

How's it going?

She thought for a moment before writing a reply: *Looks like it's going to take all night, I'm afraid.*

"Does he miss—"

Erik didn't get any further before a call came through from Ove. Hanna switched her phone to loudspeaker.

"I've sent a car over to Mille's parents' place in Färjestaden and another to his sister in Borgholm," said Ove. "Can you think of anywhere else he might be?"

"Sorry, no," said Hanna.

After she ended the call, she was keen for Erik not to fill the silence with more talk about Isak.

"Do you think we should try calling Mille?" she asked.

"Isn't that a stupid idea?" said Erik. "He'll realize we're looking for him."

"Given he still hasn't shown up here, I think he already does," said Hanna. "But you're probably right."

A car turned off onto the street and pulled up outside one of the houses on the other side. The young man who got out definitely wasn't Mille. He was carrying a vacuum cleaner, the nozzle patched up with silver tape.

"Why do you think Mille went to see Selene?" asked Hanna.

"Maybe he was afraid she would give him away? In which case he really does look guilty."

"Then why did he tell her to stop lying?"

"What else was he supposed to do? Confess to killing Thomas? He must've felt like she was really putting pressure on him. Like she'd pretty much worked out what he was up to and had probably also met one of the people involved."

"Yeah, I suppose that's possible," said Hanna. "Or Selene could have been lying about Mille."

64

Lykke sat bolt upright in bed, confused. She was only ever pulled so abruptly from her sleep when something had woken her. But what? She reached for the blind and peered out, but all she could see was the starry night sky.

Hunger gnawed at her stomach. She knew it would make it impossible to get back to sleep, so she grabbed her dressing gown from the back of a chair and got up. She walked through the adjoining room. Most people who rented the house wanted two bedrooms, so she had put some beds in it, but she still preferred to sleep in the inner room. It had been her bedroom growing up.

She walked down the curved stairs. There was a window onto the strait by the front door, and Lykke paused to peer out. The breeze was the only thing disturbing the surface of the water.

When she got to the kitchen she realized she had slept for only an hour or so; it was just twenty past eleven. She heated some water on the stove and poured it over a bag of green tea in her favorite cup. She had forced herself to go to the grocery store yesterday afternoon, and she broke off a banana that had ripened enough to eat. She didn't like brown bananas, and always chose a bunch that was still greenish yellow. She cut it into pieces, slowly pronging each on a fork and raising it to her mouth. It took her some time, but she eventually managed the entire thing.

Feeling full made her anxiety stir to life, but she needed to find another way to take control over it. She would get back to work on the garden in the morning, and she would continue looking for a job. The thought of going back to Uppsala felt increasingly impossible, but if she managed to find a job here, she could stay on the island.

Lykke went back up to bed. She thought about Hugo on the slide. He had been no more than a meter or two away from her, and if she had just taken a step forward she would have been able to touch him. She had often nagged her mother for a sibling when she was younger, but had stopped when she realized it upset her. After staring into the darkness for a while, she reached for her phone and wrote a message to Jenny.

I hope Hugo is OK. I'm so sorry that Thomas is gone, both for Hugo's sake and yours. I never got to know him.

None of the next sentences she could come up with felt right. That she still wanted to meet Hugo. That she was sorry for how things had ended up between herself and Jenny. Between her and Thomas. And between her and Hugo. Just because she was angry with Thomas didn't mean she should have raised her hand to him like that. The knowledge that Hugo wouldn't remember any of it brought her a certain comfort. He was only fourteen months old, after all. In the end Lykke sent the message as it was.

Jenny's phone call on Sunday, telling her that both Thomas and Hugo were missing, had come as a shock. Several difficult meetings with him that day, culminating in that. Given the way she had behaved toward him, she had been worried he might have taken his own life, that the police might make it seem like she had killed him.

Her anger toward Roger and everything he had taken from her flared up again. No matter which way she turned, all she could see were shadows.

Not eating wasn't going to solve anything. The sensible voice in her head had been telling her that all along, and it was time for her to start listening to it.

65

In the past ten minutes, the only movement Erik had seen outside the car was a hare bounding out into the street and disappearing between the houses.

"I don't think he's coming," he said.

"But we can't be sure," said Hanna. "So we need to stay."

Her attention was on her phone, and he guessed she was probably messaging Isak.

Erik sighed and gazed out at one of the few illuminated windows on the street. Someone seemed to be throwing together a late-night meal in their kitchen. He wanted to get home to Supriya and Nila, and should never have agreed to leave them tonight of all nights. No job in the world was worth that.

It wasn't until they actually got back to the apartment that he realized just how much he had missed them during the time they were away. His heart ached for Jenny, whose Thomas would never be coming home. Who had been left alone with Hugo.

Erik had tried to play "Hakuna Matata" on the guitar, but he had been so worked up that the tune was barely recognizable. Playing the guitar probably wasn't his thing after all. Nila had grabbed it off him once he was done, and Supriya had practically cried with laughter. *God, you really must have been bored.*

He had heated up the food he had made earlier, and it had been incredible to actually sit down and eat together. Nila had been full of stories about their time in India. About the bony, beige cows with painted horns that lay down in the middle of the road. About the trees in the park you weren't allowed to walk beneath in case the coconuts fell on your head. She had blurted out memory after memory until she ran out of air. As Supriya tidied up in the kitchen, Erik had sat down on the sofa with Nila in his lap; she wanted to watch a film where the people spoke Swedish. If he closed his eyes, he could still smell her.

"Should I give Ove a call?" he asked, unable to bear the longing.

"Hold on a bit longer," said Hanna.

Erik continued to stare out through the windshield. His phone buzzed with a message from Supriya. He clearly wasn't the only one who was missing his partner, a thought that made him feel warm and fuzzy inside.

"Selene suffers from depression," said Hanna.

"How do you know?"

"Her mother told me."

"Does it make a difference?"

"Maybe not, but—"

Ove called, interrupting their discussion, and Erik put him on loudspeaker so that they could both hear what he had to say.

"I just spoke to the hospital," said Ove. "Selene has a bleed on the brain, but she's going to be okay. They're keeping her in for the time being. She'll probably need surgery."

"Okay," said Erik. "What should we do now?"

"Go home and get some sleep," said Ove. "The others can keep looking. I've got a car on the way to relieve you outside Mille's house. It's a damn shame we didn't have time to start the surveillance on him. I want you to interview Selene on Monday, if she's feeling up to it."

"Are her parents with her?" asked Hanna.

"Yes," said Ove. "Why?"

"I can't shake the feeling that we're missing something important."

"Like what?"

"I don't know."

"Go home and get some sleep," said Ove, ending the call.

Erik turned to Hanna.

"Do you want to talk about it?"

"Not really," said Hanna. "Because I don't really know what the feeling means."

"Try."

"Why did Mille point the finger at Selene?" The words were spilling out of her now. "And why did he go to see her?"

"We've already been through this. Probably because he was worried she'd give him away."

"But why accuse her in the first place?" asked Hanna. "It just doesn't add up."

Erik didn't have the energy to discuss this with Hanna. It felt like she was rambling. Maybe she was as tired as he was. All he wanted was for their colleagues to show up so he could go home. Crawl into bed beside Supriya.

"Where should I drop you off later?" he asked.

"Kleva."

"You sure?"

"Yeah."

Hanna's phone started ringing, and she held up the display for him to see: Jenny Ahlström. After hesitating for a moment, she answered. Erik could only hear Hanna's side of the conversation.

"Calm down, please. What's going on?"

66

"You have to come over here," Jenny whispered.

Her voice was thick and croaky, likely from tears and stress, but Hanna could finally understand what she was saying.

"What's going on?" she repeated.

She was always eager to make herself available to relatives during investigations, that was why she had picked up, despite it being almost midnight on a Friday. What she had expected was an outpouring of despair, for Jenny's grief to have caught up with her. But this seemed to be something else.

"Mille is here," Jenny whispered.

"Is he—"

Jenny hung up before Hanna got any further.

"Drive," she told Erik.

Erik started the engine and stepped on the gas, almost flattening the hare that had dared hop back out into the road again. Hanna watched it bolt behind a bush in the rearview mirror. She recapped what Jenny had told her and then called Ove.

"He's called for backup," she said. "But we're the closest."

"How long does it take to get to her house?" asked Erik.

"Just under half an hour. Want me to drive?"

Erik replied by breaking the speed limit and turning on the blue lights for once. Given that Jenny had been whispering, Hanna didn't dare call or message her back. Mille might be threatening her and Hugo. Jenny had confronted him about the cigarettes, after all. Perhaps she had become yet another witness who needed to be silenced. But if that were the case, it would mean that Hanna had been wrong about Selene. She thumped the car door. Erik glanced over to her.

"Sorry," she said. "The twists and turns in this case are just really frustrating."

"We've got him now," said Erik. "Try to look at it like that."

But they didn't have him, not yet, and there was no way she could allow the investigation to end with Jenny's death. Or Hugo's.

Erik slowed down, and Hanna told him to take the next road instead, the one to Alby. As Erik turned east across the alvar, he had to switch the headlights to full beam. It was pitch-black outside. The biggest risk came from roe deer running out into the road, but there were also elk, and someone had crashed into a fallow deer a year or two ago—farther north on the island, but still. Erik reached the main road and swung south. He switched off both the blue lights and the full beams, but didn't slow down. There was almost no traffic on the roads at that time of night. When they reached Hulterstad, he finally eased off the gas, switching off the headlights completely just before they got to the turnoff to Thomas's street.

"Do you have a gun?" asked Hanna.

"Yeah, I grabbed mine at the station."

Given that they had no idea what they would be faced with inside, it felt reassuring to know that at least one of them was armed. They got out of the car and walked toward the house. The light was on in the kitchen, but it didn't look like there was anyone in the room. The gate creaked as Hanna pushed it open, and she froze, but there was no reaction from the house.

Erik gestured for them to walk around the edge of the building. For the time being it would be best for them to stick together.

Through the window at the rear of the house, Hanna peered into the living room. She could see someone hunched over on the sofa. It was Mille, sitting with his head in his hands. There was no sign of a weapon, but he could easily have one on the coffee table in front of him, or beside him on the sofa. There were just too many blind spots.

Where were Jenny and Hugo? And her parents—had they left already? Hanna and Erik kept moving around the house. The blinds were down in what was likely the main bedroom. During their earlier visits, that door had been closed.

"What should we do?" Hanna whispered.

As though in reply, they heard the sound of a child crying through the wall.

"Shit," Erik muttered.

But Hanna was relieved, because it meant Hugo was alive. Her phone buzzed in her pocket. She always switched it to silent before any sensitive operations. It was a message from Jenny.

Are you nearly here?

We're outside, Hanna wrote back. *Can we come in?*

Hold on.

Hanna held up the phone to show Erik. They made their way back around to the front of the house. The sound of raised voices mixed with Hugo's tears. Muted but intense. She couldn't make out what they were saying. What the hell was going on in there? Adrenaline was pumping through Hanna's veins, and she found it difficult to stand still. She sent a message to Ove asking how far away the backup was.

Five minutes, he replied.

A lot could happen in five minutes. Jenny had told them to wait, but for what?

Is anyone hurt? Hanna wrote to her, but this time there was no reply.

She caught a few disjointed words—"stop" and "no"—followed by silence. Hanna took a few quick steps toward the front door. It swung open, and Erik raised his pistol. Jenny came out onto the porch with Hugo in her arms. Her face was red and puffy, but she didn't seem to be hurt in any way. She flinched at the sight of the gun and clutched Hugo to her chest.

"He's in the living room," she said.

"Wait out here," said Hanna.

Jenny nodded.

Mille looked up as they came into the room. Like Jenny's, his face was red and swollen. Hanna scanned him from head to toe, taking in the room around him: the sofa, the coffee table, the floor . . . She still couldn't see a weapon.

"Are you armed?"

"No."

"Why did you come over here?"

"I didn't know where else to go," said Mille. "She's completely sick in the head."

"Who is?" asked Erik.

"Selene. Fuck! I knew she wasn't well, but not like this."

Mille spat out a whole series of incoherent expletives.

"What happened at Selene's apartment?" asked Hanna.

Mille looked up at them in despair.

"I got so scared by all this talk about you having new information. I was convinced Selene was planning to frame me, so I went over there to make her confess. The only thing that made sense was that she killed Thomas. But then she started accusing me of ruining his life, saying it was all my fault he was dead. I guess I saw red, and I hit her. I know I shouldn't have done it, but I didn't kill Thomas."

Erik took a step toward him. "We can discuss this in more detail at the station."

"I'll tell you everything about the smuggling," Mille continued. "They can do whatever they want to me; I don't care anymore. I'm the one who got Thomas mixed up in all this, he wanted to quit. I went over to the house with Oleg, and I swear . . . Thomas was already dead."

67

Hanna was standing with Jenny and Hugo on the porch outside the Ahlström family home. The blue lights swept through the night, creating ghostly shadows in the darkness. Once backup arrived, they had finally managed to get Mille Bergman out of the house and into the car. Erik was leaning back against the passenger-side door, waiting for them, but Jenny didn't want to let Hanna go yet.

"Mille didn't kill Thomas," she said.

Hugo was clinging to her, his head resting against her body. His big, bright eyes were focused on the ambulance. Fortunately it hadn't been required. Jenny said that Mille had neither threatened nor hurt either of them. He had come over because he was desperate and afraid of being blamed for the murder, that was all. The reason Jenny had whispered down the line was because Mille had begged her not to contact the police. That was also the reason they had argued.

"Mille couldn't have done it," Jenny continued. "There's just no way. It must have been Selene. I've always known there was something not quite right about her."

Mille blamed Selene, and Selene him, and it was obvious that Jenny's words were based on nothing other than sheer will. She didn't want Thomas's childhood friend to be guilty. Right now

Hanna didn't know what to think; both Mille and Selene sounded so convincing when they claimed they were innocent. Her body was tired and weary, every movement an effort. Perhaps she was the one who was struggling to let go. It didn't feel right to leave Jenny on her own after everything that had happened.

"Where are your parents?" she asked.

"They went back to Malmö today," said Jenny. "I found it so stressful having them here. I needed to be alone with Hugo."

The paramedics turned off the blue lights on the ambulance and drove away. They had probably been called out elsewhere. One of the patrol cars had already left, but the officers from the other were still busy getting the last few neighbors to go back inside. Hanna stepped down from the porch, but Jenny still wasn't ready to let her go.

"Mille didn't kill Thomas," she said again.

"I hear what you're saying," said Hanna. "We're going to get to the bottom of what happened, and in order to do that we need to take Mille back to the station. We can't talk to him here."

Hugo whimpered and reached up to Jenny's mouth as though he wanted his mother to stop talking. It was the middle of the night, and his tiny body seemed to be screaming for sleep. Jenny squeezed his hand and nodded for Hanna to go, though she remained on the porch, watching her leave.

"What's the plan?" Hanna asked once she reached Erik.

She peered into the car. Mille was slumped forward, his forehead pressed against the back of the seat in front.

"Ove wants us to take Mille into custody," said Erik. "And for us to make the most of the drive over there, since he's so eager to talk. He also wants us to interview Selene in the morning, if possible."

"Sounds sensible."

They needed a detailed account from both of them, and then they needed to compare the two versions—both against each other and against what they already knew. To force their way through to which of them was telling the truth.

"Do you feel up to driving?" asked Erik.

Hanna replied by walking around to the driver's side. The minute they got into the car, Mille leaned back and turned to look at the house.

"I know what it looks like," he said. "But I didn't kill Thomas."

"What makes you think it was Selene?" asked Erik, fastening his belt.

"Because she can never let anything go," said Mille. "She didn't stand a chance with Thomas, and she couldn't accept that. Plus she was the one who gave him the keys."

Hanna cast one last glance back at the house before she pulled away. Jenny and Hugo had gone inside, but the lights were still on. It was a slightly longer route, but she chose to drive north, toward Gårdby. She wondered what Isak was doing now. Whether he was asleep. Whether he was thinking about her.

"Who is Oleg?" asked Erik.

"I don't know his surname," said Mille. "But he's Russian, and he's the only person I've been in touch with about the cigs."

"How did you meet him?"

"At my fishing hut in Grönhögen. He showed up one day and offered me a way to make some easy money."

Mille snorted. A pair of silvery eyes stared at the car from the darkness. A split second later, they were gone. It must have been a roe deer. Mille didn't need any more encouragement to go on.

"I don't know how I could've been so stupid. I tried to stop after the raid on the fishing hut, but Oleg wouldn't let me. He forced me to find another solution. I convinced him to keep the cigarettes in the van until the buyer came to pick them up, but the cops seized an entire load."

Hanna drove past the turnoff to Södra Näsby, and the memory of Isak's body overcame her. The way it had pressed up against hers. She gripped the wheel as her body worked through the memory. The question was there again, with a note of despair this time. What was Isak up to? A large part of her wanted to turn the car around and head over there, to forget this mess with Mille and Selene and the smuggling, but she continued on toward Kalmar.

"I was desperate," said Mille. "And scared. That's why I asked Thomas for help. How fucking stupid can a person be?"

"What happened at the house in Södra Möckleby?" asked Hanna.

"Thomas was serious about quitting," said Mille. "So I got in touch with Oleg. He came out to the house with me. I was afraid he'd threaten Thomas, but it felt like the only way to get them to agree to let him quit. I convinced Oleg to let me go in alone, and it was so awful that . . . I mean, I got such a shock when I went inside and saw Thomas lying dead."

"What did you do then?"

"I went back out to the car and told Oleg."

"What did you do with the cigarettes?"

"Oleg forced me to keep them in my house overnight. He came to get them the next morning."

"How do you usually get in touch with Oleg?"

Mille reeled off a number and Erik made a note of it on his phone, likely so that he could forward it on to Ove. Mille was so eager to convince them that it was difficult to assess what he was actually saying. His claims about the smuggling felt credible, at least. It was too detailed for him to have made it up in his current state.

"Do you think Oleg killed Thomas?" asked Erik.

"You mean he might have done it before we got there?"

"I don't mean anything," said Erik. "I'm asking what you think."

Mille slowly shook his head.

"How did Oleg react when you got back to the car?"

"He muttered something in Russian and drove off."

"How did you get into the house?" asked Hanna.

"The door was open. But I'd been counting on that. I'd said seven o'clock to Thomas, but I was fifteen minutes late."

Hanna's gaze swept across the road, where the headlights were cutting through the darkness. She needed to stay alert to the sides, for everything that might come bolting toward them, but she couldn't see any more silvery white eyes. She believed Mille more than she believed Selene, but what if both were telling the truth? Or rather: What if they both believed they were? Perhaps Oleg was guilty after all, or someone else connected to the smuggling ring. According to Mille, Oleg was the only person he had ever been in contact with, so he was the person they needed to focus their efforts on.

Find Oleg, she mouthed to Erik.

He nodded and held up his phone. She realized he had already been in touch with Ove about it.

SATURDAY, AUGUST 24

68

Erik's phone clattered to the floor as he fumbled for the nightstand. He had set an alarm when he got home in the early hours, because he and Hanna were hoping to go to the hospital and interview Selene Friberg that morning. Both Supriya and Nila had been asleep by the time he got back, and though he had sent a message to his wife telling her not to wait up, he had been a little disappointed.

He managed to reach his phone and switched off the alarm. Supriya came in with a cup of coffee, and he shuffled upright in bed. She held out the cup to him.

"Thanks, sweetie," he said with a smile.

He took a big gulp of the coffee and realized just how quiet the house was.

"Where's Nila?"

"She's gone over to Sally's to play."

Sally was the only one of her friends who lived nearby, and they had ended up in the same class at Lindö School. Supriya sat down on the edge of the bed and fixed her eyes on him, her face solemn. Erik put down his cup and pulled her toward him.

"I'm really sorry, but I have to go in to work for a few hours today."

"I know you do," said Supriya.

"What is it, then?"

She pulled back so that she could look him in the eye.

"I realized something while we were in India. And, well, I suppose I really felt it while I was packing to leave."

Erik swallowed. She was finally about to confirm his fears, the anxiety her sudden silence had provoked. He nodded for her to go on.

"I realized just how much I've been longing to go home."

"This is home," said Erik.

He pulled her close again, and she let him do it.

"I know," said Supriya. "But so is Mumbai."

Erik's mind scrambled for solutions. Perhaps they could make sure to visit India every year, though that would involve so much unnecessary air travel. He didn't want to leave Sweden again, did he? He wouldn't be able to work as a police officer in India, but then again, he had only really ended up on the force because that was what so many members of his family had done. Perhaps he could try a new career, like his big brother. But he liked his job, and he couldn't think of a single thing he would rather do for a living. Damn it. Did she really have to bring this up now?

"Relax," said Supriya. "I'm not saying I want to move to India. Just that it was hard to leave."

"What about coming back to Sweden, then? Was that tough, too?"

Erik regretted his words the moment they left his mouth. The harsh, whiny side of him that she couldn't stand.

Supriya tore herself out of his embrace. "Hey, that was really uncalled-for."

"I know. Sorry."

But his frustration refused to fade away. Couldn't she have waited to dump this news on him? His phone buzzed with a message, and Erik used that as an excuse to put off the conversation for the time being.

"That's probably Hanna," he said.

"There's breakfast in the kitchen."

Supriya got up and walked away without looking at him. Hanna wrote that the doctor had said yes to them interviewing Selene. She was at the station and wanted to talk to Ove before she signed out a car and came to pick him up. Erik managed to take a quick shower, get dressed, and eat a sandwich in just over fifteen minutes. Supriya kept out of his way on the balcony. It was tempting just to leave, but he popped his head outside.

"We can talk more later," he said.

"Okay," she replied, not taking her eyes off the strait.

It was obvious she was still angry. *What about me?* he felt like shouting, but he left her alone instead. He didn't have time for this.

Hanna was sitting in the car right outside the door when he came down and got in.

"Been waiting long?" he asked.

"Just a few minutes," she said, stepping on the gas.

"Any new developments?"

"The person Mille was in contact with might have been Oleg Sokolov. He's the brother of one of the Russians who were sent down for smuggling cigarettes into Grönhögen. Ove is sending a unit over to his most recent address. Other than that, no change. Selene is still blaming Mille, and Mille is still blaming Selene."

Hanna began talking about how she was convinced that Selene was lying, but Erik didn't buy it. The murder was linked to the smuggling, he was sure of it, and the most likely explanation was that Thomas had died when Mille showed up at the house. His mind wound back to what Supriya had said. What made him most angry was that she hadn't been totally up front about her feelings. If she really felt that way, then it would only be a matter of time before she wanted to move.

"What's up?" asked Hanna.

"Nothing. Just tired, that's all. Long night."

Hanna found a parking space outside the entrance to the

hospital and led him up to the right ward. The corridor was quiet, but they could hear noises from the various rooms: coughing, a conversation about what Erik assumed was the hospital food, a scraping sound. A man emerged from of one of the rooms, pulling a drip stand behind him. The liquid in the bag was the color of charcoal.

"This is it," said Hanna.

Madeleine Friberg was sitting by her daughter's side. The other bed in the room was empty. Selene was lying beneath a yellow blanket with a huge bandage around her head. She seemed to be fast asleep. The liquid in her drip was clear.

"She's completely drained, poor thing," said Madeleine. "This whole business has been so hard on her."

She stroked her daughter's arm. Hanna pulled a chair over to the bed and sat down beside Madeleine, but Erik lingered in the background. Selene had been awake just thirty minutes earlier, and if they were particularly unlucky it might be hours before she next woke. He thought they should try to wake her.

"Does Selene ever get violent?" asked Hanna.

Madeleine's stroking came to an abrupt halt. "Absolutely not," she said.

"She broke Mille's windows when he broke up with her," Hanna continued. "How did she react when Thomas rejected her?"

"Stop it," Madeleine hissed.

Erik couldn't understand why Hanna was pushing so hard.

"We need to talk to Selene," he said.

"No," said Madeleine.

"I'm sorry," Hanna told her, in a tone that didn't sound the least bit apologetic. "But it isn't your decision to make."

Hanna reached out for Selene.

"Stop it," Madeleine hissed again. "I'll tell you everything you want to know."

"Which is what?" asked Hanna.

Erik wondered whether he had been wrong after all, whether Selene was the killer and her mother had worked it out. Selene might even have confessed to her. But instead of replying, Madeleine began stroking her daughter's arm again. She used her free hand to wipe a tear from her cheek.

"Madeleine," said Hanna, her voice much softer this time. "Talk to me."

Erik's phone beeped. He had forgotten to turn down the volume.

"Sorry," he mumbled, though neither woman seemed to have noticed.

It was a message from Supriya, saying that she loved him. Even though he was an idiot. Same, he replied, switching the phone to silent. They were usually able to talk about everything, but the thought of her wanting to move to the other side of the world terrified him.

"You're wrong about Selene," said Madeleine. "It wasn't her. She told me about the keys on Sunday, and I convinced her that Karl needed to know, too. He wasn't actually at home on Sunday evening. He left the work shed and drove off somewhere."

Erik could only see the sides of their faces. Above all Hanna's, because Madeleine kept glancing toward her daughter.

"I don't know what he was thinking," Madeleine continued. "Or what he thought he'd be able to solve by going over there to confront him."

"What are you trying to say?" asked Hanna.

"It was Karl who killed Thomas."

69

I t was Karl who killed Thomas.

Hanna wanted to feel relieved when she heard Madeleine's words, but all she felt was her weariness digging its claws ever deeper. She longed for Isak. For everything that wasn't this. She was so sick of death, lies, and families.

She had staggered into the house in Kleva at around three that morning, and after quickly brushing her teeth she had dragged herself up the stairs, peeled off her clothes, and collapsed into bed. Out for the count the minute her head hit the pillow.

Barely five hours later she had been torn from her sleep by the alarm on her phone, and after managing to make it shut up she had slumped back, rolling over onto her other side and wondering what it would have been like to wake up beside Isak. Just as the thought crossed her mind, her phone had pinged with a message: *Would you like to eat dinner with me tonight?* She replied yes without even pausing to think.

"Why are you only just telling us that Karl drove off?" Hanna asked.

"He's my husband," Madeleine sobbed. "I didn't want you to suspect him in case I was wrong."

"So what made you change your mind?"

"Selene has suffered enough. She can't handle any more. And the fact that you think she . . . that she has . . . And then I found . . ."

Madelene started crying so hard that she couldn't go on.

"What did you find?" Hanna asked once she had calmed down.

"I was cleaning the shed this morning, and I found a trash bag with a bloody hearth shovel and Thomas's phone inside."

"What did you do with it?"

"I left it where it was, so Karl wouldn't realize I'd found it."

"Why did Karl kill Thomas?" Hanna pressed her.

"I don't know," said Madeleine.

"But you must have your suspicions?" said Erik, unable to stand quietly in the background any longer.

Madeleine flinched, as though she had forgotten there was anyone else in the room. She reached up and stroked Selene's cheek.

"For what Thomas did to our daughter," said Madeleine. "He played with her feelings for months. It got to the point where I convinced Karl to fire him."

"He'd been fired?" asked Erik. Hanna turned and gave him an irritable glance.

"Yes," said Madeleine. "But when Thomas showed up at our house on Sunday, begging for his job back, Karl changed his mind. He's always been weak like that. Thomas used Selene. He threatened her to make her give him the keys."

Madeleine was getting louder and louder, and Selene stirred anxiously. Her mother immediately lowered her voice.

"Maybe we could continue this outside?" she whispered once her daughter had settled down.

"That's enough for today," said Erik. "But we're going to need to speak to both you and Selene again."

Madeleine nodded.

"Do you know where Karl is?" asked Hanna.

For the first time, she felt some kind of relief. Karl was a perpetrator she could believe in. Perhaps Selene had suspected him, too. Perhaps that was why she had been so desperate to accuse Mille.

"He had to swing by the office, but he should be back soon." Madeleine's face twisted, and she raised her hand to her mouth. "He has no idea I know, but I had to tell you for Selene's sake. For Hektor's."

Yes, lies dragged people down and ruined lives. Hanna had seen that time and time again in her work. And in her own life? She had thought she knew everything.

Fucking Kristoffer.

Hanna paused as she stepped out of the room. She needed a break from the anxiety inside before they tracked down Karl. And she had to force back her anger. Lars had sat opposite her in a supervised visitation room, wearing his green prison uniform, unable to meet her eye. She had taken that as a sign of his guilt.

"What a mess," said Erik.

Hanna nodded and called Ove. He muttered at the latest twist in the investigation, but said he would get in touch with the prosecutor right away and arrange for a search of the Fribergs' home.

"Should we give Karl a call?" asked Hanna.

Her preference was to bring him in without warning, but they couldn't do that without knowing where he was. They could always go over to the office in Färjestaden, but if they did that there was a risk of passing him en route.

But Erik didn't have time to answer her question, because the elevator doors pinged and Karl Friberg stepped out, followed by Hektor. Karl was dressed for the office, but Hektor was wearing jeans and a T-shirt. He was carrying a box of chocolates and a bouquet of flowers. Karl paused when he spotted them, and for a split second Hanna thought he was about to jump back in the elevator, but he kept walking toward them.

"Have you spoken to Selene?" he asked.

"No," said Erik. "But we have spoken to Madeleine, and now we need to talk to you."

"All right," said Karl.

"You can go in," Hanna told Hektor.

Hektor gave his father a confused glance, but when Karl nodded for him to go on, he opened the door to Selene's room.

"What do you want to talk to me about?" asked Karl.

"I think it would be best if we did this at the station."

They paused as a nurse walked by.

"I'm here to see my daughter," said Karl. "She was attacked last night."

He took a step toward the room, but Erik reached out and gripped his arm.

"I need you to come with us," he said.

The door to Selene's room flew open, and Hektor came charging out, his face the color of beetroot.

"You bastard!" he shouted. "How could you do this to Mom? To us?"

Before anyone had time to react, his hands were around Karl's throat. Hanna and Erik grabbed an arm each. Several other doors opened, and the hospital staff came running. Someone started tugging at Hanna.

"Get back, for God's sake!" she shouted. "We're police!"

The people around them drifted back. Karl's mouth was open, but he couldn't breathe. His face changed from red to blue, and his arms went limp at his sides.

"Hektor!" Erik yelled.

But Hektor's sole focus was on his father. They eventually managed to drag him away, and Erik barked for Hektor to go back in to his sister. Karl bent double, spluttering. His entire body was shaking. He opened his mouth to say something, but no sound would come out.

They straightened him up and led him down a corridor of

curious eyes, over to the elevators. A harried-looking doctor got in after them, but Erik held up his ID and told him to get out unless he was responding to a medical emergency.

"You're under arrest for the murder of Thomas Ahlström," Erik said as soon as the doors had closed.

"What? No!"

Karl backed up against the mirror, his eyes darting around.

"Selene told you that she'd given the keys to Thomas on Sunday," said Hanna.

"No, no, no . . ."

"And you weren't at home on Sunday evening. What did you do once you left your shed?"

Karl gripped the rail beneath the mirror.

"I was in the shed all evening," he said. "Who says I wasn't?"

Before they had time to answer, he realized who it must have been.

"I want to talk to Madeleine."

"I'm sure you do, but that's not possible."

"You can't stop me from talking to my wife."

Karl reached out to press the elevator buttons, but Erik blocked his hand.

"Did you go over to the house?" he asked.

"No, I didn't."

Karl tried to reach the buttons again, despite the fact that they were already moving, and Erik was rougher this time.

"What happened when you got to the house?" asked Hanna.

Karl stared at the elevator doors as they slid open.

"I'm not saying another word until I've spoken to my lawyer."

THE LAST MOMENT

Thomas looks around before he steps into the garden. A door opens farther down the street, and he pauses. The remnants of a laugh carry through the warm late summer air. The tall hedges are blocking his view, but he sees a woman with a floral dress and long dark hair emerge through one of the openings. She tosses a bag into the trash can. The green lid slams shut, and his heart skips a beat as she turns around to head back inside. For a split second he is convinced she must have spotted him, because she stops, gazing in his direction. But then she shakes her head and disappears behind the hedge.

He doesn't dare move until the woman is back in her house. A few quiet steps, and he reaches the front door. The key sticks in the lock, and he decides Selene must have given him the wrong one on purpose. A wave of stress-fueled nausea courses through his body. He hates that he got mixed up in this crap because he is incapable of saying no. Because he wanted to be nice.

This can't go on. He needs to put a stop to it, for Hugo's sake.

The key finally turns, and the door swings open. Thomas fumbles for the light switch in the hallway. The bulb on the ceiling comes on, flickers, and goes out.

Damn it.

Time isn't on his side, but there is no reason why this should take any longer than fifteen minutes. Then he can leave the house, walk back to his car, and drive home.

Without taking his shoes off, he makes his way past the fireplace and into the kitchen. He flicks the switch on the wall, but nothing happens. He glances at his watch—6:57 p.m.—and can't decide what to do while he waits. With a sigh, he slumps to the floor and hugs his knees. Maybe he should just forget the whole thing, clear off now. But no, he doesn't dare.

A few minutes later the front door opens, and Thomas jumps up so suddenly that the room sways and he has to brace himself against the wall. He staggers out into the hallway.

"We need to be quick," he says. "I'm in a hurry."

He stops dead and stares at the person in the doorway.

"What are you doing here?"

The initial surprise transforms into panic, his brain unable to piece together the swirling fragments. The anger on the face in front of him. The determination. Why? His heart is in his mouth, his field of vision shrinking. A single clear thought manages to break through: *Please, help.*

"Give me the keys," Madeleine hisses.

Thomas instinctively takes a step back. He wants to get away from the rage that is just waiting for an excuse to explode.

"How the hell could Karl be stupid enough to give you another chance?" Madeleine continues. "He should have listened to me."

The panic refuses to subside, no matter how hard Thomas tries to ignore it. Mille will be here any minute now, and Thomas can't see a single way out of this. Selene must have been calling to warn him earlier. She is the only person who could have told Madeleine about the keys. Why didn't he pick up? He's such a fucking idiot.

"How could you do this to Selene?"

Spittle flies out of Madeleine's mouth, and Thomas stares back at her.

"You know how fragile she is. You exploited that, you fake bastard."

Thomas finally manages to push back his shock enough to reply.

"I know I shouldn't have asked her for the keys."

"Asked? You forced her! It's so damn weak and sick of you to prey on someone like her. Don't you realize just how much she's struggling right now?"

At first Thomas doesn't understand. He didn't force Selene to do a damn thing, but then he realizes that she must have lied to Madeleine. Of course she didn't dare tell her mother the truth. Thomas doesn't want to be here anymore. To hell with the Fribergs, with Mille and everything else. He needs to get back to his boy, all alone in the car.

"You've been messing with Selene's emotions from the very start," says Madeleine. "Karl should have given you the boot a long time ago, but he ignored me like always. I'm nothing to him."

"I haven't . . ." Thomas begins.

But he realizes there is no point. Selene probably lied about that, too.

"Give me the keys," says Madeleine, holding out a hand.

Thomas peers over her shoulder. He wants to get out of the house. Away from everything she is claiming about him. With her other hand, Madeleine takes her phone out of her pocket.

"What the hell are you doing?" he asks.

"I'm calling the police. You're going to prison for this. For everything you've put Selene through."

"No, you can't."

Thomas tries to grab the phone from Madeleine's hand, but she gives him a shove. Thomas staggers backward, stumbling in the doorway and falling into the kitchen.

"Selene is a complete wreck!" Madeleine roars. "How could you do this to her? How?"

Thomas gets back onto his feet. He is livid now. This is the

second time someone has pushed him over today. He can take
Lykke doing it, but not this. Madeleine has no idea. He throws
himself at her. Needs to make her stop spewing such rubbish.
Needs to make sure she doesn't call the police.

Madeleine takes a quick step toward the fireplace and grabs
something long. Thomas pauses and manages to throw up his
arms in defense. The pain as the object slams into his arm is almost enough to make him pass out. He sees it coming back toward
him now, the shovel from the hearth rack, and he tries to move
backward, but the stress is making his body sluggish. All he can
think about is Hugo. How he never should have left him.

The shovel hits him square in the throat, and he feels something
warm spill down his skin. Thomas brings his hands up to his neck,
but he can't stop the blood. There is so much of it. He meets Madeleine's eye. Every last trace of anger is gone, and she looks terrified. *Help me*, he wants to beg her, but his mouth refuses to open.
It's . . . he thinks, but his legs give way beneath him.

Everything merges into one: the pain, the silence, the light, and
Hugo.

70

The half-eaten cheese sandwich lay on the plate in front of Lykke, beside her empty coffee cup. The sky was bright blue, with barely a breath of wind. The police hadn't been over again, but she was too tired to feel any relief. She was also convinced that a patrol car would pull up outside any moment, that they would force her into the back, claiming that she had killed Thomas and locking her up. Refusing to listen to what she had to say.

She hadn't been able to sleep after sending the message to Jenny. In the end she had gone downstairs and dozed fitfully on the sofa. She had taken a dip in the strait that morning in an attempt to wake herself up, but the fog in her head refused to clear. It was almost three in the afternoon, and all she wanted was for the day to be over so that she could go to bed.

Lykke took another small bite of her sandwich and opened the lid of her laptop. She would continue her search for a job.

After taking yet another bite, she logged on to the Public Employment Service website and ran a search. Clicked the ad at the very top of the list.

It was for a job at Station Linné. Till training was desired, since the position would mostly revolve around working in the shop. Language skills, too. An interest in nature and animals were bonuses.

Station Linné was a research center that organized courses and guided trips. She had visited it once before, while she was still at the university. Lykke knew she would probably fall short because of the damned till training requirement, but she opened a Word document and began writing an application. The ad had woken something inside her. Determination. Expectation. It sounded like the kind of job she might enjoy.

She heard a car pull up outside, and came close to knocking over her coffee cup as she turned around. The two police officers would appear around the corner any minute now. Demanding that she accompany them to the station. Erasing everything the job ad had stirred up.

But it wasn't the two officers. It was Hugo and Jenny. Lykke had never met Jenny before, only ever spoken to her on the phone, but she looked exactly like her photograph in the paper.

"Hi," said Lykke, sounding surprised.

"Hi. I'm Jenny."

"Yeah, I know."

Jenny glanced back at the car, just like Thomas had, then gazed over toward the water.

"What do you want?" asked Lykke.

"Have you spoken to the police?"

"No."

Her face seemed tense, and Lykke decided that Jenny must have come over to accuse her. That she had told the police she was convinced Lykke was guilty.

Hugo started squirming, and Jenny tried to resist, but it was impossible. He just wanted to be put down. The two women watched as he ran over to the net swing hanging from one of the trees. Jenny's face seemed much calmer now.

"I wanted to start by apologizing for being so rude to you," she said. "I was just so worried about Thomas. And Hugo."

Lykke nodded, but then she realized that Jenny likely hadn't seen. Her eyes were still fixed on her son.

"I understand," she said.

Hugo tried to climb up onto the swing, but fell back onto his bottom. He immediately got up again. The boy clearly had a stubborn streak.

"The police have arrested a man for Thomas's murder," said Jenny.

"Who?"

"The owner of Friberg Properties. I really don't have the energy to talk about it."

Hugo grunted in frustration. He was now lying flat-out on his stomach on the swing, but couldn't manage to turn over. Lykke didn't know what to do, how to act around Jenny and Hugo.

"Why are you here?" she asked.

"I thought Hugo should get to meet his big sister."

Big sister.

The emotions that welled up inside Lykke were just too much for her to handle. She clamped her hand to her mouth.

"I can tell you about Thomas, too," said Jenny. "About your dad. Not right now, but with time. He definitely wasn't perfect, but who is? He really did make me happy."

Lykke took a step toward Hugo, who was still struggling to roll over on the swing. She paused and glanced up at Jenny.

"Is it okay if I help him?" she asked.

"Of course."

Lykke lifted Hugo onto the swing and began pushing him back and forth.

"More!" he cried.

She was clearly being much too gentle. Lykke pushed the swing harder, and Hugo hooted with laughter. She pushed the swing over and over again.

"Thank you," she said to Jenny. "I don't think you realize just how much this means to me."

Jenny nodded, and Lykke decided that there might be a path out from Roger's shadow after all. From Thomas's.

Even beautiful things can grow in the shade. Lykke realized that her mother had never been talking about the flowers.

71

Hanna was sitting on the sofa with her legs folded beneath her. There were still another three hours to go before she had to be at Isak's place, but she was already showered and ready. She had spent at least half an hour picking out the right top to go with her jeans. Isak had a lamb stew on the stove, and it had been simmering away for hours. She was currently looking at a picture of it.

Her phone rang, and Ove's name popped up on the screen. She just hoped nothing else had happened, forcing her to cancel on Isak again. Hanna debated not picking up, pretending she hadn't heard the phone ring, though she knew she could never manage to duck a call from the boss.

"I just spoke to Daniel," said Ove.

He had gone over to the Fribergs' house to be present during the search.

"And?"

"It won't matter what Karl Friberg says now," said Ove. "The trash bag was in the shed, along with both the murder weapon and Thomas's phone."

It sounded so wrong coming from Ove like that, and Hanna's doubts came flooding back to her. She just couldn't stop thinking about it. Karl's reaction at the hospital. He hadn't admitted to a single thing, and his shock over both Hektor's attack and his arrest had seemed genuine. She couldn't ignore it any longer.

"Hey," she said, "don't you find it a bit strange that Karl took the murder weapon and the phone home with him and hid them in his shed?"

Ove's only response was to sigh, and Hanna desperately wanted to find her way back to the conviction she had felt earlier: that Karl was a killer she could believe in.

"Have you found the shoes?" she asked.

"Not yet."

Hanna's doubts continued to grow the minute she hung up. There was so much that just didn't sit right. Not only in relation to Karl's behavior at the hospital, but Madeleine's, too. The way she had essentially thrown Karl under the bus. Hanna forced back the doubts. They would be interviewing him in the presence of his lawyer on Monday. After that they would likely know more.

They were also going to interview Mille Bergman. He was being held on suspicion of smuggling and assaulting Selene Friberg. At some point during the week they would also question her. Hanna would try to make sure it took place as soon as possible.

The dark blue car Selene had spotted outside Mille's house last autumn had now been identified. It belonged to Oleg Sokolov. They hadn't managed to track him down yet, but with any luck the entire smuggling ring would be convicted this time.

Hanna's phone beeped. It was another picture, of a bowl of batter.

It's going to be even better once it's baked.

Her entire body felt like it was smiling.

I think it looks good already, she wrote back.

Hanna got up and went through to the kitchen for a glass of water. The investigation was still on her mind. The niggling doubt that just wouldn't go away. What if they had the wrong end of the stick after all? Again. Right then, it dawned on her. What Madeleine had said at the hospital: *I was cleaning the shed this morning and I found a trash bag with a bloody hearth shovel and Thomas's phone inside.*

How could Madeleine have known it was Thomas's phone? Hanna hurried back through to the living room and called Daniel.

"The phone that was found in the trash bag, what is it like?"

"Aren't you off today?"

"Come on, what is it like?"

"It's a black Samsung Galaxy S20."

"And are you sure it's Thomas's?"

"Yeah, we switched it on using the code Jenny gave us."

"Did it still have a charge?"

"Yeah."

The phone hadn't run out of battery. That meant either Thomas had switched it off, or the killer had.

"How could Madeleine have known it was Thomas's?"

There was a moment's silence on the other end of the line.

"Maybe she guessed," said Daniel. "Or maybe Karl confessed to her. Or—"

"Or maybe we've arrested the wrong person," Hanna interrupted him.

If Karl had confessed to killing Thomas, Madeleine would have said so. She wouldn't have told them a pack of lies about him driving off and her finding the trash bag while cleaning the shed. Because they were lies, Hanna was now convinced of it.

"Madeleine is sitting in the garden, staring up at the house," said Daniel. "She refused to go any farther away than that."

"Keep looking for the shoes," said Hanna. "Without them I doubt you'll be able to get anything out of her."

"Me? Don't you want to come over?"

"No," said Hanna. "I've got other plans this evening."

"Okay. I'll call Ove, too."

Hanna slumped back on the sofa and stared up at the ceiling.

She went back over the meeting with Madeleine at the hospital. What had she been wearing on her feet? Some kind of orthopedic boots. Madeleine was a tall woman, and her feet were definitely on the bigger side. The forensics database contained considerably more male shoe prints than female. Could that be the reason they hadn't managed to find a match? But why? At first Hanna couldn't think of a single reason why Madeleine might have killed Thomas. But then it came to her, Madeleine herself had said it as she was sitting by Selene's bed.

Hanna glanced at her watch. No more than fifteen minutes had passed since she last did the same. Feeling frustrated, she got up and climbed the stairs. It was even harder to pass the time now. She took off her top and tried on a different one instead. Nothing felt good enough, so she kept going. After testing her way through her entire wardrobe, she ended up putting on the same top she'd had on earlier: a simple long-sleeved green T-shirt. The color suited her.

Should she call the custodial prison and ask to speak to Karl? Or try to reach Selene at the hospital? No, it would be better to wait until the search and the interview with Madeleine were over.

Hanna went down to the bathroom and stood in front of the mirror for quite some time, studying her reflection. She was wearing the same lipstick as yesterday. Did she really want to wear it again? In the end she left her lips as they were and dug out a perfume sample she had received in the mail. She dotted it onto her wrists.

Right then, her phone rang, and Hanna jumped.

"You were right," said Daniel. "We've got her."

"Did you find the shoes?"

"Yup, they were in one of the closets. A pair of brown Ecco shoes, size forty-one. That's her size, not Karl's. I confronted her with them right away and she confessed."

"Just like that?"

"Yeah, showing her the shoes was all it took to break her. Selene never dared tell Karl that she'd given Thomas the keys. Madeleine only found out at the hospital, after you'd gone."

"Great work," said Hanna.

"Hey, same."

"How did Ove take the news?" asked Hanna.

"I'm about to call him now. Unless you want to do it?"

"No, thanks."

Hanna checked her watch again. She still had almost two hours to kill until her dinner at Isak's, and that felt like an unbearably long amount of time to be doing nothing. Maybe she should get in touch with the journalist from *Barometern* who wanted to talk about her father? No, that could wait. The more she thought about it, the more impossible those two hours felt.

What would you say if I came over right now?

She had just hit send on the message to Isak when the doorbell rang. Hanna got up to answer. She assumed it must be Ingrid, coming over to congratulate her on wrapping up the case. There had been a press conference revealing that a suspect was in custody just after lunch, and the press hadn't taken long to share the latest updates. Ingrid would likely have questions about who the suspect was, though she knew Hanna would never tell her. It would be a huge mess when the news that they had arrested the wrong person broke.

Hanna heard a ping, and saw the *YES!* from Isak as she opened the door. Her phone clattered to the floor.

Kristoffer was standing outside.

It had been two years since she'd last seen him, when she flew to London to meet his daughter Ella, who was one at the time. He had lost weight, and his once-longish hair was now cropped short.

"What are you doing here?" she asked.

Her mind was racing. She was happy to see her brother, of course, but not right there and then.

"We need to talk."

"Couldn't you have called?" she asked.

"No. I'd never be able to say this over the phone. I've . . ." Kristoffer was staring at something behind her. "I've gone over and over this in my head, and I need to tell you."

Hanna backed up and let him inside.

Acknowledgments

This is my ninth book, but it was one of the hardest to write. *The Night Singer* did so well that I set a standard for its follow-up that I found difficult to achieve at first, but in the end the story grew into something I could really feel proud of—largely thanks to those around me who remained steadfast even when I had my doubts.

I'd like to start by thanking my Swedish publishing house, Romanus & Selling. My publisher, Åsa Selling, my editor, Jesper Ims, and the rest of the gang: Lina Rönning, Emelie Hollbox, and Susanna Romanus.

I'd also like to thank my agent, Kaisa Palo, Matilda Fogelström Johnson, and everyone else at Ahlander Agency. They've done such an incredible job getting the Island Murders series out into the world. The rights have been sold to seventeen different territories so far—seventeen! Sometimes I still find myself wondering whether that can really be true.

This is the U.S. publication, so a deep thanks to Patrick Nolan and his team at Penguin Books, and of course to Alice Menzies, who translated this book into English. It feels just like the one I wrote in Swedish.

Thank you to Detectives Ulf Einarsson and Ulf Martinsson of the Kalmar police, for both answering my questions and reading my words. And to my cousin, Jessica Mo, for going over the manuscript with your eagle Öland eyes.

A number of people helped me with research for this book. Thank you to Christina Hjalmarsson from Missing People, and to Mikael Ekeberg, who took part in the search when a six-year-old vanished in Färjestaden. Thank you to Peter Hallberg, a real estate agent on Öland, for answering my questions. Considering how my real estate agents behave, I chose to come up with a fictional agency. Thank you to Pav Johnsson, who knows his birds. Without him I wouldn't have known that the birds that surrounded our car as we drove across the alvar were starlings.

I'd also like to thank everyone who has read this book and given me feedback: Björn Ekenberg, Gunnel Mo, Petra Mo, Sara Mo, Moa Olofsson, and my little writing group: Rebecka Edgren Aldén, Pernilla Ericson, and Hanna Lindberg.

Last but certainly not least, I would like to thank everyone for reading and listening, and for taking time to show your appreciation. You just don't know how much that means to me.

Johanna Mo
April 2021

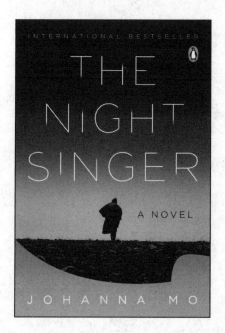